Praise for

HALLOWMERE™

"If you're looking for gothic spooky, this novel is for you. It's the kind of book that makes you want to snuggle up on the couch with

—Sarah Beth Durst, author of *Into*

"Equal parts spine-tingling and intoxicating, this is one historical fantasy I can't wait to reread."

—Jennifer Lynn Barnes, author of *Golden* and *Tattoo*

"*In the Serpent's Coils* is a rich, earthy, engrossing novel that heralds Tiffany Trent as one of the best dark fantasy writers of our time. I was completely mesmerized by her tale, and deeply gratified in the end. Bravo!"

—David Farland, *New York Times* best-selling author

"Another hot YA title, *In the Serpent's Coils* comes with a peculiarly classic set-up that is twisted at every turn."

—Cherie Priest, author of *Four and Twenty Blackbirds*

"If childhood nightmares could be alchemically distilled into prose, *In the Serpent's Coils* would be the result. Part gothic horror, part history, all dark imagination, the book is a masterpiece."

—Ree Soesbee, author of the Elements trilogy

"Fueled by mystery, fantasy, history, faeries and fear, In the Sperpent's Coils catches its audience with the perfect blend of magic and realism."

—Lee Oldoski, Young Adult Librarian

In the Serpent's Coils

By Venom's Sweet Sting
December 2007

Between Golden Jaws
March 2008

HALLOWMERE™

Volume One

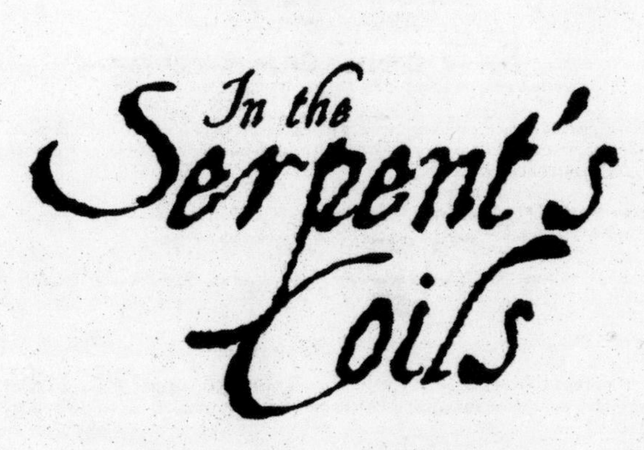

TIFFANY TRENT

Hallowmere™

In the Serpent's Coils

Printed in the U.S.A.

Cover design by Trish Yochum
First Printing: September 2007

9 8 7 6 5 4 3 2 1

ISBN: 978-0-7869-4229-9
620-95862740-001-EN

Library of Congress Cataloging-in-Publication Data

Trent, Tiffany, 1973-
In the serpent's coils / Tiffany Trent.
p. cm. — (Hallowmere)
"Mirrorstone."
Summary: After the death of her parents in the Civil War, sixteen-year-old Corrine is sent to reform school in Culpeper, Virginia, where she discovers a sinister plot involving a race of faeries and the disappearance of some of the students.
ISBN 978-0-7869-4229-9 (alk. paper)
[1. Orphans—Fiction. 2. Fairies—Fiction. 3. Reformatories—Fiction. 4. Virginia—History—1775-1865—Fiction.] I. Title.
PZ7.T314In 2007
[Fic]—dc22

2006102201

U.S., CANADA,
ASIA, PACIFIC, & LATIN AMERICA
Wizards of the Coast, Inc.
P.O. Box 707
Renton, WA 98057-0707
+1-800-324-6496

EUROPEAN HEADQUARTERS
Hasbro UK Ltd
Caswell Way
Newport, Gwent NP9 0YH
GREAT BRITAIN
Save this address for your records.

Visit our Web site at www.mirrorstonebooks.com

To the Lisas in my life:

Lisa Machi, for her unflagging friendship and support, and Lisa Stadnyk, because I promised

PROLOGUE

[Trans. note: Only surviving letter of 1285 series]

Spring 1285

To Frater Josephus, Kirk of St. Columba, from Pater Iamblicus, Kirk of St. Fillan, greetings.

My dearest brother:

I am grateful for your patience of late. By now, I hope you will have received the charm that will allow you to read this letter. I have asked you to wait before taking any action, as our dear Friend has counseled, but I believe he feels the time has come.

At Midsummer, you must enter the fallen realms of our enemy. It grieves me to place you in such great danger, who already have suffered so much at the hands of the Unhallowed. Only you can achieve this errand. You must bring the stone back to the Kirk of St. Fillan before the Midsummer-tide is done. I suppose it is needless to remind you of your duty, to beware of falling again under the spell of the witch. You of all people know her terrible fondness for revenge.

Yours in Faith,
Iamblicus

~ One ~

August 27, 1865

CORRINE TRIED TO SIT, BUT WEAKNESS WASHED OVER HER. She considered lighting a lamp to locate the source of the noise that had awakened her. Then she realized that she had no idea where the lamp was, or where she was, for that matter.

The wall behind her head squeaked. Mice. She had heard them in the walls of the rooming house where she and her mother had stayed since coming to Washington. But this room didn't harbor the sweet stink of the sewage canal outside, and there was quiet here, a deep quiet far removed from city streets.

"Mother?" she whispered to the stillness. But there was no sound of breathing aside from her own. Her mother didn't answer her call. She put her hand to her throat, but the locket she sought for reassurance was gone, the locket that her parents had given to her when she was five.

Voices sifted through the bedroom door. She tried to calm herself enough to stand. After two tries she managed. She walked unsteadily toward the line of light coming from under the door, nearly smashing into a nightstand. She ran her hand along rippling wallpaper, finding the doorknob before deeper panic boiled. Her fingers shook so hard that she could barely turn it. She crept toward the voices and crouched near the banisters, where she clung to the posts, trying to recover her shattered breathing.

Downstairs, lamplight flickered across dark blue wallpaper and the white woven flowers of a Persian carpet. A black woman, wearing a maid's dark dress with a starched apron and cap, held the door open for two men as they carried something large and heavy into the foyer. Corrine's fingers tightened on the balusters. She knew this paneled trunk. It had stood next to her mother's bureau back at the farm in Maryland. Corrine had often slipped into her parents' room to slide her hands across the trunk lid, feeling the contrast between the wooden side panels and the middle section of fern-embossed tin. It was kept locked; her mother wore the key on her charm bracelet.

Corrine had only seen inside it once, when she was four. She remembered entering her parents' bedroom and finding the trunk lid open, beckoning her like a wide mouth. The smell of every holiday combined—the spice of Christmas, the lilies of Easter—drew her to the trunk's edge. A woman looked out at her from the domed lid. Her golden hair was clasped in a pearl-studded chignon at her nape; her face shone like an angel's. But there was something decidedly wicked about the feline tilt of her eyes.

The lady in the portrait smiled at her. Corrine gasped. And then, the trunk lid slammed shut. Corrine's mother stood over her with a look on her face that Corrine had never seen before or since.

"This is not for you," her mother said, touching her head as though it ached.

"But the pretty lady, she smiled at me," Corrine said.

"Nonsense!" her mother snapped. "I will not have such fancies from you, Corrine!"

Corrine cried then. She had never seen her mother angry.

And then, her mother had enfolded her in the warm silk of her embrace. "Really darling, don't trouble yourself. Just don't look in there again."

After that, the trunk had remained locked. But Corrine had never forgotten the lovely spice drifting out from under the lid, the lady's mysterious, feline smile. Corrine would almost have said that the woman was not quite human.

And now the trunk was below. But the trunk hadn't been with them at the rooming house; it would never have fit in their tiny room.

A man entered, carrying a pair of gloves and a riding crop. As he entered the circle of light, Corrine hunkered down closer to the banister, hoping he wouldn't see her. His deep-set eyes looked hollow, and his wavy hair drooped around his cheekbones with the heat. Corrine's eyes widened. She only recognized this man because her mother had once showed her his portrait—her uncle William.

Since Corrine could remember, her mother's brother, a powerful lawyer, had shunned his sister and her family. Even when her mother came to Washington after Corrine's father had disappeared in the Battle of Petersburg, Uncle William had never once offered to shelter or succor them in any way.

"You can put the trunk over there in my study for the moment," Uncle William said to the two men.

Corrine watched as the men disappeared into the study. The maid came and took Uncle William's gloves and crop from him.

"A good journey from Maryland, Mr. McPhee?" the maid asked.

"Yes," he said. "I think the Council will be pleased." He looked up, as though he sensed Corrine's presence, and frowned. Corrine shrank from the banister, until she could see little more than his head.

"My sister's farm is in terrible disrepair," he said. "I doubt that worthless husband of hers ever worked a day on it before he went into the army. It will have to be sold."

Corrine smothered a cry of shock. Instead of staying to hear the rest of the conversation, Corrine crept back into her room and pulled herself into her bed, trying to quiet her wheezing gasps.

Sell the farm? She thought of the beautiful long fields, the Elk River that wound around them. She had begged her mother not to leave, not to dismiss Nora and Willy, former slaves who had escaped through the Underground Railroad. But her mother had been adamant. There was work to do in Washington, she had said. More nurses were needed every day to care for those still recuperating from their wounds. But her mother would never allow her estranged brother to sell the farm—would she?

The tears streamed until she was forced to smother her sobs in her pillow. The loss of the farm hurt terribly, but what her uncle had said about her father . . . She pulled the pillow from her face and stared into the darkness.

Where was her mother?

August 28, 1865

Clinking silverware rattled Corrine awake. The thin maid she'd seen the night before set a pewter tray of food on a folding table at her bedside. The room's wallpaper leaped out at her with its cigar-brown and tulip-leaf-green patterns, threatening to sicken her as she pushed herself upright.

A man entered, a white-bearded doctor who opened his black bag at the edge of her bed. He held her shoulders still as he inspected her breathing and glared into her eyes and mouth.

"Has your eye always been this way?" he asked, peering at her expanded left pupil.

He held her head so tightly she couldn't nod. "Yes," Corrine said. "My mother called it my 'fairy eye.'"

The doctor grunted and released her. Taking a bottle from his bag, he filled a tiny lead cup and gave it to her. "This should be your last dose," he said.

"What is it?" she asked.

"Quinine," he said. "You very nearly died of the ague."

"The ague?" she asked. "Swamp fever?"

"It's rare, but it can happen," the doctor said. "Your uncle tells me your rooming house was near the canal. Not a good place for children."

Corrine didn't remember when she had first felt the signs of fever, much less when she had taken her first dose of the medicine. She swallowed the quinine. Bitterness clawed at her throat until she gagged.

"Your mother was a nurse, yes?"

"Yes, sir."

"She should have known better then," he said.

Was? Should have? Why did he speak of her mother that way? She held the cup out to him. He packed it away and left the room with one last glance. She heard him in the hallway, talking, she supposed, to Uncle William.

" . . . danger mostly past. Perhaps in a day or two . . ." the doctor said.

More baritone murmurs.

The maid entered with a pitcher of water and a glass. Corrine tried to sit up again, but the dizziness capsized her into the bed.

"Where is my mother?" she asked.

"She in the grave, child," the woman said. Her accent was so thick that Corrine was not sure she understood.

The woman continued. "She die more than a week ago, and they bury her in the nurses' cemetery in Alexandria."

"Dead?" Corrine's voice cracked.

"She refuse to quit working 'til the very last. Probably what killed her, Lord bless her. They try to give her the medicine, but too late. She already too weak. And you come down with it, and they worry more over you than her. She go in a hurry, child, and that's the truth."

Corrine's mouth softened with nausea, even as she struggled against the maid's words. Her mother—dead? Despite the afternoon heat, she clutched at the covers, willing her eyes to follow the patterns in the wallpaper so she wouldn't cry.

The maid picked up the night pot at the foot of the bed. Corrine saw sympathy in her eyes, but also a very obvious frustration. *What are we going to do with you now?* the woman seemed to be thinking.

"What's your name?" Corrine asked. She tried to distract herself with something, anything, from the knowledge sinking into her stomach.

"Betsy," the maid said.

Corrine clutched at her throat and thought again of the locket. "Do you know what happened to my locket?" she asked.

"Your locket, child?"

"A gold locket on a gold chain. Shaped like a little book. My mother and father . . ." She was too shocked to say more.

Betsy shook her head. "Didn't see one." Covering the pot with a cloth, the maid glanced again at Corrine and left the room.

Corrine slid back into the bed, stiff with unshed tears. She had cried about the farm, but death was too devastating for tears. Everything was gone—her father, the farm, the locket, and now her mother.

If only the Southern states hadn't seceded. Then the rebellion wouldn't have happened. Her father would have never gone to war, her mother wouldn't have left the farm to nurse wounded soldiers. As Corrine's mind raced with what-ifs, she fell into an exhausted sleep.

She sat with her mother in a dark bower by the Elk River; night-blooming vines shed light from pearly bells. In the flower-glow, her mother's face was young and vulnerable. The iron cross she had always worn was a dark bar at her throat. Her mother removed the cross and put it over Corrine's head. You have greater need of this now than I, *her mother said.*

Eyes gleamed from the forest shade. Things flitted through her peripheral vision—nacreous wingtips, twiggy limbs, tufts of milk-weed hair. Fairies. Her mother had told her many stories of them. She wanted desperately to look at them, but her mother said, Don't look at them. Look only at me.

So she kept her gaze on her mother's eyes, watching as the pale face aged, as the skin sagged and dissolved into bone. Only her eyes remained intact, watching Corrine lovingly from their sockets while her mother's finger joints clicked toward her cheek.

She screamed herself awake, fairy laughter echoing in her ears. The dream confirmed what Betsy had said. Her mother was dead. Corrine promised herself in that moment that no one—human, fairy, or otherwise—would ever see her cry again.

No one came to her, and she drifted in and out of the fever-lands.

August 29, 1865

It was afternoon again. Uncle William was looking down at her, the same concern and consternation on his face as Betsy's had held. His bushy eyebrows winged outward like moth antennae, and below them his eyes were dark like her mother's. Now that she saw him more closely, Corrine realized there was gray at his temples. The only other family resemblance was the soft jaw, quite becoming on her mother but decidedly odd-looking on her uncle.

"I suppose you have heard about your mother," he said.

"Yes." She was proud that her voice didn't break this time.

"Most unfortunate," he said. Corrine wasn't sure if he meant for her or himself.

"Yes," she said. "How did I get here?"

"You were brought here from the hospital when the danger was past. As your father has not returned from the War, you are now my ward."

Corrine nodded. His disdainful tone when he mentioned her father was only slightly less than when he had spoken of him that night in the foyer.

"I must tell you now that I dislike children and am not accustomed to having them underfoot. You may stay here so long as you abide by my rules. These rules are simple." He held up an index finger. "First, do not interfere in my affairs. Second, act decorously and with discretion. Lastly, at all times, do as you are bid."

Uncle William paced as he lectured. "Do these things and you may stay. Do otherwise and I will send you elsewhere. Your life here will be very different from your transcendentalist upbringing. I have no tolerance for such romantic notions. You will be expected when you are of age to either make your own way in a respectable profession or, more preferably, to find a match whom I deem appropriate. Until that time, I will find a tutor to train you in a vocation."

He paused and looked at her. "Have you an idea whether you wish to be a nurse or a teacher?"

Corrine shook her head. She had never been spoken to in this way. Her parents had always believed in learning through experience, in self-cultivation through kindness and compassion.

This was so different, she didn't know how to respond.

Uncle William's brows knit. "Very well then," he said, looking around the room as if he had something more important to do. "Have you need of anything else?"

"Mourning clothes," she said in a small voice. "And . . . perhaps some books?"

"There is a library in my study on the ground floor. Betsy will show it to you when you are able. You are only to look at the books. Do not disturb my desk or personal effects. When you use the library, it would be best if you were finished before the afternoon, as I return from my office then."

He stared at her throat as he spoke, and she touched the collar of her nightgown uncomfortably.

"Corrine," he said. "Did your mother . . . give you anything before she died?"

"Only my locket a long time ago," she said. "Do you know where it is?"

"A locket?" he asked. "Are you certain it wasn't an iron cross?"

Corrine shook her head.

"You are certain?" he asked again.

"Yes," she answered, wondering why this could be so important to him.

"The cross was a family heirloom passed from mother to daughter. Did you ever see it?"

Corrine recalled her dream and shut her eyes before answering. "Yes," she said. "Mother said it was very old. She only let me touch it once."

"You don't know what happened to it?" Uncle William asked, agitated.

"No, Uncle," she said. "I don't. Mother always wore it."

There was a silence in which she gathered that he was trying to find something appropriate to say.

"May I see the trunk?" she asked.

He looked at her with fleeting surprise before his face darkened. "How do you know about that?"

"I saw you bring it in the other night," she said. "I want to see it. It was hers." She fidgeted with the bedsheets, inwardly appalled at her own impertinence.

"Do you know where the key is?" Uncle William asked.

"Mother always wore it on her charm bracelet," Corrine said.

The muscles around her uncle's right eye twitched. He swore softly.

"I would like to—" Corrine began.

But her uncle interrupted. "Until I decide otherwise, the trunk remains mine. You may enter my library for books, but you are not to go near that trunk. Do you understand me?"

"Yes, Uncle," Corrine said, wishing she had the strength to stand up to him.

"Very well," he said. His thoughts were obviously elsewhere, and she didn't know him well enough to read him. "I shall send Betsy to find suitable clothes for you and anything else within reason that you might require."

He left then, mumbling under his breath.

"My locket . . ." she said softly. But it, like everything else, was gone.

Corrine leaned back in the bed, puzzled. Uncle William was more distraught over the loss of his sister's jewelry than her death. And Corrine couldn't understand his attachment to that trunk, the only thing she had left of her mother. *If only I had the key,* she thought. But she knew where it was—six feet under the soil of Alexandria, circling her mother's rotting wrist.

~ Two ~

September 5, 1865

In a few days, Corrine was able to sit without being drowned by dizziness. In another few she was able to walk from her bed to the window and back without becoming utterly exhausted. She looked down on the sere grass, the trees weighted down with drought. There was no breeze; the window was a mouth that inhaled and exhaled heat. She watched a black cat hurry between bits of shade as though its fur would catch fire if it stayed too long in the sun. She felt almost relieved to still wear a nightgown. It was far less constricting than a proper day dress, with its crinoline and heavy skirt, which she knew her uncle would expect her to wear.

A sulky drawn by a Morgan passed, pulling with the grace of a racehorse. A well-dressed man rode in the other direction on a frothing chestnut Kentucky Saddler. Her father had bred horses on their old farm in Connecticut, before moving to Maryland. He had once told her that he admired the graceful arched neck and powerful gait of the Saddler, but his heart would always belong to the smaller, darker Morgans he had raced before the War.

She could dimly hear the din of city life far away—the whistles of ships in port, the roaring of factory furnaces. She had often been forced to pull the blankets over her ears to shut out the noises outside the rooming house. The immediate silence of this street reminded her of the Maryland farm, how it got so still that her mother said you could hear the corn grow if you put your mind to it.

But those thoughts led her toward tears, a place she had denied herself. She turned and went back to her bed. Betsy had kindly brought some books up from the library, but they were mostly subjects in which Corrine had no interest—Virginia geography, Sumerian legal codes, a biography of John Locke.

She flipped idly through the books until Betsy entered, carrying mourning clothes draped over one arm and a basket of sewing implements on the other.

"Betsy," Corrine said, "thank you for the books."

Betsy's eyes kindled in surprise. "You're welcome."

"Do you know if Uncle William has any books on poetry or . . . or . . . fairies, perhaps?"

Betsy set the basket down and spread the dress over the foot of the bed.

"Fairies, Miss Corrine?"

"You know, little people with wings who live in the woods."

Betsy looked at her curiously. "If you're talking about them evil spirits, you better not. My mammie told me they nothing but trouble, and they perfectly willing to give it to any who's interested."

"Where was your mammie from?" Corrine asked.

"Down South Carolina way," Betsy said. "Lots of ghosts and booger men down that way. Now stand up, child, so I can fit you into this here dress."

Corrine stood and let Betsy help her out of her nightgown. The crepe fell on her like a musty cloud. Betsy, pins bristling from her lips, set about making the alterations, pinning the heavy skirt to fall just at the top of Corrine's ankles.

"Booger men?" Corrine said. "What are they?"

"Bad things that live in the swamps and the woods. Just you never mind," Betsy said through her pins. "The less you know about it, the better off you are."

Corrine nodded, listening to the pins slide one by one through the fabric. Betsy probably was not one to be pushed into giving information.

"I'll bring this dress back in a day or two," Betsy said when she was done. "Then you free to go downstairs. But just remember what Mr. McPhee say to you, or you get us both in trouble."

Corrine nodded. She was ready to be free, but she wasn't sure about her uncle's orders. The trunk beckoned.

September 7, 1865

Corrine had been pacing intermittently for hours, waiting for the dark mourning dress to arrive. She had discovered her old pinafore and dress in the chest of drawers, and considered putting them on. But she sensed that would be indecorous of her, and Uncle William seemed to live by the rites of propriety. The mourning dress also seemed too old for her—she didn't feel ready for what it signified. She had still been wearing calf-length dresses and pinafores when she came to Washington with her mother, and was unaccustomed to dresses that swept all the way to her ankles.

Still, she was almost sixteen; most would say it was high time for her to dress like a young lady. She went again to the window, beyond which the September heat hung like a curtain from sky to earth. She watched the heat shimmer down the lane without interest until a man appeared—a man with dark, curling hair who shuffled away toward the river. A man who looked exactly like her father from the back, from his hair to his easy gait. He wore a blue uniform, the uniform of a Union soldier.

Betsy entered with the dress and Corrine flew to her. "Hurry, hurry," she said. "Help me put it on—my father's in the lane!"

Corrine tore off her nightgown and burrowed into the dress, while Betsy held it out in something akin to fear. Corrine wriggled up through the dark crepe, hastening through the buttons and running her fingers through her hair as she flew out the door.

"Miss Corrine," Betsy called, "your shoes!"

Corrine ignored her. She raced down the stairs, having little idea where she was going, her bare feet slapping on the polished oak treads. She was out of breath by the time she got to the bottom, and had to wrestle with the heavy front door before she heaved it open. She ran out onto the veranda and searched, leaning unsteadily against a column. Her hair streamed past her shoulders as the heat crept down the collar of her dress and clamped her lungs tighter than a corset. She looked up and down the lane, but from this vantage point could see very little—the hedge was tall and the trees along the road made a perfect screen. As she made her way down the front steps, her toes tingled from the heat of the paving stones. She stood by the gate and peered out onto the lane. Three veiled women passed, staring at her from under black bonnets that tilted forward like the prows of ships.

"Miss Corrine!" Betsy called.

Corrine leaned hard over the gate, looking up and down the street. The man was nowhere to be seen. She pushed the gate open even as she heard Betsy call her name. She ran, uncaring if people saw her bare feet, her ankles even.

"Father!" she shouted. She ran to the end of the tunnel of trees until her breath flagged again and a sharp pain in her side pulled her down to the dirt. A strange image of the trees reaching long, drooping fingers toward her made her close her eyes.

Betsy was by her side, tugging on her elbow. "Miss Corrine, wake up. If Mr. McPhee knew you was out here, we'd both of us be in a world of trouble!"

Corrine let the woman pull her up to a sitting position. Her head throbbed. "My father—" she said. "I saw him."

Betsy clucked and drew Corrine to her feet. Corrine trembled, as though the fever had come on her again.

"Miss Corrine, you're not well enough to be running after nobody. And that's hardly proper for a lady, neither."

Corrine leaned on Betsy as they made their way back down the lane. Another carriage went by, but she didn't raise her head to look at it. Betsy helped her up the steps, across the veranda, and through the front door.

"You must still be having the fever delusions, child."

Corrine shook her head, and then regretted it as the pain burst in worms of light behind her eyes. She realized she felt too weak to climb the stairs back to her room. As she leaned on Betsy's arm, she saw a doorway to her left, presumably where the men had taken her mother's trunk. She smelled leather and the musty drift of paper.

"May I go in there?" she asked.

Betsy looked her up and down, lingering on her bare feet. "Only if you let me bring you some slippers to put on," she said.

Corrine nodded. She entered the library slowly, pleased to see an old chaise lounge by the dark fireplace. She was about to sit down when a corner of her mother's trunk caught her eye, near her uncle's desk. Checking over her shoulder for Betsy, Corrine crossed the study to touch it reverently, feeling the divide between wood and embossed metal. She laid her cheek against it and thought she could smell the exotic spice of her childhood.

If only I could open it, she thought. She had heard of people using hairpins to jimmy locks before in the romance novels her mother forbade her to read. But she had run out without putting up her hair.

Then she spied the letter opener lying on her uncle's desk. She reached across, fit the slender tip into the lock. She wasn't sure what she was doing, but she could feel the mechanism within resisting her.

"Miss Corrine!" Betsy stood aghast in the doorway, holding the slippers across her chest.

Corrine put the letter opener back on the desk.

"I best not catch you doing anything like that again," Betsy said. "Your uncle William would be angry with both of us. Now come over here and get these slippers on."

Corrine slunk back to the chaise lounge where Betsy waited, avoiding the maid's eyes.

"You lie down here and take a rest, and don't even think about trying that lock again. Your uncle be home soon."

Almost unable to move any farther, Corrine sagged into the chaise as Betsy covered her with a blanket—and then she was asleep.

Corrine dreamed she was back on the lane. Her feet were bare again and the road was cool and soft under them. She looked up at the trees, the elms twisting overhead like a cathedral roof. The road was empty; no veiled women stared at her. No Kentucky Saddlers flung foam on her sleeve. Far ahead, a man in a blue uniform shimmered into view, outlined by the green tunnel, shuffling along in a gait both deceptively easy but very fast. Her father. He stopped as though he sensed her presence. He turned and looked at her.

She could barely see his smile at this distance. He urged her forward with an emphatic flick of his hand. She walked, and then broke into a run. Her long dress caught around her ankles and she lifted her skirts with both hands, uncaring if she revealed her bare ankles and calves. No one else was on the road anyway.

Her father flickered out of view again. She kept running, but the soft road became mud, and her lungs felt heavy with it. She cried out to him but he only stopped farther ahead near the end of the fence, gesturing for her to hurry. The mud sucked at her toes, then swallowed her ankles. She called again as she sank, and it was then she saw the forest thundering on the horizon. Its branches writhed and crackled like heat lightning. She was sure it hadn't been there before. Her father disappeared into its twisting arms. And she became clay.

When Corrine woke, her lungs ached and she couldn't tell if it was from running or the dream. She felt the familiar urge to cry and pushed it back. "He must be alive," she whispered.

She wanted to get up, but dizziness prevented her. At last, determined, she pushed herself off the chaise and slipped to the window between two leather-covered chairs and a table. The view of the lane was not as good here as it had been from her room.

Still, she knew she had seen him.

Corrine had watched him march away with the Union Army and had looked for his return ever since. Even when the news had come that he was lost in the Battle of Petersburg, she still had not believed it. They had never found his body. How could he possibly be dead?

She remembered how her mother had asked the same question of the soldier who had delivered the news. He just shook his head and looked down at the ground, clenching his hat in his fist.

"M-Ma'am . . ." the soldier had stuttered. "Th-There's things that could have happened too terrible to say in the present company." He glanced at Corrine, standing next to her mother. Her mother bowed her head and drew Corrine into her embrace.

Corrine had felt the steel hoops under her mother's crinoline pressing into her side.

"I see," was all her mother said.

He had apologized and left.

And though Corrine had pressed her mother for what terrible things, her mother hadn't been able to answer. Only Willy, their farmhand, had been willing to venture a guess as he and the mule rested at the end of a furrow.

"Probably blowed up, Miss Corrine," he said, shaking his head. "They use lots of cannon and mortars these days. Probably nothing left but pieces—why they can't really tell you what happened to him."

"But if they can't find him, mightn't it mean he's still alive?" she asked.

"Lord only knows," Willy said. "But I'm sure as the world, he would've returned by now if he was alive, Miss Corrine." He slapped the reins against the mule's back and the plow jerked forward.

Everyone had believed her father was dead, but Corrine couldn't. She knew that one day she would look down the road and she would see him, coming up the way, whistling and bright-eyed as always. He had promised.

She had challenged her mother on this on more than one occasion, even accusing her of lack of faith. When her mother had decided to come to Washington to help the wounded, Corrine had railed that no one would be there to welcome her father when he returned. Her mother had smiled at her sadly and said, "Darling, I think the next time I shall see your father, he will be welcoming me home to paradise." Corrine had shut her mouth then. Nothing could change her mother's mind.

But today, it had happened just as she hoped. How could she not know his walk, the slouching set of his shoulders, his dark hair? Yet he had been going the wrong direction. Perhaps he just hadn't known the proper address. After all, Uncle William had never approved of her father and she could not remember a time when they had ever visited him. It seemed likely that her father might have been searching for her, not knowing where to look.

"He'll be back," she said to herself. Doubt pricked at her; he had been missing for more than a year now. But she felt a fool for not catching up to him, and now she wondered whether he would get lost in the city. Perhaps something had happened to him, as her dream suggested. He was urging her to come find him. But under the watchful eyes of Betsy and Uncle William, she had no idea how to search for him; she had no idea where even to begin.

"Corrine," she heard her uncle say. She turned, and could see in the fading light that he was perturbed.

"You seem . . . disheveled," he said. "Are you well?"

"I saw my father today," she said, moving toward him eagerly. "He was walking down the lane. Does he not know your address?"

Uncle William's face darkened, and not because of the waning evening light. Betsy came in behind him and began lighting lanterns along the hearth and on his desk.

"Corrine, what are you saying?" He looked at her. "And why are you dressed in this haphazard fashion?"

Out of the corner of her eye, Corrine saw Betsy wince.

"I saw my father from my bedroom today, and I ran as fast as I could to find him. But he went away down the lane, and I couldn't catch him."

"Corrine," he said, running a hand through his hair, "this is preposterous. There is simply no earthly way . . . Your father died in the War a year ago, do you understand?"

"No, no," Corrine said. "Mother thought that too. But I know I saw him."

"Corrine, I think you are still feverish. Whatever the cause, you are not to be in my study at this hour. Betsy, please escort my niece to her room."

"But—"

"No more of these fancies, Corrine," her uncle said. "I know it is difficult for you to fathom, but both of your parents are gone. They are not coming back for you." He took a gold pocket watch from his coat and checked the time. "Now, I must ask you to leave. I have business to attend to here." He frowned down at her slipper-covered feet and pushed past her to his desk.

Corrine allowed Betsy to lead her away, but she was not convinced. She had seen her father. She had dreamed of him. Somehow, he was alive.

~ Three ~

September 10, 1865

After her discussion with her uncle, Corrine was forbidden to leave the house for at least a week. Though she fretted that her father might never find her and plotted constantly about how she could escape Uncle William's house to go to him, she also could barely walk, much less run. After two days of lying feverish and chilled in the heat, she was visited by the doctor with his murderous black bag and another dose of quinine. He advised her with a stern expression not to exert herself. "Swamp fever can cause many delusions, young lady," he added. "Do not succumb to them."

"Yes, sir," she whispered, her voice hoarse from the medicine. But she didn't believe him.

She heard the doctor out in the hall, telling Uncle William that she should not be excited. "Give her some methodical, quiet task when she is well enough," he said. She leaned back on the pillow, hoping Uncle William's idea of "methodical and quiet" wouldn't involve the geography and tax-code books from his study.

The dream came to her almost before her eyes had closed.

She had followed her father to the forest. The trees hissed quietly as she approached. She laid a hand on the quivering bark of the one nearest her and it bowed. All the trees bowed then, as if stooping before a great wind. With twisted hands, the trees ushered her forward. Her father was there, walking ahead, the trees parting and closing around him in curtains of green. Sunlight fell here and there, and she saw dark shapes skirting the edges of the shafts of light.

"Father!" she shouted. But the forest swallowed her call. He still wore his dusty officer's jacket, woolen trousers, and mud-stained cavalry boots. His head and hands were bare, as though he'd left his hat and gloves on the battlefield. She saw no evidence of weapons. As he walked, he whistled, and the eerie warble drifted back to her.

A face as smooth and ageless as a Greek statue's rose out of the earth. It spoke with such longing and remorse that Corrine shivered all the way to her toes. It was as though her name had never been spoken by anyone before that moment. Corrine, *the voice said beneath rolling thunder.* Come to me. I wait for you.

September 22, 1865

When she was well enough again, Corrine decided to venture forth and test the limits of her strength. The house had been extremely quiet for the past two weeks; Uncle William was apparently staying in Alexandria on business. Corrine slid on the mourning dress, still stiff from washing, and worked at the bodice buttons as best she could. She ran a brush through her tangled hair, but did nothing more than tie it back with a worn black ribbon her mother had once given her off her bonnet.

Lace-up boots sat by the nightstand. Corrine picked them up and carried them with her as she crept out of her room. She slipped down the stairs, through the foyer, and toward the front door.

"Where you going?" Betsy said.

Corrine jumped. The maid had appeared from nowhere.

"I was just—I'm . . . going for a walk outside," she said,

hoping she sounded convincing enough.

Betsy eyed the boots she held in her hand. "About time you got some fresh air," Betsy said. "Put your shoes on, child. No need to step out barefoot."

Corrine did as she was told, lacing and tying the boots sloppily and wishing she had thought to put on her stockings. Betsy opened the door for her and followed her outside.

"You don't have to follow me," Corrine said. "I won't go out of the gate." Though that was exactly what she'd first had in mind.

"I know you won't," Betsy said. "I'm here to make sure of it." Her smile was stern.

Corrine tried to return the smile. "Very well, then," she said.

She walked off the veranda, careful to avoid looking as though she was trying to search the lane, and circled the house toward Uncle William's gardens. The brown grass crackled under her boots in the morning heat. Red clay scabbed the lawn where it had once been dug up, probably for a vegetable garden during the War.

The neighbor's house loomed beyond the hedge. Two young boys played on its shadowed porches and she could hear the faint cries of agitation when one of them lost a game. A woman dandled a baby on her knee. The boys reminded Corrine of the neighbor boys in Maryland. They had often played jacks near the lane, and she had wished for brothers like them to play with. Most of all, though, the tender scene made Corrine long for her mother.

The distance across the scarred lawn to that contented family felt incalculable. Sensing that Uncle William would not like it if she spoke to them, Corrine turned back toward the gardens, where her uncle's gardener and his assistant—a small black boy named Raphael—trimmed some ancient boxwoods.

Something caught her eye as she swiveled. Just at the edge of the property grew an unruly bush that was nearly as tall as a tree, a bush that had somehow escaped the gardener's attention.

Corrine's parents had taught her the names of most of the wild things growing in the forest; it had been their game to see who could name the most plants or animals correctly on their way to a picnic spot by the river. She moved closer, feeling the sweat gliding down her neck and soaking into the back of her dress.

"Miss Corrine," she heard Betsy say. But Corrine walked deliberately, stopping before the hulking, ancient bush, amazed at how it dwarfed her. She felt its small, rounded leaves. Her palm caught on a thorn, and she knew then what she saw. *Hawthorn.* Last night's dream filtered through the small, leathery leaves. A face had spoken her name as though it were a holy word. There had been thunder in the dream, and there was thunder now. A murder of crows swept from the pines beyond the yard, protesting the oncoming storm.

"Miss Corrine," Betsy said from far behind her.

The thorn drank her blood, and she thought she heard laughter—a soft, inhuman chuckle—from the center of the hawthorn. A voice said, *What do you most desire?*

Corrine started and backed away, almost falling over her dress as it tangled around her ankles.

The thunder boiled up from the river as Corrine and Betsy hurried inside. But no rain fell.

~ Four ~

September 23, 1865

THE NEXT TIME CORRINE WENT OUTSIDE, BETSY DID NOT accompany her, but Raphael dogged her every step. He tried to make it look as though he was only trimming the grass, but since the grass seemed to need trimming wherever Corrine strayed, she had doubts as to his true intentions.

She again approached the hawthorn where it hunched smug as a toad in the unrelenting heat. Though September was nearing its end, autumn brought little relief to Washington. While all the other trees wept at the sun's onslaught, the hawthorn crouched complacently. Were it not for the thorns, Corrine thought it would be almost pleasant to creep into its dense shade.

She stood before it, listening for the bell-like laughter. So Raphael wouldn't think her too strange, she crouched and pretended to be looking at something in the grass. She leaned forward.

"Are you there?" she whispered. She had to find out if it was just a fever-dream.

We are always here, a sleepy voice said.

"Who are you?" she said.

Those who watch. Those who wait.

Corrine frowned and tore dried grass from the red soil. "That's not an answer," she said.

For the present, it is the only answer.

Corrine kept silent, unsure what to say. A breathy hissing came from under the hedge. She heard Raphael's trimmers clacking as though he worked far down the fenceline from where she squatted. "What shall I call you then?"

Your friends. There was a pause, but before Corrine could formulate another question, the voice said, *What do you desire?*

"To see my father again," Corrine said. "To speak to him."

Much laughter answered this, then a bubbling, shushing sound. *That is impossible.*

"And my mother?" she said. It was a faint hope, but she had to try.

More laughter. *Even more impossible.*

"Why do you laugh?"

Silence.

She suddenly felt dizzy and weak, and her mouth felt cottony. She stood to keep from toppling over, which she knew would draw Raphael's immediate attention. She traced her finger along a thorn hiding under a leaf.

What else? The voice sounded impatient.

"I want to be well again," Corrine whispered. Perhaps then, she could set off to find her father.

That is easily done. There is a curious stone in your uncle's study, resting on the topmost shelf by the door. Borrow the stone and place it here. You will be well again.

Corrine backed away, unsure what the voices were asking. "Borrow?" she said. There was no answer from under the hawthorn.

It sounded very much like stealing. Well, perhaps it wasn't really if she didn't remove the stone from the grounds, and wasn't one stone much like another? They hadn't said they were going to take it anywhere.

Deep in her heart, Corrine had a feeling that if her mother were here, she would not approve. Ignoring the idea, though, Corrine turned, noticing the stray stones in the red dirt of the garden plots. Why not just pick up any of these stones? Would it make a difference? Afraid to try such a deception, she walked as swiftly as she could manage back to the house, startling Raphael where he dozed over his trimmers.

That night, Corrine couldn't sleep. She curled herself into the windowsill, staring toward the heat lightning as it licked the sky above the hills. She could see the very edge of the hawthorn if she leaned out far enough. Ghostly light from the hedge flashed in response to the sky above. In one of the flashes, movement at the edge of the lawn caught her eye. A tall man stood near the hemlocks; something about his flickering shape made her feel that he wasn't exactly human. She also was quite sure he was looking at her. He raised his hand to her, and his outstretched palm glistened in the uncertain light. She slipped from the window and back into her bed, gasping in fear.

September 24, 1865

Corrine hadn't slept well. For most of the morning she sat in the window again, watching people travel down the lane, searching not only for her father but also for the tall man near the hemlocks. She could still hear the sleepy voice from under the bush asking for the stone. She wondered again if the swamp fever had indeed done something to her mind. There was only one way to be sure.

She pushed herself away from the window and stood, her muscles aching even more than usual. Despite the heat today, she felt chilly; she shoved her hands in the folds of her dress, longing for pinafore pockets or a nice fur muff. She ignored the boots and slid on the slippers instead, as her mother would have let her do at their Maryland home.

From the bottom of the staircase, she glimpsed the dining room with its chandeliers and Persian-looking wallpaper. Betsy was nowhere to be seen. Corrine examined the empty parlor with its French screens and stiff couches as she passed. She knew that her uncle entertained there sometimes, but it still held a formal, neglected air. Corrine could never imagine a family living here, certainly not a loud, informal one like the family next door or her own.

The study was empty. As silently as possible, she navigated the chairs and tables placed around the room. The trunk squatted by her uncle's desk. It drew her, made her long for her mother, but she ignored it for the moment until she was certain no one would come to apprehend her.

The familiarity of the books was comforting. Though her family had not been able to afford quite this many books, the few they had owned and the many they had borrowed were precious to Corrine. She ran her hand along the spines of a shelf full of books, pretending to be interested in them in case Betsy walked past. She wished these books were about more engaging subjects. Most of them dealt with law, geography, or an occasional translation of some Roman orator. She tried the handles of several of the cabinets interspersed with the bookshelves, but all of them were locked.

On the topmost shelf . . . Corrine looked up but couldn't see that far above her. A book ladder leaned against the shelves on the other side of the room. She would have to move it without being noticed. She gritted her teeth and crept over to the ladder. At first, it looked too heavy to move, but she pushed and it heaved forward. Her lungs fired in her chest. Despite the ladder's wheels, it was still very unwieldy. The clicking as it moved along the track made her grit her teeth that much harder. She only hoped she could come up with a convincing explanation if Betsy came calling.

At last, the ladder was in place. She waited a moment. No one came running.

The climb up to the top shelf was dizzying. Corrine had climbed a few trees in her life, and so this would have been easy, had it not been for the earth dancing under the ladder and the weakness that the swamp fever had welded into her bones. She leaned her forehead against the next rung, seeking the reassurance of hard, cool wood. Then, she pushed herself up and peered over the rim of the top shelf.

There, indeed, a stone hid under a thick coat of dust. She reached toward it and for a precarious moment imagined herself sailing out into midair. But the stone came easily into her fingers. It was about the size of an egg, with strange cuts that looked like stair steps in its side. Whether these had been carved or were natural formations of the rock, she could not tell. She took it into her palm, tracing its edges with her fingers. The tiny stair steps felt familiar.

She made her way slowly back down the ladder to the floor, then began the teeth-grinding, clicking journey of returning the ladder to its original position. When she was finished, she waited again, still surprised that no one had come running at the sound. As the silence unfolded and it seemed that perhaps she had escaped notice, she sidled over to the desk and the trunk, the rock still in her hand.

The desk was carved from one massive piece of oak. Papers and books were neatly stacked here and there; jars of ink, pens, and ink nibs stood side by side within reach. Numbers and signatures scrawled across deeds, contracts, and wills. She tried a drawer and found that it was open. She slid her free hand into the desk and touched what felt like a book. But as her fingertips explored, something on the book *moved.*

She snatched her fingers out of the drawer and opened it a little more. A small book bound in dark leather and locked with metal clasps as menacing as fangs huddled there. Two serpents—one light, one dark—twined around each other on its cover. She moved her hand closer again. The snakes twisted, their dry metal scales rasping on the leather binding. Their gem-eyes winked at her. Corrine slammed the drawer shut as though she'd been bitten.

Two framed pictures sat near the lamp on the desk. One was a black-and-white tintype of a young woman, dressed in a dark ball gown and smiling gently as if she knew the photographer well. The other was an oil portrait in an elaborate gilt frame. A girl, perhaps fifteen or sixteen, reclined on a davenport, her head cradled on her folded arms. She wore a long white dress that came almost to her toes, and her dark blond hair fell past her shoulders, while little finger-curls framed her face.

Corrine knew without a doubt that this second image was her mother, but what struck her most was her mother's resemblance to the lady's portrait in the trunk. Her mother's hair had been the same color of autumn wheat, though it had darkened in later years. Her eyes held the same intense darkness Corrine remembered, perhaps less kind here in her youth than Corrine had known. The feline look was missing, but the chin was certainly the same. She glanced at the trunk and wished there was some way to open it, even wished that wishes would open it. Perhaps she should have asked those under the hawthorn to open the trunk—

"Corrine!"

She looked up, instinctively moving the hand that held the rock behind her back.

Uncle William came into the study.

"Why are you behind my desk?" He flipped his watch from his pocket and read the time. "For that matter, why are you here at all?"

"I was searching for something to read, Uncle William."

"Behind my desk?"

"I was just going to the other side of the room to look—"

"Corrine, one thing I do not tolerate is deceitfulness. What are you doing?"

She didn't dare tell him about the voices in the hawthorn or their request to borrow the stone from the top shelf. "My mother's trunk. I wanted to see it. I was hoping maybe my locket was in it." And that was entirely true.

Before he could say anything, she added, "And you have this portrait here of her . . ."

Her uncle sighed. He looked at his watch again. "Corrine, I'm sorry, but I don't know the whereabouts of your locket. Really now, the time for this kind of mourning is past. If you are well enough to sneak about my study, then you are well enough to think about your future. I can use a clerk in my office. I will engage a tutor to help you learn the trade, but you must apply yourself earnestly. If I find you here at this hour again, it will go the worse with you, do you understand?"

She nodded, cupping the stone deeper into her palm. It seemed to shrink, as if it knew it should hide.

"Goodness knows," he said, as though speaking more to himself then to her, "I have neither the time nor the patience for dealing with children." He looked her directly in the eyes, or as directly as anyone could when gazing at her enlarged left pupil.

"No more foolishness about the trunk or your parents or that locket, do you understand? Put all of this out of your mind."

"But the trunk—shouldn't it be . . . It was my mother's."

His stare made her so uncomfortable that she found it difficult to speak.

"It's mine now," her uncle said. "If I deem it appropriate, you may receive it in time."

Corrine nodded and swallowed. The unfairness of it bit at her throat like green persimmon.

"Now go away. The tutor will be here perhaps next week if I can secure one at such short notice." Corrine slipped around the desk. The silence in the room was deep enough for her to guess her uncle's thoughts. *Your presence disturbs me.* He glanced at her one last time, a guilty look that made her feel even more certain of his thoughts.

She ducked her head and ran outside, not caring if anyone saw her running through the grass in slippers. She ran all the way to the hawthorn, though it cost her dearly as she fell to her knees before the tangled bush. Her breath gasped out of her; she felt as though she might be sick there in the dry grass.

She stood for a moment, holding the stone in her palm, contemplating. Why was this stone so important? What could it possibly mean? They had said they wanted to borrow it. But it still sounded terribly close to stealing.

You have brought us something? the voice asked.

"Why do you want it? I need to know," she said.

It was stolen from us long ago. We would like it back.

"So you don't intend to borrow, do you?" she asked.

Clever child. But know that you return something precious to its rightful owners. There was a pause, and then soft laughter. *We see into your heart. What you wish will be done.*

"What I wish?" she asked, her brows drawing down in consternation. "I just want to be well."

But there is also a secret, a secret you want unlocked, is there not?

She thought of the trunk crouching next to her uncle's desk. The trunk that by rights belonged to her, the trunk she had known all her life and now would never have the chance to open.

"Here," she whispered. She rolled the stone under the hawthorn, watching it tilt crazily into the shadows.

Silence.

Laughter built, a sleepy giggling that gave her gooseflesh. *Excellent. The bargain is sealed.*

Something rustled deep in the bush. She felt it coming toward her, but was too transfixed to move. A small packet emerged from the tangle, pushed out into the red dirt by inhuman, twiglike fingers. Corrine watched the strange fingers recede back into the shadows. Before she could think to grab them, they were gone.

"Who are you?" she said. "Show yourself."

We dare not. You will know us in time.

Corrine looked at the little packet in the dirt. She picked it up and laid it in her palm, which ached now for the stone. The packet was smaller than her thumb, made of what she'd almost swear was mouse hide, and clasped with a single black thorn. She slid the thorn free and the flaps of hide fell open to reveal what looked very much like two dried sparrow hearts.

Crush these into your tea or water at night for the next two nights. You will be well again after that. And the other desire, wait and watch. That too will be given you.

Corrine carefully reclosed the pouch.

"Thank you," she said. She pushed off her knees and left without waiting for a response.

~ Five ~

September 24, 1865

She was in her mother's bedroom. Her mother was flying around the room, frantically searching for the iron cross, while outside something large and terrible banged on the walls, the shutters, the doors. Corrine could feel its breath, stifling as the unchanging heat. Her mother threw things to the floor, shouting at her to search. She did, but only halfheartedly. She wanted to see what was outside. She tried to go to where the boards were bending and cracking under the weight of its blows, but her mother grabbed her by the arm and compelled her to dig through the bedcovers instead. As the thundering grew and the house seemed about to shake apart, Corrine's mother stretched out on the bed and died. Her last whisper: "He's here."

Corrine woke, her throat dry as though she'd swallowed blood—the taste of the curious medicine, which she'd crushed into the water she'd begged from Betsy. She felt sure she'd heard glass shattering in her sleep. She reached over to the nightstand, feeling for the water glass. It was still intact. A loud thumping rattled up from the floor, almost like her dream. She hesitated for a second, and then slid out of bed. She crept out of her room, her feet bare on the braided rugs and stairs. Something ripped and shattered things in the study. As she came down the stairs, she saw a tall form melt back through the shadows.

Steps and shouting sounded from deeper within the house, and lights bumped toward her down the hall. She froze halfway down the stairs.

"Corrine," Uncle William said from behind her on the stairs. He held a lantern aloft to look in her face, his dressing gown sleeve trailing down into shadow. Betsy, on the first floor, also held a lantern and looked up at her. Her normally hidden hair was coiled in a graying braid along her shoulder, and her face was filled with suspicion. Several of the male servants accompanied her, including the gardener.

"Did you hear the noises?" Uncle William said. "Do you know what happened?"

"I . . . heard the noise," she said. "I was just coming down to see—"

Before she could finish, the gardener said from the doorway of the study, "Lord-a-mercy, Mr. McPhee."

Her uncle brushed past her on the stairs, swinging his lantern toward the study, shoving the other men aside to look in at the study entry.

"Good Lord!" he said.

"Uncle William—" Corrine began.

Her uncle looked at Betsy. "Take her to her room," he said.

Betsy nodded and came up to her. The lantern made gruesome patterns on the maid's face as she took Corrine's arm without a word and escorted her upstairs. There was no pity in her eyes as she made sure that Corrine got back into bed and pulled the covers up to her chin. In fact, as she closed the door, Corrine was quite sure it was not a trick of the lantern light that made Betsy's gaze so accusing.

September 25, 1865

The house was unusually silent the next morning. Betsy did not arrive with breakfast. The tutor her uncle had promised wouldn't appear until next week. Thinking that perhaps she had risen earlier than everyone, Corrine decided to go down to the study and try to see in the daylight what she had not seen in the darkness. She again left her boots where they stood, hoping her silent feet might give her the advantage of more time.

She couldn't hear anything as she slid around the newel post at the bottom of the stairs. She peered into the room, and then down the hall. Trying to keep her crepe skirts as quiet as possible, she slipped into the room.

Every bit of air escaped her lungs. Cabinet doors hung crazily from their hinges, revealing skulls, feathers, books, and other strange objects she couldn't identify. Many of the books had been torn down from the shelves, their spines cracked and the pages ripped or trampled into piles. They fluttered in the breeze that streamed through the broken study window. The desk drowned in papers; several of its drawers lay broken on top of it.

The trunk sat where she had seen it before, but the dome top was smashed and the embossed tin twisted where the lock had been. The wooden staves had splintered into broken ribs. She ran to the trunk and knelt before it, running her hands over it helplessly. The spicy perfume washed over her, reminding her that her inadvertent wish to open the trunk, even unspoken, had occurred only just yesterday.

She lifted its lid slowly. The portrait, which she had expected to be cracked and yellowed by now, was still as vibrant as it had been when she was four. Only now, because of the violence done to the trunk, the lady's profile was ripped from her forehead to her chin, her heart punctured by an ancient splinter.

Tears threatened, but Corrine reached forward and removed the splinter from the portrait. She tried piecing the canvas back together and was surprised to recognize the pendant hanging from the lady's severed throat. An iron cross, just like her mother's. The lady regarded her with a twisted smile.

The ethereal perfume drifted around her. Memories of her mother wreathed her; this faint scent had always been present around her mother. It was certainly not as strong as this, but something akin to it, as soft and dangerous as nightshade.

"No tears," she said to herself. *No tears,* the lady whispered out of her torn mouth.

The trunk had obviously been rifled through, but there was no way to know if anything was missing. She had never seen anything inside the trunk except the lady's portrait. She lifted the edges of a frayed cloth that felt like silk but looked more like wool. Underneath was an ebony box with clasps white as teeth. Empty. A bottle of twisted glass with a broken stopper curved against her hand. Also empty. A thimble-size cup carved of spongy wood into the shape of a snail shell. She dug deeper. A crown of unwithered flowers came into her hands, and as she drew it up, she knew she had found the source of the scent.

She breathed deep and the air shimmered. She looked at the flowers more closely and realized she could not identify their origin or, truthfully, their color. Somewhere between corpse-white and moonlight, divided by thorns. More and deeper than silver-white. Fish scales. Pearl. The whites of eyes.

She put the crown on her head. The air rippled around her; she heard again the soft laughter from under the hawthorn. The perfume drifted down onto her shoulders like a veil of funereal lullabies.

Her fingers searched, brushing against the handle of a mirror that sent tendrils of pain through her fingertips. Somehow, she knew she should not look into its tarnished surface. She touched paper and pulled forth a packet of letters tied with a dry-rotted blue ribbon.

She observed the wax seal as she pushed the first letter open; a curious-looking figure of a seated man holding a serpent in each hand. Beneath the veil of the flowers' strange perfume, she could smell the old parchment. As she unfolded it, a slip of paper fell from it. When she held the two side by side, she could see that one was a translation of the other. The original was faded and smeared, penned in what Corrine guessed to be a Latin script so old-fashioned as to be nearly impossible to read, even if she had been able to piece together the language. But the translation said:

[Trans. note: Bottom half missing.]

May 1360

Dear Brother:

May this letter bring with it the deep peace of the Holy Spirit and of He who calls himself our Friend. I write to tell you that the child is well, that she grows faster than the flowers in her nurse's garden. We have done all we can to shield her; the wards are renewed at the full of the moon as you instructed. At your wish, she stays indoors and has little truck with those outside. But those who know her have certainly fallen under her spell. I believe she is what you say. We call her

Mary Rose, and even more so than her poor mother, we hope she will make a suitable bride of Christ in God's good time [. . .]

The rest of the original letter was tattered beyond hope of reading. Corrine put it down, still holding the translation. She looked at the portrait of the woman, wondering if she was the subject of the letter. If so, she looked like anything but a nun.

"Mary Rose," she whispered.

The lady smiled knowingly at her.

"Corrine!"

She turned at the sound of her uncle's voice. The translation floated out of her hand.

"What do you think you're doing?" His great brows bristled over his dark eyes. He stood in the doorway tall and menacing as a mountain.

"I was . . . I . . ." She felt ridiculous in her mourning clothes and flower crown.

He stalked toward her, his watch chain dangling at his waist. He yanked the flower crown from her head and threw it in the trunk. "I will not have this, Corrine," he said, as he stooped and picked up the letters that had fallen from her hand.

"I know that last night was likely quite disturbing to you. Obviously I cannot lock you out of this room, since there is no door. But I have told you before, this trunk is not for you."

Corrine could not contain the anger that flared. "This was my mother's," she said. "It's all I have left of her, and now it's ruined! Why can't I see it even for a moment?"

"Corrine." His tone was deadly. "Do you remember the rules here?"

She kept her mouth shut, afraid that anything she might say would only make him angrier.

"Do you?"

She nodded.

"Above all, you are to obey me—under *all* circumstances. I told you repeatedly not to touch anything in this room. This trunk may have once been your mother's, but it belongs to me unless and until I see fit to release it to you.

"Furthermore, this room is now the scene of a crime. The Inspector is coming today to investigate. By moving these things, you may have spoiled any chance of the Inspector discovering the criminal."

Corrine shifted uncomfortably. Her uncle retreated a little, still holding the letters he'd snatched away.

"You were coming down the stairs when this was happening. Did you see or hear anything to indicate who might have done this?"

Corrine could not meet his eyes. Her gaze fell to the floor, where the portrait of her mother lay trampled near a ripped chair. Her mother's dark eyes urged her to tell the truth.

Uncle William seized on her reluctance. "You saw something, didn't you? Corrine, I must know. It's very important. What did you see?"

"I saw a . . . a tall shape move across the study."

"What did it look like?"

"It was dark. I couldn't . . ."

"Corrine, what did it look like?"

The strange perfume from the trunk wreathed itself around her. Corrine tasted blood again.

The words came before she could stop them. "It looked like . . . like the man I saw standing near the hemlock the other day. I wanted to see inside the trunk, but I promise I didn't tell anyone."

Uncle William stared at her for a moment. Then he waded through the mess to the ladder, which hung off its track. He righted it and sent it scooting around the wall to the case where the stone had been. He clambered like a giant, leggy spider up to the top, and, as he did so, images and voices raced through her mind—the stone, how the hawthorn people had known exactly where it was, how they'd only wanted to "borrow" it, how they had given her payment for it . . .

"It's gone," he said, his voice weighted with unnamable horror.

"Just like the cross, just like . . ." He didn't finish. "It's gone," he said again. He turned and sat on one of the rungs, putting his head in his hands.

"They told me to do it, Uncle William. It was just a rock, not anything special . . ."

Uncle William dropped his hands to his knees and looked up at her. "Who are you talking about? The man by the hemlock?"

"The hawthorn people. I'm sure if you just go out to the hawthorn . . ." She barely recognized her own voice as it squeaked out the last words.

Uncle William's face paled to the color of the curtains that tangled in the broken window, but his eyes were pits of dark fire.

"Pack your things," he said. "You're leaving. Tomorrow."

Uncle William came down off the ladder, walking past her to his desk as though she wasn't there. As she left the room, she saw him pick up the portrait of her mother. She lingered around the corner long enough to hear him say, "Elizabeth, I tried. I tried to protect her. I just can't do it any longer."

She would have stayed, but Betsy came down the hall with a knowing look that sent her careening out the front door.

"Miss Corrine!" Betsy cried, but her voice was soon lost around the corner of the house.

There was no one in the back garden and Corrine wouldn't have cared if there had been. She ran to the hawthorn, reaching out impotently toward the wicked thorns.

"Why did you do this?" she shouted.

There was nothing. No whispered laughter, no slow, sleepy voice.

"Why?" she shouted again. "I demand an answer." If she had been a few years younger, she would have stomped the ground. Instead, she wrapped her fingers around the base of one of the thorns, threatening to snap it off.

The voice finally came, thick with irritation. *Unhand us, child. We have favored you. Do not treat that favor lightly.*

"Who did this?" Corrine said.

The Captain, of course.

"Captain who? Of what? Who sent him?"

He is only known as the Captain. He commands. He serves the witch.

"The witch? What are you talking about?" She dropped her hands from the thorn, wanting to sag to the ground.

Betsy came around the house shouting her name. "Miss Corrine, your uncle say to get in this house right now!"

"What witch?" Corrine tried again.

But the voice was gone.

"Miss Corrine!"

Corrine turned from the hawthorn and ran back across the rain-starved lawn, avoiding Betsy's accusing stare. Without a care for propriety, Corrine didn't stop running until she'd gotten into the house and up the steps to her room.

~ Six ~

September 25, 1865

BY EVENING, EVERYTHING WAS PACKED AND READY FOR departure the next morning. There hadn't been much to pack, really; everything Corrine owned fit into an old carpetbag Betsy had loaned her. The house had been quiet since Uncle William told Corrine of her fate. She heard the Inspector arrive and crept out on the landing to see him, but Uncle William had noticed and said sternly, "Back to your room, Corrine."

The Inspector's visit, she knew, was useless. Surely Uncle William knew it too. She guessed that he was just keeping up appearances. She imagined that the Inspector would agree to dispatch an officer to watch over the lane in case the burglar reappeared, and that her uncle would nod and say that he thought that a splendid idea. She wondered how he explained the destruction of the trunk or the revealed secrets that lurked behind the shattered cabinet doors. She imagined that he was quite clever in hiding the truth with explanations that sounded plausible. He was a lawyer, after all.

She pushed herself off her bed, where she had been sitting since she had finished packing. She couldn't say she was entirely sad to be leaving a house where she was never wanted, but the mystery of where she was going set butterflies flitting in her stomach at the horrendous possibilities. Her hand went to her throat again, searching for her locket, just as she had often seen her mother do for the iron cross. Now more than ever, she wondered what the iron cross had meant and why it had been so important to her mother—and now her uncle. She wondered why Mary Rose wore it too—she'd decided that the lady in the trunk portrait must have been Mary Rose. Was the iron cross a mark of some secret society?

She also thought about the people under the hawthorn. Had all of this happened because of her ill-fated wish to see inside the trunk? Who was the Captain? The fact that he served a witch seemed preposterous, but then she would never have believed that she would talk to twig-fingered people who lived in a hawthorn bush. She went to the window where twilight fell like a stone through the trees. She peered at the hawthorn, almost expecting to see something and relieved that she didn't.

But then she saw a dark shimmer by the hemlocks again. The tall man turned, as though he felt her gaze. He wore shadows deeper than twilight, and, as before, she couldn't see his face. But she felt his gaze, felt it through the swift gasp of her heart, the seizure in her knees. The Captain raised his hand to her, and she saw, despite the dusk, that his hand was shiny and scarlet, as though wet with blood.

She forced herself away from the window and back to the bed, hoping that when she left tomorrow she would never see him again. Surely he couldn't follow her where she was going. She sat, her knees weak and trembling, her breath catching in her lungs.

Betsy came in at that moment with a supper tray and, more important to Corrine, a lantern against the dark. Corrine knew her agitation must have been obvious, but Betsy didn't ask her what was wrong.

"You'll be getting up early tomorrow, Miss Corrine," Betsy said. "See you get good rest." She looked as if she wanted to say more as she sat the tray on the little folding table, but she didn't.

Corrine wanted to ask if she had ever seen the man with the bloody hand, but remembered Betsy had told her not to speak of "booger men." Corrine imagined she would prefer not to hear about it.

"Do you know where Uncle William is sending me, Betsy?" she asked.

"He'll tell you in the morning, child," the maid said. "Now eat your supper, go to bed, and don't do anything else foolish to upset your uncle."

Corrine nodded. With the Captain outside, she had no desire to go anywhere. She only hoped that he would not come inside of his own will again, though Corrine had a feeling he'd gotten what he wanted. Perhaps the gesture he had made to her was one of good-bye.

She looked at the little packet the hawthorn people had given her in exchange for the stone. There was one dose left, but she left it on the bedstand untouched. She ate her dinner of roast beef, overcooked string beans, and dry corn bread. In the beginning, there had sometimes been custard or cake for dessert. But not tonight.

She set the tray aside and put the lantern on the nightstand. She fell asleep to its jumping light, unwilling to succumb totally to the dark.

Her father was far ahead of her in the forest. Corrine ran after him, calling, but the trees mocked her. She heard distant cries of pain.

"Father!" she called, and tried to run harder. But the ground pulled her down, squeezing her in the deathly embrace of a constrictor.

She pushed at the massive coils as they looped over her. She screamed, but her mouth filled with soil, grubs, and rotten leaves.

This is your enemy, *she heard the trees whisper through their roots.* This is what imprisons you.

She sensed that the voices spoke not just of her, but of her father too. The terrible constriction on her lungs did not lessen. Her ribs and elbows cracked under the strain. In her terror-blank mind, she heard that voice again, the one that said her name as though it were a holy word. Corrine. Drink.

She felt fingers in her hair, fingers that drew her head up above the coils of earth long enough for her to clear her mouth and take a shallow breath. A shadowy man looked down at her; she could not see his features for all the mud in her eyes. He wiped her face with an edge of his cloak. He held a translucent cup in which rust red liquid swirled, the color of the medicinal powder she'd been given.

Will you drink now? *he asked.* Only this will save you and your father.

She couldn't say anything. She opened her mouth. The liquid soothed and lightened her so that she floated up from the soil, as though the earth was little more than water. The coils slid from her, and she was again on solid ground. In the distance, her father's screams stopped.

Do not doubt me, *the man said.* All this is for your benefit. Come to me, and you will see.

She held out her hand to him. The ageless sadness in his voice made her lungs ache. You must come to me . . .

She sat up in bed, her lungs afire. Thunder cracked and rolled all around; snakes of lightning thrashed beyond the window. She fumbled for the little packet and slipped the thorn clasp from it. In the pounding dark, she found the dinner tray and the teacup which held the remains of her tea. Her hands shook as she crushed the sparrow heart and drank the dregs. It did not taste as it had in the dream. This was rust and blood. But if it might save her father, she would choke it down willingly.

The rain came as she swallowed, lashing through the open window and onto the floor. But she was too weary to even try to wrestle with the shutters and sash. When at last the pain eased, she set the cup down, turned on her side in the sagging bed, and slept.

~ Seven ~

September 26, 1865

THE HORSES BOWED THEIR HEADS AGAINST THE PREDAWN rain, flattening their ears and chewing their bits uncomfortably as the driver forced them to remain still. Uncle William bundled Corrine into the carriage with her carpetbag, and then stood at the carriage door. The occasional flare of lightning revealed his relieved expression.

He shouted to be heard above the rain on the carriage roof. "I am sending you to a reform school run by an old friend of mine. I dispatched a courier yesterday to arrange for your express carriages and to alert Miss Brown to your imminent arrival. She will explain the school to you and help you settle."

"Where is the school?" Corrine asked.

"In Virginia," he answered. "Not too far over the border."

"Virginia?" She couldn't hide the incredulity in her voice.

Lightning twisted his mouth into a frown. "The Civil War is over, Corrine. It's time you realized that. There are much worse places I could send you, believe me."

He paused, and Corrine wished in that moment that some affection lay between them, that she could embrace him and feel sorrow at their parting as she had felt when her father had left for the War. But she felt nothing. She stared at him, wishing he would go so she could close the door and keep out the rain.

"Be a good girl," he said finally. "Do what you're told. No more of these fancies of yours, do you hear? Perhaps one day you can return here."

She didn't think he meant it. She was quite certain that she would never come back.

"Very well then," he said at her silence. He stepped back and shut the door. The carriage rocked as it released his weight. Snapping the reins, the driver called to his horses, and the carriage lurched through the mud. Corrine wrapped a rug around her knees and looked past the leather window-flap into the rain.

She watched as the darkness swallowed her uncle's house. What she longed for at this moment was the portrait of Mary Rose. She would have liked to see her again and to read the rest of the letters about her. She imagined that Mary Rose must have become a great lady at court.

The trees fell away and the red line of dawn appeared under the stormwrack. A tall, hooded man walked down the lane in the opposite direction. The Captain. She released the window-flap and wrapped the rug tighter around her, hoping she had somehow escaped his notice.

After several hours of struggling through the storm, the coach stopped in Gainesville, where the driver informed Corrine she was to change coaches. Corrine watched the exhausted, mud-caked horses as they were unhitched and led away before the tavern maid found her and offered a bit of supper.

As she entered the tavern, most people remained hunched over their plates or mugs, keeping to themselves. One woman at the end of the bar stared, her red-rimmed eyes trained on Corrine as though she'd pluck her very soul from her body.

Corrine tried to ignore her and sat as instructed by the maid. She ate quietly, her carpetbag pressed against her side. She wondered if they were whispering behind their hands about her and if they knew she was a Yankee orphan. The maid glanced at her, and Corrine stiffened her spine. War or not, Johnny Reb wouldn't see her fret.

A lanky driver entered, calling her name. She gathered her things and stood, but a shadow blocked her. The red-eyed woman grabbed her hand and pressed something into her palm, gabbling at her in words that slid from English to French and back again.

"He calls *pour tu—Ne pas faire de mal!* He calls!"

Corrine clutched her carpetbag to her, as if it could shield her. The driver pushed the strange Frenchwoman away, saying, "Get on now!" He gestured to Corrine, and she slid around the table and out the door, the edges of the thing sharp against her palm.

The smells of mud and manure greeted her as she followed the driver outside. In the weak sunlight, she opened her hand. The woman had given her a strange gift—like a playing card, only larger. On its surface, a gold-and-silver-gilded snake ate its own tail as it coiled around a young, barely-clad woman. The word *Le Monde* flowed across the bottom in elegant black script.

She remembered the serpents on Uncle William's book twisting under her fingers. The coils of the earth tightened around her again in her dreams, squeezing the breath out of her. What did it mean? The mysterious dreams, the stone, the cross—it felt as though even greater coils looped about her, entangling her in something she couldn't comprehend.

The woman followed them out of the tavern, and the driver murmured, "Best get moving."

"Where is this school I'm going to?" she asked, as he helped her into the carriage.

"On up in Culpeper."

The Frenchwoman disappeared around the corner of the tavern, and Corrine shivered. Three ladies veiled in black walked together on the opposite side of the street.

"And how much farther?" she asked.

"Twenty more miles or so." The driver handed in her carpetbag and shut the door.

Corrine settled in again to the creaking, thrashing cradle of the journey, unsure whether she wanted to go to this school of Miss Brown's. She certainly wanted to get away from the strange woman, but she wondered what she'd meant. Was something about to happen? Corrine couldn't see how things could get much worse. She clutched the Tarot card beneath the rug on her knees and was glad the rough journey made it impossible to fall asleep and dream.

Culpeper was located in the rolling hills of the Piedmont, about sixty miles from Uncle William's home in Washington, and the second coach made good time despite the muddy road. When the driver announced that they'd reached the town of Culpeper, Corrine looked out onto the evening streets, watching the women's skirts bedraggled by black water with unbecoming satisfaction.

Corrine observed the square as they passed. Signs for a milliner's, a general store, and a law office met her gaze. People struggled through the muddy walks and streets, gentlemen doffing their hats to ladies as they passed. Nothing was different about this place. She had imagined that the South would be a place of despair—the inhabitants sullen, fomenting further secret rebellions. She had expected a lynching or an illicit slave auction. She did see a few free black servants waiting on their mistresses or masters, but this was no different than in Washington. She sighed and turned away, already bored.

In the coach's twilit gloom, Corrine looked again at the card.

The girl stared up at her with such a forsaken expression, and she couldn't help but think that the serpent seemed inordinately satisfied about his captive. As the carriage passed out of the town, Corrine pushed the leather flap open and let the card flutter out on the wind, watching the flash of gold and silver sink into the mud. Then she slid back in her seat as far as she could. She didn't want to see the Captain standing alongside the road, his blood-stained hand prophesying doom.

It was not long before the carriage turned up a hill that was crowned by bristling pines and hemlocks. Corrine couldn't see the school, but sensed it brooding there in the dark trees.

When at last they topped the rise, iron gates swung open. An iron-spiked fence at least ten feet tall ran out at angles toward the rain-soaked trees. The gate clanged shut as the carriage wheels shirred across the wet gravel. The school loomed like an impregnable Gothic fortress, gargoyles and curious beasts leering down from the third-story eaves.

This is not a school, Corrine thought. *This is a prison.*

The coach stopped in front of great oaken doors. The coach door opened and the driver reached in for her carpetbag, and then helped her climb out.

A woman waited where the first step of the manor met the gravel drive. She was thin and gray-eyed, her mouth stiff as a dead fish.

Corrine shivered.

"Welcome to Falston Manor," the woman said.

Corrine heard the driver snap his reins. The carriage was gone almost before Corrine noticed.

"I am Miss de Mornay," the woman continued. She did not ask Corrine's name, nor if she needed help with her carpetbag. She simply turned and, twitching her skirts away from the steps, climbed toward the door. Corrine hefted her bag by its handles, took a deep breath, and followed.

The worn brass plaque by the door said "Falston Reformatory School for Young Ladies, 1859." By the time Corrine wrestled her way inside, Miss de Mornay was already through the foyer and climbing the stairs. Corrine glimpsed immense rooms and passages on either side of the foyer. Past the staircase in the middle of a long, shadowy corridor, Corrine saw a single light spilling onto the hall floor.

Miss de Mornay's lantern left shadows in her wake. Corrine hurried to follow, holding onto the worn, wooden banister and glancing at dusty daguerreotypes hanging on the walls. She caught up to Miss de Mornay on the third floor, where Miss de Mornay had stopped before a small door hunched under the eaves. Corrine held her carpetbag against her body like a shield, waiting as Miss de Mornay untangled a key from the ring at her wrist and unlocked the door.

Twilight crept away across the eaves, and the room was so dark Corrine could make out little more than a cot and a brooding potbelly stove attached to a chimney in the wall. The roof sloped low over the cot, and the lantern light again threw harsh shadows. A bellpull gathered dust on the wall near the door.

When she spoke, Miss de Mornay did not look at Corrine, but at a point somewhere over her head, as though she'd just seen a cobweb she would like to wipe away. "Mara will bring you supper, as you have arrived late. After that, Headmistress Brown will see you in her study." Miss de Mornay's monotone grated on Corrine's ears.

"Thank you," Corrine said. She opened her mouth to ask more questions, but Miss de Mornay was already swishing out the door, her black taffeta train trailing behind her like a dead foxtail.

The key turned in the lock. Corrine heard a distant scream, and then realized it was only the wind whipping above the chimney. Feeling her way across the dark room to the cot,

Corrine sat down and put her bag at her feet. *Yes,* she thought, *a prison.*

Steps outside the door and jangling keys made Corrine leap off the cot before she was fully awake. She'd fallen asleep, her back slumped and the top of her head resting uncomfortably against the sloping ceiling. A lantern blinded her. A girl with skin so black it could barely be distinguished from her maid's dress brought in a tray and set it on the floor near the end of the cot. This must be Mara.

"Miz Brown says to eat and then come downstairs. She's down the hall on the first floor and to the right," the girl said.

Corrine nodded. The girl swept her lantern around the room until the light revealed the curving glass of another lantern on a washstand by the window.

The girl lit it with her flame. "I'll bring up some coal and get your stove going while you talk to Miz Brown. That bellpull there's in case you have trouble. But you better not be pulling it if no trouble's to be had. Miz de Mornay'd skin you alive."

Corrine cringed, as if she was somehow guilty without knowing it. "Thank you," Corrine said. She realized she had forgotten to take off her coat. Despite being farther south, Culpeper was cooler than Washington, and the rain had brought an unshakable damp chill.

"I'm Corrine," she said. She made a little curtsy, old-fashioned as it might seem. She knew she had angered Betsy; she did not want to upset this girl, who seemed much closer to her age and might even, in time, be a friend.

"Mara," the maid said, confirming Corrine's assumption. She didn't return Corrine's curtsy but instead stalked to the door. Mara was muscular in a way that reminded Corrine of old gnarled wood. She didn't quite fit in this tiny attic room. Corrine caught Mara's eye as she left the room. The girl shook her head slightly as she closed the door behind her. This time, Corrine didn't hear the key in the lock before Mara's footsteps retreated down the hall.

Corrine sighed and turned her attention to the tray. She hadn't eaten since the stopover at the tavern. As Corrine forced down salty ham soup and bread crusts, she imagined what the rest of Falston Reformatory School for Young Ladies was like. The notion of a reformatory school, and the fact that she now attended one gave her gooseflesh.

Her mother had once spoken of schools started in New York for girls that had "problems." When she'd asked what kind of problems, her mother hadn't replied.

She went to the kitchen then to ask Nora, who had been only slightly more forthcoming as she beat cake batter in an old ceramic bowl. "Places for girls that's done bad things, Miss Corrine. Like those that's murdered or stole from people or . . . things like that," she said.

"Like Mary Surratt?" Corrine asked, speaking of the woman who had recently been hanged for conspiring to assassinate President Lincoln.

"Sort of," Nora said. "And some I'm sure that's worse."

Corrine could hardly imagine what could be worse than killing the president. She wondered if the other girls were there under such circumstances. Had these girls killed someone or stolen things? A chunk of ham lodged in her throat at the thought of attending class with a crowd of murderesses. How many were there?

She considered running away. It was said that those who went out West were allowed to claim as much land as they wanted. But somehow she doubted that rumor applied to fifteen-year-old girls. And the thought of being on a wagon train in the middle of the wilderness with no one to protect her . . . She knew if it came to the worst, she'd be the first to be sacrificed. She wished she could run away to the green fields of her father's farm, back to the days when her father and Willy had worked the land while her mother and Nora worked in the kitchen and ran the household.

All that was gone now, she knew. Uncle William had determined that the farm would be sold. And if the witch's Captain had followed Corrine from her uncle's, even the farm was no longer safe.

No, she was trapped here. She had no money and no prospects. She was as surely trapped as any slave had been in the South. She thought of the girl trapped in the serpent's coils on the Tarot card and the iron bars surrounding the manor. Did anyone ever manage to escape?

She couldn't eat much more after that thought. She stood and took the lantern from the washstand. She guessed this would be the only time she'd ever be able to move freely around this place. She would have liked to look around, but knew the lantern would make her movements obvious. Still, there was no harm in investigating the room next to hers at least, the only other room on this level as far as she could tell.

The door to the neighboring room was locked. But before she could withdraw her fingers from the doorknob, a surge of cold crept through it, freezing her fingers in place.

She wandered through a forest bright with moonlight. She looked down and saw that she wore a white nightgown that shimmered as she climbed through the branches of a hemlock. A man came through the wood then, walking slowly. He stopped under the tree and looked up. He had been following her.

Corrine nearly screamed. She wanted to go down to the man, but she also wanted to stay in the tree. She didn't know how she knew this man was dangerous, but she sensed whispers, dark intimations of talks her mother and Nora had ceased whenever she came near. Corrine shuddered so deeply that the doorknob released its hold on her.

She stood shaking, barely able to hold up her lantern with her other hand. She had never had a waking dream like this before; true terror had always been confined to sleep. And she'd never seen through another girl's eyes. This waking dream definitely felt like her vision had been exchanged with another girl's. She wondered if she was getting sick again; if in fact, as the doctor had said, she was having delusions. But as the hawthorn people had promised, she felt entirely well. There was absolutely no weakness in her lungs or body. And this dream felt different than the fever-lands of her illness. It felt all too real.

Corrine remembered that she was to go see Miss Brown and began her descent down the creaking stairs. The water-stained portraits accused her of knowledge she didn't possess. She passed Mara on her way back up the stairs, laden with a coal scuttle. The maid looked at her sidelong and shook her head again. The silence after that was punctuated only by Corrine's boots on the creaking floorboards. If this truly was a school, where were all the other girls?

At the bottom of the stairs, Corrine turned right as Mara had indicated, moving toward the doorway where yellow light flickered into the hall. She smelled the mustiness of books and unaired rooms as she passed some of the locked doors.

When she came to the doorway, she stood, uncertain what to do. Books lined the walls from floor to ceiling—the musty, leather-and-paper odor was even stronger here. Firelight from a grate threw the fronds of tall plants by the windows into high relief. A palm plant arched over the desk like a green parasol. A woman sat beneath it, writing. Besides the light rain poking at the windows and a clock ticking on the mantel, the scratch of the woman's pen was the only sound in the room. Her chestnut hair coiled in a fashionable spiral bun. The woman glanced up, and Corrine blinked in surprise at her youth. She looked younger than Corrine's mother had been when she died—certainly not the spinsterly schoolmarm that Corrine had been expecting.

And then Corrine recognized her. This was the woman in the tintype on Uncle William's desk—the one in the dark ball gown who smiled so sweetly for the camera.

Only she was not smiling now. "Well, Miss Jameson," she said, "come in. And shut the door behind you."

Corrine entered the room, setting her lantern on a nearby table that seemed only slightly less cluttered than its fellows. She shut the door and came to stand before Miss Brown's desk.

"Sit," Miss Brown said, indicating a faded brocade chair to Corrine's left.

Corrine looked around the room while Miss Brown went back to writing. A collection of strange natural objects was perched haphazardly among the books on various tables and chairs. Stones glimmered from bird's nests. A fish in a jar rested next to a pile of what looked like shed snakeskins. There were dried mushrooms and pinecones, seed catkins perched on top of seashells, feathers and teeth, bones and honeycombs. Corrine did not know what to make of it all, nor of the woman who had obviously spent so much time collecting it. She shifted her gaze in Miss Brown's direction and glimpsed gold coils on a book's cover by her elbow. Gold, like one of the serpents on Uncle William's book.

Though she did not look up, Miss Brown seemed to feel Corrine's scrutiny, for she nudged the book deeper into the pile at her elbow. She stopped writing, sighed, and sat back.

"Miss Jameson," she said, peering at Corrine as though she needed spectacles. "Do you know what brings you to Falston?"

"I think so—" Corrine began.

"Good," Miss Brown said. "Your Uncle William is a very good friend of mine." Corrine suppressed her desire to admit that she had seen Miss Brown's photograph, guessing that would be inappropriate.

Miss Brown continued, "Your uncle felt that perhaps Falston might do you good. At the very least, we will provide an education he cannot."

Corrine nodded, unsure if she should speak.

"Falston is a very special place, Miss Jameson. We take young ladies of your situation and transform them into outstanding women of means. Do you understand my full meaning?"

Corrine shook her head.

"You have come to a dangerous crossroad, Miss Jameson. One that will decide your ultimate fate. Girls like you have very few choices, and it is easy for those choices to be completely eliminated, all because of a careless mistake. Of course, most of our girls differ from you in that they have mothers and fathers. Many of the families, however, don't want the girls returned to them."

Corrine's jaw slackened. Not want them? What could anyone possibly do that her parents wouldn't want her back? Perhaps they all truly were murderesses.

"Yes, it may seem surprising," Miss Brown went on, as though she had seen this reaction a hundred times. "But this is what I mean about choices. Some of our girls have made very bad choices. We give them the opportunity to make better ones. If they follow the proper path, they can leave Falston and return to their families. Some can go on to be teachers, nurses, governesses—even headmistresses like me. Some may even be marriageable, but the best they can hope for right now is to learn to take care of themselves."

Miss Brown stood and paced over to the fireplace. She was smartly dressed in a dark blue, pinstriped jacket and matching skirt with a modest bustle. Miss Brown stared into the fire, stroking a gold timepiece at her collar.

She continued, "But there are some girls who don't make it, Corrine. Some girls come to us and refuse to change, refuse to make the right choices. Girls like that are headed on a runaway train toward their own destruction."

Corrine saw in her mind the woman who had shoved the card into her hand earlier in the day. She saw the red-rimmed eyes, the wild hair, and smelled the stink of liquored breath. She remembered the wide circle the tavern crowd had made to keep from touching or acknowledging her. The thought of such a fate was terrifying.

"Come here," Miss Brown said. "I want to show you something."

Corrine pushed herself up from the chair, carefully skirting tables and two armchairs until she stood with Miss Brown before the fire.

Miss Brown took a jar down from the mantel. "Do you see what's in this jar?" Miss Brown asked.

Corrine peered at it. It looked like a collection of twigs with a sack of silk nestled among them. "I don't know what—"

But Miss Brown was already uncapping it and pulling the sack out into the firelight.

"This," she said, "is a silk moth cocoon. The silkworm has spun herself this amazing blanket. Inside, she'll undergo a transformation the likes of which we cannot begin to comprehend. But what happens if she doesn't choose to become the beautiful moth she was meant to be?" Miss Brown palpated the cocoon, and then sliced through the silk with a fingernail. Brown fluid oozed out, dripping onto the hearth.

"She dies," Miss Brown said, "rotting from the inside out."

The stench made Corrine step back, gagging. Miss Brown threw the rest of the jar's contents into the fire. She drew a kerchief from her pocket and wiped her hands. "So much for that experiment," she muttered, and then looked up. "You understand what I mean then, Miss Jameson?"

"Yes," said Corrine.

"Then you may return to your room."

Corrine nodded and moved gratefully toward the door. As Corrine gathered up her lantern, Miss Brown said, "One more thing, Miss Jameson."

Corrine turned.

Miss Brown had seated herself again at her desk, and the palm frond loomed over her. "Forgive the impropriety, but I must ask you to put your mourning clothes aside for now. Though I understand your grief, I also must ask you not to allow it to distract you. You'll be hard-pressed to catch up since we're almost to the middle of term. But I believe if you make the right choices, you can do it." She smiled strangely, almost conspiratorially. "Remember, a woman's best work is that which is unseen by mortal eyes."

Corrine nodded again. She thought for some reason of Mary Rose's portrait, her sly cat-smile and tilted cat-eyes. The stench of the rotten silkworm hung in the air. Corrine picked up the lantern, opened the door softly, and walked back to her dark attic room, careful not to go anywhere near the door of the room next to hers.

~ EIGHT ~

September 27, 1865

THE SUN WOKE CORRINE AS IT SLANTED THROUGH THE attic window. The stove had gone out in the night, and the damp cold had seeped into her hair, her nostrils, even her ears, making the small warmth of the weak autumn sun welcome. She could not believe how completely summer had turned to autumn since she had left Uncle William's house. She sat up, wondering what time it was and if she was meant to wait for breakfast or to go downstairs. She heard something that sounded like a bell or a gong being struck and the rush of feet far below. A queasy feeling rose in her stomach; she wasn't sure whether it was hunger or nerves.

At the washbasin, she grimaced at the chilly water. She decided to forgo washing her face and scanned the corners of the room for a chamber pot. When none was forthcoming, she assumed she would have to find an outhouse of some sort downstairs. Despite this being an outpost of Southern gentility, she couldn't imagine it was modern enough to possess a water closet like Uncle William's.

She pulled on her dress and pinafore, and swapped the wool socks she'd slept in for stockings and boots. It was as though she had been on the verge of becoming a woman at her uncle's, and had now been demoted to girlhood again with the calf-length dress and pinafore. She brushed her hair and tied it back with the worn black ribbon. No fancy spiral bun here. She almost wished for invisibility. The thought of meeting the other girls, the thought of what horrible things these girls must have done to end up here, definitely made her stomach churn. She could just imagine trying to have polite conversation with an entire room of Mary Surratts.

She went to the door and found it unlocked, but no breakfast tray outside it. Unsure what else to do, she went down the stairs and crept along the hall of closed doors until she came to the kitchen. Mara was up to her elbows in flour, kneading biscuit dough with arms as muscular as tree trunks. Another girl knelt near the cookstove, carefully shoving in sticks of wood while shielding her face from sparks with her other hand.

Mara looked up and saw Corrine. "You've missed morning mass. You've also missed breakfast. And Miz de Mornay don't allow no one who's missed breakfast to have leftovers."

"I'm looking for the johnnyhouse," Corrine said.

"You've missed the time for that too," Mara said, "but I'll pretend like you didn't." She sprinkled more flour onto the kneading board and rubbed her hands together briskly until the dough flaked off.

"Siobhan," she said to the kneeling girl, "would you show her out to the johnnyhouse?"

The girl swung the oven door closed and stood. Pale wisps of hair escaped from under her maid's cap, and her blue eyes were watery and bloodshot, whether from smoke or tears Corrine was unsure. She bobbed her head at Corrine and turned to show her the way out.

Corrine followed Siobhan through the kitchen, outside down some steps and to a row of three johnnyhouses that squatted in front of the fence.

"Every time you come outside, you must have an escort or a monitor, miss. No one is to be outside unattended," Siobhan said, opening the door for her. The familiar stench hit Corrine's nose as she went in and closed the door, pondering the faint brogue of Siobhan's voice. It sounded as though she was from Ireland. She could hear Siobhan outside the door, humming something low and steady.

When Corrine stepped out, Siobhan's eyes narrowed a bit; Corrine guessed Siobhan was looking at her expanded left pupil. Siobhan shifted her feet and opened her mouth, as though she wanted to say something but shook her head instead. She led Corrine back to the kitchen, her cap bobbing at the back of her head.

As they passed a basket of old bread in the larder, Siobhan plucked a crust out and gave it to Corrine, gesturing silence and secrecy.

Corrine hid it in her pinafore pocket until they'd passed through the kitchen.

"Class has already started, miss," Siobhan said. "You'd better hurry. Down the hall two doors to the left."

Corrine nodded.

As she was about to leave the kitchen, Mara said, "Just remember: I knock when I unlock your door in the morning. That's the only warning you get that it's time to get up." She kept kneading the dough as she spoke, pushing, lifting, and throwing it on the board. "You get in the johnnyhouse line, go to mass, and get to breakfast. I'll knock louder next time, but you'll have to learn to wake up on your own. There's no one else here can do it for you, that's certain."

Corrine nodded again and scurried away, nibbling on the bread until she found the door down the hallway; she could hear the drone of a voice behind it. She took hold of the tarnished knob, closed her eyes for a moment, and swallowed the crumbs in her mouth. Taking a deep breath, she opened the door.

Nine heads swiveled to face the doorway. Nine pairs of eyes stared. Some appeared disinterested; others threatening. Alcohol stung Corrine's nostrils. She saw that some of the girls held scalpels in their hands, some odd-shaped scissors or pins. *They give a roomful of murderesses scalpels?*

And then she realized there were *ten* pairs of eyes looking at her when a voice said from her right, "Well, well. Miss Jameson graces us with her presence."

Corrine turned to see Miss de Mornay pinning her with a gray glare. The students sniggered.

"What do you have to say for yourself, Miss Jameson?"

"I—"

"In future, Miss Jameson, you will kindly remember that classes do not meet at your convenience. You will be on time or you will suffer the consequences. Come here."

Corrine walked to the front of the classroom. Her boots echoed louder than a horse's hooves on cobblestones. As she passed one of the benches, she smelled the sharp pinch of alcohol attempting to overpower a fishy smell. Something fleshy and limp huddled in one of the trays, and Corrine noticed a diagram of an eel on the chalkboard. Miss de Mornay grabbed her arm and yanked her closer. For a moment, Corrine feared the woman would strike her and recoiled in horror. She had never in her life been struck, and her parents always spoke disapprovingly of those who resorted to striking their children. Instead, Miss de Mornay held her still enough to affix a large white armband that prominently displayed the letter *D*.

"You will wear the dunce band until the end of the school day, and it will be written in the school's book of punishment," Miss de Mornay said.

"But—"

The teacher's eyes did not flash, but her tone lashed like a whip. "For speaking out of turn, you will also stay inside today during recess. Be advised that there are other, far worse punishments than what you have received." Miss de Mornay gestured toward the dunce cap and a bundle of switches standing in a bucket of water.

She turned Corrine to face the class. "Girls," she said, raising her dull voice, "this is Miss Jameson." Corrine lowered her eyes, looking at the boots peeking out from under the benches to distract herself from the stares of her classmates. Miss de Mornay led her down the aisle to where a tall girl with a dark shock of hair was gazing grimly down into her tray. "You will be Miss Takar's laboratory partner." She pulled a stained wad of fabric from under the bench and handed it to Corrine. "Here is your smock. Miss Takar," she said, though the girl barely looked up at her, "please help Miss Jameson catch up."

Corrine struggled into her smock as Miss de Mornay returned to the front of the classroom. The armband constrained her movements, making it difficult for her to adjust the ties in back.

"No wonder she's wearing the dunce band," a frog-faced girl said to her lab partner. She smiled venomously at Corrine. "Can't even put a smock on right. You sure you shouldn't be down the hall in the lower class?"

The dark-haired girl roused from contemplating her dissection tray. "Enough, Dolores," she said, her voice thick with an Eastern European accent. She twirled the scalpel in her hand. Dolores's smile froze, and she turned back to her lab tray.

Corrine felt rough hands turn her, and then tie the laces at the back of her smock.

"Thank you," Corrine said, facing her. "Miss . . . Takar?"

"My name is Ilona," the girl said. "And you are?"

"Corrine."

Corrine's new laboratory partner stuck out her hand like a

boy, and Corrine shook it. Ilona's hands were rough and large, reminding her of the boys who used to live down the road from the farm.

"You be careful of de Moray," Ilona whispered.

"De Mornay?" Corrine asked.

"De Moray, we call her," the girl said. "Like this eel."

In a glittering arc, Ilona spun the scalpel, bringing it down to slice through the eel's head in one stroke.

"Ilona!" Miss de Mornay called from the front of the classroom.

Almost simultaneously, the girl on Ilona's other side—a brunette with creamy white skin—screamed. Then she fainted. She fell between the benches, her head making a resounding *thwack* against the floor.

De Mornay galloped through the benches, shoving Corrine aside. "Christina!" she called. Corrine was surprised to hear real concern in the teacher's voice. Miss de Mornay shook the girl, but Christina didn't stir. The teacher gestured to Corrine and Ilona.

"Take her to the infirmary. Have Mara or Siobhan alert Miss Brown," she said. Corrine was relieved that de Mornay would not leave a roomful of delinquent girls alone with scalpels. While Ilona lifted Christina under the armpits, Corrine lifted the girl's ankles. Even in such disarray, Christina was lovely. Though her bow had been knocked askew, her glossy, dark hair curled perfectly. Her cheeks glowed, flushed with roses from her faint. Corrine thought she had never seen a more beautiful girl, though she had never known many other girls her age.

A vision glimmered in front of Corrine as she hoisted Christina—an image of another girl draped with a white sheet and hoisted by four bearers, as in a funeral. Corrine shook her head. Together they carried her out of the room and down the hall as quickly as they could. Ilona shouted for Mara to call

Miss Brown as they passed the kitchen.

They turned a corner in the hallway and entered one of the first rooms on the left. The infirmary's whitewashed walls reminded Corrine of a dairy. Corrine and Ilona deposited Christina on one of the metal-railed beds. While Corrine cast about for smelling salts, she pulled the crust of bread from her pocket and gnawed on it, nearly fainting with hunger and nausea herself. Ilona fanned Christina's face.

Miss Brown entered just as Corrine found the tiny bottle. Corrine hid the bread in her pocket again as the headmistress took the smelling salts from her and passed the bottle under Christina's nose. The girl choked and murmured something, a word that sounded like "Angus," though Corrine couldn't be sure. But then Christina's eyelids fluttered open and she said in too-careful English, "What happened? Miss Brown? Where am I?"

"In the infirmary, Miss Beaumont. You fainted. Again." Miss Brown held Christina's shoulders gently so she wouldn't sit up. "Stay as you are; I'll send Siobhan to watch over you until you're well."

Ilona continued fanning Christina's face, until Christina frowned and waved at her to stop. "Who is that?" she asked Ilona, gesturing to Corrine. Ilona murmured at her.

Corrine was captivated. Even when Christina frowned, a charming wrinkle formed between her brows.

Miss Brown rose, interrupting Corrine's gaze. The headmistress eyed the armband Corrine wore and raised a brow.

"I was late," Corrine said, her cheeks flushing.

"So I heard," Miss Brown said. "Best see that it doesn't happen again."

"Yes, Miss Brown." Corrine bowed her head, hoping to appear contrite. But secretly she was thinking about the portrait on her uncle William's desk, Miss Brown's serene smile and white shoulders floating above the dark dress. It was all she could do not to smile herself.

"Thank you, ladies," Miss Brown said. "Miss Takar, Miss Jameson, you may return to your classroom now."

Corrine followed Ilona back to the laboratory.

"Will Christina be all right?" Corrine asked.

"Of course," Ilona said. "She's fainted the entire term during Anatomy. She will make a very bad nurse unless she learns to loosen that corset she insists on wearing." Ilona laughed as she opened the classroom door. Corrine tried to smile, but the sight of de Mornay and the constriction of the armband as she shut the door killed any mirth she might have mustered.

After more nauseating poking at eel guts, dinner was called around noon. Corrine smelled the bland scent of parsnips before she entered the dining hall. She followed Ilona as she ducked into the low-ceilinged room and found a place on a rough bench before a trestle table. Perhaps thirty or forty girls sat at the long table, all of them varying in age from around eight to eighteen. The teachers sat apart at a round table. One of them, a man, peered at Corrine. She felt a strange tickling at the base of her spine, a needle of recognition.

Mara and Siobhan placed bowls of corn pone, biscuits, and boiled root vegetables at intervals down the table. Corrine would have found the meal completely unappetizing had it not been for her vicious hunger. She reached for a biscuit, but Ilona put a hand on her arm.

The man stood when all the girls were seated and said grace. Corrine bowed her head like the rest, realizing that she hadn't attended a service since before she had fallen ill. She snuck a glance at the priest while he prayed. He was tall and broad-shouldered, and though he looked very young, something about him spoke of incredible age. His dark glance met hers, and she dropped her gaze to her lap. She again felt the needle of recognition, as though she should know this man. At last, the prayer was over, though the priest's voice rang in her ears long after he'd stopped speaking.

She reached for the biscuits again, gulping them down one after the other until Mara chided her, "Lordamercy, girl, you plan on leaving any of those for other folks?"

Corrine looked around guiltily at the long table of accusing stares and dropped the biscuit she was holding back into the basket. Dolores, the girl from the laboratory, laughed and snatched the biscuit out of another girl's timid grasp.

"Dolores," Ilona growled.

"What?" Dolores asked, biscuit crumbs dropping from her lips.

"That was unkind," Ilona said.

"You want me to give it back or something?" Dolores opened her mouth to display a mashed wad of biscuit.

One of the teachers Corrine did not know admonished Dolores as she passed. "Miss Wilson, act like a lady!"

Dolores stuck out her tongue at the teacher's back.

"Who was that?" Corrine asked Ilona.

"That's Mrs. Alexander," Ilona said. Corrine watched the woman take her seat with Miss de Mornay and the priest.

"What does Mrs. Alexander teach?" Corrine asked.

"Dancing," Ilona said, grimacing.

"Like waltzing and things like that?" Corrine regarded the teacher with new interest. Her graying hair was parted severely and pulled into a tight bun at her nape. A pince-nez perched on her hooked nose. She surveyed her food with the dissatisfied air of an eagle.

"Yes. Those horrible things," Ilona said.

"Dancing? Horrible?" Corrine said. She vaguely remembered enjoying barn dances when she was very small and her parents lived with the Alcotts.

She was surprised to see the tall girl shudder. "I hate dancing."

Corrine couldn't help smiling. "Don't worry," she said. "You just need to find the right partner."

"No, no," Ilona said, shaking her head. "Christina says I'm terr-ible." She exaggerated the word in imitation of Christina.

To get Ilona's mind off of her terror of dancing, Corrine changed the subject. "Who are the other teachers?" she asked.

Ilona went around the table. "On Miss de Mornay's right, that's Father Joseph. He is the chaplain and history teacher. Then Miss Brown, of course. Sometimes, she teaches natural and domestic sciences. Our French teacher has been away these several months—"

Before Ilona could finish, a blonde girl entered the room with Christina. Unlike Christina, who went to the other end of the table to find a seat, this girl came up beside Dolores, clearly expecting the girl next to Dolores to make room. Dolores grinned and slid over for her. The other girl huddled as far from them as she could.

"Taking another one under your wing, Ilona?" the blonde said as she sat down. Corrine thought she looked older than most of the other girls, and not just because she wore a skirt and jacket instead of a pinafore. Something about the way she carried herself, the way she tossed her snaky, golden curls, made Corrine guess she was nearing eighteen.

Ilona didn't say anything.

"Just be careful she doesn't end up like—"

"Be quiet, Melanie!" Ilona snapped.

"My!" Melanie said, feigning surprise. "The Hungarian does have a temper like a bear now, doesn't she?"

Ilona stared at her from beneath her untidy fringe of hair.

She said in a low voice, "Recess is soon, Melanie."

Melanie gave a look of mock fright and scooped up the last biscuit. She turned and began talking to Dolores as though she were the only person at the table. The other girls were subdued for a bit, waiting for sparks to fly. When nothing happened, they resumed their own discussions. But Corrine couldn't help noticing that they all talked carefully, avoiding a secret that shouted to be heard.

Ilona didn't speak after that, and recess was called shortly thereafter. Corrine watched as Mrs. Alexander and Miss de Mornay marched Ilona and the other girls outside.

Miss Brown came to Corrine's side. "This way, Miss Jameson."

Corrine followed her silently out of the room. She caught Father Joseph's eye again as she left, and the tickle threatened to turn into a painful tug until she forced herself to look away.

I know you, she wanted to say. Miss Brown escorted her back down the hall past the kitchen and classrooms, past the open door of her office, and unlocked a new room.

"This is the library," Miss Brown said. Corrine smiled to see the rows of books wrapping from the near wall almost all the way around the room.

"Someone will return to take you to your afternoon classes when recess is over," Miss Brown said. "In the meantime, study from any of the books on these shelves."

Corrine nodded, hoping she appeared apologetic. Honestly, though, she felt rewarded to be here rather than punished. As Miss Brown left and locked the door behind her, Corrine's only wish was for a fire in the grate. Hemlocks shaded the room's windows, making it much cooler than any other room.

She walked around, pumping her arms in the chill, straining against the white armband and listening to her boots echo on the scuffed floor. She turned to the bookshelves. There were so many titles, most much more interesting than those in Uncle William's library. She removed and scanned a few of them, including *The Girl's Own Book,* a book of games and other proper amusements for young ladies. She couldn't imagine a group of girls like Falston's playing the Ladybug Game. She had no idea what any of them had done, especially not beautiful Christina, but she didn't believe that such games would delight them nearly as much as whatever had forced them to Falston.

She ran her fingers along the shelves, feeling the spines and trying to decide whether to read Shelley, Wordsworth, or Shakespeare. On the bottom shelf of one bookcase, some books had fallen on their sides. She reached in to rearrange them, knocking a wood panel loose from the side of the shelf in the process. Concerned that she'd broken something, she knelt to see what had happened. The false panel had fallen into a cubbyhole. She reached in to retrieve it, but paper came into her fingers instead of wood.

She pulled out a bundle of age-stained parchment. A faded red cord bound two letters, though the looseness of the cord made her wonder if more letters belonged in the packet. She had the strange sense that she was unraveling a spell as she gently slipped the letters free.

Each letter was accompanied by a translation, much like the one she'd found in her mother's trunk. Also written in what Corrine thought was Latin, though in a different hand, these letters looked to be translated by the same person. She wondered briefly if this were a continuation of the story of Mary Rose. She puzzled over how that could be possible. Had her mother had some connection to the school? But as she began to read, Corrine realized she'd stumbled upon something entirely new.

[Trans. note: End burned beyond recognition]

May 1356

To Sister Brighde, Isle of the Female Saints, from Brother Angus, Kirk of St. Fillan, greeting.

My beloved—

Your gentle words undid me, so that for days I have only been able to wander about in a kind of feverish bliss. I thought myself unfortunate that my father disinherited me, but then I believed myself utterly cursed when you would not see me. Now that you have deigned to speak to me again, how can I help but feel as though I am the most blessed man on earth?

You must believe me when I tell you that I will harm you neither in word nor deed, that what I tell you is true. I know that you are afraid, both of what I have said and what I have offered to show. Believe that I too feared at first. The Fey are wondrous and strange, but they have no will to harm us. Of that I am certain. They wish only to know you, as they have come to know me.

The Fey do not favor mankind easily. For all that our brave saints have done, they have also taken the sacred and holy places of the Fey, overturned their standing stones, and overrun their wild woods with sheep and cattle. Is it any wonder *that they might seem fearsome to us when we were once at war with them? But peace has been bought now, a peace that you shall surely see if you but open your heart—*

"The Fey?" Corrine whispered. She thought again of the hawthorn people, of Mary Rose's feline smile. Whatever they were, they were not human. And this Angus, whoever he might have been, corroborated these thoughts. Were these the fairies about which her mother had warned her? The twig-fingered hawthorn people who had coaxed her into stealing the stone from Uncle William's study? And the Captain who raised his hand to her in the twilight—why did the Fey fear him? Who was the witch he served? She shivered just a little, and not from the chill in the room. This letter had given the hawthorn people a name—the Fey—and established that they were other than human, but she wondered at the "peace" Angus mentioned, even as she found herself blushing at his scandalous profession of love for this nun.

She had no more time to contemplate; keys jangled outside the door. She shoved the letters in her pinafore pocket and tried to right the wooden panel.

Mara pushed open the door. She stared at Corrine, obviously surprised to see her kneeling on the floor near the bookcases.

But all she said was: "Time for dance lessons."

~ Nine ~

September 27, 1865

Mrs. Alexander was waiting in the ballroom on the second floor. She glanced at Corrine and the white armband circling her left arm as she entered, but said nothing to her directly. The room was old and smelled of dust; high windows at the far end admitted the afternoon light. A graying old man leaned against the wall near the windows, drowsing, looking like he might drop his fiddle at any moment.

White chalk marks were spaced evenly across the worn floorboards, and thirty girls, most of whom Corrine had glimpsed in Anatomy or at dinner, were lined up along a white line at one end of the room. Every other girl in the line was pulling on gloves that looked suspiciously like gentlemen's gloves.

"Miss Jameson," Mrs. Alexander snapped with a nasally, high-pitched twang. "Get in line or lose your turn."

Corrine scooted in line next to Ilona, who was flexing her fingers in the gentleman's gloves. She looked so much like an unhappy mule that Corrine wanted to pat her shoulder.

"If it helps," she whispered, "I haven't the faintest notion of how to dance."

Ilona looked at her sidelong. "No," she said, "I'm afraid that doesn't help much."

"Silence!" Mrs. Alexander yelled. "Girls, take your places." She motioned to the old man without looking at him, saying, "A waltz, please, Mr. Jefferson."

But all she got in response was a yawning snore.

Some of the girls tittered until Mrs. Alexander glared at them.

"MR. JEFFERSON!" she called across the room.

When he didn't respond, Ilona whispered, grinning, "Watch this. Happens every time."

Mrs. Alexander stalked toward the old fiddle player, all the while calling his name. When she was at last right next to him, she shouted his name so loudly that he jumped back, tangling himself with his violin and nearly falling in the process.

Mrs. Alexander got as close to him as she could. "A WALTZ PLEASE, MR. JEFFERSON!"

He nodded, his old mouth twitching, and put the violin to his shoulder, scratching out the opening notes to an old favorite for a waltz.

This, of course, forced Mrs. Alexander to rush back to the girls. She took hold of Christina, and shouted, as she began sweeping the girl about the floor, "All right now, girls, *chassé!*"

Corrine followed Ilona, shuffling first to the left and then the right. The dance continued through five movements, punctuated by Mrs. Alexander's nasal cries of *"Vis-a-vis! Chassé! Gallopade!"* Corrine let Ilona drag her through the dance, her hand clamped in Ilona's damp gloved hand, her elbows and legs tangling awkwardly with the tall girl's. Corrine found herself apologizing every few steps between breaths, but Ilona led her with an iron will, neither pausing nor hurrying. Corrine thought she saw Ilona gritting her teeth.

She asked once, "Who were they talking about at dinner?"

Ilona tried to shush her, but not before Mrs. Alexander yelled, "Miss Jameson, would you like to complete your ensemble with the dunce cap this afternoon?"

They ended their dance near the window, and as they bowed to one another, movement outside caught Corrine's eye. Just beyond the iron-spiked fence, the Captain stood, hooded and cloaked. He raised his hand, as though he knew that Corrine was watching. Although she could not see his face, she could see clearly that his palm was red and slick, as though freshly dipped in blood. She gasped and ran without thinking to the window, pressing her face against the leaded panes and craning to see him.

But the Captain was gone.

"Miss Jameson!" Mrs. Alexander said.

Corrine returned to the dance floor, uncertain which was more terrifying—the fact that the tall man had found her, that Mrs. Alexander had come to deeply dislike her already, or that her next dance partner was Melanie, who smirked and pinched her hard below the dunce band as she took Corrine in her arms.

She thought again about the Captain. Who was the witch he served? And why had the Fey wanted the stone if they had not been responsible for breaking into Uncle William's study? The only good thing Corrine could find in all of this was that the Fey medicine had worked. She felt no weakness, nothing beyond normal shortness of breath after exertion. In fact, she thought, as Melanie did her best to trip her, she was more alive, more powerful, than ever.

After supper that night, Miss Brown asked for volunteers to help with sewing for charity causes—war orphans, veterans, and the like. Corrine raised her hand, but Miss Brown said, "Next time, Corrine. You must finish out today's sentence now by signing the book of punishment."

Miss de Mornay led her back into the laboratory, which still reeked of eel and alcohol. The teacher led Corrine to her desk and opened the book of punishment that rested there, solid and imposing as the Bible.

She pointed to where Corrine should sign, not bothering to speak. Corrine took up a pen, dipped it in the ink pot on the desk, and bent forward to sign her name beside the listed infraction. She scanned the page above her and Ilona's name caught her eye. Next to Ilona's mannish signature were the words: "For striking Melanie Smith and disregarding authority. Fifty lashes with the birch switch." She could not read the date.

A great stain spread from Corrine's pen.

"Miss Jameson," Miss de Mornay growled. "Enough of this dawdling; are you quite finished?"

"Yes, Miss de Mornay."

"Very well then," the teacher said. She removed the dunce band from Corrine's arm. Corrine looked into her face as she did so, hoping to see something there—a flicker of kindness or sympathy. But the teacher's face was bland, and she did not meet Corrine's gaze.

Miss de Mornay lifted her lantern and walked out of the room without another word, looking back only as she opened the door to see if Corrine had followed. Once into the hall, she led Corrine back to the kitchen where Mara and Siobhan were cleaning up after supper.

Mara came to them when she saw them standing in the doorway. Miss de Mornay departed down the hall without saying good night. Mara led Corrine up to her room.

Opening Corrine's door, Mara said, "I don't know what you was doing in the library today, but you better not mess with nothing there. Miz de Mornay'd skin you alive, and I doubt Miz Brown would pity you much neither."

Mara's steady gaze reminded Corrine strongly of the suspicion she'd seen only too recently in Betsy's eyes. She opened her mouth, but Mara held up her hand.

"I don't want to know," she said. "I'm just warning you for your own good. Don't mess about. It'll get you in a world of trouble." Mara glanced at the little locked door next to Corrine's. As her gaze returned, Corrine again got that breathless sense of age and wisdom. A fleeting vision of twisted trees dangling bearded moss, of a giant shadow shape wading through those trees, made Corrine dizzy.

Mara's eyes narrowed. She led Corrine inside her room, lit her lantern, and saw to her stove. As she rose to leave, she shot a cold glance at Corrine that made her stiffen involuntarily. "I mean it," Mara said. "Don't go snooping about here. Or you'll have me to deal with, and I know you don't want that. Ask the girls; they'll know what I'm talking about."

Before Corrine could reply, the maid was gone, locking the door behind her. The ecstatic power Corrine had felt during the afternoon's dancing was gone. She huddled, alone and afraid, hating the smell of burning coal. Autumn was moving quickly. She dreaded the winter, especially if Mara was truly angry with her. Would she "forget" to bring the coal upstairs?

She wondered if Mara had actually seen her stuff the letters in her pocket. It seemed likely. But, if so, why didn't Mara mention them or try to search for them?

Such thoughts led her to wonder about the letters themselves. She pulled them from her pinafore and rose from her cot, wrapping the blanket around her shoulders. She retrieved the lamp and sat down with it next to the stove.

Leaning against the wall, she tried to find a comfortable position in which to read. In that moment, tendrils of cold seeped through the boards and imprisoned her.

She could not tell if her eyes were open or shut. All she saw was darkness. And then the darkness was moving, tossing its branches before a gale. She was in the tree, the moonlight flickering fitfully around her. She looked down and the man looked up, but Corrine could not see his face. Corrine whimpered in denial as she began the slow climb down, as her pale hand took the man's shadowed one.

On the ground, he led her deeper into the forest through the moonlight. Corrine looked back occasionally, as though she regretted leaving the tree. Sometimes she tested his grip, but she also knew that such struggles were futile. As they arrived at their destination, she struggled harder, a slender white shape beating fruitlessly at her captor.

Corrine's terror dissolved the vision into black splinters. She pulled away from the wall, huddling as close to the stove as she dared. She felt tears rise, but dashed them away. First the dreams of her mother and father, then the Fey, and now these visions of a girl she didn't know. Was it someone who once lived in the room next door? If the doctor came tomorrow and declared her mad, she felt inclined to believe it.

With shaking fingers, she took out the second letter and smoothed the translation across the floor near the lamp.

[Trans. note: Date scratched out, estimated June 1356]

To Sister Brighde, Isle of Female Saints
from Brother Angus, Kirk of St. Fillan, greeting.

My beloved—

It has been difficult of late to write to you; the Abbot is always about, and the Fey who delivers this message fears the iron cross he bears. You must remember not to trouble our messenger with things hateful to him, iron among them. The Fey also do not favor the burning of certain woods, especially hawthorn. While they are a peaceful folk, we should do nothing to provoke them. I have seen of late how powerful they can be.

Midsummer is soon upon us, a time most sacred to them. Again they have invited your presence, and again I entreat that you accept their invitation. That we may be able to look into each other's eyes once more will be a vast gift they want to give us, and which I desire above all things. They can achieve ways of hiding your absence, just as they can achieve ways of hiding these words from any eyes but yours.

It is my deepest prayer that your faith in me has been restored. If I have earned even the least trust in your heart, I beg you make your will known to the messenger, who will grant your desire in full measure.

I remain, as always,
Yours eternal,
Angus

Corrine scanned the document again, her thoughts lingering on the iron cross. *"They fear the iron cross he bears."* Was this the origin of her mother's iron cross? Or yet another one like Mary Rose's? But what need had anyone of offending the Fey? They had healed her—they must be good. And she heard again the man's voice from her dreams. *Corrine. Come to me.*

It had been many days since she had dreamed of him, and now the strange visions of the girl posed new mysteries to solve. She rose, her legs numb with sitting, and stumbled to her cot. As she drifted off to sleep, she hoped that there were more letters than just these two.

~ Ten ~

October 4, 1865

Corrine stepped out of the trees. The ground did not threaten to swallow her anymore; she knew herself immune. The storm had retreated to the far horizon, and a vast desert stretched to meet it. Her father walked across it just as doggedly as ever, half-turning and motioning ever so often for her to hurry. She hesitated for just a moment, before stepping out onto the burning sand and following after him. The sand was strange. Being here felt wrong. She stopped, confused. It was only then that she looked down and saw her feet were turning to stone.

Her eyes flew open and the knock on the door came just after. It had been exactly a week since her first day, and she had almost become accustomed to listening for Mara's footsteps. She sat up, realizing she'd forgotten to change into her nightgown before collapsing on her cot the night before. She didn't look at herself in the wavering washstand mirror as she ran a brush through her tangled hair and rebound it with the black ribbon. She wished she could wash her face, but no water had been left for her.

She fled from her room, hurrying to join the others who marched down the steps and into the johnnyhouse line. She avoided Melanie as much as she could, watching the smaller girls cower as Melanie jostled them out of the way. Corrine's arm still smarted where Melanie had pinched her again during dancing the other day; she could only guess what other torments Melanie might devise for her victims.

In the chilly dawn, Mara and Siobhan stood like sentinels on either side of the three johnnyhouses. Corrine looked around the school and its grounds. The house loomed over everything like a Gothic prison, its many-windowed tower and cupolas begging to be explored. Corrine was quite sure that the majority of the rooms were no longer in use. There was no telling what secrets they might reveal—though if those secrets were like those of the room next to hers, Corrine wasn't so sure she wanted to discover them. Two cabins huddled at opposite ends of the grounds. One looked like old slave quarters, while the other, with its elaborate scrollwork along the eaves, must have been a guesthouse. Corrine didn't know who used the old slave quarters, but she had heard that Father Joe lived in the guesthouse.

Someone prodded Corrine's side.

"Your turn," a little girl said. She could not have been more than eight years old, with fair hair that fell into curious, green eyes.

Mara pinned them with a stare that prevented Corrine from saying anything further. As she was about to enter the johnnyhouse, a young man appeared around the corner. She paused, staring at him. He carried a brace of rabbits over one shoulder, walking with a slight limp. He grinned crookedly from under the brim of his hat at Corrine before handing the rabbits to Siobhan.

"Coneys for the table," he said, "at no charge to Miss Siobhan." His speech carried a faint Scottish brogue, though strong enough to make Corrine forget that she was meant to go into the johnnyhouse next.

Flustered, Siobhan took the rabbits from the young man, murmuring, "Thank you, Mr. Rory," without looking at him.

Rory caught Corrine's gaze then and winked. His eyes were piercingly blue.

"Are you going or not?" the girl behind Corrine asked, poking her in the back this time.

"Oh, yes," Corrine said. She made as if to step in, but lingered a moment, watching as Rory walked away, resettling his worn hat over his black hair. His hair wanted trimming, but otherwise, Corrine could not help but think she'd just seen the most perfect-looking man on earth.

Corrine thought of the boy all through morning mass, barely paying attention to the litany Father Joe recited. At breakfast, she hurried to sit beside Ilona.

"Who is that boy who brought the rabbits to Siobhan this morning?" she asked.

"Blue eyes? Black hair?" Ilona asked.

Corrine nodded. She opened a biscuit and carved a pat of butter from the hunk in the dish.

"Rory MacLeod," Ilona said. She stuffed a biscuit in her mouth.

"Who is he?" Corrine said.

Ilona glanced at her sidelong. "He works here and lives in the old slave cabin. Keeps the grounds, takes the livestock to market, that sort of thing. His father owns the next farm." It seemed she might say more, but she grabbed a hard-boiled egg and peeled it instead.

"Oh," Corrine said.

Ilona used her thumb to separate the white from the yolk. She let the yolk roll around on the table and ate the white. "Take care around him. He's—"

"Miss Takar!" Miss de Mornay said, as she passed. "Stop playing with your food!"

Ilona snatched up the yolk and dumped it on her plate. Before Corrine could ask anything further, Christina appeared, looking feverish. Ilona slid closer to Corrine, making room for Christina on her left.

"Where have you been?" Ilona said.

"I felt ill," Christina said. The French lilt in her voice was almost as delightful to Corrine as Rory's faded brogue.

"More dreams?" Ilona said in a hushed voice. They exchanged glances, and then Christina's eyes slid to Corrine.

Ilona nodded and they said no more about it.

Instead, Christina said, "My mama has written and sent me a parcel. We shall have all manner of good things for the next Society meeting if Miss Brown can be convinced to let me have the package all to myself. Mama wants to come visit too. But Miss Brown says that might be unprofitable for both of us."

"I wish my mother wanted to see me," Ilona said wistfully.

I just wish my mother was still alive, Corrine thought, but didn't say aloud.

Breakfast was over more quickly than Corrine expected; she was only halfway through her grits before Miss de Mornay called for classes to begin. Christina's low murmurs intrigued her—what dreams did she suffer from, and were they as terrible as her own? What was the Society? It bothered her that the girls had ignored her; like everyone else, they were intent on keeping secrets from her. Rebuffed, she put her hand on the pinafore pocket containing the two precious letters. *Let them have their secrets,* she thought. *I have plenty of my own.*

Corrine fell into line behind Ilona as Miss Brown led the girls out of the dining hall, through the kitchen and into a mudroom where everyone began unlacing their boots and seeking out wooden clogs that rested side by side under a bench. One girl handed out straw hats with wide ribbons; another handed out leather gloves.

Ilona must have sensed her bewilderment because she whispered, "It's our class's turn for gardening." She crammed the straw hat over her hair and tied the ribbons under her chin.

"Whatever for?" Corrine asked.

"Your education," Miss Brown said, coming up behind the two as she pulled on her gardening gloves.

Corrine joined Ilona in picking up a basket and following Miss Brown down the stairs, around the corner of the school to an immense garden plot that Corrine hadn't seen yet. Plants tangled across its expanse—a jungle of vegetables. Some of them had seen better days—the cucumbers, for instance. Sunflowers mourned over the end of the growing season, their seed-laden heads drooping. Pumpkins sprawled on great, curling vines, just beginning to turn. Crookneck squash poked yellow horns from beneath broad leaves.

Corrine looked beyond all these things, past the iron fence to where the hemlocks and pines crowded at the school's perimeter. She half-expected the bloody-handed Captain to be there, watching her, but he wasn't. Instead, she saw Rory, his hat cocked to shade the sun from his face, working in the corn at the far end of the garden.

"Girls, start here," Miss Brown said. "I must speak with Mr. MacLeod, and then I'll return. Ilona, you are in charge."

Corrine was impressed that Ilona had the grace not to puff up and make the others take notice of her, but simply nodded and bent to her work. Miss Brown departed down the rows, disappearing among the cornstalks.

Corrine followed Ilona along the row of crookneck squash, working from the other side. She was accustomed to this sort of work, having helped her mother in past years, even plucking the tomato hornworms from the plants and squishing them enthusiastically in the dirt. The squash was full and golden and her basket was soon heavy.

"Why do we seldom eat vegetables like this?" Corrine asked.

Ilona grimaced and flicked a bug off her arm. "The school sells all this in town. We eat it sometimes, but not often. That would be wasted money," she said.

"Do you ever go into town to help sell things?" Corrine asked.

"Sometimes. If I'm really good. But usually Rory does it."

"Oh." Corrine kept her eyes focused on the squash in front of her.

She was surprised to hear Ilona laugh, a low whinny.

Corrine looked up and saw a dark, sparkling eye under the straw hat.

"Don't even think those thoughts, Corrine," Ilona said. "Melanie has her eye on him. And"—at this her smile faltered—"he is not to be trusted."

"You said that before. Why?"

Ilona regarded her for a moment, and then dropped her gaze to the plant between them. "It's just a feeling I have. Christina says—"

But whatever Christina said was lost in Miss Brown's return and her ardent observation of the girls' work. She strode up and down the rows, chastising Dolores for her slowness and Melanie for her idleness. Corrine looked up at this and saw Melanie watching Rory at the end of the garden, her lips parted and the tip of her tongue showing.

Christina was nearby, working in the tomatoes with one of the younger girls. Suddenly, she collapsed to the dirt, fainting neatly between rows.

"My Lord!" Corrine said, starting toward her. But Ilona's dirt-caked glove held her back.

"Somebody probably squashed a bug. Miss Brown will see to her."

Rory had seen too, for he had dropped his hoe and was running or, rather, rocking down the row toward them. Corrine guessed his gait was awkward due to whatever injury caused him to limp—most likely a war wound. And she could guess, from Melanie's rapt attention, on which side he had fought.

As he entered the row where Miss Brown was fanning and murmuring over Christina, he was near enough that Corrine could see his forearms bulging out of his rolled-up sleeves and the long, dark sweat stain on his back between his suspenders.

"Miss Brown," she heard him say, "is the lass—"

Miss Brown murmured something that answered his question before he finished. But he stood there, staring, Corrine thought, as though he had never seen Christina in his life. Or, as if he had not seen her in an eternity. Melanie saw it too, apparently—her face darkened and she muttered something Corrine couldn't catch. Melanie bent and plucked an eggplant viciously while Dolores spoke to her.

Rory was limping steadily toward the barn when Corrine turned to look at him again, as Miss Brown helped Christina to stand.

While the sun circled the house, the girls worked halfway down the garden, carrying vegetables and depositing them in giant baskets before the noon bell finally rang. Rory drove up with a team of horses hitched to a wagon as Corrine was emptying her last basket of beans into a larger bushel basket. He climbed off the driver's seat and began hoisting the baskets onto the flatbed.

"And are you coming to market today, lassie?" he asked.

"Me?" Corrine said. "No!" Her face got so hot that it must have been the color of a beet.

"Such a pity," he said and winked.

Not knowing what else to do, she turned and walked back to the others. Melanie gave her an evil look, and Ilona shook her head.

Miss Brown hurried them back toward the kitchen door. As Corrine fell into line behind Ilona, Christina whispered, "You should volunteer for sewing tomorrow night, Corrine. We must learn more about you." Corrine allowed herself a small smile as she entered the mudroom and dropped her hat, gloves, and basket on the table with the rest.

When recess was called after dinner, Corrine watched as Ilona and Christina rushed out of the dining room together before she could catch up to them. Jostled to the back of the gaggle of girls, she emerged to find Christina and Ilona on the far side of the yard, playing graces with an energy that did not invite her participation. Ilona used two wands to flip a beribboned ring toward Christina, who would catch it with her wands and flip it back. The object was to keep the ring moving without dropping it on the ground or getting it tangled in the wands. Though she'd seen it played back in Maryland, Corrine had never played before and guessed she wouldn't get the chance now. Everyone else was similarly engaged and looked askance at Corrine as she passed. Since there seemed to be no enforced calisthenics—at least, not today—Corrine decided to steal away and explore the grounds if she could.

Christina had been assigned as the monitor, but she was clearly not paying attention. Corrine slipped around the edge of the house. The barn was close enough to hear the recess bell when it rang. She'd start there.

As she rounded the hog shed, she saw several things at once. A group of four girls were rolling and smoking cigarettes against the fence. Among them, Dolores lit a cigarette in

Melanie's pouting mouth. And on the other side of the fence, Rory sat astride a black mare, laughing at something one of the girls had said. He glanced at Corrine as she approached, and she saw his blue eyes and crooked grin from under his hat brim. Corrine considered leaving, but Melanie called her forward.

"Why, look," said Dolores, "it's Duncinea. Or Duncine. Or perhaps Duncey would do nicely."

"Oh stop it, Dolores," Melanie said, holding Corrine's eyes with her own. "As if you've never worn the dunce band before. Like a smoke?" Melanie took her cigarette from her lips and reversed it, thrusting it in Corrine's direction. The smoke trickled over Corrine and she coughed, her lungs constricting as though she still suffered from the swamp fever. She turned a little away, just in time for a sharp breeze to whisk Rory's hat off, up over the fence, and into her hands. She tried not to crush the worn felt.

"You'll not mind returning that to me, there's a good lass," he said.

"What are you doing here?" Corrine said.

"My father's on the way to market with the wagon, but the harness snapped, and I rode back here to fetch another. I saw the present company on the way up the hill and stopped for a chat."

He raised the harness in his hand so she could see it, but she was not entirely convinced. Why would he lurk on the other side of the fence unless he didn't want to be seen?

"What a lovely Morgan," Corrine said, her eyes trained on the mare as she handed the hat through the fence. A twinge of pain richocheted from her fingertips to her elbow, causing her to almost lose her grip. Rory looked at her closely as he resettled the hat over his black hair, but he made no mention of her reaction. Instead, he asked, "How'd you guess the breed? Most girls don't give a hog's arse for such things."

"My father used to raise them. Sometimes raced them as pacers," Corrine said, blushing that he had sworn.

"Ah," he said, his little smile creeping back. "No wonder then." He doffed his hat. "My apology for the cursing. What's your name again?"

"Corrine," she said, unable to keep herself from grinning back.

"Corrine," he said. His faint Scottish brogue nearly sent her heart through the roof of her mouth. She was reminded strangely of the shadow prince of her dreams, the one who said her name as though it were a holy word.

"Well, ladies," he said, "I must be off before the Moray Eel finds me." He tipped his hat to all of them. "We'll speak later, Melanie," he said, and a look passed between them that Corrine couldn't quite discern. He turned the mare and sent her trotting down the hill through the pines.

When Corrine turned back to the girls, Melanie contemplated her with the cold look that Corrine was coming to know all too well. Before Corrine could blink, Melanie grabbed her wrist and held a cigarette close enough that Corrine could feel its heat. "If you tell anyone what you saw today, I can do much worse. Do you believe me?"

Corrine couldn't say anything, and wondered if she meant the smoking or Rory. Probably both.

"Do you?" Melanie pressed closer.

"Yes," Corrine stammered, just as the bell to end recess rang.

"Good." Melanie took a last puff on her cigarette, releasing Corrine's wrist. She blew the smoke in Corrine's face, and then tossed the cigarette to the ground and stubbed it out with her boot heel. The other girls followed suit. She put an arm around Corrine and led her back toward the manor. "I may lie about lots of things," she said, smiling sweetly, "but I'm not lying when I say that I will hurt you if you cross me. You won't, will you?"

"No," Corrine said, smothered by Melanie's golden curls, the arm wrapped firmly around her waist. "Not at all." She tried to produce a smile.

"Good," Melanie said, pinching the flesh beside her elbow so hard that Corrine almost gasped. "Because, in addition to all that, my daddy is quite a powerful man. He owned a plantation with a thousand slaves not far from here. During the War of Southern Independence, he was a lieutenant in the cavalry."

Melanie's dark eyes held hers, making her feel like a bird hypnotized by a snake. But part of her wondered how Melanie had ended up here if she had such a powerful, prestigious father.

"Believe me," Melanie said, as Dolores giggled next to her, "I may be here now, but I won't be for much longer. My daddy would see to it that you'd regret tattling on me."

Corrine nodded.

"What does your daddy do?" Melanie asked.

"He was in the War," Corrine said. She wanted to grit her teeth against what she knew was coming, the inevitable question about which side he fought on. Here, she had a feeling, the Union was not the right answer.

They rounded the school building and the recess bell rang again.

Melanie released her with another hard pinch that Corrine knew would draw a bruise. "Back to class, ladies." She joined a bevy of older girls going to Domestic Science class.

Dolores laughed and pushed at Corrine's arm. "Time for French, Duncinea."

Corrine hurried ahead of Dolores to avoid any pinching from her too, looking for Ilona and trying not to think about what Melanie might do when she found out Corrine was a Northern carpetbagger.

Corrine found the French classroom only by dint of being herded by Dolores through the halls. She scooted into a seat near the front of the classroom, hoping to avoid sharing a desk with Dolores. Most of the girls in this classroom were younger—she recognized the green-eyed girl who had prodded her at the johnnyhouses. As she looked up at the teacher, she held in a gasp of shock. Christina stood up from the teacher's desk.

None of the other girls seemed surprised, and Christina went straight into the lesson without preamble. The little girls piped their conjugations like birds, and Corrine tried to follow along, though she had no idea what she was doing. Her mother had once tried to teach her French, but had despaired of it when Corrine clearly showed no ear for languages. Though she loved the way they sounded, she could not make a passable imitation to save herself. She could tell that Christina also thought this was a problem. She looked at Corrine with an expression of consternation and spoke more loudly and forcefully above the others to help Corrine hear.

Christina turned to the board and began writing some verb forms: *elle a mangé* (she ate), *elle mangeait* (she was eating), *elle avait mangé* (she had eaten)—

Christina's body stiffened. Corrine watched as the chalk took on a life of its own. It wrote in fluid characters across the board, dragging Christina's hand with it in a language that was definitely not French. *Dominus Deus vallo mihi.* Christina gasped and pulled her hand away. She tried to erase the foreign words, but Corrine could see that her arm was refusing to cooperate; it was as though the eraser was made of lead. Christina tried to cross them out, but then the chalk pulled her hand across the board, drawing a thicket of crosses over everything.

The girls began laughing, especially Dolores who pointed and screwed up her face in imitation of Christina as she drew helplessly. A dangerous anger built within Corrine. She turned to the green-eyed girl.

"What's your name?" she said.

"Penelope," the girl said nervously.

"Penelope, go find Miss Brown."

"But, we're not supposed to—"

"Go find her now!"

Penelope slid out of her desk and hurried out of the door.

Corrine rose and walked to Christina, who was trying to hold back tears as she wrestled with the unwieldy chalk. Corrine put her hand on Christina's arm. A flash of vision surged through her. *A dark, howling night surrounded a woman who ran through the rain. She wore strange clothing—a filmy gown with many layers. Her long hair wrapped in wet ropes around her belly, swollen in the last stages of pregnancy. Corrine watched in horror as something tall and twisted, like a walking tree, came up behind the woman, who obviously could not hear it in the storm.*

This was a new vision, different from the girl who had been taken into the forest. Corrine tried to shut her mind against the woman's terror and pulled Christina's arm from the board. The laughter in the room had stopped, and Miss Brown was there beside them.

"Girls, what is—?" She stopped speaking and stared at the board.

Corrine saw the headmistress's face tighten; her normally generous mouth compressed in a thin line.

"Take her to the infirmary, Corrine, and wait there with her. I will finish the lesson here."

"Yes, Miss Brown."

Corrine helped Christina out of the door, ignoring Dolores's whispered taunts as she passed.

Out into the hall, they nearly collided with Mara, who had just turned the corner of the hall.

The maid stopped just in time and said, "What are you two doing out here? Miz de Mornay catch you, she punish both of you."

"Christina had an . . . accident," Corrine said. "Miss Brown told me to take her to the infirmary."

Mara came closer. She slipped her fingers around Christina's wrist. She put her other hand on Christina's cheek, looking closely into her eyes. Christina submitted to Mara's inspection without complaint. Corrine thought Christina might faint.

"Yep," she said. "You ridden, child, and no mistake."

"Ridden?" Corrine asked. "What do you mean?"

Mara stared at her with the same inscrutable look as the day she'd caught her with the letters. "Ridden by spirits. Plain as day in her eyes."

"Spirits?" Corrine said. "How do you know?"

Mara stared like she might laugh, but she said only, "Some things as I just know, Miz Corrine." She let go of Christina's wrist and stepped back. "You take her on to the infirmary. I'll bring something to fix her right up."

Corrine nodded, perturbed at Mara's easy diagnosis of Christina's affliction. With all she had witnessed thus far at Falston—and before at Uncle William's—she did not doubt that it could be true; she was just not certain that Mara or anyone could find a cure.

She guided Christina down the hall and back into the infirmary. As she helped the girl lie down, Christina asked faintly, "What did she say is wrong with me?"

Corrine shook her head. "Don't trouble yourself, Christina. Just lie still."

But Christina gripped her forearm with a strength that

made Melanie's pinching seem mild. "What did she say?" the girl said.

"That—that you were possessed by a spirit," Corrine said.

"What kind of spirit?"

"I don't know." Corrine pulled against Christina's grasp and the girl let her go.

"She's a witch, you know," Christina said, her voice slurring toward sleep. "She knows everything." By the last word, Christina was fast asleep, Corrine sitting stunned beside her.

~ Eleven ~

October 5, 1865

CORRINE STILL CARRIED THE DISTURBING IMAGES OF Christina's possession with her the next day. Father Joe was just beginning his history lecture when Corrine entered the classroom. A board sat on the teacher's desk in the front, covered with miniature armies made of twigs and flannel that faced each other around the contours of paper mountains. Father Joe began explaining in great detail how the armies were positioned.

Corrine found the lesson dull and largely incomprehensible. What Father Joe really needed was a classroom full of boys. She noticed, surprisingly, that Ilona leaned forward a few rows ahead, hanging on every tiny twig's movement, every twist of the arduous battle tale. Corrine had yet to see any other subject move Ilona quite this much.

Contemplating Ilona and Christina, Corrine lost track of the lecture. But Father Joe quickly snapped her back.

"And do you know why the Confederates managed to take Cedar Mountain on August 9, 1862?" he asked, his voice rising ominously.

Some of the girls shook their heads. Melanie shook her curls and was most likely gritting her teeth. The former belle apparently did not like it when the War was discussed, especially when mention was made of the Confederates.

Father Joe raised a portrait. Quiet shivers poured down Corrine's arms, shivers that had nothing to do with the day's chill. A young man with a broad, white forehead and close-set eyes peered out from the picture. He had wide shoulders and full lips, which were compressed as though he withheld dangerous thoughts. His crisp gray uniform revealed his affiliation with the Confederacy.

Some of the girls sighed.

"This is Lieutenant Colonel John Pelham," Father Joe said.

"A hero of our country," Melanie said to Dolores. Dolores nodded.

Father Joe kept talking as though he didn't notice the girls' rudeness.

"John Pelham was often called the Boy Major. He was also known as the Hero of Fredricksburg. He held off the Union Army with just two guns, even though an entire battalion had its guns trained on him. He wouldn't leave until his ammunition ran out.

"He was foolhardy, brave, and ambitious—"

"He was a hero," Melanie muttered through clenched teeth. Corrine wondered why she was so passionate about this man.

"But," Father Joe raised his voice, "he died fighting for what he believed."

Melanie muttered something else Corrine didn't catch.

"Do you have something to add, Miss Smith?" Father Joe asked. His gaze was trained on Melanie in a way that made Corrine intensely glad she was not the object of his attention.

"Why, no sir, Father Joe," Melanie said in her thickest Southern-belle accent. All she needed to do to complete the image was twirl a golden ringlet around her fingers.

"Good, then," he said. "I've asked permission to take you all to Kelly's Ford next week," he said. "As some of you may become nurses, it may give you some idea of what it's like to work on the field of battle. And, you will hear the end of the story of the Boy Major."

Excited whispers erupted. Many of the girls had never left Falston since their arrival. The idea of a trip somewhere, anywhere, filled their heads with dreams of all the picnics and cotillions they were missing.

"Miss Brown and Rory MacLeod will go along to ensure your protection and cooperation. If anyone is caught acting out of accordance with school rules, she will be returned to the manor and summarily punished."

Corrine listened to the list of rules that followed, but she was more interested in watching Father Joe's expressions as he talked. He clearly had a distaste for discipline or punishment. She wondered how he got along with Miss de Mornay in private.

Something still felt familiar about him, as familiar as the language—Latin, she now realized—that had written itself on the board through Christina's hand. He met her gaze and she felt the needle again in her spine. Who was he and why did his presence spark something she couldn't name?

When class let out for dinner, Corrine approached the desk where Father Joe was removing the twig figures from the war board.

"Father?" she said, her voice squeaking embarrassingly.

"Yes, Miss Jameson." He concentrated on the figures, avoiding her eyes.

"Do you know Latin?"

Clearly, he was not expecting this kind of question, for he lifted up his head and laughed. From the sound, Corrine guessed he hadn't laughed in a long time.

"Forgive me, Miss Jameson. I suppose I was expecting a much more dire question." He took off his wire-framed spectacles and polished them on his cassock. "Yes, I speak Latin."

Corrine went to the board and picked up chalk. She wrote the phrase *Dominus Deus vallo mihi.* "What does this mean?"

He replaced his spectacles and read the words on the board. "Lord God defend me," he said. "Why?"

And, suddenly, without meaning to, she was telling him about Christina, about how the chalk had driven her hand to write those words, about the crosses that covered the board in a thicket of white when Christina tried to refuse it. "And," she finished breathlessly, "is Mara a witch?"

Father Joe went noticeably pale. He looked at her for a moment, focusing on her strange eye. Then, he took his spectacles off and polished them again. "Let us say that Mara has certain . . . instincts and talents about these things."

"But she said a spirit was possessing Christina!"

"Did she?" He swallowed and took one more pass on the spectacles. He looked very old, not hale and ageless as he'd appeared the first night Corrine had seen him. "Yes, well," he continued. "These are probably things best left alone, Corrine. The proper authorities will sort them out, I'm sure."

"But Father—" Corrine began.

"Hadn't you better get washed up for supper, Miss Jameson? I'm quite certain all of this will take care of itself in good time. Have no fear." He put his spectacles back on and smiled absently. "Off you go, now."

Dismissed, Corrine turned and left the room, puzzling over what Father Joe might be hiding.

That evening after supper, Corrine remembered that Christina had asked her yesterday to attend the sewing circle. She raised her hand promptly when Miss Brown asked for volunteers. Dolores and Melanie snickered at their end of the table, something about "the spinsters' sewing circle," but Corrine ignored them. Miss Brown escorted her, Ilona, Christina, and Penelope to the chapel room while the rest of the girls were sent to bed. Mara laid a fire in the grate and brought several sewing baskets from the hall closet.

"Christina," Miss Brown said. "Are you sure you feel well enough tonight?"

"Yes, Miss Brown. I think I'd rather sit up for a while," Christina said.

"Very well," Miss Brown said. "I'm leaving you in charge then. I will return in two hours' time to make sure everyone gets to bed. In the meantime, I will be in my study should you need me."

"Yes, Miss Brown," Christina said.

The headmistress stroked the timepiece at her collar thoughtfully, and then left the room, her taffeta skirts whispering around the corner. Corrine wondered for a fleeting moment if Miss Brown was ever lonely, and she thought again of the picture on Uncle William's desk of young Miss Brown in her ball gown. Were she and Uncle William ever sweethearts?

For a long while, there was silence except for the crackling of the fire and the slide of thread through wool and linen.

"Are you truly all right, Christina?" Corrine asked.

Christina smiled. "Yes, truly. Thank you for your help yesterday."

Penelope piped up, "Someone said you was possessed by ghosts!"

Christina's expression looked pained. "I'm afraid not," she said. "Just a passing fit. I've had them since I was young." She blushed. Corrine could tell she was telling the truth, but not all of it. Then Christina said, "So, Corrine, tell us how you came to be at Falston."

Corrine's hands stilled on the blanket she was sewing. She had hoped that the others would talk and she could listen. "I—"

Christina's eyes were wide and dark; her expression as inviting as Melanie's had been that first day in the play yard, but without the accompanying malice. Corrine realized that she had never really explained even to herself how she had gotten here.

"My uncle was angry with me. He's a friend of Miss Brown's and thought this would be a good place for me." For some reason, she could not tell them about Miss Brown's picture on her uncle's desk.

"What about your parents?" Christina asked.

"They're dead," Corrine heard herself say. But even as she said it, her mind screamed that it couldn't possibly be true. She wanted to say that her father had meant to come find her, but now he never would. And, as for her mother, she realized that she had never actually seen her buried. What if all of this was a hoax? What if she had been tricked into being put away where no one would ever hear of her again? Her attention on her fears, she slid the needle into her finger. The pain erased her thoughts as a bright bead of blood welled on her fingertip. Ilona saw it and took her hand, wiping the blood away and pressing down hard.

"I'm terribly sorry," Christina murmured, looking down at the shirt on her lap. Penelope also murmured her sympathy, but Ilona remained silent, squeezing Corrine's finger.

"How about you?" Corrine asked Christina.

The fire sizzled. The blood stopped, and Ilona released her.

When Christina's gaze met hers, she feared she'd asked the wrong question. There was a hardness in the girl's eyes that she had never seen before. When Christina answered, though, her tone was light. "The same as anyone else," she said, the soft French tones clinging to her words. "Someone wanted me here."

Corrine nodded. She sensed that further inquiry would not be appreciated.

After a moment, Christina continued. "My mama wishes very much to have me in Washington with her. My papa is still unconvinced of my innocence. He considered sending me back to France to live with my grandparents, but is afraid to, since the trouble began there. So, he sends me here."

"But—but—" Corrine spluttered. "Surely you will not be a teacher or a nurse!"

Christina laughed. "Oh no!" she said. "I'm sure papa will make a good match for me. He is an ambassador here, after all. It is just better for him to have me out of his sight and still be able to humiliate me at the same time." She stopped as though she said something she shouldn't have. Then she smiled. "My father is a cunning diplomat. I do not believe he likes to see himself mirrored in me."

Corrine nodded. She wondered if something similar was part of Uncle William's abhorrence to her. She guessed, from the way he spoke to her mother's portrait that final day in the study, that her resemblance to her mother unnerved him.

"Ilona, tell Corrine how you came to be here," Christina said. "It makes a charming tale."

Ilona cast her a dark glance. She bent closer to her sewing, as if to avoid what had to be said, and then relaxed again. Her stitches were uneven, zigzagging from here to there without much order.

"I hit a girl in my boarding school," she said. "No other school would take me after that."

Corrine remembered what she had seen in the book of punishment on her first day. Penelope corroborated this by saying brightly, "And she hit Melanie too! Right in the face!"

"Hush, Penelope," Christina said.

Ilona went bright red. She continued, her voice huskier than usual, "I was defending another girl, a friend, who had been bullied. The girl I hit had taken to cutting off my friend's hair at night and accusing her of doing it herself. My friend was too afraid to say anything, and kept getting in trouble for it. And the other girl began threatening worse things with the scissors. I hit her in the face and broke her nose. Perhaps the worst of it was that I spoiled her beauty." Ilona grinned behind her hair.

"Ilona!" Christina said, in false shock.

"Her parents were angry. They threatened mine, and made it so that no other school in Norfolk would take me. So I am here."

The girls fell silent again, until Christina asked, "Were you ever injured, Corrine?"

"Injured?" Corrine said. "I—no."

"She's asking what happened to your eye," Ilona said in an aside.

"Oh." Corrine thought about it. "I've always had it for as long as I can remember. My mother called it my 'fairy eye.'"

Penelope interrupted, "My mommy didn't want me!"

"Hush, Penelope," Christina said again.

"It's true," the little girl said. "She said she hoped the fairies took me away, because she didn't want me."

Corrine remembered her mother's instructions to her about fairies when she was about Penelope's age. "Did she give them your name?" she asked.

"Them who?" Penelope said.

"The fairies," Corrine said.

"I don't think so."

"Then you're safe," Corrine said. "As long as they don't have your name, they can't harm you."

"Oh," the little girl said. Then she said, "Is that what happened to Jeanette? Did they get her name?"

Both Christina and Ilona tensed. Ilona jabbed at her fabric as though her needle were a sword.

"Penelope," Christina said.

The little girl opened her mouth, but at Christina's warning look, closed it again.

Christina turned to Corrine, with a smile that seemed forced. "And you believe in such stories, Corrine?" she asked. Her voice was carefully neutral. It was difficult for Corrine to tell whether Christina was baiting her or asking sincerely. And though her curiosity ate at her, Corrine sensed that she should not ask about Jeanette.

Corrine stared hard at her sewing. She decided to take a chance. "I think so," she said, without looking up. "My mother always believed in them, and I thought of her as a very wise person."

Christina didn't reply, and the girls continued to sew in silence for some time. The fire continued to crackle beside them, and Penelope, closest to it, slowed in her sewing.

"Do you ever have dreams that you cannot explain?" Christina asked, breaking another long silence. The tone in Christina's voice compelled Corrine to look up. Her dark eyes were intent, frightened. Corrine sensed confusion there, and an abiding sense of shame, as though a young lady of her station should not fall prey to such fancies.

"All the time," Corrine said, thinking of the dreams of her father, the shadowy prince, and now all the visions of the girl in the forest, the pregnant woman running from the trees.

Ilona said, "Perhaps we should not speak of this here." She tilted her head toward Penelope, who was now drowsing, staring with half-closed eyes into the fire.

Christina looked toward the door. "Perhaps," she agreed. "But—"

"We have a Society," Ilona said in almost a whisper, "where we can discuss such things. Now is not the time."

Miss Brown appeared in the door then. "To bed, ladies," she said. She crossed to where Penelope sat nearly asleep in her sewing pile and helped her to stand.

"I must finish some business before retiring. Help Penelope and then make your way to your own rooms," Miss Brown said. "I shall lock your doors in ten minutes."

The girls nodded as Miss Brown disappeared down the hall. Corrine rose, trying to pile the blanket neatly back into the basket. She took a lantern from the table and helped Penelope with hers as the others went ahead into the hall.

"You know, she cut all her hair off after the fairies took Jeanette," Penelope said solemnly.

"Who?" Corrine said, as she took the little girl's hand.

"Ilona," Penelope said. "That's why her hair looks so funny."

Corrine didn't know what to say. Jeannette must have been the girl in Corrine's visions. She took Penelope to the foot of the steps where Ilona and Christina waited for them.

"Off you go," Corrine said to Penelope. The three older girls watched Penelope as she climbed to the second floor, her lantern dancing like a will-o'-the-wisp.

"Good night, Corrine," Christina said, smiling.

"Good night," Corrine said, with a sudden feeling that she should kneel and cross herself. Mystified, she longed to ask what Christina had meant about her dreams, but the girl shook her head slightly, the fear still in her eyes. She departed up the stairs.

Ilona nodded at Corrine, her short dark hair bobbing like a duck's tail in the shadows of her lantern. Corrine sensed that she was still disturbed by the mention of Jeanette.

"What happened to Jeanette, Ilona?" she asked, her whisper skittering between banisters and daguerreotypes.

Ilona frowned. "I will not talk about this now."

"But I just think . . . it might help." She couldn't reveal that she had seen Jeanette in visions, that the room next door forced her to see through the eyes of its former occupant with chilling regularity.

"Another time," Ilona said. She turned swiftly and took the stairs two at a time to the second floor.

As Corrine slowly followed, she wondered what had given Penelope cause to believe the fairies had stolen a Falston student. Why would the Fey steal a child? In the visions, a man had stolen her; this was clearly a human problem. Yet the visions themselves were of an inhuman influence, weren't they? If she wasn't crazy, she was definitely experiencing something otherworldly.

When she entered her room, she was pleased to see that Mara had already lit a fire for her, and the room, despite the perpetual draft that leaked through the window frame, was almost cozy.

The water pitcher was also full. A flannel cloth and a sliver of lye soap had been left on the washstand. She removed her clothes and washed briefly, hurrying into her nightgown to stand by the stove. She longed to soak in a tub full of hot water, like her mother used to fix up for her. Sometimes her mother would put stems of lavender and hyssop in the water, and she remembered as a child pretending they were fairy wands. As always, such thoughts led her to long for her mother.

She went to the window to try and shake them off. She looked out over the roof, down past the barn into the forest. Clouds raced across the face of the full moon, but there was enough light to see him there, waiting. And, as always, he knew that she watched. He raised his hand. Sickened, she turned away and blew out the lamp.

~ Twelve ~

October 10, 1865

Her father waited for her in her dreams. He came back to her as stone crept up to her knees. She could see him clearly; he wore his blue cavalry uniform, ragged now, the buttons dull and tarnished with what looked like blood. A rusty sword hung at his side. Tremors shivered through her stone feet, not quite like the prickling feeling she felt whenever she focused on Father Joe, but similar. This feeling, though, was almost nauseating. She would have liked to run, but could not.

He waits for you, *her father said. His voice was flat, a monotone wrenched from somewhere deep within him.*

She knew that he was asking her to choose between going with him or staying rooted in the sand.

The stone crept higher above her knees. It seemed there was really no choice to make. She nodded, and her father bent and put his hand around her left ankle. Life returned to her feet. She looked down and saw a ring of red roses circling her ankle, blooming obscenely against her skin.

He waits.

Corrine stepped forward and she was light as milkweed down. They floated together over the desert, and she watched their shadows make strange shapes upon the sand.

Gray dawn light filtered through Corrine's window. Mara had not yet knocked. The chill in the air told Corrine she hadn't banked her fire properly. She sat up, reaching to scratch her left ankle beneath her wool socks. The skin felt odd—almost puckered. She pushed down the sock and traced around a thin red manacle of seared flesh with a fingertip. It was as though someone had put a branding iron to her, drawing a molten line around her ankle with it. She scratched at it until it almost bled.

The knock came then. Corrine hurried to dress and get downstairs for the johnnyhouse line. As she was rushing down with the other girls, she bumped into Melanie.

"Watch it," Melanie hissed. There were dark patches under her eyes, and her normally vibrant curls seemed limp and unkempt. In fact, Corrine thought she even saw pieces of straw in them.

Ilona confirmed this by saying as she passed, "Is that straw in your hair, Melanie?"

Melanie gave Ilona a blood-freezing look, but she was already down the stairs. Melanie dusted at her hair in frustration while Corrine let the tide of girls carry her past. Corrine couldn't help wondering how the girl had managed to get straw in her hair, fastidious as she normally was. Certainly she didn't have a straw mattress? As far as Corrine knew, everyone had a cot like hers.

At morning mass, Corrine's ankle itched appallingly, but in a way she was grateful, because it was the only thing that kept her awake. She followed the line to receive the host, kneeling before Father Joe. When she looked into his eyes, her spine twitched and she nearly toppled over with the pain. *A woman with golden hair and amber eyes bent over Father Joe, caressing his cheek with a dark feather. He stared at the woman helplessly, lost between enchantment and terror.*

Corrine shuddered. Father Joe put the cup on the altar and steadied her. She felt his touch vibrate through her bones until she thought her teeth would rattle, but she remained upright.

He removed his hand, opened his mouth a little to signal that she should do the same. He laid the host on her tongue and held the cup to her lips, and she tried not to feel the strange buzzing, which stayed on her tongue even after she'd swallowed.

"*In nomine Patris et Filii et Spiritus Sancti,*" he said, and made the sign of the cross over her.

She imitated him, still mesmerized by the woman's amber eyes. She wondered about the woman, about Father Joe's relationship with her.

As she moved into line with the rest of the girls, Corrine noticed for the first time a tapestry that hung in the alcove behind the altar. Its colors were indistinct at first, but as she looked closer, she drew in a breath. A woman, her long, dark hair covering her otherwise naked body, reached up to a blue-green python coiled among the leaves of an apple tree. Eve tempted by the serpent. As Corrine watched, the serpent's coils seemed to expand and flash, as though the snake breathed.

She moved on with the rest of the girls to the dining hall for breakfast.

"Are you well?" Ilona asked, as they sat down.

Corrine reached to scratch her ankle, trying to hide the fear she felt from her dreams and this morning's vision. "Yes, why?" she answered, still irritated at Ilona for silencing her about Jeanette, and even more frustrated that she couldn't talk about all the things she had seen since coming to Falston.

"You seemed . . . odd when you took the Eucharist."

"I'm fine," she said. Ilona turned a little away from her.

Chagrined at her short tone, Corrine put a hand on her arm. "Ilona," she said. Ilona looked at her, and she felt the arm stiffen. "It's just that—" Corrine began.

"Shush," Ilona said. "Not here."

Corrine dropped her hand.

Ilona leaned forward and whispered in her ear, "At the meeting tonight."

"Miss Takar!" Miss de Mornay was on her feet and moving toward them, her gray eyes expressionless as always. "Did I see you whisper in Miss Jameson's ear?"

"Yes, Miss de Mornay."

"You will not sit together during classes today, and during your recess hour you will each write me an essay about why whispering is rude."

Corrine made sure she didn't look at Ilona, but stared at a fleck in her grits. She heard Dolores and Melanie tittering at the end of the table.

"Yes, Miss de Mornay," Ilona said through gritted teeth.

"Melanie," Miss de Mornay said, "you will be class monitor for today."

Corrine sighed.

"And, you and Miss Jameson will be laboratory partners."

"Thank you, Miss de Mornay," Melanie said.

Corrine glanced up in time to see Melanie's sweet, wicked smile.

In the laboratory, even the chilly air could not quite dim the smell of decaying flesh. The girls were to begin work on new specimens—frogs, this time.

Melanie was unwilling to reach into the jar for their frog and forced Corrine to do it. The flesh was cold and rubbery, and as she lifted the frog from the alcohol fluid spilled out of its mouth. *If Christina doesn't faint at this, I'll be amazed,* she thought. She put the frog in the tray, while Miss de Mornay revealed a diagram of how to make the first incision.

Melanie folded her arms across her chest. "Go ahead," she said.

"But—" Corrine began.

"Do you want even more trouble than what you've got now?" Melanie asked. She picked up the scalpel and waved it suggestively at Corrine, and then put it into Corrine's hand.

As de Mornay began her monotone lecture, Corrine set the scalpel against the frog's throat. She didn't know why she had to do this as part of her training as a potential nurse; she had never heard of any other school doing this sort of work. But she guessed that this was Miss Brown's idea of progressive education; maybe Miss Brown even had some idea that this would allow the girls to go to medical colleges and become doctors. The idea seemed fairly preposterous to Corrine.

As she sliced the frog's skin, she could have sworn that it turned its head and sighed. A little bubble of fluid burst out of its mouth and suddenly the frog emitted a raucous croak from its slit vocal chords. Corrine stepped back. As one, the class stopped, scalpels raised, and stared at her. Miss de Mornay turned toward Corrine, her eyes narrowing.

Melanie smothered a laugh behind her hand and forced a horrified look onto her face.

Miss de Mornay came to stand before Corrine's bench.

"Miss Jameson, whatever do you mean by making such rude noises in my classroom?"

"Miss de Mornay—"

"That was a rhetorical question, Miss Jameson. Put out your hand."

Corrine saw the ruler at the same time that she extended her hand. Before she could withdraw it, Miss de Mornay grabbed the tips of her fingers and brought the ruler down on Corrine's palm.

The pain was shocking, but the fact that no one had ever

struck her in her life made it even more so. Tears started, but she pushed the feeling back when she saw Melanie smiling from the corner of her eye.

Miss de Mornay made a red stripe on Corrine's palm before she released Corrine.

"No more of this behavior, Miss Jameson, do you hear?"

Corrine nodded, swallowing against the horrible gritty feeling in her throat.

Miss de Mornay went back to the front of the classroom, opening the book of punishment and writing Corrine's indiscretion and punishment in it.

"Carry on, ladies," she said, her eyes on the paper.

Corrine lifted the scalpel in her burning hand. Her fingers trembled. She looked at Melanie, who was watching her with a triumphant look in her eyes—the look of a cat who'd just nipped up a helpless canary.

"Get on with it," said Melanie.

Corrine controlled her hand and returned to the incision. She concentrated as hard as she could on keeping the knife true. The frog remained still and silent. Melanie looked disappointed, and Corrine swallowed her tears with a sigh of relief.

Dinner went quickly. Corrine said nothing, hoping to escape further notice from the Moray Eel. She sat apart from Ilona, and went along just as quietly when Miss de Mornay led them to the library.

"Miss Jameson, you shall stay here. Be finished with the essay by the end of recess, or it will go the worse with you. There are pencils and paper there on the table."

Corrine nodded.

"Miss Takar, come with me."

Corrine glimpsed Ilona's face. She was surprised to see a sparkle in her eye, a little smile playing about her lips. She winked at Corrine as she followed Miss de Mornay from the room, and Corrine remembered the whisper at breakfast that had gotten her in trouble in the first place. Was the meeting that Ilona had mentioned for the Society? Where and when would it take place?

Miss de Mornay shut and locked the door.

Corrine exhaled the breath she felt she'd been holding since before dinner. She half-smiled at the thought that what Miss Brown and Miss de Mornay considered punishment—locking her alone in the library during recess—was to her the greatest reward. She sat down at the table and picked up a pencil, but her palm smarted so much when she gripped it that she set it down again.

She wandered along the library shelves. She knelt and tested the cubbyhole where she'd found the first two letters, but it was still as empty as she'd left it. She considered replacing them, but felt she wanted to hold onto them a little longer. Perhaps she would even reread them, guilty as that made her feel.

As she rose, though, she noticed a book on the shelf to her right that was pulled out farther than the others. She went to push it in and noticed a bit of paper sticking out of its pages. When she took the book down and opened it, two letters fluttered out.

Nearly laughing in her glee, she replaced the book and took them back to the table. She smoothed the first letter down on the table.

[Trans. note: Substantial portions missing]

June 1356

To Sister Brighde of the Isle of Female Saints, from Brother Angus at Kirk of St. Fillan, greetings.

My beloved—

I write to you with no expectation of response, but I have every hope of one. I know that your gentle heart is troubled by what you saw. I cannot explain why you saw or felt what you did. If you would but drink and eat with the Fey, I believe that would lessen their timidity with you. And who could resist such a repast as they offer? Only you, my love, who are as pure of will as the highest saints.

[. . .]

But I fear that you will anger them if you persist in this course. You have [. . .]

[. . .]

They wish but to serve you; they would even make of you a queen in their lands. All that is required is your pledge of faith, to be given even as I have given it. I know you fear that such pledges are against the will of the Church, but do we not also swear allegiance to king and country, as well as God? The Fey were here long before any human king, long before the saints, even. I honor their longevity and wisdom. They have much to teach and much they are willing to give.

Corrine wondered if Brighde had felt as much conflict in her heart as she did. Though the Fey had truly helped make her well, she still could not help fearing them, at least a little. If they had some connection to the disappearance of Jeanette, she felt even more frightened. But their involvement with Jeanette's kidnapping must surely be no more than an eight-year-old's fancy. Everything else had happened because of the Captain, and the Captain served the witch.

She had no gauge of time, and desperately wanted to read the next letter. But she remembered the birch switches resting in their jar in the laboratory. She set herself to the task of writing the essay. She pulled her sleeve down over her palm, holding the pencil as loosely as she could. Thus awkwardly, she began her essay, "Whispering is rude because . . ." But all the while, she was thinking of Angus's words and Brighde's fear of the Fey and feeling perhaps that it was well deserved.

When Miss de Mornay returned to escort her to French, she handed her essay over without looking in her teacher's face. In her expressionless voice, Miss de Mornay said, "Your penmanship is deplorable," before leading her to the room where Christina had already stood to begin teaching.

Corrine tried not to let the Moray Eel's flat words sting, and instead listened carefully to the girls around her. Pronouncing the foreign words felt like forcing her tongue to speak through molasses. Penelope spoke perfectly in her high, birdlike voice, and Corrine could not help but envy her. She noticed throughout the class, though, that Christina refrained from writing on the board. Corrine almost smirked to see that when Dolores tried to tease Christina, she stood her ground and stared back at Dolores defiantly, almost singing the words in her sonorous voice, until the toad-mouthed girl gave up.

There was no request for sewing on that night, so Corrine went to her room after dinner, intending to study French, read the next letter, and stay well away from the wall. She didn't think she could bear to know more about Jeanette tonight, if there was truly anything more to know.

The dark came down faster every day; autumn was moving on quickly. She was sure the time would come when the room would be completely dark when she returned from dinner, a very unpleasant thought.

She studied French until she couldn't pronounce the painful words any longer, and then took the second letter she'd found out of her pocket. This one seemed to be a little earlier than some of the others, and the original didn't seem to be missing anything.

April 1556

To Sister Brighde Fional, of the Isle of Female St., from Brother Angus, Kirk of St. Fillan, greetings.

My beloved—

It has been long since we exchanged letters, much less glances or, dare I think of it even, a touch of hands. After the righteous anger of the Abbess, I had no hope that I would write to or see you again. But hope lives forever so long as there is faith. And my faith was rewarded last night.

I do not know how to explain this except to say that the herbwives of my father's villages must have told truth.

Last evening I walked along Loch Tay after Vespers, my heart heavy with thoughts of how I have offended you, and even God, with my desires. A light came from the trees, and between them was set a glorious feast as from some lord's gracious hall—music and the smells of food never tasted on earth drew me hence. It was like all the old tales we hear in childhood and put away as men and women. 'Twas the Fey welcoming me as blessed, and they bid me stay with them. It seemed ages that I sat with them beneath the roofs of trees, delighting in their music, observing dancing grace in their every movement. They perceived my sorrow and asked after it—what cause had a monk who lived by the Holy Well to grieve?

I told them of you, of how I love you despite myself, of how if I truly cared for you I would leave you be. And they said if God would not have us love, then why did we? If you would not have it so, why did you lift your lips to mine that day? Theirs is a wisdom my heart would gladly follow. They have said that there are many roads to God, and have said they would teach us these paths if we are willing. Often, I fear them—what heresies have they kept alive under the hills? Yet their wisdom rings more truly in my heart than any other. Why should children of Christ not love one another? Why does love spring between us if God did not wish it to exist? Surely you also ask these questions in your heart.

The Fey said they could not bear to see a child of earth grieve. And so they have sent a courier, one who will bear messages between us in secret, if you will it. No other eyes but mine and yours will look upon the words we exchange. Perhaps in this way we can discover the meaning of what God has opened to us. You have but to leave your response with a bit of bread by the window of your cell before you sleep, and your words will be swiftly delivered to me. Trouble not the messenger with iron or cross; these things disturb the Fey and have often kept them from doing the good work they wish to do among us.

I trust that you will have faith in what I have seen, for I swear by the waters of St. Fillan, I have not dreamed. I shall eagerly await your reply and even more the sight of your face again among the novitiates.

Yours Eternal,
Angus

A loud knock at her window startled Corrine so badly that she dropped the letter on the floor. Fearing it was the Captain finally coming for her, she huddled on her cot, hoping he'd go away. Or perhaps it had simply been a bird; one had flown into her bedroom window one day at home, and she'd gone outside and held its stunned body in her hand until it warmed enough to fly again.

But then the knock came again, and she thought she heard her name garbled through the glass.

A dark shadow took shape against the darker night and crept closer. She nearly screamed when Ilona's pale face appeared, framed by one of the windowpanes.

"Open the window," Ilona said.

"But it's—"

"Just open it!" Ilona said. Corrine saw her shape now, crouched down on the slanting roof next to the attic eaves.

Corrine got her fingers as close to the bottom edge of the window as she could and pushed. The window groaned and stuttered, but she definitely felt it move. Wind spat through the opening.

She heaved one more time, and as the window went up, she could feel Ilona from the other side, helping her to raise it. At last, there was room enough for Corrine to slip through.

"They lock the doors, but not the windows," Ilona said. She grinned in the faint moonlight.

The way across the roof was treacherous, but the wind was mild, for which Corrine counted her blessings. She didn't ask how Ilona had gotten out or why the Hungarian girl had chosen this route over sneaking through the manor. With de Mornay's sharp senses, she had no doubt that the teacher would be immediately alert to any movement at night.

They came to the edge where they were to begin their descent.

"This is how it goes," Ilona said, crouching. "You must put your foot here on this strut, and swing down. Use the drainpipe to climb down, but don't bang about. Someone could hear you. You can rest on the ledges if you need to."

Corrine nodded and swallowed. It was a long way down. She was grateful that the night obscured just how long. She could just make out the pipe, like a faint bone column, disappearing into the darkness before ground level.

Ilona swung over. "One more thing," she said, her head rising eerily above the eaves. "Climb off on the woodshed. We don't want any footprints to be seen at the bottom of the pipe."

Corrine nodded and watched her for a long time, until she disappeared.

She heard Ilona's hiss come from far down the pipe. "Come on, you yellow Yankee!"

Gritting her teeth, Corrine reached under the eaves and swung herself down below them. For a moment, she hung in terrifying space until she found the ledge with her feet on either side of the pipe. This was nothing like climbing a tree or even the ladder in Uncle William's study. The idea of falling three stories from a drainpipe paralyzed her for a moment. She clung to the gutter, her arms trembling. She considered climbing back into her room, shutting the window, and sleeping safely through the night. But she was certain that Ilona would never speak to her again if she did.

She began the slow climb downward, praying that the pipe wouldn't dissolve like the earth in her dreams. *Or strangle me or turn me to stone,* she thought.

When she neared the woodshed, Ilona hissed again. "Be careful. Move your hands sideways across the ledge, and very gently move your feet until you feel the roof under them."

Corrine did as she was told, fearing that her toes on the boards sounded like the drums of an army brigade. When at last she stood solidly next to Ilona on the woodshed roof, her arms trembled so much she wondered how she would ever climb back up.

"Come on," Ilona said. And she jumped off the roof without a thought, landing on the ground almost soundlessly. Corrine did not follow quite as gracefully. She had barely picked herself up out of the grass before Ilona disappeared toward the barn.

Corrine followed her as quickly as possible. When she entered the deeper darkness of the barn, she waited a moment for her eyes to adjust, massaging her fingers in the cold. The carriage horses and the cow stirred in the straw, but she also heard whispering. Corrine followed the sound until she came to a stall from which a faint light gleamed, as from a shuttered lantern. There, she could just barely make out the figures of several girls—Christina, Ilona, and a few others that she didn't recognize. But not Melanie or Dolores, thankfully. She sank into the clean straw near them. They had gathered it around them like blankets to keep warm.

Christina put her hands near the lantern to warm them. "Welcome to our little Society, Corrine." She gestured toward the shadowy faces of the girls she didn't know.

"This is Abigail," Christina said. Corrine saw the girl nod slightly. "And this is Hannah, and Olivia."

Corrine greeted each of them in turn, wondering if she'd remember their names properly when she saw them in daylight.

"Would you like a *petit four?"* Christina asked. "My mama sent them from a bakery in Washington."

Corrine held out her hand and Christina dropped a little cake into her palm, a perfectly shaped treat that rested there like a baby bird. Sugared violet sparkled in the lantern glow.

"Well, eat. And then you must tell us a story," Christina said. "You're new, so it's your turn."

Corrine slid the cake into her mouth, letting her teeth sink slowly into its softness. It felt like the utmost act of rebellion, even more forbidden than smoking cigarettes or climbing down the side of the manor. This little cake was all that had been denied her, all that would never be hers again. She let the almond paste and sugar dissolve on her tongue, felt the violet petals melt into lingering sweetness.

When Corrine could speak again, she said, "Your mother sent you these?"

"Mama always sends me something around this time of year. She is lonely for me, you see," Christina said.

"Oh," Corrine said. A pang of loneliness for her own mother

made any other response impossible.

"What about your parents, Corrine?" one of the other girls asked. "Why did they send you here?"

"I wasn't—They didn't . . ." Corrine sighed.

"It doesn't matter," Ilona said from the shadows. "Let her tell her story."

"What kind of story?" Corrine said.

"A scary one, you ninny," Christina said. "As scary as possible."

Corrine smiled. She knew a story that would serve. She decided to change the names of the characters, in case it was familiar to anyone else.

"Once there was a young monk named . . . Nigel . . . who fell in love with a nun. He knew that he should not love Elizabeth because they were both sworn to God, but he could not help himself. He could not forget about her."

She heard appreciative sighs from her shadowy audience.

"He began writing letters to her, begging to see her again. Elizabeth refused at first, knowing that her duty was to God. But soon she could not deny her feelings and wrote back to him."

Corrine decided to add a little spice from her own recent frightening experiences. "At about that time, Elizabeth began seeing a strange man, usually at twilight, who stood outside the convent. He seemed to be waiting for her, though she could not say how or why she thought so. This went on for several days until one evening, Elizabeth saw him raise his hand to her, as if in greeting. She went closer to try to see his face more clearly, but he turned and walked away."

That felt a little *too* real. Corrine could almost see the Captain waiting for Brighde beyond the convent walls. "Nigel kept writing letters, begging Bri—Elizabeth to see him. Again, despite her conscience, she went to meet him beneath the town bridge one night." Corrine shivered and decided to shift the story more toward a fairy story her mother had told her.

"Only it wasn't him," Corrine said, half-smiling in the dark. "It was the man who had raised his hand to her. And when she opened her lantern, she saw his hand, and that it was covered in blood."

Hannah half-shrieked and dove beneath Abigail's arms.

"The man seized her, putting his bloody palm over her mouth to keep her from screaming, and carried her off into the forest without a word. When they got to the forest, he set Elizabeth down and said a magic word that opened a gate into the earth.

"She asked, 'Who are you? Where is Nigel?'

"He laughed at her then and changed his shape to look like Nigel. He said, 'I am the Fairy Prince, and this was the only way I could bring you to my home beneath the earth. Now you will be my wife and give me many strong sons.' "

"Scandalous!" Abigail exclaimed.

"At that," Corrine continued, "Elizabeth screamed in terror, but he said another magic word and the blood on her mouth sealed her lips shut. Then he picked her up and carried her off with him to live in his evil underground kingdom forever."

The girls all sat quietly, unmoving in the shadows. Hannah still had her head buried under Abigail's elbow. Corrine could not help but be pleased. It was enough to have had the chance to talk about Angus and Brighde and the Captain in some way, even if much of it was imagined. No one, she knew, would ever believe the letters or the other things she had seen. She certainly didn't want anyone to discover that a semblance of these things had happened to her. They'd think her mad and truly lock her away forever, either here at Falston or some place worse.

Corrine's teeth chattered, despite the straw she had gathered all around her. Abigail shuddered with cold.

"Well," Christina said. Her voice sounded oddly troubled. "It's terribly cold. Have you all had enough?"

"Yes," soft voices said. "Enough." "Yes." "Let's go back inside."

"Right, then," Christina said. "Thank you, Corrine, for your wonderful story. You shall have to tell us another when the Abandoned Angels Society meets again."

"Abandoned Angels Society?" Corrine asked.

"Yes," Christina said. "That is what we call ourselves. We meet as we can throughout the year, and we induct new members at Hallowe'en. It's fortunate you came to us this time of year."

"Yes," she said hoarsely, trying not to think of all that had brought her here. She cleared her throat. "Yes, it is."

"Sometimes," Christina said, "we have emergency meetings. A member may call a meeting by using the code to alert us."

"Code?" Corrine asked.

"You ask Ilona or Christina if they have a pair of stockings you can borrow," Abigail answered. "And if they say they've got a hole in the left, that's 'yes, we can have a meeting.' And if there's a tear in the right, that's 'no.' "

"Oh," Corrine said. "I'll remember that."

They all stood.

Corrine watched as they joined hands across the circle. She put her hands in among them. Icy fingers clasped hers.

"Victory, memory, hope, perseverance," Christina said. The others followed her in the remainder of the chant. "We shall never forget. We shall never forgive. We shall prosper."

They squeezed hands, and then let go. Corrine heard them go, singly or in pairs in a ritual that apparently had had many rehearsals.

"Only one or two at a time," Ilona said. "Otherwise we might get caught."

"Have you ever been caught?"

"I? No. Christina—once. But she was able to lie her way out of it." Corrine heard the smile in Ilona's tone. "As she does with everything."

Corrine and Ilona waited together until everyone had gone. They retraced their steps to the woodshed. Ilona's room was on the second floor, so she had no need to climb back up the roof.

"Can you do this by yourself?" she asked.

"I think so," Corrine said, though she felt absolutely no confidence that she could. Coming down, she guessed, was easier than going up.

"I can lift you up to the woodshed roof," Ilona said.

"All right," Corrine said. She was not quite ready when Ilona's strong hands circled her hips and pushed her up into the air. She flailed onto the woodshed roof and pulled herself up, turning so she could look down at Ilona's shadowed face.

"All right then," Ilona said. "Sleep well."

"Yes," Corrine said. "Good night."

She heard Ilona's steps whispering away around the building. In the distance, the lights of the old slave quarters, where Rory lived, and Father Joe's cottage winked at each other. She wondered what they were doing at this hour. It wouldn't have taken much to coax her into trying to peer through their windows, but she was glad that she didn't have the choice now. She would never have been able to get back up on the woodshed roof by herself.

She worked her way up the cold stone, hauling herself onto the roof with aching fingers. She rolled onto her back and sat up by degrees, looking out upon the darkness. The cool air sailed past her cheeks, the stars distant in their fevered glitter. The splintered cradle of the moon rocked low over the hill.

Something caught her eye then, a shape at the edge of the forest near Falston's iron fence. She knew it was the Captain, even before she felt the sensation racing up from the ground—the same feeling she'd been able to avoid when she'd changed the direction of the story. The surge of power was violent, and she splayed her hands against the roof to keep it from bucking her off. A mist rose around him that glowed and shifted with purpose, as if it were alive. She wondered why he didn't come for her if he wanted her so much. Thinking of Jeanette, she retched with fear and clutched at her mouth to keep from vomiting the precious *petit four.* Her ankle burned. She scrambled backward up the roof, before turning and crawling through the dark mouth of her window.

~ Thirteen ~

October 11, 1865

Corrine's sleep was fitful. Between bursts of fearful clarity, she sank into a vivid world of colors she had never before seen, textures she had never before encountered. *She stood with her father at the edge of the desert beside a boulder warped by heat. The roses bloomed against her ankle even in the desert. Her father pointed at the shadow of the boulder and a hole opened in the earth, a wound that exposed a glistening city of towers and domes beneath the ground. Corrine peered within, fascinated.*

He waits for you, *her father said.*

"Father!" She gasped awake, her throat dry, her fingers clutching the blanket tight around her. Her body was cold, except for her ankle, which burned so fiercely that she wiggled her foot out from under the coverlet, longing to tear the wool sock from it.

Then she breathed deeply and sank toward sleep again, lured by a beautiful, familiar voice. Once, she even thought she felt a warm, endless embrace, the reverent shadow-whisper at her ear: *Do not fear me, Corrine. I have sent a token, something that will help you believe. You will see. And then you must come to me. I wait for you.*

A kiss whispered against her forehead, burning like the

roses about her ankle. And with it came every sweet smell she had ever known—lilacs and honeysuckle, lilies and lavender. In that kiss was more sorrow and love than she had ever seen in her mother's dark eyes and more yearning than she had ever felt for her lost father.

When the knock at last came, she rose, hoping day would chase away the dark's persistent hold. But through the johnny-house line and morning mass, she felt dull, her feet dragging across the floor. Father Joe's forehead wrinkled with concern as she received the host, for she forgot to cross herself when she rose. The wafer burned on her tongue; it took all her composure not to spit it out.

When mass was over, she followed the others to the dining hall and went through the motions of eating breakfast. Ilona was cheerful, but Corrine could not rise to her mood, nor did she give any indication that she heard Melanie and Dolores's whispered taunts. She noticed Father Joe looking at her from the teachers' table, worry plain on his face, but it was as though all her senses were muffled in cotton.

Her dull gaze met Siobhan's as the maid brought another bowl of grits to the table. Siobhan's eyes widened; her face pulled taut with horror. The ceramic bowl slid from her fingers and shattered on the floor, splashing hot grits all over Corrine, the table, and the bench. The high titters of her classmates and the soggy heat seeping through Corrine's clothes roused her. She pulled herself off the bench. Her sleeve and pinafore dripped with grits and butter. Siobhan crouched on the floor, sobbing and muttering. Corrine heard the word "marked" among Siobhan's tears and the clatter of ceramic shards, but couldn't understand anything else the girl said. Miss de Mornay and Miss Brown rushed over.

"Miss Jameson," Miss de Mornay began.

"I hardly think this is Miss Jameson's fault, do you, Marguerite?" Miss Brown said.

Corrine caught the look that flashed between them—a deadly look that almost made her forget the hot grits burning through her clothes.

"Siobhan," Miss Brown said, "take Miss Jameson to the laundry room and help her clean up. When you are done, Miss Jameson, please report to the garden."

Corrine nodded and followed Siobhan down a series of corridors until they reached the laundry room, which she guessed was at the very back of the old manor house.

Siobhan carefully avoided her gaze and knelt at the washing tub. Bloomers floated like intestines in the gray water. She put the washboard into the tub and picked up a bar of soap. "Just leave your pinafore there, miss," she said, pointing to a nearby pile of pinafores.

Corrine pulled the pinafore off and used it to dab at the rest of the grits soaking into her sleeve. Her arm hurt, and she guessed the grits had burned it but decided not to say anything.

"I think my dress may be dirty too," Corrine said, pulling at her skirts, "but it's mostly wet, I think."

Siobhan stared at her with the same look of fear and revulsion she'd had before she dropped the bowl of grits.

"What?" she said.

"You're marked," the maid whispered. "He's been at you. You try to hide it, but I see it there on your forehead, plain as day. Any of Them would know you in a hobgoblin's wink."

"Who?" Corrine asked.

"The Fey," Siobhan said. "The Unhallowed Ones. They want you. And they'll be coming to get you."

Her face crumpled, and she threw herself at the washboard, grabbing the bloomers and furiously scrubbing them until Corrine feared her knuckles would bleed.

Siobhan sobbed, "I knew as I shouldn't have taken this job!" She looked up at Corrine. "How could They have followed us all this way?"

"Who? What are you talking about?" Corrine said. She had never yet heard anyone living mention the Fey. Only Angus had spoken of them in his letters, and he had never said anything about any "Unhallowed."

But Siobhan would not answer her and refused to look at her, muttering softly to herself, while her tears dropped into the gray water.

Corrine didn't know what else to say. She laid her pinafore carefully on the pile.

As Corrine turned to leave, she heard Siobhan mumble, "Not like you'll be needing it anyway, where you're going."

She whirled back to Siobhan. "What do you mean?"

Siobhan's red-rimmed eyes looked up and she cowered, as if she expected Corrine to strike her. "Oh, miss, I just meant—"

"What? What do you know?" Corrine's voice was strident. She knew she had no reason to yell at a poor, frightened maid. Her mother would have been ashamed.

"Just that . . . They always come for the ones they mark, miss," Siobhan said. "They take them away under the ground."

"Where?"

"I don't know, miss. They just do. Always. They always come." Corrine could see her gaze growing distant. Pushing Siobhan further would result in nothing.

"We'll see," Corrine said, feeling the ridiculousness of her situation—standing over a maid in a sodden dress yelling about fairies, while somewhere Miss Brown was ticking away the moments it took for her to arrive in the garden. She left the laundry, trying not to hear the girl's frightened sobs as she passed into the hall.

She found the mudroom and pulled on her hat and gloves in confusion. How did Siobhan know about the Fey? And why was she terrified of them? As far as Corrine could tell it was the bloody-handed Captain who was to be feared. The hawthorn people had said he served a witch, so perhaps he was a ghost or controlled by some sort of spell. Perhaps the Fey were mischievous and even misleading, but never malevolent. Sometimes they were even helpful, as when they had healed her of the lingering effects of the ague. All the stories she could remember involved some helpful or tricksy fairy.

She remembered the dream in which her mother had frantically searched for the iron cross and then said in her dying breath, "He's here." At the time, she hadn't understood it; she had assumed it was yet another fever-dream. But now she wondered if the dream referred to the Captain, who surely could not be Fey. He felt much more evil than tricksy. Or could he? Was he one of the Unhallowed that Siobhan spoke of?

Out into the sunlight, the other girls whispered over the pumpkins as they straggled along the rows. Corrine looked for Rory in the corn but didn't see him anywhere. Miss Brown showed one of the girls how to pick the last of the okra, while others cut late crops of greens.

Though she saw Ilona working among the dying tomatoes, Corrine did not join her, staying instead among the withered green beans and trying to untangle the knot of thoughts in her mind. Mara came outside and spoke to Miss Brown in a low voice. Her black eyes snapped across the girls with equal disdain, and Corrine remembered Christina's "possession," how Christina had openly called Mara a witch before she fell asleep, and how Father Joe had tried ineffectually to evade discussing Mara at all.

Corrine watched Mara from under the brim of her hat as she returned to the manor. Miss Brown assigned Christina the position of monitor while she went inside. Corrine patted the pinafore pocket where she normally kept the letters for reassurance, and then slowly realized she had neither a pocket nor a pinafore. The horror of what would happen if the letters were discovered or even destroyed in the washbasin slipped down her spine all the way to the soles of her feet.

She set her basket at the end of the row and went to Christina, who was struggling to break up a clod of earth with a hoe. She stared at the dirt as though she would conquer it, and her brow beaded with sweat under her hat. Even so, Corrine still thought her beautiful—her cheeks glowed with exertion and her chestnut curls framed her face charmingly under her bonnet. Corrine could well see why Rory was taken with her.

"Christina," she said in a low voice, trying to draw her attention without alerting Melanie or Dolores.

Christina ceased hoeing and straightened to look at her. "Yes?"

"I need to go inside. I forgot my pinafore. My dress will get dirty without it."

Christina's gaze ran over her, looking at the shrinking wet spots on her sleeve and dress. She wasn't sure if Christina believed her, but she didn't dare tell her about the strange letters out here where someone else might hear.

"I shouldn't let you go in; if you're caught, we will both be in great trouble," Christina said.

"But my dress—"

Christina thought for a moment. "Just don't let anyone catch you, especially not the Moray Eel," Christina said.

Corrine nodded. She untied her hat and removed her gloves as she walked, placing them by her basket at the end of the row of beans. She could only hope Melanie and Dolores didn't see her leaving and remark upon it; she hated giving them such easy ammunition. But if Siobhan found the letters. . . .

In the mudroom, Corrine paused in the doorway to listen for voices out in the hall. Then she began the long, slow creep through the corridors back to the laundry room. She slipped into the laundry room entry without incident and stood listening for telltale sounds of water splashing. When she heard nothing, she walked in and said a silent prayer as she dug through the pile of pinafores and bloomers. She had dropped them on top, but it looked as though in the interim Siobhan might have brought in more laundry. She came up first with a pair of bloomers monogrammed with the initials MS. Melanie Smith. She threw them down in disgust and continued shuffling through the clothes until at last she found a pinafore that felt heavier than the rest. She slid her hand into the left pocket and sighed with relief as she drew out the slim packet of letters.

"Thank you, Lord," she said under her breath.

She rifled through the pinafores again, trying to find one that seemed less stained than the others. They all looked virtually the same, so no one would suspect anything. She found one and pulled it on, adjusting the ties and sliding the letters in as quickly as she could. She hurried to leave, not wanting to find Siobhan or endure her disturbing stares again.

So much was Corrine's hurry to get back to the garden before Miss Brown that she barely paid attention to anything around her. As she turned the corner, Mara and Miss Brown emerged from the chapel room. Mara held something in her hand—what looked like a crude doll made of black flannel.

"I almos' forgot," Mara said. She handed the doll to Miss Brown. Red flashed on its left hand, and something silver, like a pin, stuck out of it. They both saw Corrine at the same time, too late for Corrine to duck back around the corner.

A chill sliced down Corrine's spine. She had heard whispers of things found when the slaves of the Deep South had been liberated by the Union troops—voodoo dolls, chicken's feet charms. "Things as no good Christian would keep in they homes," Nora had once said to her mother. Christina had said that Mara was a witch, and what better proof than this voodoo doll? For all its crudeness, Corrine could not miss the significance of the red hand. Corrine thought again of what the Fey had said. *The Captain serves the witch.*

Mara nodded to Miss Brown and, casting a smoldering glance at Corrine, took her leave.

Miss Brown turned her gaze fully on Corrine, holding the doll casually around the throat as if it was a dusting rag. Corrine saw that it had white thread crosses for eyes.

"Miss Jameson, what are you doing here? I told Siobhan to send you to the garden."

Corrine didn't know what to say at first. The doll stared at her from Miss Brown's grasp.

"Miss Jameson?"

"I . . . came to get another pinafore, Miss Brown. I felt uncomfortable without one, especially in the garden. I didn't want to dirty my dress." She clenched her teeth and prayed silently that somehow her mother could not hear all her lies in heaven.

"And Christina said this was all right?"

"Yes," Corrine said.

Miss Brown sighed. "You seem to be having a difficult time of it, Miss Jameson. I can only hope you will adapt soon. Next time, wait until I return so that I can escort you. No students are to be wandering the halls alone, day or night."

Corrine could not help but look at the red-handed doll. *I can guess why,* she thought.

"Do you understand, Miss Jameson?" Miss Brown asked.

She considered asking Miss Brown about the doll, about those Siobhan had called the Unhallowed, but all she wanted right now was to return to the garden unscathed.

"Yes, Miss Brown," she said.

"I shall trust you to make your way to the garden on your own," Miss Brown said. "I will follow you momentarily."

Corrine nodded. Miss Brown stepped back into the doorway of the chapel room to let Corrine pass. Corrine felt as though the doll watched her all the way to the next turn in the corridor.

Corrine was silent throughout the rest of gardening and even through Father Joe's religion class. She successfully avoided Melanie and Dolores, who teased Penelope about her inability to pronounce the names of the saints rather than torment the new girl. Ilona cast a worried glance at Corrine, but knew better than to draw attention to her.

By the time the dinner bell rang at noon, she was ready to speak to Ilona, ready to have answers.

She looked carefully around to make sure that Miss de Mornay wasn't watching. "Ilona," she said, "is it true that Mara's a—"

Just as the word hit the tip of Corrine's tongue, Mara appeared, bearing a heavy Dutch oven full of beans.

Ilona shook her head in warning.

Mara set the pot at the far end of the table between Dolores and another girl whose name Corrine had not quite caught yet.

"You expect us to eat that slop?" Dolores said.

Mara didn't reply, just drove the metal serving spoon she held into the beans as though it were a knife. But she fixed Dolores with such a hard look that Corrine's fingers twitched as she reached for a corn muffin.

"Cooking was evidently not one of her duties when she was a slave," Dolores mumbled after Mara disappeared into the kitchen. No one said anything in response. Perhaps, Corrine thought, they were all too wise to speak.

"Is she, Ilona?" Corrine whispered, after Mara had gone back into the kitchen. She lowered her whisper to a bare breath. "A . . . wi—"

"I told you," Ilona said. "Be careful of her. She knows things."

"What kinds of things?"

"Things it is better to know nothing about. Dolores will regret that, believe me."

"Why?" Corrine asked.

"Wait and see," Ilona said. "But I'll bet you a game of graces that Dolores will be too unwell to go to the battlefield tomorrow." She glanced at Dolores as she shoveled beans through her wide lips. "She should know better by now."

"What will happen?" Corrine asked, also trying to keep her voice low.

"Who knows?" Ilona said. She pushed her dark hair out of her eyes. "Something always does."

"Where did Mara come from?" Corrine said.

"Later," Ilona said. Her eyes were on Miss de Mornay, who had just entered the room. "The Eel is watching."

Corrine nodded and ate the rest of her dinner in silence, the questions in her mind tangled beyond hope.

At recess, Ilona scooped up a worn leather ball and gestured for Corrine to follow her to the edge of the play yard. Miss Brown watched from the steps for a bit until Siobhan took over. Ilona bounced the ball to Corrine and Corrine sent it back.

"You want to know about Mara?" Ilona said.

Corrine was close enough that she didn't have to shout. "Yes."

"All I know is that Father Joe risked his life to save her from a plantation just before the War. She ran away and he lost track of her. He finally found her again after a few months in New Orleans, and by then all the fighting had gotten pretty bad. He brought her back here, right through enemy lines."

Corrine could hear the unabashed joy in Ilona's voice at the talk of battle. *Are you sure you're not a boy?* she wanted to ask. She had never seen a girl revel so much at the thought of combat. Instead, she asked, "Why?"

"No one knows," Ilona said, pushing the ball at her. "But what I do know is that if she wants something to happen, it does. If you make her angry, you will pay."

"I saw her with a voodoo doll," Corrine said.

"When?" Ilona asked.

"Today when I went inside to get a pinafore. She was giving it to Miss Brown," Corrine said. "What do you think she was doing with it?"

Ilona caught the ball and held it for a moment. She turned it over in her hands before looking up at Corrine. "Corrine, you should ask no more questions," she said, reminding Corrine of the night when she had asked about Jeanette.

"But don't you want to know what's happening here?" Corrine said. "What if Mara really is a witch? What if Jeanette disappeared because of her?" Her voice was rising. A few nearby girls turned to stare.

"I said no more questions," Ilona said. She turned, clutching the ball to her abdomen, and stalked away across the play yard. Corrine stared after her, dumbfounded. The other girls snickered, but she barely heard them. How had this happened? In one moment, she and Ilona were talking and playing like good friends. The next, Ilona was storming away from her. But she wouldn't follow the tall girl, who had already joined another group of girls playing blindman's bluff.

She stared after Ilona for a few more minutes, but there was nothing to be done. She decided to slip away and reread one of the letters before classes resumed. Siobhan was watching them, but made a concerted effort to avoid looking in her direction.

Corrine edged farther from the play yard until Siobhan's attention was occupied by a group of shrieking girls. Corrine definitely would not make the mistake of going to the barn, as she had last time, though she saw that Melanie and Dolores were occupied with graces at the other end of the yard. Nevertheless, she went the other way toward Father Joe's cottage, watching Siobhan carefully to make sure she remained distracted.

As she turned the corner, she ran into something solid, something that gasped.

"Heavens, you'll leave a lad with no breath at all!" Rory said.

Corrine looked into his face, aghast. He smiled and clutched his chest in mock pain. Then he winked and touched his hat.

"Miss Corrine, if I remember correctly."

"Yes, sir," she said, lowering her eyes.

"There'll be no 'sir'-ing me," he said. "I'm barely older than you. Call me Rory."

She looked at him and nodded, but didn't say his name. He looked older than she could imagine being, and she couldn't decipher whether he was making fun of her or simply telling the truth.

"And what are you doing sneaking off during recess, lass? You're not wanting the Moray Eel to find you, are you?"

"I was just—" Naturally, she couldn't tell him she was seeking a quiet place to read letters she'd stolen from the library. She felt small and strange. She disliked imagining how she looked to him—strange eye, straggling hair, stained clothes. "—going to the johnnyhouse," she finished.

"Well, the johnnyhouse is that way," he said pointing in the opposite direction. "But no matter. You're new. Perhaps you lost your way?"

Corrine nodded.

"It's just as well," he said, taking something from his pocket. "I'm glad I found you. I have a token I was told to give you."

A familiar gold locket shimmered out of his fingers and swung in the sunlight. She heard his last words as though they were drops of water falling into a well. The shadow prince's voice whispered, *I have sent a token, something that will help you believe.*

"What?" she managed to whisper, stunned.

"He sends this to you. As a token of his goodwill."

Rory must have sensed her shock, for he grasped her forearm with his free hand and lifted it, pouring the locket into her palm.

"Where did you get this?" she whispered. She feared to open it, but her thumb depressed the clasp of its own volition. Inside were pictures she'd never forget, though now they seemed even older than the portrait of the lady in the trunk. Her mother smiled at something distant, her eyes kinder and gentler than they had been in the youthful portrait on her uncle's desk. Her father's portrait included Magellan, his favorite horse. Horse and man looked out at her with a similar expression that had made her and her mother laugh when first they'd seen it.

"You know where I got it, lass," Rory said.

She looked up. His eyes had lost their casual cerulean glow, becoming deep as the ocean and just as mysterious. He seemed untroubled by her strange eye, but focused on her completely, as few people ever had been able to do.

"Corrine," he said, and in his voice she heard echoes of the way the shadow prince spoke her name in dreams.

"I am a friend of the prince who sent this to you. When you are ready to believe the truth, you have but to speak the words. As our good Father says, 'Ask and ye shall receive.' "

The bell clanged for the end of recess. Corrine backed away, clutching the locket. Rory tipped his hat to her again and limped off toward the barn before she could say anything.

She slipped the locket over her head and arranged it under her collar so it wouldn't show. It glided into its old place over her heart. For the first time since waking at Uncle William's, she felt close to whole—and ashamed that she had doubted the Fey, that she had allowed Siobhan to disturb her peace. All of the horrible things that had happened, from the violation of her mother's trunk to the oddness here at Falston, could be traced to one source, the Captain. And the Captain, as the Fey had told her, served the witch—a witch who could be Mara. But what did the Captain and the witch want? And who else was involved with them?

Corrine pondered these questions all afternoon as she struggled over the pencil sketches Miss Brown asked her art class to compose. Ilona seemed bent on ignoring her, so Corrine did her best to focus on committing the still life of fruits and vegetables onto her paper. What she got in the end, though, was a drawing that looked like a lopsided head with large ears, rather than a melon and crookneck squash. Exasperated, she could only pray that Miss Brown was lenient in her grading.

Christina sat ahead of her. Corrine leaned out from her row to peer at what was on her easel. It was certainly not a still life like any Corrine had ever seen. Instead, a nun knelt, her arms spread in supplication, before a tall, cloaked man. Christina was sketching this so rapidly and perfectly that it was almost as though she'd sketched this before. Corrine glanced at Miss Brown as she maneuvered through the easels like a cruising shark. Corrine clenched her pencil more tightly, hoping that Christina would not be embarrassed again in front of the class. But Miss Brown simply bent and whispered something in Christina's ear, then moved on. And though Christina's hand trembled a bit, she was allowed to continue her drawing in peace. Corrine gritted her teeth to think of what would have happened if Miss de Mornay administered this class. She was quite sure things would have gone differently.

"Corrine, is there something wrong with your pencil?" Miss Brown spoke from behind her.

"I just can't draw," she said. The girl next to her, who had managed to sketch a passable squash, looked at her sidelong.

Miss Brown took the pencil from her and made some corrective strokes, turning the lopsided head into a passable melon. "With practice, it becomes easier," she said. "We often feel we can't do what we're called to do, but that should never prevent us from doing it. The secret is that if we weren't meant to do it, we wouldn't be called." Corrine didn't miss the hint at something deeper than vegetable sketches in Miss Brown's words.

"What am I called to do?" she whispered.

Miss Brown smiled. "Right now, I charge you with drawing a better squash. But later on, we'll see." Miss Brown fixed her with an inscrutable gaze. "Just know that the first step is believing in your worthiness. You are worthy, Corrine."

Corrine nodded. Even as she felt buoyed by these words—words her mother might have said to her—the locket, secret and heavy, weighed against her heart.

October 13, 1865

As on most Friday nights, the girls were asked to tidy up the chapel room to prepare for Sunday mass. Tonight, Miss Brown also asked for volunteers to help clean in the library. Corrine raised her hand at the mention of the library and was gratified when she was asked to form a line with the two other volunteers.

Melanie and Dolores didn't volunteer, as usual, and Dolores looked almost green as she filed out of the dining room toward the stairs with the other girls. Corrine wondered again if what Ilona had said was true, but then she remembered the black voodoo doll and supposed it was only a matter of time before she found out. Ilona still avoided her and Corrine decided it would be best to leave her be.

She entered the library with Abigail and Hannah, the girls she had first met at the Society meeting. Abigail winked at her as she handed out dust rags from a cleaning basket. "The sooner we're done," she said, "the sooner we can talk."

Corrine nodded and went to the far end of the room, while Abigail and Hannah concentrated on the shelves near the door. There were no book ladders here, but a sturdy stool helped her reach the top. As she dusted, she felt along the panels of the shelves to see if any were loose or missing. She was disappointed to find that they were all solid. While dusting above the books, however, she heard paper rustling. She felt along until she found the paper sticking out of a book. Quickly, she pulled the book from the shelf. Its title—*De Historia Caledoniae*—meant nothing to her. But the piece of paper itself was another letter. Two, actually, folded together. She looked around. Abigail and Hannah were poring over a book together and ignoring her. Corrine put the letter in her pinafore.

There was unfortunately no chance to discuss the Society, for Miss Brown came shortly afterward to escort them to bed. As Corrine shuffled up the stairs, she tried not to smile about the letter riding securely in her pocket.

The lantern in her room danced with flames and the stove was already warm. Mara had been here. Now that Corrine knew Mara was a witch, she shivered a little at the thought of Mara's presence in her room. *But is she* the *witch?* The black voodoo doll with its red hand suggested that she was.

She went to her window, expecting to see the Captain in the fading dusk. But he was not there. Instead, something white caught her eye. It drifted across the yard and veered behind the barn. She saw it reappear beyond the fence, a girl in white walking deep into the wood—a girl Corrine couldn't recognize from this distance.

Actually, she didn't seem to walk so much as float. Her form flickered, yielding to the breeze and to the dark, until at last it drifted beyond Corrine's vision. The Fey, witches, and now ghosts? Corrine splayed her palm against the glass, needing to feel something real and solid. She considered investigating but instead turned her back on the dark and fished a letter from her pocket.

Late May 1356

To Sister Brighde, Isle of the Female Saints, from Brother Angus, Kirk of St. Fillan, greeting.

My beloved—

It seems, no matter my resolutions, that I cannot cease writing to you. I saw the one I spoke of again—the man who watches from the wood. I worked in the monastery garden, and I felt him standing there through the ground. I looked up and realized he had meant for me to see him this time. He did not leave the shadows of the trees, only raised his hand to me, and moved farther back into the leaves. I realized in that moment that the world had receded. It was as though I alone had stepped into a shell and could hear the waves crashing all around me.

I pray you do not think me mad for these things I say to you. The Fey have revealed a realm that I believed was false. But they have shown me that there is more to this earth than what we have been taught, that even the least whisper of the old herbwives must have been true. I do not know who this man is who watches—I believe that he may be the one the mad have often called "the Captain."

I do not know how it is that I am preserved of my sanity when others are not. Perhaps it is the protection of God or my nearness to the Holy Well; perhaps their minds are too fragile to encompass his presence. However it is that I have escaped this madness, I am grateful for it, and even more grateful for your faith in me. I know you sometimes fear what I have witnessed. I assure you that if you will assent to come with me at Midsummer, all will be clear to you, my love.

[Translation note: rest of letter lost]

So Angus had seen the Captain too. How could they both have seen him? If Mara was the witch and she had summoned this demon or spirit or whatever he was . . . Corrine shook her head, too confused to try to sort it out. She returned the last letter to the packet unread, suddenly frightened of the information it could hold.

She changed into her nightgown and socks, and turned down the lamp wick until the light died. She stretched out on the rickety cot and drew the wool blanket to her chin.

Ask and ye shall receive, Rory had said. She held the locket as though it was the iron cross, as though her parents could somehow protect her from the dark. "I ask for no dreams tonight," she said.

That night, there were none.

~ FOURTEEN ~

October 14, 1865

MORNING CAME JUST AFTER CORRINE LAID HER HEAD ON the flat feather pillow. The sense of urgency as the girls rushed down the stairs was even greater than usual. After all the girls hurried through the johnnyhouse lines, Siobhan and Mara handed them bandana-wrapped biscuits and salt pork for breakfast, and a dinner pail for later.

"You'll be back for a late supper," Miss Brown said. "Just be sure not to eat all your food too quickly, else you'll be hungry."

Some of the girls grumbled as Miss de Mornay ushered them out the front door, fearful because they could not go to mass or confession. Corrine, however, was glad. She was afraid she would end up telling all the secrets knocking around inside her. Judging from her earlier attempt to confide in Father Joe after history class, she wasn't sure she could trust him any more than Miss Brown or Mara. But she feared she couldn't hold onto these secrets much longer anyway, confession or no.

Two wagons were parked outside the school's front entrance. Father Joe drove one and Miss Brown took the reins of the other. Miss de Mornay stood on the top step, surveying everything with her usual flat stare, her long, black skirts the only funereal spot in the brilliant, if chilly, day. Miss de Mornay was staying behind, for which Corrine was very glad. That happiness grew when she saw Rory astride his black Morgan, trotting toward them from the gates. Rory wore a brown huntsman's coat and his old felt hat. An engraved brass plate shone on his saddle horn, but Corrine couldn't make out the letters from where she stood. A long pistol hung in a holster from the saddle, and Corrine wondered if the gun had accompanied Rory to war. She had no doubt on which side he'd fought, but even in a gray uniform, he would have been quite handsome. Their shared knowledge of the Fey and his gallant gesture of returning her locket deepened her feelings for him into something far beyond mere admiration.

"The road looks clear, Father," Rory said to the priest. "No downed tree limbs or bad ruts."

"Good," Father Joe said. "Thank you, Rory."

"All right, girls. Let's load up," Miss Brown called.

Rory dismounted and limped over to lend a hand to the girls as they climbed up a set of portable steps into Father Joe's wagon. Corrine watched Melanie smile at Rory and toss her curls as he helped her up. Rory's reaction to Melanie seemed no different than his reaction to anyone else he helped. She also realized at that moment that Dolores was missing—Dolores who was never far from Melanie's side. She looked around but didn't see Dolores anywhere.

When Father Joe's wagon was full, Rory moved the steps to the back of Miss Brown's wagon. Ilona was next and then Corrine.

"Miss Corrine," Rory said. He took her hand and helped her up, bowing his head before her as if she were nobility. She blushed.

She settled herself next to Ilona who looked at her sidelong and smiled. "Good morning," she said.

"Good morning," Corrine said, somewhat perplexed. Ilona acted as though nothing had happened yesterday. Corrine decided it would be best not to remind her. Before she could say anything else, Christina nestled down beside her.

"Bonjour, mon amie," she said. Her cheeks held a flush that didn't seem to come from just climbing into the wagon. Corrine looked at Rory, and she saw his glance dart away from Christina as he helped another girl into the wagon. Something ghosted across his face. If she had known him better, she would have called it longing.

"Bonjour," Corrine replied. She still felt the French vowels twisting away from her, even in so easy a word.

Her face must have shown her disgruntlement, for Christina patted her forearm and said, "It is all right. You will learn."

"I don't know," Corrine said, shaking her head.

Miss Brown clucked to the horses and the wagon jerked forward.

"I will help you," Christina said.

All down the hill and toward Brandyville, the town between Falston and Kelly's Ford, Corrine practiced declensions and conjugations with Christina over the jerking and jolting of the wagon. Though the words still slid away from her, they distracted her from the fear that accompanied passing out of the iron gates. She was fair game again for the Captain, though she still did not understand why he could not enter the school grounds, if he served the witches. Corrine remembered that Jeanette had been lured beyond the fence. Had he taken her then? She pushed her thoughts away in favor of conjugating *avoir.*

As they moved out of the pines and hemlocks of Falston Hill, the oaks and maples showed that autumn was indeed well on its way. Scarlet, orange, and gold tipped the edges of the leaves. Some shrubs had gone brown already, their flowers spent, their leaves unable to resist the hammering heat of the last few months. Daylilies withered alongside the road, and the milkweed pods were cracked, revealing their silky inner floss. Occasionally, an orange monarch butterfly floated by bound for some unknown destination.

Everyone fell silent, lost in the freedom of being outside the school grounds. Melanie unfastened her bonnet, letting the sun lighten her hair to pure gold. Undoubtedly this was a tactic to attract Rory, but he sent his mare up ahead of Father Joe's wagon again, and didn't seem to notice. Seeing Melanie's failed attempt at attracting his attention for some reason reminded Corrine again of Dolores' absence.

"Where is Dolores?" Corrine asked Ilona as quietly as she could.

Ilona gave Corrine a warning glance. "Ill, so I hear."

But Penelope had heard her from across the wagon and piped up, "They said she upchucked toads all night long!"

Miss Brown half-turned her head and Corrine cringed, but the headmistress didn't say anything. The other girls giggled.

Ilona said to Penelope, "She has diarrhea. No toads, silly girl." But she glanced at Corrine as if to say, "I told you so," and Corrine got an uncomfortable feeling in the pit of her stomach that had nothing to do with the wagon ride. If Mara was the witch and she could do this sort of thing *and* control the Captain, what could possibly stop her? Corrine needed more proof than a voodoo doll, as alarming as that was. If the Fey knew something . . . Rory claimed to have answers if she was ready to hear them. But how could she be sure? Her hand lifted to the locket for reassurance.

The wagons stopped in Brandyville, and the girls were allowed to get out of the wagon and stretch their legs. There was a public johnnyhouse at the edge of the market square, and Miss Brown and the older girls shepherded the younger girls in that direction. Over on the boardwalk in front of the general store, Rory spoke to the sheriff, who laughed in great booming cascades like a bullfrog. Father Joe perused the market, pausing at a basket of apples with a look that was almost lustful.

Corrine held her nose throughout the dismal experience of the johnnyhouse, wishing she could have just gone into some bushes as she used to do when she played near the Elk River at home. When she emerged, she saw that Melanie was hanging on Rory's arm, chatting animatedly with the sheriff.

"Back into the wagons, girls," Miss Brown called, and Melanie slipped her arm from Rory's as naturally as breathing. Rory borrowed a crate from the general store, and helped the girls climb back into Father Joe's wagon, sometimes having to lift the smallest ones up. Ilona helped the girls up into Miss Brown's wagon to speed things along. Corrine was both disappointed and relieved when Ilona's rough hands propelled her forward.

As they set out again from Brandyville, Corrine opened the bandana and munched on her biscuit, wishing she had a cup of water to wash it down. She had given up on French, for Christina dozed next to her, her head falling close to Corrine's shoulder. Corrine had no idea how anyone could sleep through such a rickety ride.

They passed through some hills into a low, broad plain. Corrine smelled pungent river mud nearby. She could see nature's slow recovery from the recent insults of the War—splintered trees healing, scorched earth fading into the fields, tumbling walls covered with vines. Men, white and black, working the fields reminded her painfully of her father. He had loved this time of year. "Nothing like seeing the fruits of your labor," he'd often said around harvest time. Even during the hot, itchy work of gathering and storing hay in the haymow, he had still maintained his joy, whistling and singing softly to himself.

She looked back down the road toward the town they'd just left. A man was walking in the opposite direction toward Brandyville, kicking up dust in little puffs. He wore an old Union cavalry coat, and his dark hair, frosted with gray, tumbled over his collar. Corrine stiffened and inhaled so sharply that Ilona turned to her.

"Corrine?"

"That man," she said. "Do you see him?"

A few of the other girls in the wagon looked at her and looked back down the road.

"Where?" Ilona said.

"Down the road there, walking away toward Brandyville."

"I don't see anyone," Ilona said.

"But, he's right there," Corrine rose on her knees, torn between jumping down and running after him or asking Miss Brown to stop the wagon.

"I see no one. And, besides, we would have passed him on the road. It must be a shadow." Ilona settled back against the wagon's rough boards.

"But—"

"Miss Jameson," Miss Brown said, glancing back at her, "You need to sit down. We don't want you falling out of the wagon."

"But, Miss Brown, I just saw—"

"Remember what we talked about on the day you arrived, Miss Jameson. No more flights of fancy."

". . . my father," Corrine whispered, sitting back down between Ilona and the drowsing Christina.

Once again, she had seen and lost him. He was gone before she had even been able to call him. She felt the tears she had forbidden herself to shed turn her vision to water.

"Corrine," Ilona said.

Corrine shook her head and rubbed at her eyes. If she spoke, she knew she wouldn't be able to hold herself back.

Ilona didn't press her further.

Corrine stared out at the fields, trying to force her sorrow back down into the anguished hole in her chest. She touched the place where the locket rested for reassurance. At least this much had come back to her. She wished the Fey could bring back her father as well. But they had said that was impossible. Still, she wondered. If they had found the locket, why couldn't they find a person? That he had appeared again, much as it filled her with grief, also filled her with a wild hope that he truly was alive somewhere. And if that was so . . .

The questions quieted her tears. As the road widened and the river appeared through the trees, Father Joe and Miss Brown drove their wagons toward a stopping point in the field. Each of them climbed down and began helping the girls out of the wagon beds. Rory circled the field once before coming alongside them and dismounting.

"Care for the horses, would you?" Father Joe said to Rory, and Rory nodded.

"Leave your dinner pails here, girls," Miss Brown said. "Mr. MacLeod will have everything arranged for us to eat our dinner when we return."

Rory touched his hat in acknowledgment as he bent over the harnesses. Corrine smiled at how the black Morgan stood so quietly, her reins touching the ground. She could not help but think of Magellan, who had known intuitively what her father wanted, whether it was to stand still while he worked or to gallop with him across the fields chasing rabbits.

Father Joe led the group toward a bridge that spanned the Rappahannock River. The wooden planks creaked under Corrine's boots. The river was clear and broad; sycamores and willows turned gold all along its banks. Wagons had recently crossed the river through the shallow ford just below the bridge;

one wagon had apparently lost a wheel.

"This is Kelly's Ford," Father Joe said, "one of the closest battlefields to Falston. Not far from here, the young Boy Major, John Pelham, fell."

He began describing the setting of the battle, how Fitzhugh Lee and William Averell, the two armies' commanders, had known each other at West Point. "Fitz taunted Averell, telling him, 'If you won't go home, return my visit, and bring me a sack of coffee.'"

Most of the girls laughed at this, except for Melanie. Her face looked harder than usual, and when Father Joe mentioned John Pelham again, her expression grew even stranger—perhaps even on the verge of crying. Corrine remembered how Melanie had defended the young major in class. The look on Melanie's face right now was one of a lover mourning her beloved. But when Melanie caught Corrine's glance, her face resumed its normal belligerence.

Corrine looked away, as Father Joe continued. "John Pelham was in Culpeper at the time, attending to certain . . . matters." He glanced at Melanie and then Miss Brown. A look passed between the two of them that Corrine couldn't fathom. "When he heard the guns going off here, he left his . . . engagement and rode with all haste to the battlefield.

"He led the charge of the cavalry along that wall there," Father Joe pointed at a low, crumbling wall that ran the length of an adjacent field. "When the Fifth Virginia found a hole in the wall, Pelham rushed through. An exploding shell rained the Confederates with metal, and Pelham fell, injured by a sliver of metal in his skull."

Some of the girls winced. Others shuddered. Corrine looked again at Melanie. The golden-haired girl looked far out over the river, her eyes wide and distant.

Father Joe finished describing the battle, including the

sack of coffee left behind by Averell as he left victory to the Confederates, despite their heavy losses. Corrine's attention drifted. Ilona was rapt, looking up and down the ford as Father Joe illustrated how Johnny Reb managed to push the Federals back across the Rappahannock over two years ago.

Something moved through the golden leaves on the near bank. Corrine watched as it shifted through the underbrush, thinking at first perhaps it was a deer, maybe even a bear. And then she realized the form could not possibly be anything but human. She glanced around, her fingers tightening on the thick bridge railing. A flash of dark curls and muddy cavalry boots and she was ready to leap off the bridge after him. She didn't question how he'd gotten here when he had been heading the opposite direction. She glanced around. No one else had seen him. He was a sign, and only she was meant to follow where he led.

When Father Joe led everyone across the echoing planks, Corrine edged to the back of the group. Miss Brown walked in the middle, so there was no rear guard. Corrine slipped off the bridge and crouched near the pilings, looking for Rory to make sure he wasn't nearby. It was only a short distance between the open shore near the bridge and the cover of underbrush. Corrine knew she would have to be quick; it would be very easy to spot her from the other end of the bridge.

Her heart thrashed as though gripped again by the fever. She plunged across the rocks and into the brush. She picked up a faint deer trail that she assumed her father must have used and followed it along the river, hoping it was far enough into the thicket that she wouldn't be seen. Nettles stung her hands as she passed; grapevine and Virginia creeper tangled in her hair. She could just make him out ahead, flickering through the falling leaves. The base of his skull was dark and matted with dirt.

"Father!" she said, trying not to shout.

He didn't stop, didn't hear her running behind him. Thorns caught her pinafore and pricked at her stockings. Ash and beech whipped her face until she could barely see. She glimpsed his head and shoulders as he knelt by an eddy of the river, a place where a creek flowed out of the flatlands into the Rappahannock. His coat looked mysteriously gray.

"Father," she said, barely able to speak for the fire in her lungs.

But when she came into the clearing a little below him, to the stream's muddy bank, it was not her father that knelt there. The man rose and turned.

She fell back a step. It was as though a void had opened in the day, tearing everything into silence and stillness. Even the stream ceased. The river was voiceless. Cold seeped into the clearing, rooting Corrine where she stood near two boulders.

John Pelham smirked at her. He looked as solid and real as the trees by the river. Even more real, because he alone could move. He took a step toward her, and she could see how even the dust motes hung around him, turning the air a ghastly green. His gray officer's coat was covered with dirt and horsehair. His narrow eyes appraised her and his wide nostrils flared as he inhaled her scent. She thought she might be ill, but she couldn't move.

"Fairy girl," he said. His voice wavered, as though forced through layers of dirt.

He lifted his arm, but a strange noise, like thick paper dragged over wood, distracted him. He looked toward the creek, and Corrine saw where the blood and dirt had caked in the wound on the back of his head. Father Joe had said that he might have been saved if people had not believed him dead.

Something rose between the two boulders, and Corrine found she could move her head enough to look. She immediately wished she hadn't. Two of the largest copperheads she had ever seen—perhaps the largest serpents in the world—lifted from a fissure between the two boulders. She was reminded of the serpent-bound book in Uncle William's desk, the two serpents twining around each other. But then she realized it was not two serpents, but one. A giant two-headed snake loomed over them, and Corrine screamed.

The snake growled—some garbled language that Corrine could not comprehend—and one of its heads lunged toward Pelham. Corrine could only focus on the cat-slitted eye as one head moved toward its target. She saw the copper dimples around the golden jaws, the flat armor of the wedge-shaped head. The mouth opened, the fangs descending from the rose pink upper jaw. She had a sudden memory of the Tarot card that the strange woman had thrown at her—the girl surrounded by a giant serpent on the World card. Had she been warned? What could she have done?

Pelham snarled. Corrine thought she heard the rusty scrape of a drawn sword.

Movement caught the corner of her eye. Pelham evaporated. The serpent retreated toward a defensive position behind the rocks. Corrine glimpsed Rory leaping toward the copperhead before she fainted among the stones.

~ Fifteen ~

October 14, 1865

"Corrine!" Rory's hands were on her shoulders, shaking her gently. He helped her sit. She felt again as though she might be sick. She saw that a slick liquid shone along his jaw and across his coat. He smelled strongly of cucumbers.

She tried to focus on the trees. They were naked, as though a great frost had stripped them of all their leaves. Leaves scattered around her like golden scales.

"Rory? What—?" Her throat felt raw and leathery.

"Corrine," he said. "Are you well? What were you doing here by yourself?" He backed away from her. He held a huge knife, which he cleaned on his boot, wiping away more of the shining liquid. He sheathed the knife in a holster under his coat.

"I—" Corrine couldn't speak; all the words twisted inside her like the serpent's vanished coils.

He knelt near her and took her trembling hands into his own. He looked into her eyes and said, "Now you begin to understand. But I wonder if you understand fully?"

"What?" Shivers made her teeth knock together like wooden clappers.

"Corrine, you are not the only one in danger here. If something is not done to stop these witches, every girl in this school may suffer. Do you think Jeanette is the only girl who has disappeared?"

Corrine gasped, but before she could reply, Father Joe emerged from the underbrush.

"Corrine! Rory!" he said. "Thank the Lord! We heard screams."

Rory looked at Corrine for a moment longer before saying, "'Twas nothing, Father. A copperhead startled Miss Jameson here. I killed it." Rory helped Corrine stand.

"Very good," Father Joe said. The priest wandered down to the shore. Corrine saw a rainbow stain spreading on the muddy water where the serpent had been.

"Where is the snake's body?" he asked, turning to Rory. "It is rather late in the season for snakes to be out."

Rory looked at Corrine. "I threw it out into the river, Father. It frightened the lass so."

"A pity," Father Joe said. "We could have used the skin for a specimen."

His voice held an edge that Corrine didn't understand. He seemed both angry and grieved.

"My apologies, sir."

"Come," Father Joe said. "Let's return to the bridge." He took one of Corrine's hands and led her forward, so that she lost her grip on Rory. She felt the shock of Father Joe's anger sparking down her spine like lightning. "What were you thinking, Miss Jameson, coming out here on your own?"

Corrine started to speak, but at Rory's glance, she fell silent.

"There will be punishment, I'm afraid. I hope this encounter has taught you a lesson, Miss Jameson."

She looked up at him, but didn't know what to say. His expression was so tight with anger she feared it would break, though she sensed that the anger wasn't entirely directed at her. What was hidden behind that ageless face? He dropped her hand, but made sure that she was in front of him along the trail. She felt his gaze burning her back until they emerged next to the bridge, where the rest of the class waited with Miss Brown.

Everyone immediately clamored to know what had happened, except Melanie, who looked terribly bored with the whole affair.

"It was a snake," Corrine said. "Rory killed it."

"Why were you in the woods?" Abigail asked.

Miss Brown's expression demanded an answer.

"I thought I saw something," Corrine said, meeting Miss Brown's gaze. "But it turned out to be nothing." She bowed her head. "I'm sorry."

"So you should be," Miss Brown said. Corrine glanced up and saw anger akin to Father Joe's, an anger that seemed laced with grief. It was as though Corrine had done something far more serious than run off into the woods by herself. The two-headed serpent? But how could they possibly know about it or be angry about it even if they did? It had clearly been some evil, malformed thing; she was glad Rory had killed it.

Miss Brown turned and Corrine caught a glimmer of what looked like tears in the headmistress's eyes. "Come along, girls," she said. "Let's go have dinner. Mr. MacLeod, you've prepared a place for us?"

"Yes, ma'am," Rory said. "Follow me."

He led them off the bridge and back to the edge of the field, where he had taken the horses to keep them out of the sun.

Corrine made sure she was somewhere at the back of the group, but not the very last. Ilona walked next to her, looking at her with concern.

"Corrine, are you well? Were you bitten?"

"No, Ilona. I'm fine." Corrine couldn't look at her for very long.

"You're certain?" Christina asked, falling back to walk on her other side.

"Really, yes," Corrine said. It felt terrible to lie, but she had learned now that it was even more terrible to tell the truth.

"What were you doing in the woods?" Ilona said.

"I just thought I saw something."

"The man you thought you saw down the road?"

"Yes," Corrine almost whispered.

"What are you talking about?" Christina said. "What man?"

Corrine looked ahead to where Miss Brown was standing aside with Father Joe, talking to him, while the other girls settled on picnic blankets with their dinner pails. She glanced at Christina and Ilona. "Please don't ask me any more." She broke into an awkward run toward the wagons.

Corrine spent the rest of the afternoon trailing after the group, trying not to make eye contact with anyone, while Father Joe discussed the rest of the battle. Everyone kept her at a distance, including Ilona and Christina. She knew she had offended them, but she also knew they would not believe what she had seen. They probably would not want her to talk about it, even if they did believe. She avoided further contact with Rory, afraid that she'd tell him everything and uncertain why this bothered her. She wanted to trust him, but her doubts crept in again.

But the deepest hurt, what kept her silent and still, was the thought of her father. Why had he appeared on the road again without speaking to her? Was it really him? The second appearance was obviously John Pelham tricking her into thinking he was her father so she would follow. She wondered what John Pelham wanted and why the serpent had tried to attack them both. It must have been something planned by the witches to frighten her—or worse, hurt her. But she was more baffled by her father than the persistence of the witches.

It was late afternoon by the time Rory had the horses hitched and the wagons loaded. The girls climbed into the wagons quietly; there was much less talking and laughter than there had been that morning. Father Joe and Miss Brown were even more silent than usual, and their melancholy sent a deeper pall over the girls. Corrine looked out into the fading afternoon light, wondering if her father would appear again, but knowing that he probably wouldn't.

It was only as they passed Brandyville and entered the last turn toward Falston's hill that Corrine noticed Penelope was missing.

Corrine looked at the girls alternately dozing or staring blankly at the darkening countryside. She craned her neck to look ahead at the girls in the other wagon, but still she did not see Penelope.

"Miss Brown," she said. Her voice cracked, and the headmistress didn't turn.

"Miss Brown," she said, forcing her voice above the rattle of wagon and harness.

The headmistress half-turned. "Yes, Corrine?" Anger and sorrow were still apparent in her set mouth, the way her brows drew down over her icy eyes. Corrine couldn't believe this was the same woman as the one whose portrait graced her uncle's desk.

"Miss Brown, I think Penelope is missing."

"Penelope?" Miss Brown turned quickly and searched the the wagon. She turned forward again and scanned the back of Father Joe's wagon.

She pulled the horses to a halt. "Father!" she called.

He looked over his shoulder, saw that she'd stopped, and halted his wagon as well. "Thea?"

"Penelope's missing," Miss Brown said. One of the horses tossed its head and the harness jangled like splintering ice.

"Penelope . . ." It took Father Joe a few moments, but

Corrine could see recognition dawn slowly. She saw the instant he thought of Jeanette, and recognition shifted to horror.

"We must find her before full dusk," he said. He told his group of girls to stay in the wagon and climbed down. Miss Brown made as if to do so also, but Father Joe hurried to the wagon and prevented her.

"You should stay here with them," he said, looking up at Miss Brown with an expression of concern—Corrine might have called it love, if he weren't a priest. "It's too dangerous otherwise."

Miss Brown looked as if she wanted to say something, but rearranged the reins in her hands instead.

Rory rode up at that moment; he had been scouting ahead on the road. "Is something wrong, Father?" he asked.

"One of the girls is missing," Father Joe said. "Would you help?"

"Yes, sir," Rory said. "Why don't you just let me look for her and you all keep moving on? You don't want these girls out after dark. If I find her, I'll bring her to you. If I don't, I'll get the sheriff from Brandyville and see what we can find out."

"But—" Father Joe began.

"Mr. MacLeod's idea is very logical, Father," Miss Brown said. "We must get these girls back to Falston. If we need to return to help, we can do so after the other girls are settled. You'll send someone to inform us, Mr. MacLeod?"

Rory nodded.

"Very well, then," Father Joe said, his shoulders tense.

Rory kicked the mare's sides and sent her back the way they'd come, pulling off his hat and stuffing it behind him in his saddlebags. He urged the mare into a full gallop as he passed the last wagon, his damp hair clinging to his face. Corrine watched in admiration as he swept away into the twilight.

"Get settled, girls," Miss Brown said. "We'll keep going." She clucked and twitched the reins and the wagon surged forward. "Let's just pray Rory finds her," she said under her breath.

Corrine happened to catch Ilona's eye as she settled more comfortably between Ilona and Christina. Ilona was listless, her fingers clenched on a blanket. She didn't have to say it. She was thinking of Jeanette.

"If only I were a man," Ilona whispered. "If only . . ."

Corrine did not know what to say to her, so she offered her hand. Ilona took it, her large hand nearly crushing Corrine's smaller one. A vision opened of Ilona at battle. *She wore a battered helm and breastplate. She cast her shield aside and lifted a notched sword against a great darkness that the vision could not penetrate. A girl in a torn dress cowered behind her.*

Corrine gasped.

"Corrine?"

She squeezed Ilona's hand. "It's . . . nothing. I just hope Rory finds Penelope."

"Yes." But Ilona didn't sound confident he would. "Before it is too late."

Corrine tried to fill her voice with as much optimism as she could muster. "Whatever happened before, Ilona, it won't happen now. Rory will find her. I'm sure of it."

Ilona sighed and shook her head.

Cold fell with the night, and the girls huddled in blankets and rugs that had been left in the back of the wagon. Corrine strained to hear hooves above the din and rattle, but she was only rewarded as the horses began the slow climb up the hill to Falston.

The mare galloped out of the night, slowing to a trot as she approached the wagons. The lather on her chest glowed strangely under the stars, reminding Corrine of the shining blood of the two-headed serpent. She peered at Rory, whose face she could not quite make out in the darkness. But there was a small form perched in front of him on the saddle. He had found Penelope.

Miss Brown stopped her wagon, while Father Joe lumbered ahead. Rory handed Penelope over into the wagon bed, and Christina and Ilona made room for her between them. Penelope immediately tried to begin the long, complicated tale of her rescue, but Ilona murmured, "Wait a moment. We must thank your rescuer."

"Thank you, Mr. MacLeod," Christina said, standing and turning Penelope to Rory to encourage her echoing thanks. There was something more in Christina's voice, a catch that had nothing to do with the faint French lilt of her words.

"My pleasure, Miss Christina," he said, a surprising anguish filling his voice. In the dark, Corrine couldn't see anything, only the vague outlines of his cheekbones and shadowed eyes.

"Yes," Miss Brown added, "we do thank you, Mr. MacLeod, for returning Penelope and for aiding Corrine earlier today. Please ride ahead and have Mara bring you some supper."

"Thank you, Miss Brown," Rory said. A moment more and he was gone up the hill toward the distant lights of Falston.

Christina sat down hard, with what almost sounded like a sob.

"Christina?" Corrine said.

"I just feel like I know him—and I do not know why it makes me sad. I had never seen him before I came to Falston last year," Christina said.

But before she could continue, Penelope broke into her tale. "The fairies tried to take me! They made me go into the woods and I fell asleep, and then Mr. Rory came and he had a argument with them—"

"Penelope!" Miss Brown interrupted. "I don't know who is worse with these fancies, you or Corrine! Be quiet!" Her voice was almost strident, and she slapped the reins so hard the horses bolted in surprise up the hill.

Penelope quieted, but Corrine heard her mutter, "They did. He told them they weren't to have me as yet."

Corrine felt a chill that had nothing to do with the night air. What had happened today? She felt as though she was looking at the experience in the same way she viewed the French primer. It sometimes seemed like she understood the words or experiences, but then something shifted and she realized she didn't understand after all. Was it really the Fey who nearly took Penelope, or the Captain? Was Penelope really imagining things? *What is my part in all of this?*

She found it difficult to believe that after what the Fey had given her—health, the locket—that they were responsible for Penelope's disappearance. Could it be that the witches were trying to get rid of her? For what reason? Miss Brown had looked genuinely frightened.

Confused, Corrine shook her head as the wagon at last crested the hill and the manor loomed before her with glowing eyes. The gates whined shut behind them. She felt a great relief that they shut out at least some of what hid in the dark.

Supper was very quiet. Even Melanie wasn't up to her usual spleen. Dolores joined Melanie at the table, but they didn't speak to each other. Dolores looked pale and unsteady, and she shrank a little whenever Mara passed with a plate of food or an empty bowl. Even Penelope seemed to have lost her desire to tell her story, pushing her spoon around in her soup bowl with uncharacteristic silence. The girls who had stayed behind for whatever reason prudently didn't ask much about the trip.

At the end of supper, Miss Brown announced there would be no volunteer sewing that evening, and Corrine stifled a sigh of relief. She wasn't sure she wanted to try to answer the questions that she knew would come when she was alone with the other girls.

Corrine fell in line to return to her room, but Miss Brown stopped her.

"Come with me to my study, please, Miss Jameson," Miss Brown said.

Corrine stepped toward Miss Brown while the other girls filed past. Ilona gave her a fleeting look of compassion before leaving the dining room. After all the girls were gone, Corrine followed the headmistress down the corridor to her study, feeling the locket like a leaden weight against her chest.

Mara had lit the lamps in Miss Brown's study, and the unsteady yellow light flickered out across the dim hallway. When Corrine entered, she saw that a fire also burned in the grate. She thought again of the wrecked silkworm and shivered.

"Please sit, Miss Jameson," Miss Brown said, as she seated herself behind the mahogany desk.

Corrine noticed a photo she hadn't seen the last time. A boy with eyes like Miss Brown's dressed in Confederate gray.

"Now," Miss Brown said, jerking Corrine's attention from the photo, "perhaps you'd care to explain what really happened today."

Corrine was surprised that Miss Brown looked not angry, but tired. There were lines on her face that Corrine had never seen before, though perhaps they were all tricks of the dim light. A hazy image appeared—of Miss Brown walking along a lake in a dark dress, the mist rolling around her. Behind her, the gunmetal gray lake boiled.

"Corrine?" Miss Brown said.

Corrine's fingers twitched against her pinafore.

"I just thought I saw someone in the trees is all," she said. "I went to see who it was, and it turned out to be no one. Then, I saw the snake, and when I screamed was when Mr. Rory came and killed it."

"Did the snake look . . . unusual?" Miss Brown asked.

Corrine felt the words burning like acid on the tip of her tongue. *It was huge and had two heads. Is that what you mean by unusual?* Corrine swallowed the bitterness. She shook her head. "Just a big, mean copperhead, Miss Brown."

Miss Brown nodded, but she seemed unconvinced.

"And who was it that you thought you saw in the woods?"

Corrine hesitated. She did not want to be accused of fancifulness again. "Miss Brown, I really—"

"Who was it?" Miss Brown's tone cut. Corrine dropped her gaze to her lap, unable to look into those bitter blue eyes.

"John Pelham, Miss Brown."

"John Pelham? The Hero of Fredricksburg?"

"Yes. He said—he . . ." Corrine couldn't finish. It sounded ridiculous, even to her.

"You saw a ghost, but you screamed at a snake?"

"I screamed when he came toward me, when he spoke to me."

"He spoke to you? And what did the dashing Boy Major say to you?"

"He called me . . ." Corrine watched her fingers knotting themselves in panic. She couldn't think of any way to elude this.

"Yes, well?"

"Fairy girl," Corrine said, looking up.

Miss Brown sat very still. The fire threw a lacework of shadows over her face so that she seemed wreathed with cobwebs. She said nothing for a long while, then finally, she said, "Corrine, I want you to do two things. First, forget about this.

Forget John Pelham, forget the copperhead, forget all these things. Clearly, your mind is still extremely fragile from the ague."

She shuffled a few papers on her desk as though she did not know what to do with her hands.

"Second, I want you to avoid Rory MacLeod. Do not speak to him; do not even look at him. Do nothing to invite his attentions."

Corrine was surprised by the second admonition. Avoid Rory? Hadn't he helped save her and Penelope? And yet, of course the witches would fear him if they suspected he was a friend of the Fey. Of course they would want to maintain control by forcing her to avoid him. Then why, she wondered, did they keep him around?

"Do I have your cooperation in this, Corrine?" Miss Brown asked.

"Yes," Corrine said, hoping the headmistress was convinced.

"As for your punishment for running off this afternoon, I shall require an essay from you by breakfast next Sunday explaining reasons why wandering away by yourself is dangerous and what you have learned from this experience." Corrine wondered if these reasons should include being assaulted by ghosts and two-headed serpents, but said nothing to indicate her thoughts. She also wondered if a day would ever come where she would know the truth about Miss Brown, the witches of Falston, and the Fey.

"I will escort you to your room now," Miss Brown said. She rose, and the fire cast a shadowy net over her entire body. Corrine saw her again in a vision, this time wreathed in a corona of fire, and a wave of pity she didn't understand washed through her.

"Are you coming?" Miss Brown asked from the door.

Corrine blinked and followed.

Corrine worked deep into the night on her essay, half-hoping that Ilona would come to her window and rescue her. But the night remained silent. When she was too tired to think anymore, she took the lantern to its place on the washstand and blew it out. She looked out expecting to see the Captain, but what she saw made her grip the window sash even more tightly.

A familiar form caught the moon's glimmer, a woman, in clothes as white and funereal as a bride's. She drifted across the grounds and through the fence. Corrine watched as the ghost disappeared again into the forest. The blackness of the forest turned into the black holes of John Pelham's eyes. *Fairy girl,* she heard him snarl again. When she could move, she crawled into her cot, too frightened even to change into her nightgown.

~ Sixteen ~

October 22, 1865

Corrine knelt in a tunnel, compressed and constricted by its thick muscular walls. Hands came through the wall, and then a face. Her mother stood before her again, looking at her so tenderly that Corrine had to look away in grief.

"Why are you here, my child?" her mother said.

Corrine shook her head. She didn't know. The walls expanded enough that she could stand.

"Come," her mother said. She took her hand. The iron cross about her throat glowed white-hot as she tried to lead Corrine through the wall. But Corrine could not pass through it. Her mother turned and Corrine followed her gaze to where the roses bloomed around her ankle.

Corrine's mother bent to touch them. Vicious thorns emerged from beneath the petals, as wicked and curving as claws. Corrine felt them testing her skin. If anyone tried to pull them off, she was quite certain they would bite deeply into her flesh.

"Oh, what have you done?" her mother said. Her sad eyes looked up at Corrine from where she knelt.

Corrine could hear wind gathering and roaring farther down the tunnel.

Her mother glanced down the tunnel at the sound. "Run," she said.

But it was on them before Corrine could even take a step. Her mother was shredded to colorful ribbons, like a portrait torn into confetti. All that lingered of her was a sigh that crested the roar.

Oh, what have you done?

The walls of the tunnel blew outward and Corrine stood on a green hill in the middle of the desert. The shadow prince's voice came from the ground. Come to me . . .

A hole opened in the ground and she peered down into it. A city rose under the earth, its towers glistening like the inner organs of some great beast. Before she knew it, she was floating down toward it. She followed an empty road that wound like a great worm into the heart of the towers. They glowed with hidden light, a shimmer that reminded her more of water than stone. Deserted gates opened at her approach and she drifted like a ghost beyond a fountain that gave forth only dust, past balconies of skeletal flowers. Feathers blew like milkweed fluff, catching on her arms and in her hair. She looked down and saw that she wore a dress that clung and moved like sunlight over her body. She thought she should feel ashamed, but could not. Instead, she drew a fold of the dress like a hood over her hair, sinking deeper into the city's shadows.

She realized she was being drawn to a particular place when she skimmed through a doorway and hundreds of masked eyes turned upon her, their waltzes arrested by her passing. They soon resumed their dancing, the swishing of women's skirts and the soft tap of shoes the only sounds in the room. Corrine watched them from under her hood. Ribbons trailed from their horned masks; feathers sprouted from headdresses. Hooves or clawed hooks took the place of feet and hands. She was sure she glimpsed tails—elegant and feline or the lovely brush of a fox. Forked tongues scented her while owl-eyes followed her passage across the floor.

She only saw the dais as she was climbing it, and the shadow sitting on a shadowy throne. She could not see his face, but she gave him her hand and he drew it toward his chest. A gaping darkness beat there as hard as a heart. And she knew without knowing how that he wanted her to give his heart back to him, that his heart was a stone only she could bring to him. His power had been stolen, and now he sat alone on his throne of thorns, watching his courtiers waltz endlessly in silence until they became dust.

He wept a single tear of blood that fell on her palm. It burned so deeply that it stung her awake.

Corrine sat up, unsure whether the knock had come yet. She tried to shake the dream from her body, but she ached in every joint as though she'd just been dragged through the earth. At last she had met him, the prince who haunted her dreams. She felt his sorrow sweep over her again, a sorrow as vast and unending as the sea. It was too heavy to bear, too heavy even for tears.

When the knock came and her door was unlocked, she rushed down the stairs to flee his grief. But echoes of her mother's voice dogged her—*Oh, what have you done?*

Corrine filed with the others into the chapel room, her stomach rumbling. Father Joe was already there in his vestments. He glanced at Corrine and she felt the familiar sensation arcing along her spine. But his gaze did not linger long, and as Corrine followed the others in crossing herself and kneeling, she saw a watery image of him, traveling through a great, dense forest like that of her dreams at Uncle William's. She had the strange feeling that this had happened centuries ago in a distant place. She saw a great dark beast hurtling toward him through the forest long before he did. She nearly cried out, but came back to herself in time to find that she was the only one still kneeling. Father Joe stared at her. She slid back into the pew as quickly as she could.

At breakfast, Corrine took the essay she'd finally finished

to the teachers' table and waited quietly until Miss Brown acknowledged her. She was afraid to look Father Joe in the face, afraid that she would see something else about him that she didn't want to know at present. Miss Brown took the essay and said, "You may return to your seat, Miss Jameson," before turning back to her strong coffee.

Corrine went back to the table. Ilona had saved her a seat on the bench and she slid in beside her. They were silent for a while, until Ilona whispered, "May I borrow a pair of stockings? I'll need them when you can see the moon in your window."

Corrine nodded at the code for a meeting of the Society. Miss de Mornay's gray glare almost stopped her heart. She reached for a piece of salt pork to put into her biscuit, and the Moray Eel's gaze swept elsewhere.

Sundays were usually reserved for studying. Occasionally, some girls went with Miss Brown or Father Joe to deliver blankets and produce to shut-ins in Culpeper, but not on this particular Sunday. Groups of girls were ushered to various rooms about the manor for study; Corrine was glad that her group included Christina but not Melanie. Mara led them to the library and sat in the corner to monitor them. Mara had a basket of knitting with her to occupy the time, and her needles clacked together like the pincers of a giant crab. Whenever Mara's flat, black stare fell on her, a chill passed through Corrine. She wondered if Mara knew that Corrine had dealings with the Fey. If so, Corrine feared Mara would do something even more horrible to her than what she had done to Dolores. Would Mara make another voodoo doll meant to torment her rather than summon the Captain?

Christina helped her study French for several hours until her accent was at least passable.

"*Excellent, mon amie,*" she said after the last round of

pronunciations. "I am glad you are doing so well. You will be all ready when the new French teacher comes tomorrow."

"New French teacher?" Corrine said.

"Do not be so dismayed, Corrine. I am sure you will do well."

"But I prefer learning from you." The admission forced her to blush.

Christina smiled, that dazzling smile that Rory seemed to find so profoundly troubling. "It is kind of you to say so, Corrine, but I am really not the best teacher. I believe Madame DuBois will be much better for you. She will come from Culpeper twice a week to take my place."

Corrine nodded, overwhelmed at the thought of having a new teacher—yet another person to scorn, mock, or scold her.

Christina put her hand over Corrine's. "Don't worry; I will still help you if you need it."

"Thank you," Corrine said, but she couldn't release the doubt that settled in the pit of her stomach.

For the rest of the afternoon, Corrine studied anatomy, trying to drill the Latinate names of body parts into her brain. Everything tangled in her mind until all she wished for was to find another letter. It had been over a week since she'd found the last one and she missed the secret thrill of reading about the illicit love affair between Angus and Brighde and finding out more about the Fey. She imagined that Angus's voice sounded very similar to Rory's, though she knew that in truth she could only understand what he'd written because someone had translated the letters and may have changed the phrasing. She wondered if Father Joe had translated them and if so, how he'd come by them.

She thought back to the very first letter she'd read, the one from her mother's trunk about the mysterious Mary Rose. Had Father Joe translated that letter too? The handwriting was too similar to think otherwise—if Father Joe were indeed the translator, were the letters linked? More and more she was finding that everything was connected. Make a wish to open a trunk and it was opened. Speak of John Pelham and his ghost appeared. She feared to think about Angus; who knew what might come to her as a result?

Late in the afternoon, Miss Brown came to relieve Mara and take the girls for a turn around the grounds. Corrine was glad of the fresh air, but the chill made her wish for her coat. As they walked, the group passed Rory returning through the gates. He was dressed in his Sunday best, his boots so polished that Corrine could see the sky reflected in them.

He tipped his hat to Corrine and Christina, but before Corrine could say anything, she saw Miss Brown's warning glance. She didn't acknowledge him, but backed out of the way so the black mare could pass. Christina took her arm and they walked quietly together for the rest of the way, trying to seem interested in the bits of natural history that Miss Brown pointed out to them.

Corrine was glad when evening came and she could ascend quietly to her room. She'd avoided rereading the letters the entire week since the trip to Kelly's Ford, but today her curiosity once again overtook her caution. For want of a new letter, she took out the last letter she'd read last week and read it again as night tumbled through her window.

[Trans. note: Beginning charred, as though letter was burned. End is also lost. Date believed to be June 1357.]

[. . .] I have felt that fear as well, but I must question it—for why did the Lord reveal your face to me that day in

Kenmore if He did not mean for me to love you? You are the reason I was sent into exile. And the Lord has given me a sign of surety that this is so. You must believe this.

The Fey have taken me to their city, Brighde, a city so fair and wondrous as would make your heart weep with gladness. The man I spoke of has proven to be an even greater friend than I would have dreamed. He showed me this city. Like Moses parting the waters, he stretched forth his hand and the earth drew back to reveal its shining towers. There were lights there that reminded me of the light in your eyes, palaces and ramparts like the morning upon your face [. . .]

[Middle burned]

What I have seen none can refute. If you would but try to receive dispensation for me to see you, I could tell you more of the wondrous things I have seen [. . .]

[End lost]

Corrine wondered why so many of the letters were missing parts or had been burned. She couldn't imagine that Brighde, as gentle as she seemed, would ever do such a vicious thing. She thought again of the city in her dreams, of the dancers turning to dust in their quiet revels, of the prince who had wept tears of blood on her hand. Angus had said it was a wondrous city, a city of lights and music. What had happened? Why was it now a city of dust and tears? It saddened her to think that the Fey had helped her when perhaps they could little afford it. And the prince, with the gaping hole where his heart had once been—what did he want of her?

She shook her head and felt the locket against her skin, proof of his trust in her. Now that she was forbidden to speak to Rory, she didn't know what she could possibly do to help the Fey. She sat down near the coal stove for warmth, carefully avoiding the wall. She wanted no frightening visions of Jeanette before she had to climb off the roof. She half-dozed; the prince and his courtiers danced through her mind, quietly dissolving into dust.

The moon slid into her window and pierced her consciousness. She put on her coat and lifted the window sash. The night air was crisp, smelling of burning leaves and wood smoke, as she climbed out and shimmied across the roof to the pipe. She wished briefly for Ilona; her confidence was immensely heartening. But there was no one, and Corrine swung down over the edge by herself, longing for mittens as soon as her hands touched the cold metal. She climbed down carefully until at last she came to the ledge near the woodshed. She scooted to the edge and dropped off. Her right ankle threatened to twist under her at first, but she righted herself and headed toward the barn.

The girls were already assembled there, circled together in the straw—Ilona, Christina, Abigail, and Hannah.

"We were beginning to think you'd fallen off the roof," Ilona said.

"It was only by luck that I didn't," Corrine said. She sat down in the straw near Ilona, wishing for something softer and less itchy.

"Ladies, the meeting is opened," Christina said. "Would anyone like to begin with concerns?"

"I would," Ilona said. She turned to Corrine. "I would like to know what really happened at the battlefield."

Corrine looked at her incredulously. "You expect me to tell you about this, yet you will tell me nothing?"

Before Ilona could say anything, Christina interjected, "Corrine, to be inducted, every member of the Society must tell a truth and a lie. After that, you may simply withhold information. It's one of our rules. Ilona has already done both, so she is free to withhold information if she chooses, especially from a new member." Her eyes brightened. "You already told us quite a fantastic lie—your frightening story. Now you must tell us the truth."

Corrine absorbed this for a moment. No one had said anything about rules for being part of the Society, but she should have expected it, she supposed. She sighed. Their friendship, their trust was too important. Yet, she was quite certain that she couldn't talk about the two-headed serpent. Anyone might believe in a ghost, but a two-headed serpent? They would think her mad.

"Well," she said softly. "If I tell you, will you promise not to tell me to be quiet?" She said this mostly to Ilona, who bowed her head in the shadows.

"I am sorry, Corrine. I should not have said that to you. But you must understand how dangerous it is to discuss these things where others can hear them. Even now it is not truly safe."

"I understand that now," Corrine said.

So she told them what she could bear to tell, of how she had followed the man into the forest, only to be confronted by the ghost of John Pelham, of how he had called her fairy girl, and how Rory had come to her rescue. She hoped her mother would forgive her when she altered the story to say that Pelham had turned into a copperhead, which Rory then killed. The two-headed serpent was just too incredible.

They were all silent for a moment.

"Have you always seen ghosts, Corrine?" Christina asked.

"It only just started," Corrine said. "Since coming to Falston. I could do with seeing them a little less."

"Yes," Christina said softly. "I understand."

"Do you see them, Christina?" Hannah asked.

"Not ghosts," Christina said. "But my dreams—you know, I've had them since I was small."

"What are the dreams about?" Corrine asked before she realized that perhaps she'd breached Christina's right to withhold.

But Christina said, "I dream always of a nun—at least, she seems to be a nun—and she is greatly tormented by something, perhaps a man she loves? Like Heloise and Abelard in old France." Corrine thought she heard the trace of a smile in Christina's voice.

"Do you know her name?" Corrine asked.

"Her name? No, I . . ." Christina fidgeted in the straw. "She is just a dream."

The straw poked Corrine too, but she tried to ignore it. This revelation was too important to worry about scratchy straw. "Brighde?"

There was a pause as the name seemed to hang like a bright echo in the air. The straw rustled as Christina shivered.

"I don't know. *Mon Dieu,* I do not want to think about it anymore."

Corrine resisted the urge to push her further. She knew Christina was sensitive and ashamed of these visions. "Are the dreams better since Mara helped you?" Corrine asked.

"Yes. A little better," Christina said. "They no longer come upon me in the day." She stopped speaking abruptly, as though she couldn't bear to discuss it further.

Ilona broke in, holding her arms out to Christina and Corrine. "Enough. Let us think about the induction. What will we do this time?"

"Induction?" Corrine asked.

"We induct new members at Hallowe'en," Christina said. "And you, Corrine, will of course be our new member."

"So what shall we do?" Ilona said.

"Do?" asked Corrine.

"Every new member must do something to prove her worth. Hallowe'en is always a night full of mischief. We, however, try to do something good, like the little brownies or fairies of old times."

Corrine wondered how Christina would feel if she actually met the Fey. She half-smiled at the thought of Christina fainting at the touch of one of their knobby fingertips. But there was no denying the old stories; they were helpful. Corrine just wished that their help had not somehow also attracted the attentions of the bloody-handed Captain.

"Last year, we made dolls out of rags in the sewing circle and left them for the little girls," Christina said. "What shall we do this year?"

Mittens, Corrine thought, rubbing her freezing hands. But then she imagined trying to learn to knit so many pairs of mittens in only a month. She remembered the delicious sweetness of the *petit fours* Christina had shared and said, "How about something small and sweet, like what your mother sent?"

"But where would you get it?" Ilona asked.

"I have an idea," Corrine said.

"Good, then," Christina said. "Corrine, as our next sister, this will be your task. We will adjourn until next time."

They each rose, said their parting litany, and one by one left the barn. Christina went before Ilona and Corrine, who crept back to the woodshed together.

"Do you want me to lift you up?" Ilona asked. "We can also

put a block of wood here to help you."

"That will work," Corrine said. She didn't want to trouble Ilona any more than was necessary.

Ilona turned before she left. "I will tell you one day, Corrine. It is just—" She broke off.

Corrine reached for her in the dark and took her hand.

"I promise," Ilona said. And then she was gone, climbing up the woodshed to slip into her own second-story window.

Corrine moved a block of wood to where she thought it would be best for her to climb. She was reaching for the top of the woodshed, trying to pull herself up, when a sound made her turn.

It sounded like metal grinding against itself, a rusty squeal that caused Corrine to flail off the stump and nearly fall into the mud. She crouched in the shadows of the shed, looking toward the barn. A flicker of white moved beyond it into the hemlocks that surrounded the fence. The ghost.

If Corrine were wise, she would simply climb as fast as she could into her room and shut the window. She had had her fill of ghosts, and there would be no Rory this time to save her. But she couldn't help herself. She ran as quietly as she could, ducking around the barn to see which way the ghost had gone.

It was vanishing into the forest. She raced across the frozen ground to the fence. Even though the iron bars had pained her on her first day, she tested each of them, pushing and pulling until her arms trembled and her breath burned in her throat. She could hear the iron protesting, perhaps loud enough to wake a light sleeper, but she prayed she would get through before then.

There was one bar that gave more than the others. She pushed harder and it gave more, but the horizontal bar that joined all the bars at their tips held it fast. She ran her hand up and down the bar, and it moved at her touch. She worked it up some more, watching in surprise as it slid all the way up as high as she could lift it, leaving enough space between the remaining bars for her to step through the fence. The pain of it nearly knocked her senseless. A ghost wouldn't have needed to move this bar. Was she, in fact, following a human being?

An unnatural gleam floated at the foot of the trees, like the mist the Captain had summoned that night after the first Society meeting. The mist wove around the white figure as if in greeting. Corrine followed at a distance. She realized, her heart thundering against her tongue, that she was outside Falston. Free. If she wished, she could leave this life. But answers were more important to her now than her own welfare. She had to know what was happening.

She followed the figure at a distance as it moved down the hill. It disappeared into a grove of hemlocks and pines, where the gleaming mist thickened and swirled. Corrine crept as close as she dared beneath the boughs of a large hemlock. She shivered with the chill, hoping the mist would not also find her. In the clearing, a woman was waiting by a giant tree stump, shrouded in a dark scarf and coat. The mist made her pale face visible: Miss de Mornay.

Corrine felt a faint tinge of vindication to know that the Moray Eel was involved in these sinister nighttime intrigues.

The other figure, the one Corrine had been following, approached Miss de Mornay and knelt. The mist-light transformed Melanie's features; she looked groggy and unkempt, as though she had been sleepwalking and was only just beginning to wake.

Corrine watched, digging her cold fingers into the craggy bark as the mist crept around Miss de Mornay and Melanie. Sibilant whispers and strange faces swirled in the rising mist. Bark splintered under Corrine's fingernails as a tall form stepped into the mist. The Captain came to Miss de Mornay. He forced her to kneel, but he said nothing. Still Corrine could hear Miss de Mornay whispering answers to him. Her gray braid uncoiled from her scarf like a dead snake.

"Yes, my lord," Corrine heard Miss de Mornay whisper.

Melanie looked up, and Corrine was surprised to see tears on her face. She held up something shining. Corrine peered at it. It looked like a coin or perhaps a button.

"Bring him back," Melanie said.

Miss de Mornay took the object from her and passed it to the Captain.

Corrine heard his thoughts as clearly as if he whispered into her ear, *Now, bring me the girl.*

She thought she saw his head turn in her direction, as though he had sensed her presence. She scrambled backward, but hit something solid—something much softer than a tree. It grabbed her, clapping a hand over her mouth to stop her scream. The smells of horses and leather surrounded her as the man dragged her back out from under the hemlocks.

"Miss Corrine," Rory said in her ear.

She struggled against him, and he released her.

"Don't scream," he said. He had brought her several hundred yards away from the hemlocks into a rhododendron thicket. A little breeze made the dead leaves clack like beetle shells.

"What are you doing?" she said.

"I might ask the same of you, lass."

She glanced again toward the clearing where de Mornay and Melanie knelt entranced. It looked as though the mist was slowly twining around them, creeping over their arms and heads in a glowing shroud.

"Except," Corrine said, gathering her courage, "I asked you first." She could smell him through the cold—leather, horses, and the taint of peat moss. She had the sudden strange feeling that the person she spoke to was not Rory at all, but someone else, someone she had never met and yet knew intimately. She thought of Angus, wondering if he had been as handsome as Rory, and then shook her head.

"Keeping the grounds safe," he said. "I saw Melanie come and then you. And the mist." She thought she heard the grimace in his voice.

"Have you ever seen this before?" she asked.

"Aye," he said. "Another of the witches' tricks. This is where the girls come who disappear."

"Disappear?" Corrine said.

"I don't know where he takes them; I've tried to save them, but—"

"Takes them?" She could not stop repeating his words.

"Yes," he said. "But we must get you out of here. If he knows you're here, he'll come looking for you."

"But Miss de Mornay and Melanie . . ."

"I'll come back for them, I promise. These things take time; the witches are cunning. Why do you think I've never been able to stop them myself?"

"But—"

His mouth on hers was so swift she almost didn't realize what was happening, except that her lips no longer felt numb with cold. They buzzed and swelled, stung by a thousand benevolent bees.

He stepped back. "I'm sorry," he said. She could not see his face in the dark, only feel the cold dividing them again. "I care for you, Corrine. I will not see you hurt by those evil witches."

She didn't know what to say. All this time, the way he'd looked at Christina with such longing, Corrine thought he loved Christina. But he had kissed her. She let him lead her back up the hill, away from where the glowing mist curled.

"I see you finally found the loose bar," he said. "Took you long enough. Melanie found it in no time."

She looked at him in shock, but couldn't see his expression in the darkness.

When they got to the fence, Rory lifted the iron bar for her. She stepped through, and he slid the bar down between them. She wished very much that she could see his face. She wanted to reach through the bars and touch him, to know that he was real, but she couldn't bear the queasy iron feeling.

"You still don't quite trust me, do you?" he said.

"It's just that—well, Miss Brown told me not to speak to you."

"Ah, so that's why you've been avoiding me. Well, understand this—the Fey and I are the only true friends you have in this place, Miss Corrine. The Fey want to protect you. They want to help you. But only you can allow it."

She was tired and confused. Tired of ghosts, fairies, witches, and two-headed serpents. Tired of fancies and shadows and vague warnings. "Prove it," she said.

He half-laughed. "Proof? What more proof do you need? When you were dying, they healed you. When your uncle sent you here with nothing, they sent you a token of their affection, something lost to you. When you were plagued by ghosts and two-headed serpents, I came to save you. What more do they need to prove?"

"If they care for me, I want them to bring something to me."

"It is not ours to make demands of the Fey." His tone was dark and unsettled.

Corrine continued as though she hadn't heard. "They will bring me the finest box of confections on earth, and they will deliver this to me by Hallowe'en." She reveled in finally being able to command something.

Rory threw back his head and laughed. She began to feel embarrassed, but stood her ground.

Rory finally said, "Is that all it takes to buy your loyalty, Miss Corrine? A box of chocolates?"

"Enough for the entire school," she said, her breath frosting the air.

"I'll see what I can do. Our friends the Fey do magic of a sort, but I'm not sure it extends to confections."

Corrine was silent. Her authority failed her in the face of his amusement.

"And now," he said, "I really must go. Hopefully, Melanie and Miss de Mornay still have a chance."

"Yes," she said. He turned and limped away into the dark. She put her fingers to her cold lips, wishing there was some way to feel his kiss again.

~ Seventeen ~

October 23, 1865

Corrine was up before Mara's morning knock. She smiled when she walked downstairs and ended up at the back of the johnnyhouse line, and she smiled during the mass she barely heard. She smiled when she soaked a tasteless biscuit in watery gravy for breakfast. She even smiled during Anatomy, and could only look upon Miss de Mornay with pity when the woman threatened to take the switch to her. Even Miss de Mornay could be excused, helpless slave that she was to the witches' dark magic. Rory had kissed her, and that was all that Corrine knew.

Even Ilona took note.

"You are different," Ilona said during recess. She picked up the hoop and wands for graces, handing two of the wands to Corrine. "What has happened to you?"

"Nothing," Corrine said, smarting under the lie. Corrine threw the hoop from her wands, hoping the questions would end with the beginning of the game.

"I know untruth when I see it," Ilona said, looking out from beneath her forelock of dark hair. She tossed the hoop to Corrine, who just barely managed to catch it with her right wand.

"I am just . . ." Corrine thought of telling her, but realized that it would be foolish to tell anyone. Ilona's dark eyes searched hers as Corrine felt the hoop slide down over the wands toward her wrists. She hoped fiercely that she never made Ilona angry.

"Just?" Ilona said.

" . . . happy," Corrine said, hoping that would suffice.

"Happy? Why? What causes this happiness? You were attacked by a ghost not long ago!"

Corrine tossed the hoop back. "I just feel that good things will happen soon."

"Like what?" Ilona said, catching it high.

"You'll see," Corrine said.

"I'd guess the only thing worth looking forward to after Hallowe'en, of course, is the Thanksgiving," Ilona said longingly.

"What happens then?" Corrine asked. She was surprised to hear that the school celebrated it. Many Southerners were so devastated by the War that they couldn't celebrate Thanksgiving, even had they wished to follow a holiday instituted by President Lincoln.

"Sometimes, there is a turkey, sometimes two!" Ilona said, as she tossed the hoop back. "And the gravy is thicker and tastier, the biscuits softer. Once, there were potatoes. Pumpkin." Ilona paused reverently. "Indian pudding."

Corrine smiled. She remembered her mother's Indian pudding—warm and dense with molasses and ginger. She thought back to the *petit four* she'd had and the secret treat that was coming on Hallowe'en. But she thought there was nothing sweeter than Rory's kiss in the dark, and felt herself blushing.

But as the time came for French class, Corrine's euphoria settled into a strange melancholy, almost disbelief. How could it be possible that Rory cared for her? Especially when he had so many other, better choices, like Christina with her dark, beguiling eyes and lovely smile, or Melanie and her serpentine curls and perfect figure. Despite all he had done, she still didn't know if she could trust him. And did any of it matter anyway? The Captain had told Melanie and Miss de Mornay to bring her to him. He had been dogging her steps since she'd been at Uncle William's house, and it seemed he was done with merely watching her. Would Rory be there to save her when at last her time came?

She was musing over these thoughts as she settled beside Penelope in French class. The new teacher had finally arrived and was writing something on the board. Corrine opened her primer and arranged her notebook and pencils, looking up as the teacher turned from the board. She gasped. The wild-eyed woman who had accosted her in the way-station tavern stood at the front of the room. Though she looked more sedate, Corrine could still see the madness hiding at the back of her eyes. She stared at Corrine for a moment, and then looked around the room.

"I am Madame DuBois," she said.

Without bothering to ask her students' names, she immediately began declensions. Corrine could barely mutter them because she was trying to understand how a drunkard like Madame DuBois could be the beginning French teacher at Falston. Even now, it appeared that Madame DuBois was intoxicated, though perhaps less than when Corrine had last seen her. The woman was distracted, her voice breaking on the repetitive words, her eyes wandering around the room without apparent focus. The sense of strangeness that lurked in every corner of the school was unbearable, but Corrine was too exhausted now to puzzle out the details. She clung to the fact that Rory and the Fey at least were her friends.

In the evening after supper, some of the girls were sent to tidy the chapel room. As Miss de Mornay's favorite, Melanie had been assigned to oversee the cleaning, and of course, she would do none of it herself. She perched on the back of one of the pews, making comments about everyone's handiwork. Melanie's upbringing as a Southern belle probably qualified her perfectly for such a role. Corrine kept as far away from her as she could, sliding around the lectern and dusting there.

As she picked up the old Bible to dust under it, a bit of folded paper slid out. It huddled against the podium, flopping open like an untidy handkerchief. Corrine picked it up, and could not help but notice the familiar translator's note and even more familiar words. *My beloved,* it began, *I feel that it has been an age since I heard your voice, much less read your words. Why will you not write to me? What I have done was done for both our sakes.*

Angus. Corrine refolded the letter abruptly. She could feel her cheeks heating at the anguished passion of his words. Ever since the last letters she'd discovered in the library, she had hoped to find another. And there it was. Glancing around, she slid the letter into the front pocket of her pinafore, and bent her head to continue her dusting.

"What's in your pocket, Corrine?"

Kneeling to reach around the bottom of the lectern, Corrine looked up into Melanie's curl-framed face. Melanie had seen everything.

"Nothing," Corrine said. She thought of how Melanie had knelt on the frozen ground last night, begging the Captain to bring back someone she obviously loved. Such an image seemed incongruous with the Melanie who stood over her now, her blue eyes vibrant with malice. Corrine stood, so that Melanie couldn't loom over her, and put the lectern between them.

"You're lying," Melanie said. "I saw you take something out of Father Joe's Bible. You wouldn't want to be accused of stealing, would you?" She smiled her dangerous, sweet smile.

Corrine shook her head, feeling her face grow hotter. She knew she was a terrible liar, but she could not bear to have Melanie read Angus's letters. "I don't have anything," she said. "I just dropped my dusting rag."

Melanie laughed. "You've really got to come up with something better than that. Do you think I'd believe that?"

Ilona had apparently heard trouble brewing and edged between them. Corrine held in her sigh of relief.

"Leave her alone, Melanie," Ilona said.

She stood to her full height and crossed her arms across her chest, looking more like a solemn knight than a sixteen-year-old girl. Corrine saw her again as she had in the vision, defending a frightened girl against an impossible darkness.

"Fine," Melanie said. "But, someday, little scalawag, your henchman won't be around."

Corrine was about to retort, but Ilona shushed her with a backward glance.

"Melanie," Christina called from across the room. "Come play baccarat while we wait for Miss Brown. We're all finished over here."

Melanie scorched Corrine with another glance before she and her golden curls bounced across the room to Christina.

"I'm not a scalawag," Corrine said.

"If she knew you were a Northerner, it would be all the worse for you," Ilona said. "She does not take kindly to your folk coming down to her country."

"Well, she'd better get used to it," Corrine muttered.

"I do not understand this about your country," Ilona said. "Why not let the Southerners go? We Hungarians fought for centuries to keep our country together, at the cost of many lives and much bloodshed. Why not just let the South be its own land?"

Corrine did not know how to answer. The War of Southern Rebellion had gone on since she was ten. She could barely remember what it had been like to live in a country without the rumor of war. In the years before her father's disappearance, whenever she had complained about his absence in the War, her mother had explained to her how numerous families had been abused and destroyed for years because of the Southern need to hold and sell slaves. "Your father has gone away from us to help make these families whole again," she had said. "That's a small sacrifice for us to make."

Corrine gritted her teeth. She saw again the dream in which her mother became nothing more than colorful ribbons, borne along by a thundering wind. *Was your death also a small sacrifice?* she thought at her mother's spirit.

"I thank you for your thoughts," she said to Ilona, as her mother had taught her to say to someone with whom she disagreed. "But I have no sympathy for Johnny Reb. He got what he deserved."

Ilona looked at her curiously; Johnny Reb was apparently not a familiar phrase. "I don't know if anyone deserves the destruction of their homeland," Ilona said slowly. "People should fight for what they believe."

"Even if that belief is wrong?" Corrine asked.

But Ilona had no time for further comment, for Miss de Mornay entered, clapping her hands for the girls to go upstairs to bed. As Corrine placed her rag in a basket by the door, she slid her hand into her pocket and felt the letter resting there. It pleased her that Ilona had put Melanie off the scent. She shuddered to think of what might happen on the day she was by herself. She kept her eyes down to avoid Miss de Mornay, who swept past her, leading the girls to the stairs.

After Corrine entered her room, she lit her lamp from the stove fire and set it down near the stove. She wrapped her blanket around her shoulders and slid down onto the floor, careful to avoid the wall, and removed the letter from her pocket.

[Trans. note: Date missing. Believed to be August 1356]

To Sister Brighde, Isle of Female Saints, from Brother Angus, Kirk of St. Fillan, greetings.

My beloved—

I feel that it has been an age since I heard your voice, much less read your words. Why will you not write to me? What I have done was done for both our sakes; it does not in any way impede my service to God. If faith is the measure of a true servant, then how am I to convince you of the truth? Isaiah says, "Unless you believe, you shall not understand." If we are to understand the Fey, we must believe them, even as we do the doctrines of God. Are they not also of God? I cannot believe anything so fair and wondrous as their domain could exist on the borders of damnation.

I took the oath to them because it is the only way I can convince them to trust me, to have faith even as I do that mortals and the Fey can again be allies. Think of all the wonders we could do with their help, if we only acceded to even the least of their demands! Once we lived in harmony with one another. It is my dream that we do so again.

But that oath is as nothing compared to the oath I would swear to you, if you would have me do it. I will swear with blood, body, and heart—whatever you would ask of me. I cannot now take back the fealty I have sworn to the Fey—it is a blood oath—but I can swear again to you and pray that you would not find me forsworn.

Yours Eternal,
Angus

She pondered what Angus had done to anger Brighde. She didn't know what he meant by a blood oath, but she could guess, and the thought chilled her. Why would the Fey require such a thing? Would they ask the same of her? Corrine sighed. It seemed she was not the only girl having difficulty trusting a man. But she had bigger problems, like how to put these letters back without anyone noticing. And how to keep the witches and their Captain from stealing her away.

~ Eighteen ~

October 30, 1865

The next week passed in a blur of attending classes, studying, and attempting to avoid Melanie at all costs, even and especially during dance class. Corrine barely had time to think about Rory, the Fey, the disappearance of Jeanette, or anything else. Before Corrine came to Falston, it had been quite some time since Corrine had had any schooling, and it certainly showed. Madame DuBois's presence did not help matters; she shifted from topic to topic so fast that Corrine could barely understand her. Corrine did not join the sewing circle again for fear she'd fall impossibly behind. With midterms coming up, and the angry image of her uncle looming in her mind if she failed, she tried to keep herself placed firmly in her textbooks.

She was also managing her confessions with less trouble than she expected, though it troubled her to think that perhaps she was just becoming a better liar. Father Joe seemed more nervous about it than she was, in fact. He gently instructed her through the confessional screen, explaining the proper prayers and responses for her confession. The idea seemed so strange that she hardly knew what to say to him, though she found herself longing to ask him questions about himself: why he was here, who the woman was she had seen with him in her visions, if Mara really was a witch. But she kept her silence and tried to do what she was told, sure that he would never answer her questions anyway. She wondered if her transcendentalist parents, focused as they were on finding spirit through self-growth, would also find confession strange.

The brief autumn had succumbed to the freezing temperatures and foul weather that made it often impossible to stay outside for very long. Society meetings were cancelled until the Hallowe'en induction meeting.

Corrine learned to bank her fire so that her room stayed relatively warm throughout the night, though the attic window seemed to do little to keep out the screaming wind. Freezing rain and snow fell alternately with a fierceness that Corrine had never before witnessed. Coal was running low and the evening soup seemed to get more watery by the day. Corrine sometimes saw Mara trudging wearily from the kitchen to the barn for milk, her skirts weighted down by mud and ice and her face obscured by a thick wool scarf. Corrine guessed that even witches were affected by the weather, and she certainly did not envy Mara such chores.

The weather broke the day before Hallowe'en, and the girls were at last allowed out for recess. The cold had abated somewhat overnight so that the ground was not quite as frozen. Corrine had not seen Rory except for brief flashes when he delivered something to the kitchen or took his supper. The memory of his kiss seemed like a dream, one of the fancies sent her by the Fey.

She was heartened, therefore, when she saw him driving the hogs past the muddy play yard to market. He winked at her from under the brim of his hat as he passed. She hoped this meant good things—that he had not forgotten her, and that perhaps the Fey would honor her request. She watched him go, wishing she had as much leisure to leave Falston as he had.

She was completely unprepared when someone grabbed her arm and spun her around, throwing her off balance so that she sat down hard in the mud. Melanie glowered down at her, her curls hissing with fury. Corrine squinted against the sun, trying to see her face. Dolores stood beside her, but Corrine couldn't make out her face either. She imagined she was leering.

"Oh dear," Melanie said to Dolores, "look what just jumped up out of the mud."

"Our little scalawag, Duncinea," Dolores said.

"Now, Dolores," said Melanie, "that really isn't very kind of you. Turns out we were wrong about her. You're not a scalawag at all, are you?" Melanie said to Corrine. The blonde leaned closer, her curls dangling above Corrine. Cold mud soaked through Corrine's coat. "You're a carpetbagger, a damn Yankee." Melanie made the words sound like the foulest things imaginable. Corrine felt more soiled by them than she did by the mud.

"I'll tell you this, Yankee," Melanie continued when Corrine said nothing, "I don't know who thought it was a good idea to send you down here, but they were dead wrong. We may not be far south of the Mason-Dixon Line, but we're still in Dixie. And if you got your carpetbagger eye trained on Rory, you got another think coming."

Corrine wished fervently that Ilona would appear, but prospects for her timely arrival looked grim. "Rory is a Southern gentleman, born and bred, a Confederate veteran," Melanie declared. "He wouldn't take to the likes of you. If you know what's best for you, you'll leave him be. And if you don't, I'll tell de Mornay all about your nightly expeditions to the barn."

Corrine's body turned to stone. How could Melanie possibly know about that? Had she seen her in the thicket the night the Captain had been in the grove? What else did she know?

Before she could say anything, Miss Brown appeared. "Girls! Girls! What is going on here?" she said.

Melanie drew back, adjusting her hair and her coat.

"Melanie," Miss Brown asked, "what are you doing? Why is Corrine sitting in the mud?" She stooped over Corrine. "Are you quite well, Miss Jameson?" she asked.

Before Corrine could say anything, Melanie said smoothly, "It's all right, Miss Brown. Corrine here just tripped and I was asking her if she needed help."

Corrine nodded. She let Miss Brown help her up, trying to lean on her as little as possible.

"Well, Melanie and Dolores, you two go on and get some fresh air until recess ends. Corrine, let's go inside and take your coat to Siobhan—maybe she can wash it out."

Corrine acquiesced, trying to ignore the notion that she had no idea which would be the lesser of the two evils—being escorted alone by a possible witch or being left outside with a bullying Southern belle who certainly served the witches.

When Melanie and Dolores had gone far enough away, Miss Brown asked, "Are you really all right, Corrine? I know Melanie can sometimes be a bit . . . overzealous."

Corrine eyed Miss Brown as she walked up the stairs, feeling her sodden clothes clinging uncomfortably to her backside. The look the headmistress returned was one of genuine concern; she saw nothing sinister in the woman's face—certainly nothing to suggest that she was at all connected to Mara or the other witches at Falston.

"I'm fine," Corrine said. She couldn't bring herself to tattle, and furthermore she knew that she could not afford the retribution that awaited her if she did. Though Melanie had also been out at night, Corrine felt certain that she would receive the greater punishment for her failings.

"Well, then." Miss Brown patted Corrine's arm softly as they stopped by the laundry room in the hall. Remembering the voodoo doll, its red hand and white-stitched eyes, Corrine did her best not to shrink from her.

"Siobhan," Miss Brown called.

Siobhan came, her rolled-up sleeves dripping with wash water. When she saw Corrine, her watery eyes grew frantic. She looked as though she would run straight out the door and all the way to Culpeper. "Yes, Miss Brown," she said.

"Miss Jameson had an unfortunate accident in the play yard. I'm wondering if you could help her find fresh clothes, and then take her to the library for the rest of recess. Afterward, please launder her coat and dress so they can dry as quickly as possible."

Siobhan bobbed an abbreviated curtsy to both of them. "Yes, Miss Brown."

Miss Brown turned to Corrine. "Take care, Corrine. And don't be afraid to speak up if something is wrong."

Corrine nodded.

Miss Brown left them, and Siobhan led Corrine in silence down the hall and up the stairs to her room.

Siobhan waited outside the door while Corrine changed her clothes. She remembered the letters just in time. Being in the library meant that she would have the opportunity to return them to their hiding place, which relieved her immensely. She slipped all of them into her pinafore pocket except the last one, wondering when or if she would ever be able to return it to Father Joe's Bible in the chapel room.

She brought her mud-drenched clothes back out to Siobhan.

"I'll take those, miss," Siobhan said, not looking in Corrine's eyes.

Corrine handed them to her. Siobhan started down the stairs, but Corrine stopped her with a hand on her arm.

"Siobhan, why are you so afraid of me?"

Siobhan flinched at her touch, much as Corrine had done with Miss Brown.

"It's nothing, miss," she said. "Let's get you to the library like Miss Brown said."

"No, really," Corrine said. "Last time you said something about . . . the Unhallowed, you called them. You said I was marked. What does all that mean?"

"Oh, miss, I . . ." Siobhan looked horrified. "I didn't mean anything. Just talk, that's all. I didn't mean no offense." She started swiftly down the stairs.

But Corrine didn't give up. "You can tell me, Siobhan. I won't be upset. I just need to know. Things are happening that—"

Miss de Mornay passed below them. She looked up, her gray eyes searching for trouble, and stopped to wait for them at the bottom of the stairs.

"Not here, miss," Siobhan said in a low voice.

"What are you girls doing?" Miss de Mornay said, fixing them both with her cold stare.

Corrine and Siobhan looked at each other.

"I fell in the mud, Miss de Mornay," Corrine said, keeping her eyes lowered. "Miss Brown asked Siobhan to escort me to get fresh clothes and to the library for the rest of recess."

"Well, then," said Miss de Mornay, "carry on. But I should advise you, Miss Jameson, to be very careful where you step. Very careful, indeed."

Corrine looked up. Miss de Mornay smiled an eely smile that sent cold daggers into her chest. Then, the teacher turned and Corrine watched her taffeta bustle disappear down the hall like a giant spider.

"May I drop these in my room, miss? It's closer to the library than the laundry," Siobhan said.

"Of course," Corrine said.

She followed Siobhan around the stairs to a room with two beds, a couple chests, and a worn wardrobe. It looked like an old parlor that had been converted into servants' quarters. Rory's cottage had been the slaves' quarters; since he could not be respectably housed in the same building as women and girls, Corrine understood why this arrangement had been made. Father Joe, in the guesthouse, was in a similar situation.

Siobhan seemed to pick up on her thoughts, for she said, "Miss Brown has said that when you are moved downstairs next year, Mara and I might have the attic rooms. But then," she said, as she set the clothes down by her bed, "we probably won't all be here by then."

"What?" Corrine said.

Siobhan turned fearful eyes on her. "Just a feeling, miss. May not be true."

Corrine stepped closer. "You see things. What have you seen?"

"Oh, miss, please," Siobhan looked down and clenched her hands in her apron. "Please don't ask. I don't want to make no trouble. I need this job."

"I won't get you in trouble, Siobhan, I promise," said Corrine. "I just need you to explain to me what you meant before about the Fey."

Siobhan looked up at her, and Corrine saw a nervous twitch start in her arms and face, much like the last time Corrine had been in the laundry room with her.

"If the Fey hear as I've talked to you—" she began.

"They won't," Corrine said. "I won't tell."

"But they have ways," Siobhan said, her face twisting. "They have ways of knowing even when you don't tell. Just don't trust them," she said at last.

Corrine looked over at the bed that must belong to Mara.

"And you trust Mara more?" she asked. "Surely a witch is worse than the Fey?"

Siobhan's eyes widened at that, and she said, "Don't be talking about Miss Mara either. She has her ways, Lord knows, but the Fey have ways that's much worse."

She straightened then, as if she'd shaken off a chill, and said, "Now, miss, I think I should be taking you to the library. If Miss de Mornay finds us here, you know how much trouble we'll both be in."

She walked past Corrine and out the door, clearly expecting her to follow. Corrine looked around once, seeking evidence of Mara's witchery, shocked at Siobhan's dismissal of it, and then hurried out of the room.

Siobhan left her in the library without another word, and Corrine was too stunned to thank her. That Siobhan would be so terrified of the Fey and so dismissive of Mara's obvious witchcraft . . . Corrine did not know what to think. Then she remembered the letters and decided to return them before recess ended and she lost her chance.

It took a while to find the right panel, but she crawled along the bottom shelves, pressing against the wood until at last one panel gave. She was placing the letters back in the cavity when the library door opened. She started, losing hold of the panel so that it clattered out onto the floor. Her heart hammered at the thought of the Moray Eel catching her in yet another scrape.

Father Joe looked at her kneeling on the floor and smiled. "So it was you who took the letters. I was rather hoping so," he said.

She felt her skin blaze like a bonfire. "Well, I . . . This panel, you see—I was looking for a book, and—"

"It's all right, Corrine. No sense in lying to me, is there?"

"No, Father," she said.

He came and knelt next to her, fixing the panel back in place.

"Would you also happen to be the one who took the letter out of my Bible?"

She imagined that she now looked like a boiled lobster, so hot were her cheeks. "Yes, Father."

"Will you return that to me also?"

"It's in my room, Father," she said, still unable to look at him.

"Really, Corrine, it's all right. I'm glad it was you. Perhaps you are learning something from them. At least, I hope so."

He helped her rise, then went over to another bookshelf and took out a book from the top shelf. He pulled a folded letter from between its pages. "Here is the last one we have," he said, giving it to her. "You can return it to me with the other when you're done."

She stared at him, unable to think of a thing to say. *She saw him again, looking up at the woman with amber eyes as she rode a white charger, flowers raining from her hair down around his shoulders. He caught one in the air and gave it back to her. She smiled, cruel and satisfied as a cat.*

"Corrine?"

She shook herself. He looked concerned.

"Are you well?" he asked.

She nodded, still speechless.

He reached around her for a book, and she felt the usual shiver of power that she always felt in his presence.

"Well," he said. "I leave you to the letters. Let's keep it our little secret, shall we?"

She nodded again, holding the letter as carefully as she could. She wondered if the amber-eyed woman was also a witch, like Mara and Miss Brown. She wanted to ask him, but found she couldn't. Instead, she said, "Have you ever seen a voodoo doll, Father?"

He stopped looking at the books and peered at her through his spectacles. "Why do you ask?"

"A while back, I saw Mara give Miss Brown a voodoo doll, a black one with a pin stuck in it." She longed to say more about the Captain, but waited to see what Father Joe would say.

He cleared his throat. "I—well, I have seen such things in the deeper South. But I'm sure what you saw was not really a voodoo doll. Perhaps Mara found it somewhere on the grounds. Who knows? What we see is sometimes not what is. Probably best just to forget about it."

"But aren't you afraid that something bad might be happening?"

He frowned a little. "Like what?"

"Well, like witchcraft or—or—devil worship." She thought of Miss de Mornay and Melanie with the Captain. Obviously, they had been swearing some sort of fealty to him. But she didn't know how to talk about the incident without implicating herself. "I mean, Miss de Mornay, she—"

"What about Miss de Mornay? Are you saying she worships the Devil?"

"Er—"

"That is a very serious accusation, Miss Jameson. Very serious indeed. Many people died in Salem, Massachusetts, unnecessarily because of similar accusations." Father Joe's frown deepened even further and he bent toward her in a way that seemed almost predatory.

Corrine didn't know what else to say. If she couldn't talk to him about the voodoo doll or even hint at the possibility of witchcraft at Falston, there was no chance she could talk to him about the Captain or any of her visions. As usual, he had deflected her questions, leaving her nowhere closer to the truth.

When she remained silent, his stance relaxed, though his face was still clouded with skepticism. "Bring those letters back when you're done," he said, and left the library, closing the door behind him. Corrine sat at one of the tables. She put the letter before her, but stared at it without seeing. She had thought nothing could be stranger than John Pelham appearing to her at Kelly's Ford or seeing Miss de Mornay and Melanie with the Captain, but this encounter with Father Joe had been stranger by far. Clearly, he knew something, something that he seemed to want her to discover in the letters. Why, then, did he refuse to give any credence to her questions? When the bell rang, she still had not read the letter. She shoved it in her pocket, confused.

That night, Corrine settled into her cot to read. The lamp cast leaping shadows on the ceiling and the words danced in time to them.

[Trans. note: Possibly July 1357]

My beloved—

I swear to you that I meant no harm in what I said or did the night you so innocently came to me. Is any man to be held accountable for word or deed in his darkest hour? What I said was but an extension of the darkness that lives and breathes in me now, the terrible heaviness of this mortal life. Can you now see why I am willing to throw it all away? Without you, there is no reason to stay. Yet you still refuse the gifts that might be.

[Words blurred, scratched out]

[. . .] you think, you must blame me, not the Fey. They are a fair people, a just people, and they wish only our happiness. The thing they ask of you is so very small, yet infinitely precious to Them. Did you not willingly give Our Lord all, even your soul? Yet have you ever seen Him, ever once felt His presence? Perhaps I am the most ill-favored of men, but I have not. Oh, aye, I know how we eat of His flesh and drink His blood at every Communion. And if that is truly so, why is it an abomination that They should do so? What they offer you is far beyond what the Abbess or any of the cold saints of your chapel ever could. And the love I offer cannot possibly be less.

Perhaps I do not know how best to teach you of their ways; I am the most inept of disciples. But I assure you, beloved, the Fey are our only path to togetherness. You have said you wanted this, and I believe it still. Come to me again and I swear upon all we hold dear in this life, that you shall have no cause to fear. For my path of salvation is in you. There can be no other.

Yours in love eternally,
Angus

Corrine lay back on her cot, letting the letter fall to her chest. She smoothed her fingers along the parchment, feeling Angus's pleas burning into her heart. She had never been allowed to read fanciful or romantic novels. She remembered her mother once finding her in possession of Charlotte Dacre's *Zofloya, or, the Moor: A Romance of the Fifteenth Century.* Though there had been no punishment, her mother's disappointment had stung her deeply enough that she had ceased reading it. "We must pity Miss Dacre," her mother had said, "that she is forced to earn her bread through such lewd inventions. You, I know, will be a wiser, stronger woman. And if you choose to write, let us hope that like Miss Alcott, you will inspire girls to be better and truer women than those in the pages of this book."

She remembered her shame, but she had often secretly wished she had read the rest of *Zofloya.* Victoria's passion, the watery avenues of Venice, the Moor's demonic hold on Victoria—all had conspired to set her longing for such excitement. Angus's letters reminded her of those forbidden words, long forgotten in the desire to fill her mother with pride.

She wondered what Brighde had chosen, and if Angus was truly talking about the same people to whom Siobhan had referred. *The Fey. The Unhallowed Ones.* How could they possibly be the same? What did he mean about the Fey and Communion? Did he mean that they drank blood? Corrine sighed. Surely that could not be so. And why was Father Joe glad she had stolen the letters? That was still the strangest thing of all.

~ Nineteen ~

Hallowe'en 1865

Hallowe'en morning came at last, and Corrine awoke jittery and exhausted, as though she hadn't slept at all. She had taken her midterm exams but dreaded the results; she didn't feel confident about any of them. She also had not seen Rory and didn't know if he or the Fey would fulfill their promise—hence jeopardizing her induction into the Society. Since speaking to Siobhan, she doubted her judgment in trusting the Fey. Her dreams lately had been vague, mostly images that jumbled together and vanished with the morning.

She moved through her day like a sleepwalker, narrowly avoiding Miss de Mornay's ruler and rousing Mrs. Alexander's ire in the ballroom. Ilona had to pinch her more than once as they danced to keep her feet moving.

"Are you a young lady or a slug?" Mrs. Alexander yelled in her ear. "Step lightly!"

At last the day was done. Corrine sat morosely at supper, pushing at her food. Nothing had come from Rory. And the Fey could not bring it to her themselves; the iron fences warded the school as tightly as a prison.

Christina nudged at her, smiling. "Why are you not happy, Corrine?" she asked.

Corrine couldn't bear to say. She shrugged and spooned mashed squash into her mouth.

Before Christina could say more, the outer door of the dining hall banged open. Rory entered in a blast of snow. His hat and shoulders were lightly powdered, so that he shone in the lantern light. He took off his hat, dusted at his coat, and wiped his boots on the braided rug. Something large and square protruded from under his coat.

Corrine could not help the smile that spread across her face as he came to her. "A package just come for Miss Corrine," he said.

He looked into her eyes as he handed her the silver-wrapped box. And though he smiled his crooked smile, his gaze was grave.

"Thank you, Mr. MacLeod," she said.

He nodded, his eyes straying for a moment to Christina. Then, wishing everyone a good Hallowe'en, he departed back into the night.

Out of the corner of her eye, Corrine saw Miss Brown stop Miss de Mornay, presumably from coming and taking the package from her. She turned the shining package over in her hands. A sealed note was attached to its sparkling wrapping. She pulled it off and it opened of its own volition in her hand. At first, she couldn't make out the spidery letters, but then they resolved themselves into words she could understand.

Now, do you believe? Much more than this is possible, if only you believe in it.

"What does it say, Corrine?" Christina asked, her face alight with excitement. "I can't read it; the letters seem all smeared."

Corrine thought fast. "I think it says, 'From a fairy godfather to all the girls at Falston.'"

Christina practically grinned. "Your uncle must have sent

it!" The teachers, including Miss Brown and Father Joe had come to stand around the table.

"Well, open it, you ninny," Ilona muttered.

Corrine stuffed the note in her pocket, and then opened the shining outer wrapping with slow reverence. She had never in all her life received such a gift and certainly never one wrapped this beautifully. She pulled off the silver paper, revealing a box of shimmering green satin. She opened it carefully, and a delicious, almost unearthly smell drifted from it. All who looked inside drew in gasps of delight. Nestled in the box were at least fifty confections, each one exquisitely shaped and decorated. Here was a chocolate truffle shaped like a heart and decorated with swirls of raspberry sauce. There was a perfect white cake on top of which sat two tiny white doves. Corrine marveled at the richness and delicacy of it, more perfect than she could possibly have dreamed.

"My, Corrine," Miss Brown said, her voice rich with admiration, "your fairy godfather certainly has taste." Her smile seemed a faint echo of the photo on Uncle William's desk.

"Yes," she said, smiling back. "May I share these with everyone, Miss Brown?"

The rich smells of chocolate and cake, strawberries and hazelnuts, drifted around the table.

Miss Brown looked at Father Joe and the other teachers for corroboration. Miss de Mornay seemed to be having trouble maintaining her dour expression, which made her countenance truly frightening. But she did not object.

"Very well, then," Miss Brown said. "Let's clear a place on the table for everyone to try a piece. If there's more afterward—"

But the girls had already cleared the space and helped Corrine lay the box on the scarred table. One by one, they took whatever they most desired, and Corrine stood back and watched, her heart swelling with renewed faith.

"However did you do it, Corrine?" Christina asked, her mouth smeared with strawberry sauce. It looked a bit like blood, unsettling Corrine.

"Oh . . . magic," she said.

Ilona invited Mara and Siobhan in from the kitchen to share in the festivities. When Mara stepped up to the box, her gaze darted to Corrine. Mara pinned her with a flat, dark stare. She stepped back.

"No thank you, Miz Ilona," she said. She turned quickly and went back into the kitchen.

But Siobhan twitched when she looked at the candies.

"Try one, Siobhan," Corrine said, moving to stand next to her.

She moaned. "No," she whispered. "No, nothing but death and maggots in there. Nothing but rotted bones and blood. What have you done?" she said, looking at Corrine with her wild, watery eyes. "What have you done?" And in her voice, Corrine heard the echo of her mother's ghost: *Oh, what have you done?*

Miss Brown shook herself, as though she'd just awoken from a dream. She looked hard at Siobhan, Corrine, and the box with its crumpled green lid lying innocently on the table.

"All right, girls. Enough. Off to bed with you," she said, sounding almost frightened. But who wouldn't have been frightened by Siobhan's queer remarks?

Corrine filed out with the others, smiling at Christina and Ilona's conspiratorial winks. There was no doubt that tonight she had earned her place in the Society. And in a matter of hours, she would be inducted as one of them.

While she waited on the moon to fill her window, Corrine drowsed by the stove. A beautiful dream filled her. *The Fey city stood ablaze with lights and music. The perfume of a million unearthly blossoms wreathed her like smoke. She drifted toward the masked revelers revolving across the floor in a perfect waltz. And then he was there, his face shadowed by a mask peaked with bells.* Corrine, *he said.* Come to me.

She opened her eyes to the moon staring blindly at her through her window. Slowly she crawled toward it, lifted the sash, and began her climb across the roof. With each step, she felt lighter and the roof felt less solid. She nearly lost her grip as she slipped over the eaves and down the ledge. She stopped and looked up, trying to use the moon as a reference point. Two moons wavered over the roof. She shook her head and breathed deeply to steady herself. She managed to clamber down and was almost to the woodshed roof when she looked up again. The sky was filled with lights that trailed rose and silver sparks as they flew. She tilted her head all the way back to watch the colors. And then all the lights went out.

Someone was shaking her. "Corrine! Corrine!"

Rory.

She opened her eyes. Clouds boiled across an orange moon. She could dimly make out his face.

"Rory?" He helped her sit. And then she realized that she hurt.

"Can you stand, lass?"

With his help, she stood slowly, but her spine felt as though it had been beaten with a hammer. She winced.

"What were you doing on the roof?" he asked. "You should have been sleeping and having sweet dreams by now."

"I was, but there was a meeting—" She clapped her hand over her mouth.

"A meeting?" he said. "Well, there's only one meeting going on tonight, but it won't be with your friends. They're all fast asleep in their beds."

"They are?"

"The only way the Fey could protect them from the witches this night. A brilliant stroke on your part, I must say," he said.

"But I didn't—"

"Let's walk a bit, shall we?" he asked. "Did you hurt anything else besides your back?"

She shook her head and felt a spark of pain.

"Eh?"

She realized he could not see her as she could see him. His back blocked what little light the moon gave through the clouds. "No, I don't think so. At least, everything hurts now."

"But you're walking. That's good," he said.

They walked around the corner of the manor, toward the play yard. She blinked against the colors that streamed from the sky.

"What other meeting were you talking about?" she said.

"I'll show you, if you really want to see," he said.

"Yes."

He helped her limp over to where candles floated like giant lightning bugs inside the chapel room. He lifted her up on the stone ledge and she winced with pain. What she saw nearly made her lose her grip in shock.

Three dark figures bore candles as they circled a table in the chapel room. They placed them in iron holders on the table, and then stood back to where the light hit their faces. Corrine could see Miss Brown, Mara, and Madame DuBois. She tried to shrink down onto the ledge to keep from being seen while Rory held her off the ground.

With perfect clarity, almost as though she were inside the room, she watched Mara take a stone from the pocket of her robe and place it in the center of the circle of fire. Miss Brown placed the familiar serpent-bound book on the table near it. She could see the serpents on the cover raise their heads as the women began to chant. The words were slurred and strange; she could not make them out. Just as she was wondering if this stone was like the stone she had taken at Uncle Willliam's, a golden light emanated from it, turning and coiling into a tangible golden serpent at the sound of the witches' chant. The serpent grew to a dizzying height, and then spread its golden hood and turned, looking straight through Corrine. It pierced her with a lidless glare as fierce as that of the two-headed serpent at Kelly's Ford, so powerful that she felt herself sliding off the ledge, almost into unconsciousness.

Rory pulled her down and away from the window to the corner of the building.

"Corrine," he said. "What did you see?"

"A—a golden serpent," she said faintly. "Even more powerful than the one that came when John Pelham . . ."

"Rest here," he said. He took her into his arms then, rocking her as though she was a small child. She was so happy to be held that she nearly sobbed aloud.

"What are they doing in there?" she said against his jacket.

"The same as at every Hallowe'en," he answered. "Worshiping the Devil."

"What?" she said. She disengaged herself from his embrace.

"Haven't you seen signs of the serpent everywhere here?" he asked. "Weren't you attacked by one of their minions at Kelly's Ford?"

"Yes, but—"

"They are our enemy," he said. "And the enemies of the Fey. They must be stopped."

"How?" she asked doubtfully.

"We need your help."

"Why not just go to the deputy in Culpeper?" Corrine asked.

"Because this deals with more than just ordinary life, Corrine. Even if the deputy arrested them, they would still have their power. It's the power that must be destroyed, not them. Even Father Joe is on their side."

"Then how have you escaped?" she asked.

"The Fey protect me," he said. "As they would protect you, if you would allow it."

"But—"

"Do you realize how many girls have disappeared from Falston, Corrine?"

Visions of Jeanette flashed through her mind. She felt gooseflesh rising on the back of her neck.

"No," she said slowly.

"You saw de Mornay with that man. And I know you've seen him before. He's the one who takes them."

"Who is he?" she asked.

"One of the Devil's henchman, most like. They call him the Captain. The witches give him the girls to maintain their power—part of their bargain with him."

All Corrine could hear in her mind was Nora clucking to herself and saying, "Lord-a-mercy," as she had once done when Corrine had fallen and torn open her knee. "Lord-a-mercy," the woman had said over and over, pouring whiskey on the wound while Corrine screamed.

And this is where Uncle William sent me? And then a deeper chill ran through her as she remembered the book with the serpent on the cover, which he'd hidden away from view—the same book that Miss Brown had placed on the witches' altar. And Miss Brown was an old friend of his. Was he in league with them?

She put a hand against the frozen stone to steady herself. "What do you want from me?"

"I want to know if you will be one of the disappeared, or if you'll help me in our fight to stop the witches."

"Why me? How could I possibly stop them?"

"Because you have not yet fallen prey to their spell."

"How do you know?" she said.

"I've worked for this place for many years," Rory said. "I've seen how the girls become docile and biddable. But you—you've still got fire, spirit. I can see it in you. I can only guess what you were sent here for, but I'm sure it wasn't for obeying."

She quieted the flutter in her chest with some effort. "So?" she said.

"You saw that stone the black girl had, right?"

"Mara," Corrine said. "Her name's Mara."

"Yes, well, you saw that stone?"

"Yes." The cold worked itself into her jaws. Her teeth began to chatter.

"That stone is the key to the witches' power. If you were to bring it to me, I could take it away and destroy it. All you need to do," he said, "is just find where they hide the stone and take it. Tie your handkerchief around the fence to let me know you've got it, and I'll come to meet you that night."

She stood up, her toes freezing in her boots, her hands numb against her coat. The sky was awash with flame. She heard the voice of the hawthorn people again—*Bring us the stone . . . The Captain serves the witch . . .* She remembered the shattered trunk, the lady's torn smile, her uncle's head in his hands.

"Will you do it?"

She thought of all the girls who must have disappeared, of Jeanette's poor ghost doomed to haunt Falston forever. The Fey had been good to her. They had healed her of her terrible illness. They had given her the locket, which hung again against her heart. And tonight they had given everyone a heavenly satisfaction, and, apparently, protection, which they might never enjoy again. It hadn't been their fault that the Captain had vandalized her uncle's study.

But the thought of her friends finally made her say yes. How else was she to protect them? Penelope's disappearance, short as it had been, was frightening enough. But the thought of losing Ilona and Christina . . . She swallowed hard.

"Yes," she said, her voice cracking. "Yes."

"Good," Rory said. He sounded so ecstatic that she thought he might laugh. "The Fey are never wrong when they choose someone. I knew you were the one they sought." He touched her on the cheek, but she longed for his kiss. "Now, let's get you back up to your room."

He helped her up on the woodshed and gave her a boost toward the first ledge. Weakly, she worked her way up the frozen stone, hauling herself onto the roof with aching fingers. Compared to the task Rory had set before her, climbing onto the roof and into her room seemed trivial.

~ Twenty ~

November 6, 1865

In the johnnyhouse line a few days later, Corrine made sure she was behind Ilona. It had taken Corrine that long to work up the courage for this. She nudged Ilona as they stood mutely in the cold. Mara watched over all of them with a disinterested, yet predatory gleam in her eye.

Ilona looked back at her, her dark hair shading one eye.

"Do you happen to have any stockings I could borrow?"

The other eye widened questioningly.

"Mine have a hole in the left toe," Corrine said.

"I'm sorry," Ilona said. "Mine have a hole too."

Corrine hid her sigh of relief. She had remembered the code correctly. Ilona would call a meeting for tonight.

"Oh, what a shame," Corrine said.

"All right! Quiet!" Mara said, giving them a pointed look.

Ilona hurried into the privy, and they didn't speak again for the rest of the day.

That night, Corrine climbed off the roof reluctantly. She was still sore from her fall, but she knew she had no choice. She had to explain to the girls what she'd seen. She reached the ground without much trouble, though the cold made her fingers ache and her legs stiffen. She leaped off the woodshed, managed not to fall in the frozen mud, and tried to make her way to the barn as quietly as possible. Not all of the girls were there, but most were, including Christina and Ilona.

They all sat in a circle, their eyes gleaming in the light of the shuttered lantern. The cold transformed Corrine's breath into a column of smoke. She didn't know how to begin.

"Listen," she said, at last, "Hallowe'en night, I saw something—something really terrible, and I just felt all of you should know about it."

"First tell us, Corrine," Christina said, "is this a lie or another truth?"

For a moment, Corrine thought she could see malevolence in their eyes, like animals stalking around a fire.

"Truth," she said. She swallowed and plunged forward. "This school is run by witches. On Hallowe'en, I saw them practicing some kind of evil ritual—calling up some kind of spirit. I think we are all in great danger here."

Whispers broke out amongst the girls.

Finally, Christina said, "You brought us out of our beds to tell us that?" Corrine could not see her face, but her tone was flat, with just the slightest edge of incredulity.

"I—"

"Did you think we did not know that?" Ilona said.

"What?" Corrine said. Her tongue went numb in her mouth.

"We have known this for a long time," Ilona went on. "We know what danger we live in every day."

Corrine's mouth dropped open. "You do? But—Why didn't you tell me?"

"You were new. It was not time for you to know," Ilona said.

"Besides," Christina said, "most girls would rather not know. Some leave the school without ever knowing."

"But don't you want to do something about it?" The hopelessness of the situation seemed as empty and cold as the stall in which they huddled together.

"What do you think we could do?" Christina said. "We are locked up here. There is no way to escape. Our parents don't want us"—Corrine felt the sting in that—"and no one cares about us. Who would care if these witches did whatever they wanted with us?"

"All the more reason to do something on our own!" Corrine said. "I know that part of their power rests in a stone they use for their rituals. Mara brought it to the ritual on Hallowe'en. If we could just get that stone and destroy it, maybe we could stop them."

"What you are talking about is insane," Ilona said. "Can you imagine how angry they would be if we did that? I told you not to cross Mara. She is the strongest of all of them! Don't you remember what happened to Dolores?"

"But—" Corrine said.

"And how do we know you aren't in league with them?" Christina asked.

"What?" Corrine said. She was so shocked that her voice almost squeaked.

"Wasn't it you that gave us those magic candies?" Christina replied. "Our induction was to be on Hallowe'en, but instead we were all dreaming of sugar palaces and plum-pudding clouds! Why would you do that unless you were working with them? Fairy godfather indeed!"

"Christina," Ilona said in a low voice.

"But I didn't mean—I didn't know—" Corrine began.

"The best we can hope for is to get out of this place one day," Ilona said, her tone edged with steel. "The best way to do that is to do exactly what the witches tell you to do, maybe even make them like you, if you can."

"But—"

"Corrine," Christina said, "I don't know what you've done or what you're trying to do by bringing us here. But as of tonight, I move that you will not be inducted into our Society. You will not attend further meetings and you will not reveal any knowledge you have of these meetings. If you try, we will deny anything you say. We survive by silence. That's the way. All in favor, say aye."

One by one, around the circle, she heard their voices speak against her. But when Ilona's turn came, she said gruffly, "Abstain."

"So noted," Christina said. "By majority, Corrine, you are cast out."

Corrine opened her mouth to protest, but the blinding light of a lantern eclipsed whatever she might have said. She cringed, squinting, dread filling her with cold.

Miss de Mornay stared at them. She clutched her coat closed over her flannel robe and nightgown, her grayish hair straggling out of its braid over her left shoulder. A smiling Melanie followed her.

"Well," Miss de Mornay said, "I would have expected this from the likes of Miss Jameson. There has been nothing but trouble from her since she arrived. But I did not expect this from you, Miss Beaumont, or you, Miss Takar."

Corrine moved her mouth, but no sound came.

"Don't speak!" Miss de Mornay said, rounding on her with a force that sent the lantern shadows dancing crazily across her face. "You, dear Corrine, will explain the entire story to Miss Brown tomorrow. We will decide punishment for the rest of you in the morning, as well. Now, back to your rooms!"

As they all filed past Miss de Mornay and back toward the house, Corrine glanced at Melanie. Her triumphant expression was ghastly in the lantern light. In a flash, Corrine saw her, chased by sleek, ghostly hounds across a meadow. She was wearing a strange outfit—something that reminded Corrine of the ancient Greeks—that was torn and bloodied.

Melanie's smile broadened as Corrine passed, but Corrine, the vision still jarring her senses, looked away.

November 7, 1865

In the morning, Mara led Corrine to Miss Brown's study. As on Corrine's first night at Falston, Miss Brown was seated at her desk in the smart, pinstriped jacket with puffed sleeves. But she was studying a book of curious line drawings, and her hair was not as tidy as Corrine remembered from her first interview. The book with the serpents on its cover was nowhere to be seen.

Miss Brown glanced up and her eyes were like ice. "So, tell me, Corrine, what prompted you to leave your room, gather your classmates, and sit out in the freezing barn together in the middle of the night?"

Corrine had been rehearsing what she might say all night but none of her answers had sounded very convincing. She thought of being flippant like Melanie, demure and sweet like Christina, or even strong and silent like Ilona. But none of those appealed to her. Her mother had told her that the truth should be her guide in all things.

"Danger," she said.

"Danger?" Miss Brown said. Corrine realized that she had never seen the headmistress this angry. Now that she was about to, she was quite certain she did not want to.

"Danger?" Miss Brown said again. "Were all your beds simultaneously infested by bedbugs? Were the barn animals in danger of dying of loneliness? I should hope you have a good explanation for this, because I doubt my more fanciful ones do it justice."

She leaned over the desk. "Tell me, Corrine, what danger forced you to choose to break Falston's every rule last night?"

Corrine wanted to squeeze her eyes shut, so that she couldn't see Miss Brown's expression when she said what she knew she had to. But Miss Brown's blue eyes held hers with their violent cold.

"You," she said.

"What?" Miss Brown sat down, hard enough so that her skirts rustled alarmingly.

"I know you're a witch," Corrine said. "And I thought the girls should know it too." At last, she had said it. She felt again her shock at Christina's rejection. And then a smoldering anger grew—she could not be sorry about this, no matter how hard she tried. The truth was, in fact, getting her into the deepest trouble imaginable.

"Why, Corrine, that is perhaps the most fantastical accusation I have ever heard," Miss Brown began.

Corrine's anger boiled. "My mother told me never to tell lies. You know I'm telling the truth. I saw you with the other witches in the parlor on Hallowe'en! How can you lie about that?"

Miss Brown's face, a little sallow already, went nearly white.

"What do you think you saw?" she said in a low voice, full of murmuring threats that set Corrine's hair on end even more than de Mornay's dull remonstrations.

"I know I saw you in black robes, in the chapel room. Mara carried a stone, and you chanted." She felt herself babbling, but the words would not stop. "There were candles and a—a—a golden serpent. And before, I saw you and Mara with a voodoo doll!"

Miss Brown raised her eyebrows, and Corrine's voice ceased.

"Now, Corrine, let me tell you two things. The first is that eavesdroppers never, ever prosper. Whatever you thought you saw, I am quite sure it was nothing like what you believe.

Second, I thought your parents, or at least your uncle, had taught you not to leap to conclusions. As Goethe said, 'Misunderstandings and neglect occasion more mischief in the world than even malice and wickedness. At all events, the two latter are of less frequent occurrence.' "

Corrine remained silent.

"Corrine, the fact is that you are prone to flights of fancy, which are the reason that you find yourself here. Imagination can be a splendid thing, but it must be used properly. I will not lend credence to your ideas by trying to help you determine what you might have seen. What I am more concerned about is your sneaking about the manor at all hours of the night. I want to know how you and your compatriots are accomplishing it."

If Miss Brown was not going to tell her the truth, Corrine did not see why it was important for her to do so. The truth had already gotten her in enough trouble with everyone as it was.

"I—The door is just unlocked somehow. And then I go out and find them in the barn."

"The door is unlocked? Your room? And the hall door? And the outer doors? Really, Corrine, you must think me absolutely daft."

"No, it's true," Corrine said. She was not about to tell Miss Brown about the unlocked window. Nor her climb off the roof.

"Well, I have quite a different story from Melanie," Miss Brown said. "I'm more inclined to believe you, but it appears you are choosing not to tell me the truth."

Corrine held her tongue. There was a long silence in which the clock ticked on the mantel and wood sizzled in the grate.

At last, Miss Brown said, "I am sorry to have to resort to such harsh measures, but I must uphold Falston's rules and your uncle's expectations. You will be placed in isolation and given bread and water for three days. Your cot and a chamber pot will be brought into your detention room. Your teachers will give you your lessons as they are able. In the meantime, French being your most trying subject, you will study for a French exam to be proctored by Madame DuBois at the end of the third day. When you return from isolation, you are not to speak of your fancies again to anyone, nor are you to leave your room at night for any reason. Am I understood?"

"Yes, Miss Brown." Corrine could feel the tears starting. She widened her eyes as much as possible, tried to press covertly at the edges of her eyes with her fingertips.

"What I do is for your own protection," Miss Brown said. "There is more to this than you could possibly guess, and you are far too young to be involved in it. Now, go to the chapel until Mara can arrange your isolation room."

Corrine fled from the chair, the room, and Miss Brown's icy blue stare.

In the chapel room, the tears that she had controlled in Miss Brown's study fell freely. She took several steps into the room before she realized someone else was there. Father Joe rose from behind a pew, his arms full of hymnals.

Corrine dashed a hand over her eyes. The feeling was there, the tingling in her spine, a memory too long unremembered.

"Corrine?" Father Joe said. He set the stack of hymnals on the pew near him. Winter light filtered in through the window, setting the dust motes dancing around him. Corrine saw another version of him, a younger version, walking in that timeless world beside the amber-eyed woman. The delicate image shattered.

"Corrine?" he said again.

"Father," she mumbled, dropping her eyes to the worn floor.

"Isn't it a bit early for recess?" he asked.

"I'm to be placed in isolation for three days," Corrine said. And saying the words aloud brought fresh tears. She fought them back. "Miss Brown told me to wait here."

"Oh, dear," Father Joe said. "I hardly would have expected such a thing from you. What happened?"

And then she could not fight anymore, and the words flowed out with her tears, startled and bitter at once. She told him of the witches, of the girls' betrayal at the meeting, and how Melanie had led Miss de Mornay to find them in the barn. "And Miss Brown told me I wasn't to share my flights of fancy with anyone anymore." Corrine finished "But they weren't fanciful, Father, I swear!"

Father Joe came to her and took her by the elbow. When he touched her, the familiar buzzing started in her bones and worked its way into her nerves. He took a handkerchief from the pocket of his cassock and handed it to her.

"Thank you," she said, scrubbing angrily at her eyes. She could not believe she had broken her prohibition against crying.

He helped her settle into the pew and then sat beside her. She was surprised at how comfortable this felt, despite the buzzing that warmed her fingers and toes.

"Corrine," he said when she'd calmed a bit, "I'm afraid Miss Brown is right."

She looked up at him then, all feelings of comfort fading away. Amber swam deep within his eyes, and she felt a twinge of fear.

"In this case, I can assure you that you only know half the truth. And what you do not know is for the protection of you and everyone here at Falston. There are strange things afoot, Corrine, things from which Miss Brown is trying to protect you. 'There are more things in heaven and earth, Horatio, than are dreamt of in your philosophy.' "

Corrine looked at him blankly.

"Have you not read *Hamlet?"* he asked.

"It was next," Corrine said in a low voice. "My mother was reading Shakespeare to me before—before she . . ."

Father Joe sighed.

"All I am saying is that you must believe that the adults here at Falston know what they're doing and are doing what they can for your best interests."

"That's what Miss Brown said," Corrine said. "But—"

"But, you must believe her," Father Joe said. What he said next was barely a whisper. "I think you know now what the Fey are capable of."

"The Fey?" Corrine said in shock.

He shushed her. "I asked if you had learned something from the letters. Have you or have you not?"

"I . . . suppose," she said, not sure what he wanted her to say.

"Then you know or can guess of what I speak. The Fey are real, Corrine. And they are relentless. Surely you know that by now." And a strange look came on his face that reminded Corrine of the amber-eyed woman.

"You knew in your heart these letters were not just fairy tales. Why else would you have been drawn to steal them? They are real. Angus and Brighde were real. And their tale should be a lesson to all of us. The Fey are not to be meddled with."

Before she could say anything, Mara spoke from the door. "Miz Corrine," she said. "Your room is ready. You're to go there now."

Corrine nodded.

"Thank you," she said to Father Joe. She handed the handkerchief back to him.

"Keep it," he said, closing her fingers over it. There was sadness in his smile, a sadness that made her wonder if this was how angels smiled at mortals, with the knowledge of dust and eternity behind their eyes. "Let us hope that all will be well."

Corrine didn't have the heart to say that she thought that was a false hope. "Let us hope," she said.

~ Twenty-One ~

November 10, 1865

It was the third day of what Corrine had come to think of as her incarceration. She had spent most of it daydreaming of Rory and studying French, to little avail. She had become used to the routine of Mara bringing her bread and water three times a day, removing and returning the chamber pot. The stench of her own bodily emanations sickened her, and the room was colder than even her attic room, as there was no stove or fireplace here. She wore her coat at all times.

On the scarred table, a French poem sat before her, its words nearly as incomprehensible as the fairy note had been at first. Madame DuBois was to come in and give her an examination on it later that day. Since Corrine normally relied on Christina to help her, translating an entire poem on her own seemed a marvelous feat that she could not imagine performing.

Si jamais il y eut plus clairvoyant qu'Ulysse,
Il n'aurait jamais pu prévoir que ce visage,
Orné de tant de grâce et si digne d'hommage,
Devienne l'instrument de mon affreux supplice.

"Something about Ulysses being clairvoyant?" Corrine said to herself. The French words were just close enough to English to confuse her. She sighed and looked at the door. Madame DuBois would be coming soon; she could hear the sounds of girls out in the play yard, and the teachers normally visited her when they had no other students.

The door opened. Madame DuBois swept in, her eyes as red-rimmed as ever, her blowsy hair done up in a loose bun. Corrine still could not reconcile the wild-eyed woman who'd accosted her in the tavern with Falston's French teacher. Taffeta rustled ominously as Madame DuBois seated herself. She looked at the paper on the table.

"What have you completed?" she asked.

Corrine stared down at the inscrutable poem. The words all ran together. "It's—is it about Ulysses?"

She glanced at Madame DuBois's face, saw it twitch as though the woman might either laugh or groan.

"No," she said.

Madame DuBois read the first stanza in mellifluous French. Corrine felt herself shrinking into her chair. She wished she could become as tiny as a dust mote and sink straight through the floorboards into the dark, forgiving earth.

"Can't you feel this poem?" Madame DuBois said. "It was written by Louise Labe to her lover."

"And he traveled like Ulysses?" Corrine ventured.

Madame DuBois muttered something to herself in French. Then she translated:

Not Ulysses, no, nor any other man
however astute his mind, ever longed for
that holy face shaded with grace, honor,
respect, more than I sigh for you. Nor can

I turn my gaze, Love, from your handsome eyes,
which wound me deeply in my innocent chest;
and though I have food, warmth, and tenderest
relief, without your hand all my hope dies.

Corrine tried to make sure her mouth was closed. It was as though the poet had looked in her heart and seen what she could barely acknowledge, her feelings for Rory. And she had written it all down, for everyone to know and feel.

"I cannot examine you on this," Madame DuBois said. "It is obvious you do not know it."

But Corrine was thinking that she knew it all too well. She looked down at the paper, unwilling to see the disdain in Madame DuBois's eyes. Something slid into her vision. A card, on which lightning cleaved a great manor in half. Tiny people—women with trailing hair, demons with pitchforks, ascending angels—rained through the air. *La Tour* was inscribed at the bottom.

Corrine looked up.

"Unless you stop this madness, destruction will come for all of us," Madame DuBois said. She held Corrine's eyes for one more moment before rising and going to the door, her taffeta train hissing behind her.

"What do you mean?" Corrine asked.

The teacher paused at the door, glaring at Corrine with those disturbing eyes. She glanced at the card again and swept out of the room.

Corrine sat still, watching the manor catching fire, hearing the silent thunder. The World card with its serpent had been a warning, a warning that she had not heeded. She thought of the golden serpent and shuddered. Clearly, Madame DuBois was expecting her to stop her dealings with the Fey. But why should Corrine listen to her? Madame DuBois had been there on Hallowe'en, with Miss Brown and Mara. *Without your hand, all my hope dies.* She thought of Rory. There was no one else to trust and no one else to believe.

That evening, Miss Brown herself came to release Corrine from isolation.

"I trust you've had some time to think, Corrine," she said. "In the meantime, know that the locks on all the doors have been changed, including your own. There will be no further midnight excursions. If you are caught outside again, I'm afraid we will have to resort to much sterner measures than this. I hope this was enough."

Corrine nodded. She knew what she had to do. She had made her peace with the fact that it might entail much more artifice than her mother would have liked.

Miss Brown looked at her with concern, as though she was unsure whether to believe that Corrine would hold to the proper path. She patted her on the shoulder, and for the first time, Corrine wondered if, in fact, Miss Brown felt an affection for her that she was reluctant to show. Perhaps Miss Brown had neither given nor received affection, no matter how she felt, in a long time. This made Corrine feel guilty, but she pushed the guilt back with the knowledge that what she did would ultimately free Miss Brown from whatever evil spell held her. Of that, Corrine was convinced.

Corrine's return to the supper table was met largely with silence, except for giggles and whispers between Melanie and Dolores, of course. The others would not look at her or speak to her, especially those who had been caught with her in the barn. Ilona wouldn't even make room for Corrine to sit, so Corrine went to the end of the table closest to the teachers where the little girls sat. She ate in silence, looking only at her plate. If this was the way of it, then so be it. She could work better alone anyway.

She did not volunteer for sewing after supper, but went straight to her room. Mara hauled in a fresh load of coal and made a new fire for her. She did not speak to Corrine, as she had not for the last three days. Her occasional glance dared Corrine to say anything. After Mara left, Corrine studied French listlessly, wondering how she would ever get through it without Christina's help. She went to the window, watching the night creep up through the forest.

Still not quite warm, she wrapped her blanket around her, coat and all, and lay down as near to the stove as possible. In the middle of the night, the heat drove her to roll away in her sleep. She half-woke when she realized that she had rolled up against the far wall.

The cold seeped into her back and galloped up her neck and across her face. Darkness stole her sight. But this time, Corrine did not see through Jeanette's eyes.

Corrine saw Jeanette from above, struggling with the man. He dragged her just a little farther over the lip of a dell, and Jeanette's struggles ceased.

A tree in the center of the dell reached toward the moon like an ivory tower. Lights hovered and buzzed around it, as though the stars had come to dance in its branches. Jeannette ran forward, entranced. The man did not follow. And then the lights stilled their shimmering dance. As one they turned and swarmed down like hornets, a torrent of toothed light aimed at Jeanette. Corrine knew Jeanette was too enchanted to move. The hornet lights stung and entered Jeanette's flesh until she screamed; then she and her tormentors were invisible. She was there. And then she was not. Her scream still echoed.

The tree went dark. The familiar form of the Captain stepped out of the shadows. He strode toward the man who had brought Jeanette to the tree, whose back was turned to Corrine. He put his hand upon the man's head, forcing him to kneel, as Corrine had seen him do to Melanie and Miss de Mornay.

In sheer terror, she pulled herself away from the wall. She stood, shedding her blanket and coat, and went to the window. The Captain was there, closer than she'd ever seen him to the iron fence. The gleaming mist whirled around him like a tornado, and in the mist-light she could see a small figure, reaching up to hold his hand. He lifted his other hand to Corrine, and though she was high above him, she could see his scarlet palm in the ghastly light.

Bring the girl to me.

She thought of Penelope again, saying how "the fairies" had tried to steal her away, how Rory had saved her from them. She looked closer at the figure reaching for the Captain's hand, and stark recognition horrified her.

The ghostlight whirled up into the sky, and the Captain and Penelope disappeared.

"No!" she said, putting her fists to the glass. "Penelope!"

She turned and saw the dusty bell pull hanging on the wall, the one that was only to be used during the direst emergencies. She ran to it, ready to pull it as hard as she could. And then she realized that no one would come. This was what the Captain had asked of the witches. They had given him Penelope as they had given him Jeanette and others she probably did not know about. There was no one to help.

She went back to the window and stared out at the stillness. She wondered what she would do now that she knew what had happened to Jeanette, now that she had seen Penelope taken by the Captain. She knew that no one would ever believe what she had to tell. Or worse, they would not care. Tomorrow, she would get the stone.

~ Twenty-Two ~

November 11, 1865

WHISPERS RIPPLED THROUGH THE PEWS AT MORNING MASS discussing Penelope's disappearance. Shortly thereafter, Rory and Father Joe went to Culpeper to seek help in searching for her. Melanie feigned sorrow at breakfast, laying her hand over her heart and declaring what a precious child Penelope had been.

Ilona peeled her egg with shaking fingers, and Corrine gritted her teeth as she watched from down the table, praying that Melanie would not provoke Ilona into hitting her again. But for once, Melanie seemed to sense that no one would rise to her taunts, and she finished her breakfast primly, content as a kitten.

As had become the norm since the last botched Society meeting, no one spoke to Corrine throughout classes. When she turned to go to the library for recess, she was surprised when Ilona followed her a few steps down the hall.

"Corrine." The tall girl fidgeted, and Corrine could not shake the image of her in armor with a sword in her hand. Her pinafore and dress seemed ridiculous by comparison.

"Listen, Ilona," she said. "About that night, I—"

"It is enough. Let us not talk more about it." Ilona turned

toward the corridor to go outside, as though someone might discover her talking to Corrine.

"I never meant for anything to happen. You don't believe that I did this, do you?" She paused to clear her throat, which had gone very dry. "Because it's not like Christina said."

Ilona stepped a little closer. She said in a low, careful voice. "I believe you. I know that Penelope is not your fault. I believe that you are very stupid and very innocent. I believe you think you know what is happening here, but you don't. None of us should. The best thing is to just get through this. Alive."

"Ilona—"

"If you want to be my friend again, you must do this. No more silly plots. No witches. No fairies. No spirits or stones. Understand? If you want to survive here, promise me that you'll just get through this."

Ilona's eyes were round and wet, as though she was holding back tears. "Otherwise, you might be the next one," she whispered.

Corrine thought about last night's vision of Jeanette. "I know what happened to Jeanette," she whispered. "That man took her—"

Ilona leaped at her, took Corrine's upper shoulders in her great hands and shook her. "Be quiet! Do you hear?" she said, her voice grating. "If you want to live, please be quiet!" She pushed Corrine away from her and ran outside.

Corrine stared after her. This had to end. Quietly or no, she had to end it.

Father Joe came in from outdoors, looking ruffled from his ride. "Corrine?" he said. "I just saw Ilona. Is she well?"

"I think so, Father," Corrine said. She did not like how natural it was becoming for her to lie.

"Ah." He turned to go toward Miss Brown's study, but then turned back. "You will return those last two letters soon?" he said. His stare pinned her like a butterfly to a board.

"Yes, Father," she said.

"Good," he said. He hurried away and Corrine continued to the library, but she felt his presence in her spine all the way down the hall.

Later that evening, after she had washed up and was about to return downstairs for supper, Corrine remembered Father Joe's request and set about searching for the letters. But they were nowhere to be found. Her pinafore from yesterday—it was gone. Washing day. Siobhan must have taken her dirty clothes either to the laundry room or to the room she shared with Mara. Siobhan and Mara were serving supper now. This was probably the only opportunity she'd have.

She finished tidying herself and walked downstairs at a normal pace, hoping that the Moray Eel wasn't lurking at the bottom of the stairs to point the girls in the direction of the dining room. She felt it a stroke of luck, some kind of sign, when de Mornay wasn't by the newel post. All the other girls crowded out of their doors. Corrine slipped quietly among them, and then slowed until she reached the back of the line. She ducked around the corner and into the converted parlor as quickly as she could.

The servants, Corrine thought, as she entered their tiny room with its high window, had just the opposite problem of the school's boarders. At least, with the enforced evening curfew, the students did not have to anticipate unwanted visitors or attention after lockdown. In this room, however, Mara and Siobhan couldn't lock anyone out. They had no privacy whatsoever. As she crossed the floor, Corrine twitched when the floorboards protested.

The clothes were, as she had guessed, in a small pile of laundry at the foot of Siobhan's bed. Corrine found the letters easily and placed them in her pinafore pocket.

Twilight was edging in, and she would be missed at supper if she didn't hurry. Her gaze traveled over Mara's bed, and the scarred wardrobe the two servants shared. On the washstand, she saw a bent, withered corn dolly, reminding her of the black flannel voodoo doll. It seemed unlikely to her that Mara would keep the stone here. *It can't hurt to look, though,* Corrine thought.

She crept toward the wardrobe, trying and failing to think of a good excuse for doing this in case she got caught. She would just have to do this fast. The wardrobe doors were the first problem. They were sticky and she had to force them with all her wiry strength. And suddenly, they popped open like a shot. She caught her breath for a few moments, before feeling along the top shelf. She leaned in and breathed the scents of old cedar and well-worn clothes tainted with a whiff of onion. She felt along the boards beneath the clothes, seeking any irregular cracks. Nothing. She closed the doors and looked in the drawers.

At last, in the back corner of the top drawer, she uncovered something strange. Beneath a pair of old bloomers was a small box surrounded by dried herbs and sigils made of thorns. She opened the box, which was carved with a large pentagram. Indeed, inside was the stone Mara had held during the Hallowe'en ceremony. Surprisingly, it was simply a pocked pebble, like every other piece of gravel or river stone. She had expected that it would look like the stone she had taken at Uncle William's. As she picked it up, she felt a powerful prickling in her hand, as though she'd suddenly been afflicted with poison ivy. She put the stone in her pocket, rearranged the bloomers over the box, and shut the drawer. She left the room, trying to not to feel the burning itch beginning in her palm.

~ Twenty-Three ~

November 25, 1865

Despite all attempts, no trace of Penelope was found. A few days passed while Miss Brown waited for some word from Penelope's mother, but none ever came. Father Joe held a memorial mass for her on the following Sunday. Corrine and Ilona knelt side by side. And while Ilona wept, Corrine couldn't. Her eyes remained dry and gritty, and she stared at the serpent tempting Eve with revulsion. The witches had let the Captain take those girls away. Their power had to be broken. And as she clasped her itching palms together, she knew she could do it.

Inclement weather caused recess to be held indoors for a couple weeks, and Corrine was unable to signal Rory that she had procured the stone. She had not seen him since Hallowe'en, and though she considered climbing off the roof and taking the stone to his cottage, she feared her aching palms wouldn't allow it. On the first night with the stone, she had scratched her palms so hard they bled, and she had been hiding her hands as much as possible to keep Mara from seeing them. She didn't know how she would fare if she tried to climb down the pipe. The notion of another fall did not sit well with her.

Mara watched everyone even more carefully than usual, and Corrine walked on eggshells wondering how she would keep the stone hidden from the sharp-eyed girl or her dark magic for much longer.

At last on Thanksgiving, the gloomy weather broke. A longer recess was held before the sermon and then dinner that would follow. Mara and Siobhan, and even Madame DuBois, were occupied with fixing the school's version of a Thanksgiving feast. At recess, Corrine sneaked to the iron fence and with trembling, burning hands managed to tie her handkerchief around the bars.

The sermon after recess was long and drowsy. Corrine felt the sparkling in her spine only once when Father Joe looked at her as he praised the unity of the nation. "And though," Father Joe concluded, "this day was first meant as a day of fasting and prayer, let us also keep it in celebration and joy for the continued healing of our great nation." Corrine heard some snorts; she guessed Melanie and Dolores were not pleased with the thought.

But Thanksgiving dinner at Falston was all Ilona had intimated it would be and more. Corrine supposed that because Father Joe had given a special sermon the women felt compelled to cook especially for him. There were, in fact, two turkeys; their aroma had been taunting Corrine since her meager breakfast early that morning. The sideboard was loaded with mashed pumpkin, beans cooked with salt pork, mashed potatoes with giblet gravy, and the cherished Indian pudding. Corrine's mouth watered when she discovered a steaming pie made with wizened apples that Mara was rumored to have charmed or frightened out of the storekeeper in Culpeper. A jar of pickled eggs stood on the teachers' table, for which Corrine yearned, but they stayed right where they were and were mostly consumed by Father Joe.

Due to the plentiful food, the girls served themselves from the sideboard under Miss Brown's watchful eye. Dolores was of course the first to be admonished for taking more than her share. As the serving spoon made its fourth trip from the beans to her plate, Miss Brown said, "Dolores . . ." and the girl slammed the spoon back into its pot and marched to her bench, grumbling. Corrine was surprised to see Miss Brown smile as she passed. She returned the smile hesitantly, wondering if Miss Brown thought her finally reformed.

She settled herself at the bench and leaned toward her plate. A shadow loomed over her and dropped a white cloth in her food. She recognized the little yellow flowers embroidered in the corner. Her handkerchief. The one she had tied on the fence.

Melanie arched over the table menacingly. "I'd reckon being found out by Miss de Mornay and Miss Brown once would be enough for you, little dunce-girl," Melanie said. She bent closer. "But perhaps not. I promise I can do much worse." Corrine kept her eyes on the handkerchief, watching as the brown food stains slowly rose up through the white linen. She knew it would go extremely ill with her if Melanie ever found out that Corrine had seen her in the grove, or that she suspected Melanie had aided in Penelope's disappearance. And if Melanie learned Rory had kissed her . . .

"Melanie!" she heard Madame DuBois call. Melanie backed slowly away, smiling sweetly though her gaze was full of poison.

Corrine caught Ilona looking at her sidelong. She didn't know what to say, and de Mornay was looking in her direction anyway, so she concentrated on her plate. She removed the gravy-soaked handkerchief and wadded it into a ball, laying it beside her on the bench.

After a few moments of silently passing fork to mouth, she

heard Ilona whisper, "What have you done now?"

A couple of the other little girls looked at her. Christina was on the other side of the room, laughing at something one of Melanie's friends had said. She no longer spoke to Corrine, though she did not participate—at least not directly, as far as Corrine knew—in any of the hostilities Melanie and her friends liked to visit upon Corrine.

"Nothing," Corrine said.

"Then why did she just drop a handkerchief in your food?"

"She just thinks I'm trying to take Rory from her for some reason." Much as it was killing her to maintain her silence, she knew it was the only way to do what had to be done. Corrine continued, "I must have dropped it outside and she got the notion that I left it there for him on purpose. I don't know."

Clearly, Ilona didn't believe her. "Be careful," she said. "Melanie has had her eye on him for quite a while."

"Guess he's really the only man around," Corrine said.

"There is Father Joe," Ilona said, her mouth crinkling in the beginning of a smile.

"I suppose," Corrine said, smiling back. "I wonder . . ." she said, lowering her voice and sliding a little closer to Ilona. "Do you think Father Joe has ever been in love?"

"You are wicked," Ilona said, smiling and pushing at her arm. "He is a priest."

Corrine thought about the woman with the amber eyes. "Still, surely he has loved someone, don't you think?"

They looked at him, talking in a low voice to Miss Brown across the mound of turkey. "Perhaps," Ilona said. "Perhaps he does even now."

"Is that why Miss Brown isn't married?" Corrine asked.

Ilona chuckled. "Corrine, you are truly wicked."

Corrine grinned. For the rest of the meal, they discussed the possible romantic lives of priests. And when Ilona asked Corrine to play hearts with her afterward, Corrine did not say no.

November 26, 1865

Corrine had passed the city gates, the dusty, glittering streets. She moved up the dais now, to the beautiful face eternally shadowed, eternally weeping tears of blood. Something burned in her hand and when she looked down, she could see straight through flesh, bone, and blood to the hectic star clasped in her fingers. No more a pebble, but a hot diamond, which stilled the eerie waltz and made the silence roar in her ears. The silence grew its own rhythm, barely perceptible until she felt her heart beating in time to it.

She was at the throne. She held her hand out to him, the prince of shadows. His chest opened to her. She watched her hand put the diamond-heart in it. The rhythm became stronger, coercing oaken ribs to close over the spot. Ivy and hemlock flesh followed. He pushed himself from the throne, and she turned in time to the thundering heartbeat. She could not see him, but she felt his hand like living wood on the back of her neck.

He held her so that she could watch. Her forehead burned with the mark of his kiss. Slowly, the cobweb glamour that she had seen before melted. Masks collapsed like brittle cocoons. Tattered vines and withered flowers fell from the dancers' agate eyes. Some of them fell under the weight of rotting moss, once a gown of the most exquisite silk or a suit of fine velvet. Wood creaked and broke, bowed as though under an ice storm. In the end, only a few broken wooden skeletons jerked to a screeching waltz. The sulfurous decay of peat clutched at Corrine's nose until she was gasping for breath. The prince's wooden fingers curled just where her head joined her spine, casually poised as if to snap her neck. His fingers sank through her, roots and tendrils questing behind her eyes.

See now . . . *his fingers said.*

The rhythm of his heart spread from where it contained the two of them, reordering the waltz, making the music warm and resonant. Dancers rose from the dead with new coats of flesh, new gowns, and even more grotesque masks. Then, they turned and looked at her, and came toward her, their gleaming, new eyes upon her. She was among them, and his hand was no longer at her neck. Thank you, Corrine, *he said. He knelt, and she felt a numb pain against her wrist. Blood trickled into her palm, turning her hand as red as the Captain's. Then she looked up and, as though her thought had called him, the Captain stood before her, his cloaked form shimmering with heat. She still could not see his eyes, but she saw him smile. He had thorns for teeth.*

She sat up in bed, hitting her head violently against the sloping ceiling. She fumbled out from beneath her blankets and sat on the edge of her cot, breathing hard. "This has to end," she said out loud. "Now." She dressed quickly, scrambling into her boots and coat. She fished the stone out of her pinafore and placed it in her coat pocket, her palms throbbing. Pain or not, she was climbing down. She pushed up the window sash, crawled across the roof, and began the descent.

She reached the ground and made for Rory's cabin, kicking up the most recent snow in little white puffs before her. She knocked several times, but his cottage remained dark and silent. She felt the indecency of it—a young girl knocking on a man's door in the middle of the night—and shame burned her cheeks. What was she to do now?

She turned and leaned against the wall of his cabin looking out at the night. In the distance, she heard great horned owls calling across the hill. She remembered times when she and her father had gone out in the winter to hoot them up, listening to their eerie calls in the stillness of midnight.

The moon appeared through restless, scudding clouds. She looked across the grounds, half-afraid that she would see the

Captain waiting for her. Just as she began to wonder if she should return to her room and try again another night, a pinprick of light near the barn caught her eye. Perhaps there was some trouble with one of the barn animals? She hurried across the snow, the cold seizing her legs through her stockings.

The lantern hung on the outer barn post, flickering low in the stillness. She stepped inside and listened. She heard a rustling and a faint giggle from the back of the barn. Perhaps the Society was meeting. If she went to talk to them, if she showed them the stone, maybe then they'd believe her. Even if she didn't find Rory tonight, at least she could try to win back Christina's regard.

She took the lantern from the outer post. She crept through the barn as quietly as she could, listening for the next giggle to lead her to the proper stall. As she neared the back of the barn, it sounded as though the giggling was coming from above, up in the hayloft. She shuttered the lantern and climbed the loft ladder as silently as she could, hoping to surprise the girls and perhaps make them laugh.

As she emerged into the hayloft, she threw the shutter open and almost dropped the lantern at what she saw. Melanie and Rory lay entwined in a nest of hay. Melanie's nightgown was pushed off her shoulders. As the light fell on him, Rory lifted from her exposed throat. The look he turned on Corrine was truly the only thing that saved Corrine from dropping the lantern. His face was so twisted by vice and derision that she hardly recognized him. She hurried back down the ladder.

"Corrine!" he shouted, coming after her. She made it to the floor and began to run. But he was faster and leaped straight to the ground from the hayloft like a cat. She had only a moment to notice that his limp was gone before she tripped over a pitchfork handle and nearly fell. He caught her, closing his hand over hers on the lantern handle.

She glimpsed the curve of his triumphant smile, but could not look at him.

"Best not to drop this, lass," he said. "Could start a nasty fire. Someone could get hurt."

That drew her, chilled by the implications of his voice. His eyes said he would certainly do what he promised, if she did not cooperate.

"What are you doing here?" she said. "With her!" She was appalled as the sobs came.

"Melanie? She's nothing to me, Corrine," he said. And she wanted to believe him, except for the truth she had already seen in his eyes.

Melanie had come down the ladder. When she heard this, she shouted, "Rory, you no-good son of a—You take her to the Captain now, and bring back John like you promised!"

But Rory ignored her, focusing on Corrine.

"Nothing, Corrine," he said. He looked deeply in her eyes and she heard him mumble something—a soft, cloudy word that made her feel strange, almost sleepy.

"Do you have the stone now?" he said.

"Yes," she said, in spite of herself.

"Good. Our friends will be pleased."

But then Melanie was on him, beating at him. He turned. He said a harsh word, something Corrine couldn't make out—all consonants and rough clicks—and spat on her. Melanie slumped to the floor.

He turned back to Corrine, still holding his hand over hers. The lantern light swung between them, promising an inferno with its dance.

"Corrine," he said. "The stone."

"But she said—you—you would have given me to the Captain?"

"No," he said, his voice taking on a strangely familiar

cadence, like a long-unremembered heartbeat. "No, that isn't your fate, lass. I wouldn't have it so."

"Then, what?"

"This is all part of the witches' magic. Making you see the worst in me. There is only one way to break their power, Corrine. Give me the stone."

She wanted to say no, but she felt a warm drift of air, like a sleepy summer afternoon creeping around her father's barn. She could smell the hay, the grain in the bins, the clover fields beyond the door. Milkweed seeds drifted like white feathers.

And then his hand was in her coat pocket and the stone was in his hand. He winced, ending her dream.

"Thank you, Corrine," he said, tying the stone into a handkerchief. "Without you, this never could have been." He kissed her—a hard, ruthless kiss that spun her until she felt a stall door against her back.

He was gone.

She tried to catch her breath. Corrine went to where Melanie lay on the cold floor, set the lantern down, and shook her.

"Melanie," she said.

Melanie rose on her elbows, and then slowly pushed herself to a sitting position.

"Melanie, are you—"

Before she could finish, Melanie's palm struck her mouth into silence. "Don't speak to me, you Yankee whore!" she said, her voice low and venomous as always. "You may have given him one thing he wanted, but he'd never want *you*."

"Melanie, what have you done?" Corrine said. Her jaw throbbed.

"What I had to," the girl said, refusing Corrine's help to stand.

"But why?" Corrine said. "You gave Penelope to the witches? Why?"

"The witches? I don't know what you're talking about. The Fey wanted the girl. It was the only way to bring John back," Melanie said. Her face rippled as if she would cry, but she reined herself in. "And I will do anything to bring him back. Do you understand?"

Corrine could not help but feel pity for the girl. Melanie must have loved John Pelham indeed, and seen Rory as her only means of regaining the life she'd hoped for with the Boy Major. But she'd sacrificed an innocent little girl in the process. And what did she mean when she said the Fey wanted the girl? What about the Captain?

"Melanie—"

"Don't speak to me, damn it!" Melanie patted her hair and arranged her nightgown carefully. "You will pay for this like you've never paid for anything in your life."

Corrine remembered the vision of phantom hounds chasing a terrified and helpless Melanie across an unearthly green meadow.

"So will you," she said softly.

Melanie grabbed her and pushed her into the barn wall, grinning triumphantly before stalking out of the barn and into the cold night.

Corrine slumped to the floor by the lantern and wept.

~ Twenty-Four ~

November 26, 1865

Corrine did not move when she heard the footsteps coming across the snow, nor even when the footsteps came into the barn. She half-hoped that it was the Captain, that he and all the witches, if there were any, would come end her life. Rory and the Fey had betrayed her. They'd manipulated her all along. Even if Miss de Mornay came, she would seem like a gnat in comparison to that horrible fact.

"Corrine!"

Father Joe. She curled tighter around herself, hating the hope that sprang and died at her core. Even now, she still wished that Rory would return.

Father Joe took her shoulders and pulled her upright. "Corrine," he said again. He brushed a hand through her hair, and the gesture, so reminiscent of her father, undid her. He held her while she sobbed.

"Come with me," he said.

He lifted the lantern and led her out into the snow to his cottage. A fire danced in the grate in his sitting room. He helped her into an easy chair near it. The room smelled of leather and cigar smoke and applewood burning on the hearth.

He went to a sideboard and she heard him pouring

something into two glasses. He returned and handed one of the glasses to her. The smell of whiskey stung her nose.

"Father?" she said uncertainly.

"Medicinal," he said. "To calm the nerves."

She took a tiny sip, her eyes watering. It stung all the way to her stomach, as though she'd swallowed the stone Rory had just taken away.

"Now," he said, after she'd handed the glass back to him. "Why did I find you, despite all of Miss Brown's warnings and punishment, huddled on the barn floor after midnight?"

Corrine sat in her silence, the whiskey burning pleasantly in her belly.

"And why did I run into Melanie, storming back toward the manor like Medusa herself? I feared that I'd be turned to stone with the look she gave me!"

"Father, I think I may have done something very bad," Corrine said.

"Let me judge that," he said. "Tell me."

And so she told him, from the beginning. Some of it, especially at the beginning, she could see that he already knew. The rest of it . . . Despite the whiskey, she gripped the arms of the chair as though bracing herself for a blow.

At last, he said, "And he took the stone from you? You are certain of that?"

"Yes," Corrine said. "He took it from my coat pocket, after he said a—a spell . . . or something . . . to take it from me." She fought not to cry again, not to blubber on about how she hadn't known he would betray her. She knew it would do no good.

"Corrine," he said, "what you have done is very serious. You have put the entire school in mortal danger, including yourself."

"But Rory said that . . ."

"Need I remind you to whom you owe your present circumstances?" Father Joe said. "It's time for truth, on all our parts. And I believe you have told me your truth. Now, let me tell you mine.

"I am a good deal older than you would ever guess. I will not tell you what I am, nor how I came to be that way. Suffice it to say I have fought the Unhallowed Fey for most of my life at the behest of the Elder Fey, those we call the Hallowed Ones. The Unhallowed were once like their siblings, spirits of the natural world who filled it with beauty and goodness. Like us, they were mortal, though they lived ages beyond our normal lifespan. But the Unhallowed turned from the ways of their brethren and became corrupted by their lust for immortality and power, and now their dealings with humankind involve nothing but treachery. The Hallowed Fey, the Elders, have little to do with the human world these days.

"I am a member of the Council of Elaphe, a secret society that keeps the Unhallowed Fey from taking control of all Fey lands—raths, they call them—and mortal lands too. The stones you have taken are keys to these raths, necessary elements in the schemes of the Unhallowed. With it, they will further their push to control all raths and bring mortals completely under their sway."

It was too much to contemplate all at once. Though Corrine had experienced so much strangeness and horror in the past several months, she wrestled with the notion that what Father Joe said was true, that everything she thought she knew had been turned on its head.

He must have guessed at the thoughts behind her expression for he said, "The Unhallowed are very real, Corrine, and they are extremely dangerous. All the stories you've ever heard about evil fairies, about bogeymen in the dark, about spirits whisking off children in the night—they all are true. These are all the workings of the Unhallowed Fey, who learned long ago that drinking mortal blood would grant them the immortality they sought. The red-handed man you have seen—he is Captain of the Unhallowed army. He has the power to go where the prince cannot."

"But the Fey said that the Captain served the witches!" Corrine said.

Father Joe shook his head. "One thing you will learn about the Unhallowed is that they are adept at telling half-truths. What they told you was somewhat true. The Captain once served a Fey witch named Leanan, but she has given him command over the prince's armies now." The witch's name elicited a desolate look on Father Joe's face. He sipped at his whiskey to hide it.

"The prince . . ." Corrine said, almost to herself. There was still something about the prince's sadness that undid her, something about the way he said her name . . .

"The Fey Prince is perhaps the most dangerous of the Unhallowed, but he is also—or was—the weakest. He seduced you into giving him the stone in your dreams, did he not?"

Corrine nodded. "He made me feel—I mean—I thought that I was helping to heal him and that somehow made it seem right, in the dreams."

"And Rory made it seem right in real life by telling you that you could save Falston from evil witches single-handedly," Father Joe said. He took off his spectacles and polished them with an edge of his cassock. It was as though a glamour had torn away. The prickling in Corrine's spine became a burning. She glimpsed him looking up into the woman's face, the one whose golden hair was like a net of sunlight.

"You are one of them," she said. "You are Fey."

His fingers abruptly halted their circling motions. He held his spectacles carefully by the wire rims. "No," he said. His voice was edged, daring her to cut herself further on the truth. "I told you. We will not discuss my past. Let it be enough that

I know more than anyone living about the Fey."

Corrine considered probing further, but his gaze made her refrain.

"Corrine, one of the most important lessons you have to learn in life is who to trust. What was trustworthy about Rory?"

"He knew what he was talking about. He saved me from the ghost and that copperhead." She would not say, *His eyes, his smile—of course you trust those you love.* "And he gave me this," she said, fumbling the locket out from under her collar and pulling it over her head.

Father Joe set his spectacles on a sidetable and took the locket from her.

"It's a locket I lost when I was sick. It has pictures of my father and mother."

Father Joe said a few words over the locket. It shimmered and melted into a collection of mouse bones, bits of moss, and twisted wire. He looked up at her. "This is what he gave you."

Corrine stared at the remains of the locket, horrified.

"And on Hallowe'en night, he brought you a gift, didn't he—a box of unearthly delights that you shared with the entire school?"

Corrine felt her face flushing with more than the whiskey. "I just asked because—"

"Even I was fooled by the glamour. We all thought it was a present from your uncle, until Siobhan saw it for what it truly was."

"Siobhan—how does she know these things?"

"She has what some would call a gift of Sight. But doubtless most of us would find it a torment," he said. "No glamour can shield the truth from her."

"She tried to tell me, but I wouldn't believe her," Corrine said. "She was so cryptic."

"Of course you didn't," Father Joe said. "This," he said, throwing the bones and wire into the grate, "kept you from it."

"And Rory?" she asked.

"And Rory. Did you never wonder why he was always present wherever you were? Or why he was always about the grounds at all hours of the night? Did you never see him as a possible threat?"

"No." Corrine was getting angry. "No, but if he was such a threat, then why didn't the school do something about him? Why did you let him stay around instead of just telling me not to talk to him? You made it seem like *I* was the danger, when it was him all along!"

"Rory's family owns much of this county and has the sheriffs of two towns in their pockets. We were never certain if Rory was in league with the Unhallowed or operating on his own. We were hoping that Melanie would soon tell us—"

"Melanie?" Corrine said. "You were using Melanie as bait to lure in these evil—fairies?" She could not help herself. "And you think *I* was acting dangerously?"

"In this battle, you use every asset available. I am sorry to say so, but it is the truth. Melanie agreed to help us at first. She had certain talents that were useful in this case. But over time it became clear that Melanie was too swayed by her emotions. We could not trust her to help us. When we lost Jeanette last spring, we realized that we could not use the girls to further our aims. Melanie acts on her own now."

"What happened to Jeanette? I need to know the truth. No one will tell me."

"She lived in the room next to yours. And like you, she was fond of exploring. We still do not know how she got out of her room at night"—he looked at Corrine pointedly—"but we know that she disappeared last spring around the first of May. We think that Rory brought Jeanette to the Unhallowed as tribute, but we cannot prove it. Her body was never found."

The man in the visions, Corrine thought. *That was Rory?* Her heart hurt as she drowned in information. All that she had so carefully been trying to discover was now pouring out on her in a torrent. The Unhallowed Fey, the Hallowed, the raths—she did not know how to absorb it all. Jeanette and now Penelope must have died horribly at the hands of the Unhallowed. Melanie's case also concerned her, since the Council had apparently used and discarded her. She wondered if she was in danger of the same fate.

"And so now that I have given the Unhallowed the stone, will you also give me to them?" Corrine asked.

"We must seem ruthless to you," Father Joe said. "But we are not that ruthless. Melanie was a mistake I greatly regret now. As for Jeanette and Penelope—" He looked up at Corrine, transfixing her with a look that could have stopped Death in its tracks. "This is why we must stop them, Corrine. This is why the Council exists. To destroy the Unhallowed. We have watched and waited for far too long. Now is the time for action."

"And how do I fit into your schemes?" Corrine said, unable to keep the bitterness out of her voice. There were traps on every side now, and all she wanted to do was escape to her old life, back to the farm with its tall oaks and gentle breezes, with her parents and Nora and Willy and dear old Magellan.

"We are not yet certain." He gave her a long, measuring look. "You have caught the Prince's interest, and that is both dangerous and noteworthy. When did you first begin dreaming of him?"

Corrine thought back to her recovery at Uncle William's. "It all started with seeing my father," she said. She felt tender about admitting it, almost afraid that Father Joe would react as her uncle had.

"Your father?" Father Joe said. "Wasn't he killed in the War?"

"No," Corrine said, gritting her teeth. "He disappeared at the Battle of Petersburg."

"Disappeared?" Father Joe said. "Corrine, are you certain you saw him?"

"Yes," she said, fighting back indignation. "I saw him."

"Tell me what you saw."

Corrine described how she had seen him first on the road, then in her dreams. "It was then that the prince came to me," she said. "In a dream when both Father and I were being crushed in the earth."

"And have you seen your father again?" Father Joe said.

"I saw him the day I saw John Pelham," she said.

Father Joe grunted. He seemed to be thinking deeply about something, swirling the dark whiskey in slow circles, staring into it as though he searched there for answers.

"Do you know what's happened to him?"

"No," he said finally. "And I think you should not worry over it just now. You have much bigger problems. Your Uncle William tried to shield you for a long time, I think, but when you gave the stone he held to the Unhallowed Fey, it forced his hand. He sent you to Falston for protection, but it appears we have come very close to failing."

"My Uncle William? He wants to protect me?" she said, incredulous.

"He sensed that you were special. He also saw the Captain and knew that he had come for you. He knew he could not protect you by himself. When you gave the stone to the Unhallowed, it became a good, if unfortunate, excuse to send you here. We never imagined that you would take the stone we held here, as well!"

"So all this time, when everyone said I was lying or being 'fanciful,' you all knew I was telling the truth?" Corrine felt the tears coming again. This betrayal, heaped on top of Rory's, was too much to bear. "You let me think I was all alone in this?"

"Yes," Father Joe said. "I'm afraid so."

Her tears came again. Just this night, she had broken her old prohibition more times than she could count.

Father Joe sat forward in his seat, dug for a handkerchief, and very gently wiped the tears away from Corrine's face. "Perhaps, in my old age, I've forgotten the pain of youth. I know it will be difficult to trust us, Corrine, but you must. The Unhallowed want you and they will not stop until they get you. We will do all we can to protect you, if you will let us."

"How"—Corrine hiccuped—"how can I trust you now?"

"Because I am telling the truth and admitting that I did wrong." She heard him slide something from his pocket. "And I am giving you this." He laid it on her knees. A familiar book, bound with dark and light serpents, rested there. Its energy raced across her knees and up her spine. She wiped at the tears and touched the cover. It was as soft as suede. The serpents writhed under her hands, shifting position and eyeing her, but never losing their grip on each other's tails.

She started, but her fingers had already fallen in love with the book. She could not stop touching it.

"See if you can open it and read."

She slid her hand along the edge. Something pricked her; she felt stinging as though she'd brushed against nettles and was reminded of the way she'd felt after taking the stone from Mara's wardrobe. The book opened, choosing the page it wanted her to see. The words danced in front of her, as they had with the fairy note. She put a hand on the page to soothe them. It was like touching water without the wetness—a slick silk that pulled her hand deeper into its pages.

The first words swam up. *Let this be to the eyes who see it a history of the true Lords of the Earth, the rightful rulers of Hallowmere.*

"Hallowmere?" she said, looking up.

Father Joe's face held a triumphant smile that frightened her.

"Let us save that for another day," he said. "For now, it is enough to know that the book agrees with you."

Corrine nodded. She was tired and a chill sank in her bones that even the whiskey could not displace.

"I don't know how you are still getting out of the manor—" Father Joe began.

"I climb," Corrine said wearily. "Over the roof and down the drainpipe to the woodshed."

Father Joe looked at her in amazement. He swirled the rest of the whiskey in his glass and downed it.

"I don't have keys to the manor, so I shall make you a pallet here by the fire," he said. "I can escort you to mass in the morning and no one will be the wiser."

She nodded, too tired to climb anyway. He went into another room and she heard him rummaging in a chest for blankets. Corrine moved her hand to the book's cover and felt the serpents slide in protest.

Before he left her alone, he said, "That book is both precious and horrible to me. If you would judge the cruelty of the Unhallowed, know that this book is bound in human skin, the skin of the one who wrote the letters you have been reading. The Unhallowed are very displeased that this is in my possession. If you feel compelled to give it back to them, through dreams or other methods, please return it to me immediately. But for now, read and learn."

Corrine could only stare at him as he departed with the lantern into his bedroom, shutting the door behind him.

She smoothed her fingers in scintillating horror across its covers.

"Angus," she breathed.

~ Twenty-Five ~

November 27, 1865

The quality of the day seemed different to Corrine when she entered the classroom in the morning. She had stayed up for much of the night reading the curious book by the light of Father Joe's fire, and her eyes swam from focusing on the wavering words. That Father Joe would share such a book with her puzzled Corrine; it was obviously dangerous. It pulled her into its world and would not let her go, even more so than the letters of Angus to Brighde. The magic of it suffused her veins with a prickly shiver, like songs carved from ice. The logic of the Unhallowed fascinated her; their belief in their precedence over the human world reminded her very much of plantation holders from the old South. To the Unhallowed, she now understood, she was little more than livestock, a beast to be used, eaten, petted, or disposed of as they saw fit. Just as the Negroes had been. The new knowledge sickened her, but the powerful certainty of the voices compelled her. She needed to understand them.

Of course, there had been some things she could not read. There were things that were locked even from her eyes—spells perhaps, or darker, deeper secrets. She was unsure. The only thing she did know was that she longed for the key to unlock these mysteries, even as she knew she would probably never acquire it.

"Corrine." Ilona nudged her and made a small gesture in de Mornay's direction.

Corrine smiled her thanks and tried to focus on her notebook. But every now and then, her hand strayed to her pocket to stroke the incredible terror of the book's binding.

Corrine noticed that Dolores seemed more subdued than usual. As the day wore on, it became clear that this was because Melanie was nowhere to be found. The teachers tried to keep it as quiet as possible, announcing her disappearance only at dinnertime and only as part of a prayer that Melanie be restored to them. Corrine felt sure that she knew what had happened to her, but didn't dare to suggest it as the girls whispered over their bowls. All she could remember was Melanie leaning over her and hissing, "You will pay." If she had gone to the Unhallowed, Corrine could only imagine what that payment would be.

She was on her way to her room that evening when Mara stopped her. "You're wanted in the chapel room," she said. Her voice was flat and defiant—her normal tone. Her black eyes gave away nothing.

Corrine nodded, sure that Mara must know now that she had stolen the stone. She went down the hall to the chapel. Mara followed silently. When Corrine entered, she was surprised to see Miss Brown, Madame DuBois, and Father Joe all there, seated around a small table. Two chairs were empty.

"Ah, Corrine," said Miss Brown. "Welcome."

"Hello," she said uncertainly. She almost felt as though she should curtsy or something, but kept her hands by her sides and tried to seem small.

"Come sit," Father Joe said, indicating the chair next to him. The floor creaked as she crossed to him. Mara took the other chair.

After she was seated, but before she could ask why she had been called, Miss Brown spoke, "We call this meeting in the name of Elaphe to induct our new sister, Corrine Jameson, into the Council."

Corrine looked around the circle, trying to keep her mouth from dropping open.

Miss Brown continued, "We call this meeting in the name of Elaphe to persecute traitors and visit the justice of His law to the Unhallowed Fey."

Corrine shivered.

"Our sister Corrine unknowingly has given our greatest protection to the Unhallowed. Now we must use every means to get it back. Mara," she said, "please begin the ritual."

Mara eyed all of them, especially Corrine, with a piercing disregard. She wondered if Mara would ever be her friend, if Mara would ever forgive her for her unwitting transgression. She longed to apologize, and felt the words bubbling up in her throat, but the ritual tension in the room made her choose to remain silent.

"Bring me the coat you wore last night," Mara said to Corrine. "I need a hair, an eyelash, anything that belongs to Mr. Rory."

Corrine blushed.

"Anything to make the magic stronger," Mara said. She eyed Corrine dubiously, "Though there probably ain't much stronger than whatever mojo you got."

"What?" Corrine said.

"The bad root I put on that stone should've turned you beet red and covered you with boils for days. Someday you have to tell me how you got around it."

Corrine felt her blush deepening. Without answering, she turned and went up to her room to retrieve her coat.

When she brought it back, everyone had risen and pushed

the chairs back from the table. Several objects were spread across the table—a crystal ball; what looked like an assortment of bones; a chicken's foot bound in raven feathers with a leather cord; a bottle of yellow powder; a black candle; a spindly, dried plant; and the black flannel voodoo doll. It leaned against a crucible surrounded by bent nails, its red hand touching the table.

Corrine stared at the doll. "A binding root," Mara said.

Corrine's incredulity must have spread quickly to her face, for Mara said, "You thought it was a summons, didn't you?"

"They said he served the witch," Corrine whispered.

Mara shook her head. "Not this witch. Though to control something that powerful . . ." Corrine saw the girl shiver slightly, more with delight than fear.

Mara directed Corrine to spread the coat across the back of a pew, and then told her to hold a light close by. Mara ran her fingertips over the coat, dusting off flecks of dirt. The tips of her fingers made pink moons against the worn wool, and Corrine felt the familiar tingle of recognition, as though Mara was much more than a human girl who practiced hoodoo. Corrine was about to touch the girl and see if her theory was true. But at that moment, Mara plucked a dark hair from the fabric.

"Let's hope this don't be a horse's," she muttered.

"Why? What will it do?" Corrine said.

"Melt his bones to jelly," Mara said. "Or feel like it, leastways." She grinned. It was the first time Corrine had ever seen Mara smile. She wasn't sure she liked it.

As Mara carried the single, curling hair to the table, Corrine felt a strange sense of betrayal. These people were cursing Rory. If this was an even darker curse than that placed on the stone, if he was more helpless than she apparently was, then she could only imagine his suffering. Though he had betrayed her, even used spells to take the stone from her, she was not sure she could condone this kind of revenge magic. She could almost see her mother shaking her head sadly and reminding her that charity was the greater part of humanity.

"Wait," Corrine said.

Everyone stared at her.

"Is this really the best course?" Corrine asked. "I—I just—aren't we supposed to love our enemy?"

"Corrine," Miss Brown began. Her voice rose with impatience.

"Wait, Thea," Father Joe said, laying a hand on her elbow. "Corrine has the right to ask, and we must answer. After all, it is our fault that she is embroiled now in this struggle."

He came to Corrine, and she saw again that agelessness and kindness that made her long for her father. "I know what you have been taught, Corrine. And I believe it, all of it. I am a priest, after all! But the existence of the Unhallowed, their very nature, cannot be fought with noble human values. We must meet them on their ground. And that ground is magic."

"But Rory's not Unhallowed," Corrine said.

"No, but he is under their control. I have been trying to research his family bloodline. I believe they are tied to the Unhallowed Fey in some way, perhaps by a *geas,* a magical bond that forces them to serve the Fey. Even if that is not the case, we know that he is certainly under their protection. I cannot explain how important it is that the stone does not get into the hands of the Unhallowed. I'm afraid we must use any means necessary."

"Even if that means hurting him?" Just the faint promise of tears made Corrine's eyes sore.

"Even so," Father Joe said.

Corrine bowed her head.

Madame DuBois came then, crouching awkwardly in her swath of skirts so that she could look into Corrine's face.

"Corrine, we have lost too many people. First Jeanette,

Penelope, and now Melanie. We cannot afford to lose you, as well. If we do not curse Rory, if we do not get the stone back, we cannot protect you. Surely you would not choose the life of one who betrayed you over your own."

More of Louise Labe's poem echoed in Corrine's head. *Suffering the scorpion to feast on me, I seek protection . . . by appealing to the beast that stings me.*

She shook her head.

"Corrine," Madame DuBois said, "look at it this way. The curse will wear off when he returns the stone to us. If he gives it to the Unhallowed, then he could suffer an even worse fate at their hands."

Corrine thought of the skin-bound book and shivered. What Madame DuBois said made sense. And though Corrine felt the others shifting in impatience over her stubbornness, she wiped at her eyes and thought. It appeared that Rory was enslaved, bound by powers darker and stronger than she expected. Perhaps this little hurt now would turn him away from the darkness. She hated herself for the tiny voice within that said, *And I will see him again.*

"Remember the book?" Father Joe said softly, as if he knew what she was thinking. "They can devise worse than that, believe me."

He was about to say more, but Corrine stopped him.

"Yes, sir," she said. "I understand." Madame DuBois stood to her full height next to her.

"Hurry," Mara said. She was obviously displeased at Corrine's delaying the ritual.

A circle of salt had been sprinkled around the table. Corrine was given a candle and told to stand in a ring with the others for the duration of the ceremony. Madame DuBois went around the outer circle, lighting the candles with her own already-lit candle, while Mara stepped within the ring of salt.

At first there was silence. Then Mara spoke in a language that Corrine could not quite catch but that filled the seat of her spine with power. Miss Brown stepped forward to the edge of the salt, and Mara dipped her black candle into Miss Brown's flame. Miss Brown stepped back. Still holding the hair, Mara opened the jar of powder with one hand. She cast the sulfur in the cardinal directions, chanting each time she did so.

She turned back to face the crucible, lifting her hands and throwing back her head. She spoke softly, and the words brought all the hairs along the back of Corrine's neck and arms to attention. Mara put the hair in the crucible, along with a bit of the sulfur powder and a couple of the bent nails. She used the feathered chicken's foot to stir the contents. She lifted the dried plant to her lips, kissed it, and put it in her mouth. She chewed it as she lit the contents of the crucible.

When Mara began the chant again, Corrine felt the spell. She felt the burning, twisting pain seeking out Rory wherever he was and settling in his bones. She felt the knowledge cramping his innards that if he just returned what he had taken he would be released. She swayed a bit with nausea, and Miss Brown steadied her.

Mara's eyes rolled, and juice from the plant foamed from her mouth. She collapsed. Corrine started toward her, but Miss Brown placed a warning hand across her. "A revenge spell cuts both ways," she said, keeping her voice low. "She will feel the pain she has dealt. It is the way of things. She must be left to recover by herself."

Corrine nodded and relaxed. Miss Brown's hand fell away from her. Slowly, everyone in the outer circle blew out their candles. Corrine followed suit.

Madame DuBois came to her. "How many times did I try to warn you, Corrine? There were forces at work around you that you would not admit." Corrine was reminded of the very first Tarot card with the girl encircled by the body of a great serpent, the World card that she had thrown away. She thought of the two-headed serpent and sighed.

Miss Brown said softly, "We are all in the serpent's coils."

"Yes," Corrine said. But she still was unsure if that was a good thing or not.

"Yes," Madame DuBois echoed, her gaze keen and unreadable. "Now, off to bed with you."

Corrine sensed they had things to discuss, things that they did not want her to hear. She retrieved her coat. Mara was still huddled on the floor like a wrung-out rag, though her convulsions had eased. The seeming disregard the others showed the girl disturbed Corrine, but she was beginning to believe them when it came to magic. There were powers one had best not toy with.

Miss Brown herself escorted her up the stairs, saying nothing, holding her skirts stiffly before her as though she fought a flood rather than a few flights of stairs.

She made sure Corrine's stove and lantern were lit. As Miss Brown left, she turned to Corrine, and the shadows on her face made Corrine think that perhaps Miss Brown, like Father Joseph, was older than she'd guessed. The headmistress tried to smile, but Corrine saw a deep sorrow in her eyes. She put a hand on Corrine's hair briefly. "Go to sleep now, little spy. Let us hope the Unhallowed have no further use for you."

December 2, 1865

A few days later, Corrine heard that Miss Brown had driven into Culpeper to place a report with the deputy regarding Melanie's disappearance. The sheriff promised a few volunteers from the town to help. Once the posse was gathered, classes were suspended for a day so that the older and reliable girls could begin the search. Apparently, the Council felt that leaving the search for Penelope entirely to the sheriff hadn't been wise. Nothing was said about Rory.

Mara watched the little girls, while the other teachers and Father Joe fanned out around the woods of Falston with small groups of girls who could be trusted not to run off by themselves. Corrine hoped that everyone was too concerned about Melanie to even consider escaping.

As they set out in Father Joe's group, Ilona looked even more distant than usual, her hands stuffed into her coat pockets and her shoulders hunched like a brooding crow's.

"Ilona?" she said.

Ilona ignored her at first. As they trudged out of the gate and down the frost-hardened road, she said, "This is just like what happened with Jeanette. We will never find her."

Corrine squeezed her elbow in sympathy.

They combed the hillside for hours, the girls shouting Melanie's name in a confused chorus that echoed over the countryside. The sheriff's men arrived toward late afternoon, and Corrine could hear them galloping up and down the road, adding their strange male voices to the din. Some of them worked their way down toward the river, their cries like remnants of an all-too-recent battle.

Afternoon filtered away and there was no sign of the girl, not even a lock of hair or item of clothing to signal where she might have gone. Corrine knew that the search was futile, and as the afternoon wore on toward twilight, she wished that everyone could just return to the manor.

She strayed a little from her group, but tried to keep them in her line of sight. She almost asked Father Joe why the Council couldn't just do some spell to determine where Melanie was, but he forbade her with a look, as if he knew what she was about to say.

So, she wandered idly, stabbing halfheartedly at the leaf

mold with a stick she'd picked up. She looked up occasionally, watching for Ilona or Christina and always finding them. This time, though, she realized she had no idea where she was or how she had gotten there.

A white shimmer in the near distance drew her; she wondered if she'd come to the river, and could then ride back up the hill with the sheriff's men. Only she didn't remember going down the hill to get there. She pushed through the hemlocks, the tiny needles breaking off into her hair and the crevices of her sleeves. When she got to the other side, she stopped, unable to keep her mouth from falling open in sheer wonder. The stick fell from her fingers. It made no sound when it hit the forest floor.

An unearthly white tree grew at the center of the hemlock grove. Its branches were myriad; her eyes wandered over it until they were lost in her attempts to mark where one intricacy ended and another began. Mist obscured the topmost branches. Revolving in a soft trance, little lights pulsed around the mist-shrouded tree like lightning bugs. She saw that odd flowers grew over the tree's roots, flowers that moved and crept up and down the trunk like animals, their blood-black petals questing for hidden things. There was a music to their movements, a harmony that reminded her of the Fey Prince's heartbeat.

She shivered in horror. She knew this tree. And then the tree noticed her.

The lights all drew together to a blinding point. The flowers turned. An angry buzzing, as of a million hornets, eclipsed the faint music. The mist grew, swirling around the tree like a tornado. The sun vanished all at once. Corrine's mouth closed.

She stood transfixed. If she moved, she felt certain she would either be caught or she would release something that had previously been confined to the tree. She thought of crying out, but knew that no one would be able to hear her over the droning. The lights arrowed toward her, a million angry little faces humming down on her like battalions of bees. Out of the corner of her eye, she saw a tall, hulking shape step from behind the tree. The Captain did not bother extending his hand, but strode in her direction while the Unhallowed hornets descended in a frenzy of light.

A cold certainty washed down Corrine's back. They had done this on purpose to lure her out of the iron gates. They had Penelope and Melanie, and they were after her. They had the stone; they could take whomever or whatever they wanted.

Corrine could not move. Her legs were rooted in place; her mouth would not open to scream.

Something dark and wavering rose before her. Her heart leaped against her ribs as the form took shape.

Mother?

Her mother looked at her, her great, sad eyes speaking what no words could. It was like the fever-dream she'd had the day her mother was buried. *Don't look at them,* she seemed to be saying. *Look only at me.* Around her mother's neck, the iron cross burned like a dark star, and it was this that barred the Unhallowed horde from its victim. The Captain stood blockaded from her by a smoky wall. He beat at it with his bloody palm, and Corrine watched as her mother shuddered beneath his onslaught. The hornets wormed their way through the smoke in beads and knots of light.

Run.

Corrine found that her legs could move and she turned and ran shouting back through the woods.

She found Father Joe first. He took her by the shoulders and held her steady while she caught her breath.

"Corrine?" he said.

"We must get out of the woods. Now," she said.

"Why?"

"The Unhallowed. I think they used this search as an excuse to lure everyone out into the forest."

Father Joe's face went almost as white as the unearthly tree. "Get the others in our group and take them back to the manor. I'll alert Miss Brown."

Corrine nodded. She was glad he hadn't asked for further details. She couldn't talk about her mother's ghost without crying.

She managed to find Ilona and Christina not far away, sitting together on a boulder and imagining all the wonderful things they could eat if they ran away to a large city like Washington or New York.

Christina fell silent when Corrine came into the clearing. She was still not speaking to Corrine, and was still angry about the Society meeting Miss de Mornay had discovered. Ilona fidgeted by peeling lichen from the boulder.

Corrine said, "There's trouble. Father Joe said to get back to the manor at once."

Ilona slid off the rock, but Christina did not move.

Corrine didn't know what to say. She cared deeply what Christina thought, and every recent snub had been like a little barb to her heart. She could only hope that Christina would understand the danger someday and be grateful. "Listen to me," Corrine said, "there's no time for this. It's not safe here."

"What has happened, Corrine?" Ilona said.

Corrine shook her head. "Not now. Just go."

Ilona believed the urgency in her voice, and Corrine hoped that it was enough to convince Christina. She ran on to where she thought Miss Brown's group had gone, her breath coming in trembling gasps. When she finally did find Miss Brown, her throat was so dry that she could barely talk.

Miss Brown clearly believed that something was wrong, but

her frown forbade Corrine to give details that might frighten the other girls.

"Come, girls," Miss Brown said, "time to go back to the manor. Mara will have supper for you, I'm sure."

"Won't that be a treat?" Dolores said.

But before she could say more, Corrine was off again.

When at last she'd warned everyone she could, Corrine returned up the hill by herself. It was nearly full dark now. She knew that she was still in danger, but it seemed remote. She didn't know how long her mother's ghost had lasted, but she still felt her protection and love. At that moment she knew with a certainty that she'd never quite been able to embrace that her mother was dead. Even when she'd heard it and known it the first day, she'd never quite accepted it. She fantasized that her mother had gone away wherever her father had gone and that one day they would come to take her along with them. In either case, she had always carried a tiny seed of hope that perhaps her mother was still alive. But now, she acknowledged, even that small hope had been fancy; she could never rescue her mother from the grave.

And even as she knew all this, she still wished that she could see her again. The thought of the Unhallowed tormenting her mother's spirit made her want to rush back to her mother's aid. She realized she knew nothing about how to fight the Unhallowed Fey or keep them from harming her. And she knew now why Uncle William must have been so upset about the iron cross. It seemed as though it was the one thing that might have protected her from the Unhallowed, possibly even from Rory's trickery. Too tired to weep, she struggled up the hill, determined to do better.

~ Twenty-Six ~

Early December 1865

The next two weeks were relatively quiet. Corrine spent the hours studying for term exams, trying to cram everything into her brain that she'd missed while reading the skin-bound book or searching for Rory and Melanie. There was still no sign of either of them. When Miss Brown wrote a note inquiring about Rory's whereabouts, his father politely replied that he had been sent to Scotland on extended holiday and was not expected to return for a long while. Hope that the stone would be returned flickered and went out. Corrine was secretly grateful, for it gave her hope, much as she could never admit it, that the curse had not harmed Rory.

But she felt for Mara, who had undergone great pain to put the curse in place and did not like it when her magic went awry. Since the ritual, Corrine had heard the girl mutter on more than one occasion, "It should've worked. It should've." She tried to stay out of Mara's sight as much as possible, because the girl's dislike of Corrine seemed palpable. It was a hot, dry energy that Corrine did not want to get too near, though she could not blame Mara's feelings in the least.

Corrine had noticed, however, that Siobhan was much more at ease. The laundry maid seemed to smile more, and there was a light in her eyes that didn't dim even when she saw Corrine.

Siobhan bounded into Corrine's room one evening, carrying a pile of stiffly pressed and folded laundry. "Here's your things, miss," she said.

"Thank you," Corrine said, looking up from her book. Siobhan smiled at her.

"They're gone, ain't they, miss?" Siobhan asked.

Corrine no longer tried to press Siobhan for information. "Yes, yes, I think so." She hesitated. She thought of telling Siobhan that they were gone because the stone had been taken, because Falston was now completely unprotected. But it didn't seem fair to dampen the girl's mood in that way. Siobhan was terrified of the Unhallowed, and though Father Joe had only hinted as to why, it seemed cruel to keep reminding the girl of her misfortunes.

"Yes," Corrine said again, "They're gone."

Siobhan's smile grew into a toothy, almost comical grin. She skipped when she left the room.

December 14, 1865

Toward the end of the exam period, when Corrine felt that her brain could not be asked to do anything more ingenious than wash her face, Miss Brown called her into her study again. The tintype of the young man in Confederate gray caught Corrine's attention again.

Miss Brown noticed her gaze this time. "My brother," she said. "He was lost in the War. He fled from our home in Maryland to join the Rebels at Petersburg. I never saw him again."

"My father was at Petersburg," Corrine said softly. "He was a Union lieutenant." Miss Brown's eyes held hers. Corrine felt a chill as she continued, "That's where he disappeared."

Miss Brown shook her head. "Will these wounds ever be healed?" she said, almost to herself.

Miss Brown assumed her normal neutral expression and said, "I have a letter from your uncle William."

"Oh," Corrine said. She thought about the fact that her father and Miss Brown's brother may have seen each other at Petersburg, that her father might even have killed Miss Brown's brother. Shifting her thoughts to Uncle William seemed an impossible task. She wasn't sure how she felt about him now, knowing that he had kept the truth of the Unhallowed a secret from her.

"He says that he hopes you are well and are receiving a proper education."

Corrine nodded.

"He also says that he would prefer that you stay here for the holidays, as he fears he cannot protect you in Washington. I suppose our letters must have crossed in the post; I had hoped he would have realized that we are less safe than we once were when he received my letter."

She did not say anything to indict Corrine for that lack of safety, but Corrine still felt guilty. Though she knew that she had been terribly misled and though Father Joe said he did not truly think her at fault, she could not help blaming herself. She knew some of the Council—Mara and Madame DuBois especially—were angry with her for falling for such an easy trick. Twice. There was nothing in Corrine that would have made her suspect Rory's actions to be manipulations to further the aims of his masters. She had always been encouraged to trust people. "Faith is never misplaced," her mother had said. She wished she could still believe that.

"There are always a few girls who are not asked to return home," Miss Brown said. "We generally have a fine Christmas, and the rules here are much more relaxed during the holidays, so the girls who stay feel freer to make merry. It's really not such a hardship," she said, as though she heard Corrine's distant thoughts.

"Who else is staying?" Corrine asked. The dull tone in her voice made her feel selfish.

"Probably Dolores," Miss Brown began.

Brilliant, Corrine thought.

"Christina generally goes home, but last year Ilona was asked not to return home for Christmas. That could have changed this year. And some of the little girls stay, though this year it looks like all of them will be going home. And Siobhan, of course, stays. Sometimes we go into town and buy roasted chestnuts—the milliner's wife sells them for extra income."

Despair descended. Not even the thought of roasted chestnuts could comfort Corrine. She looked down at her hands, laced quietly in her lap, as though they could tell her what she would do. She thought again of running away and joining a wagon train. How much worse could that be than dealing with the Unhallowed?

"Unfortunately, this time I will not be here for Christmas," Miss Brown said.

Corrine looked up.

"I am leaving in a week for Scotland on the next steamer ship from Baltimore. The Council has decided. Mara and I believe that Rory has fled to Scotland. We'll find Rory and retrieve the stone from him. Father Joe will stay here to protect you from the Unhallowed should they return. He will also train you in a few elementary magics, things that can protect you from dreams, for instance."

Corrine nodded. "What about Melanie?" she said. "Is anyone still looking for her?"

"We believe that all three girls' best chances now lie with finding and questioning Rory," Miss Brown said. "He can at least lead us to the Fey who took them, or possibly take us into the rath where they've taken them."

"The rath?" Corrine said. She remembered Father Joe mentioning this before, but hadn't completely understood.

"Yes," Miss Brown said. "The world in which the Unhallowed live. The Fey have always inhabited other . . . places, other spaces in time. Once these worlds touched ours, and were thus easy to enter. But when Elaphe sent his power into the rathstones and had them scattered, he shattered many of those connections. Some raths were closed forever. Others will only open at a specific place and time or on a certain night with special incantations to open the gates between earth and rath."

Corrine nodded.

"We're certain the Unhallowed have taken both girls into their rath, but we do not know how to open it without the stone. As I said, we think finding Rory is our best chance." She leaned forward, balancing a pen between her fingers. "Believe me, Corrine, we'll find him. And we'll learn what happened to the girls. We haven't forgotten them."

"But what about their parents?" Corrine said. "Don't they want to know what happened?"

"Are they angry at us, you mean?" Miss Brown said. "No. Because they don't care. Jeanette's mother wanted her gone. She never responded to any of our messages about Jeanette's disappearance and she has apparently left their home for goodness knows where. Nor did Penelope's mother respond, as you probably know. And Melanie was a charity case. I rescued her off the streets of Culpeper, where she was . . . working. There's no one for her to go back to."

"But Melanie said—She said her father had a big plantation, hordes of slaves," Corrine said.

"In her fancy only, I'm afraid," Miss Brown said. "No one knows who her family was."

Once again, Corrine found this hard to believe. She knew the pain of being an orphan by circumstance, but she could not imagine being an orphan out of sheer abandonment.

"You seem surprised," Miss Brown said.

"Yes," Corrine said. "My parents would have never—at least, I believe they would not have abandoned me. They loved me." It still felt strange to speak of them in the past tense; it was as though all of this—Falston, the Unhallowed, even the palm looming over Miss Brown's head—were part of a nightmare that would soon dissolve beneath her father's hand, waking her in the morning. But reality and nightmare had traded places. This nightmare was now truth; her old life an unattainable dream.

"You are fortunate," Miss Brown said. "War makes people do terrible things. Many of these girls have never known what you have, even for only a moment."

Corrine bowed her head. She wanted to say that she had trouble feeling lucky, but something about Miss Brown's tone didn't invite the confidence.

"In any case," Miss Brown said, "the girls, whose families do want them home, will be leaving in the next few days, so I will help those who remain with Christmas preparations. I'll see to it that you're moved downstairs for the duration of the holiday, so you can be closer to everyone. Try to enjoy it."

"Thank you, Miss Brown." Corrine fidgeted with the edges of her pockets, feeling the strangeness of this—knowing that Miss Brown was and was not a witch, wondering still whether she could or couldn't trust her and knowing that, in the end, she'd have to make her own choice in the matter.

"You may go, Corrine," Miss Brown said.

Corrine stood, trying to muster a smile, but her gaze fell on the portrait of Miss Brown's brother—proud, young, and dead.

She left in silence.

December 19, 1865

The carriages had come and departed; no new snow had fallen to prevent them. Corrine watched the girls go from the front hall, trying not to feel desolated. Their faces were alight; they were going home to family and friends. Perhaps their families would be unkind to them, but they would be home, a place Corrine knew she would never see again.

She felt a hand on her shoulder and turned. Christina smiled at her, the luminous smile that Corrine knew could make princes swoon in her presence.

"Well," she said, "I suppose that will be the last of them."

Corrine turned as Christina took her hand. "What do you mean?" she asked.

"I'm staying here, with all of you this Christmas."

"You are?" Corrine tried not to gape.

"Mama would like me home, but Papa is not as eager. We quarreled last time we saw each other, and he is not known for letting go of his grudges." Christina shrugged. "This way at least, we will have more time to play baccarat."

Corrine smiled. "Yes," she said, squeezing Christina's hand. "We will." Gladness surged to replace her desolation. Of all the things that had hurt her about discovering the secrets of the Unhallowed, losing Christina's friendship had grieved her terribly. Losing Rory was also a deep wound, but the daily shunning by someone she admired had left scars.

They turned to go back to the parlor where Miss Brown and Father Joe were waiting. Ilona joined them. When they entered the room, they could see Miss Brown and Father Joe sitting by the fire. Their easy chairs were pulled close together, and they leaned forward eagerly, their eyes intent on each other. Miss Brown laughed, laying a hand on Father Joe's forearm, as the girls approached them. Ilona nudged Corrine's side, and she half-smiled. Yes, those two had to be in love.

Corrine envisioned for a moment a cobbled-together family, with Father Joe and Miss Brown as parents and herself, Ilona, and Christina as siblings. As Father Joe and Miss Brown turned, their expressions settled again into professional detachment, and Corrine's cozy vision evaporated. Dolores also stalked into the room, reminding Corrine that the holiday would not be as pleasant as she would have liked to imagine.

Miss Brown and Father Joe stood. "All right, girls," Miss Brown said, "we haven't much time, as the afternoon is getting on. But we need to decorate the chapel room for the holidays. So, let's go into the forest around Falston and collect what we can. We want boughs of pine, holly, mistletoe, anything green and fragrant. If you find something too big to tear off by yourself, just ask one of us to cut it for you. Father Joe will carry the hacksaw." She gestured toward the table, on which a number of baskets waited. "Baskets are there," she said. "Go get your coats and we'll be off."

When everyone was ready, they set off from the manor house and went through the gate. It was afternoon—chilly, but not as cold as it had been. The snow had largely disappeared except for in the deepest shadows under trees.

Corrine caught up to Miss Brown, who looked at her questioningly.

"Is this safe?" Corrine said, in as low a voice as she could manage.

Miss Brown smiled. "Entirely," she said. "We took care of the problem, I assure you."

Corrine nodded, hoping that Miss Brown was correct.

Halfway down the hill, they left the main road and went in among the trees. Miss Brown was in her element, happily naming trees, listening for bird songs, and identifying the birds that flitted among the tree trunks. She told them where the spring would bring squaw root and hepatica, wild ginger, and bloodroot. Dolores rolled her eyes.

They came to a clearing where several tall oaks were clothed in mistletoe. Miss Brown looked so excited, Corrine was surprised that she didn't clap her hands in glee.

"Mistletoe was considered sacred by the ancient druids," Miss Brown said, as she approached the trees. "They used to cut it with a golden sickle, and it was never allowed to touch the ground once it had been cut."

She spoke reverently, her eyes on the trees. Corrine saw her in that instant, robed in thin white linen, running through a hall of glittering mirrors. She saw with a kind of double vision as the headmistress went forward. *No!* she wanted to shout, but she was rooted to the spot. Miss Brown ran and a white tide chased her in one world. But in this one, the headmistress found a bit of low-hanging mistletoe and cut it with her scissors.

"Girls," she said, as she turned to them, smiling, "go on and find some things. Just don't stray out of earshot."

Corrine closed her eyes for a moment. When she opened them again, Miss Brown was putting more mistletoe into the trug basket at her elbow. Ilona and Christina moved toward the edge of the grove, and Dolores had already passed the line of trees. Corrine wondered at Miss Brown's trust—how did she know Dolores, or any of them, would not run away? How did she know they were safe?

She moved toward Ilona and Christina. She heard a faint buzzing, a sound that might have reminded her of bees, had it not been the dead of winter.

"Ilona, wait!" she said. Something floated by her, white as a snowflake, but with more certain intentions. The buzzing intensified. She felt something on her arm and looked down. A frost-white hornet sat on her coat, its abdomen pulsing as it palpated her sleeve with its forelegs. Then, it lifted off, ostensibly to join its fellows.

Corrine caught up with Ilona and Christina then, and the

buzzing was so loud that she had to shout. "We need to get back to Miss Brown now!"

Then they heard Miss Brown shout, "Girls! Girls! Back to me, please!"

Twilight had fallen faster than Corrine could track. Even the muted green and brown of the trees bled out to gray and shade. A deep concussion sounded nearby. The trees shook. There was a whistling noise and a crack of white smoke and flame off through the trees.

Christina screamed and almost fell. Ilona and Corrine grabbed her by the elbows and dragged her until she could get her feet under her again.

"Is that cannon fire?" Ilona asked, as they ran back to the clearing.

"Miss Brown!" Corrine shouted.

Miss Brown ran to them, and Corrine could see she was trying hard to hold in her fear. "Have you seen Dolores?" she asked frantically. They all shook their heads.

"Father Joe!" Miss Brown shouted.

Another explosion sounded, this one a little closer than the last. The buzzing was so loud that Corrine turned. Her mouth dropped in horror at what she saw. A white torrent tore through the woods, coming toward them in a wave of ghostly hornets.

"Run, girls! Run!" Miss Brown said. "Back to the manor house!"

Corrine, Ilona, and Christina dropped their baskets and ran. Out of the corner of her eye, Corrine saw Father Joe coming from the left, rushing toward Miss Brown. When they got to the road, Christina's breath was rattling so hard in her chest that she begged the others to stop.

Father Joe and Miss Brown burst out of the trees behind them.

"Keep going, girls! Up to the house!"

Corrine pulled at Christina, but she saw Christina's eyes were locked farther down the road in terror. The blizzard of hornets came on, and the shattering explosions made the trees jitter in the gloom. Beneath the buzzing, Corrine could now hear shouting, perhaps what had caught Christina's ear and compelled her to look. And now, Corrine could see an entire army of ghosts pouring up through the twilight—their pale horses materializing in the sunset, their hollow eyes searching for the enemy. She heard someone shout "Old Napoleon!" as the cannon fired again.

"John Pelham," she heard Miss Brown breathe. "They've raised John Pelham."

Corrine saw him again as he had appeared to her on the bank of the Rappahannock—leering, his dark eyes silvered by ghostlight. She remembered Melanie's tears over him and a glimmer of something—Melanie handing what looked like a shiny button over to the Captain. And now the Unhallowed had raised John Pelham and his artillery.

And then Corrine saw something even more horrible. Down the hill, Dolores was running, stumbling, her fat legs unable to carry her very far. Her frog-mouth was wide with screams, but they couldn't hear anything over the oncoming explosion. They watched as an old pine rocked crazily nearby.

"Dolores!" Father Joe shouted, bolting toward her.

The tree fell, sweeping Dolores beneath it as it crashed into the road.

Father Joe was too far away. He turned, and the look in his eyes made Corrine's spine flare. "Get back to the house now. I will deal with them."

"Joseph," Miss Brown said.

"Thea, go!" he said.

They all turned, sprinting up the road toward the house. Corrine could not tell whether her lungs were burning from exertion or the smoke. A white frost chased them, cracking the trees on either side of the road with deep cold. As they rounded the last bend up the hill, they were assailed by thick waves of black smoke.

"The manor!" Miss Brown said. She sped ahead of them, gathering her skirts as high as she could. Her stockinged calves flashed ahead of them. When they topped the rise, Corrine could see flames spurting from the windows, curling out of the chinks in the walls.

Marguerite de Mornay came to meet them. "What happened?" Miss Brown shouted. "Why is the house on fire?"

But Miss de Mornay did not answer her. She passed her and walked toward the gate, where she stood staring down the road, a bemused expression in her dull eyes.

The sound of the oncoming ghost army was like a rushing train.

"Marguerite!" Miss Brown went to her and shook her. "Help me close the gates! We must not let them in!"

Marguerite ignored her. And when Miss Brown reached to shake her again, Marguerite grabbed her by the forearms and threw the headmistress into the mud and gravel of the driveway.

"You think you can defeat my masters?" de Mornay said. "They are coming, witch! Nothing you can do will stop them."

Miss Brown hauled herself to her feet. She was about to say something more when her face froze.

"Girls," she shouted, running toward the manor, "go to the fence! Take hold of the iron, close your eyes, and do not let go!"

Corrine watched to see where she was going, and saw that Mara and Siobhan were in the yard, throwing soot-stained buckets of water helplessly against the conflagration.

She looked again down the road. Frost crackled a challenge to the sunset along the road as the Confederate cavalry thundered up the hill. Corrine could see now that the Unhallowed rode with them—gripping the throats of the soldiers in skeletal glee, whipping the ghost horses with thorn crops. Tiny, wizened fairies hung from the lead horse's martingale, giggling as the horse rushed onward. And behind them all, Corrine saw, came three tall women—spirits or fairies, she was not sure—dressed in mourning clothes, trailing their black lace veils behind them. Miss de Mornay did not move, except to open her arms in welcome.

Corrine, Christina, and Ilona ran to the fence. Corrine grabbed the iron, sliding to the ground in pain as it burned into her flesh. The other two girls held on, crouching next to her, staring at her. Despite Miss Brown's warning, she could not close her eyes. The train blast of air poured through the fence, buzzing like a thousand hornet nests. Miss de Mornay froze in a glittering column of ice. As the fairy-spurred cavalry rushed through the breach, the buzzing rose to a painful whine. Miss de Mornay shattered into sparkling bits of ice that showered the gravel.

The Unhallowed cavalcade poured through the gates. It tumbled about the foundations of the house in a white torrent, causing the house to shiver and dance as though made of matchsticks. When the stones collapsed on themselves, Corrine fainted.

EPILOGUE

December 19, 1865

In the dream, the Unhallowed poured through the gates. Miss de Mornay became ice and shattered. But this time, Corrine did not faint. This time the three women in mourning surrounded her, the veils blowing around her like black mist. She had an intense desire to know what was beneath their veils, but a terrible revulsion also made her shrink away.

She saw herself as from a great distance in a broad marble hall. She approached a statue from behind and she trembled as though in the presence of a goddess. She saw the three women veiled in gloom sweeping toward her from the other end of the hall, and she knew that she needed to hurry. But her feet were like lead. They reached her before she could round the statue.

Then she was beneath the veil of one of them. She looked up, trying to see the woman's face. The woman wore a mask, as the Fey dancers had in her other dreams. Yet this mask was like no other she had ever seen. Its tusked teeth grimaced; ribbons flowed around it in snakes of energy. It was so horrible, so entrancing, that she felt herself turning to stone.

She shook out of the dream. Or rather, she was being shaken. A faint light dazzled her. A dark form bent over her, gripping her shoulder gently. When at last she could see, she realized it was Miss Brown. Her cheeks were smudged with soot, and her usually carefully coifed hair straggled about her shoulders. Corrine noted with surprise how beautiful she looked.

She didn't have to ask where they were. The sweet, gagging stench of pig manure overpowered her. She started up again, hoping she wasn't actually lying in manure, but Miss Brown halted her.

"Rest," she said. "We're next to the sty, not in it."

Corrine heard the sow grunt in her sleep on the other side of the wall.

"It's the only building that wasn't damaged," Miss Brown said.

Corrine nodded, and then had another thought. "The library!" She started up, but Miss Brown held her still.

"Gone. I trust you still have the book?"

"Yes," Corrine said, "but the letters—I have only the last two," she said.

"There are two full translations. Your uncle has the only other copies. They are safe, for now."

Corrine thought of the thundering cannons, the wave of white frost sweeping through the gates with the ghost cavalry. "Why did they do this?"

Miss Brown sighed and shook her head.

Corrine heard someone come closer on Miss Brown's other side. Father Joe said, "They did this to frighten us, to flaunt their might. The Unhallowed have never been content to simply take what they want."

Corrine was too tired for her anger to flare. But she couldn't resist making one thing known. "I tried to warn you about Miss de Mornay."

"I know," Father Joe said, "I didn't listen. I thought I had protected us well enough. I didn't think the Unhallowed had regained quite so much power. Especially after Mara—"

Miss Brown put her hand on Father Joe's shoulder. "Don't blame yourself, Joseph. The fault lies with all of us, especially for not listening to Corrine."

Miss Brown looked at Corrine, her gaze turning sharp and probing. "Has your left eye always been that way?" she asked.

"The enlarged pupil?" Corrine asked. "Yes."

"Yes, I know that," Miss Brown said. "But this looks like . . ." She turned toward Father Joe. "More light, please, Father."

The priest reached back and found the lantern, then held it over Corrine. She blinked and Miss Brown turned her chin, so that whatever was in her eye could reflect in the light.

"Do you see that?" Miss Brown murmured. "Is it—"

"It's possible," Father Joe said. "I have been so inclined."

Corrine saw a glance pass between them. "Miss Brown?" she said.

"A blood-mark in the center of your left pupil. Do you feel any pain?"

"No," Corrine said.

"Perhaps you got soot in your eye. If it doesn't clear, well then . . ." Miss Brown fell silent.

For once, Corrine did not want to know. She believed she'd seen and heard enough for one day.

"Can you sit?" Father Joe said. He sat the lantern down beside her, and offered her his hand. Miss Brown slid her hand behind her shoulders and helped her sit up.

"Be careful of your head," Miss Brown said. "The ceiling is quite low."

"Indeed," Father Joe said, glancing upward ruefully. "All well and good if you're a pig, not so if you're trying to hide in a pig's house."

Corrine smiled. She heard other voices, some soft sobbing, and a cough.

"Who else is here?" she said.

She felt someone crawl forward and take her hand. The grip was strong, the hand large and rough for a girl.

"Ilona?"

"Corrine." Ilona released her hand and settled beside her. "Are you all right?"

"Fine, I think." She tried to shake off thoughts of the Unhallowed cavalry and the dream, but felt so bruised that she stopped midshudder.

"Who is here?" she asked again.

"Mara, Christina, Siobhan, and you two," Miss Brown answered.

She remembered the tree falling and Dolores disappearing beneath it. "Dolores?" she said.

Father Joe shook his head.

"God rest her soul. She's gone," Miss Brown said. "Along with Falston—and my reputation." The last bit was said almost under her breath. Father Joe touched her arm briefly.

"What will we do?" Corrine said. "Where can we possibly go that they won't find us and cause trouble?"

"Where they least expect us," Miss Brown said.

"Girls," she said, pitching her voice so that everyone in the hog shed could hear, "how do you feel about studying in Scotland next term?"

AFTERWORD

As a work of historical dark fantasy, this series relies heavily on real people, places, and events interwoven with the bright threads of imagination. Culpeper, for instance, is a real place with a rich history; Falston, of course, is not. John Pelham was known as the Boy Major and died of shrapnel wounds, but I'm quite certain his vengeful ghost has never terrorized young girls at Kelly's Ford.

The Civil War and the resulting Reconstruction were difficult periods in American history. Though I'm no Shelby Foote, I've tried to render it as accurately as possible on a compressed writing schedule. I hope historians and residents of the places mentioned herein will forgive my iniquities and indulge my fantasies.

There is much that is fascinating, disturbing, and amazing about the Civil War and its effects on modern life. To delve more deeply, read:

A Diary from Dixie, Mary Boykin Chestnut and Ben Ames Williams

The Civil War: A Narrative, Shelby Foote

All Things Altered: Women in the Wake of Civil War and Reconstruction, Marilyn Mayer Culpepper

ACKNOWLEDGEMENTS

Like many books, this one didn't come into being without a great deal of help. Many thanks to Stacy Whitman and the editorial team at Wizards. This series wouldn't have been born without all of you. I want to especially thank Shannon Hale, for her continued support; Holly Black, for her friendship and wonderful critiques; and Nancy Brauer and Janelle Dvorak, for fun with name-storming. Thanks to Michelle Smith and her family in Culpeper, who provided much of the inspiration for this tale. Thanks to Cheryl Ruggiero and Sue Hagedorn, for their continued enthusiasm and interest in my work. Thanks also to Jeff Mann and John Ross, who know that a writer requires art in the dining room as well as the soul, and who have feted me royally more times than I can count. Appreciation also goes to Kim and Dom Borkowski, who have fed me and taken care of my feline children on numerous occasions. I'm sure there are many more I could thank, especially for good laughs—you know who you are. And, of course, my abiding thanks to my husband, without whom I would lose whatever tiny shred of sanity I possess.

Read a sample of the exciting sequel to Tiffany Trent's
In the Serpent's Coils!

Tiffany Trent

Following the destruction of Falston and the loss of the rathstone, nothing can keep Corrine safe. The Fey have spies everywhere. And they are determined to find Corrine wherever she may hide.

With no options left, the Council of Elaphe takes Corrine and the rest of the Falston girls to Scotland where they can fight the Fey on their own terms. As the Council struggles to come up with a battle plan, the girls become immersed in preparations for their first ball. There, a mysterious young man soothes Corrine's heartache and she begins to let down her guard—perhaps sooner than she should. For there is a new danger lurking on the Scottish moors, a danger more sinister than any Corrine has faced before.

Available December 2007

HALLOWMERE™

Volume Two

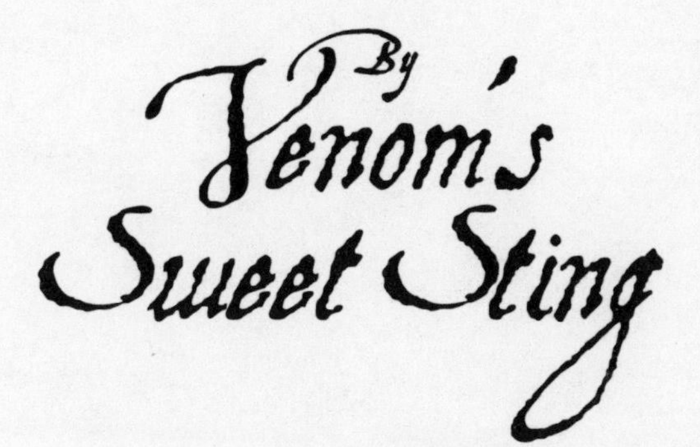

TIFFANY TRENT

~ Chapter I ~

Christmas Eve, 1865

Corrine listened by the newel post as the voices upstairs rose and fell—Miss Brown and Uncle William arguing. Since they'd arrived at Uncle William's estate two days ago, the tensions between the adults had mounted like an afternoon thunderstorm. But it had all been furious whispers, intimations, glares behind napkins. Today, Father Joe had gone out on an errand and all the servants were occupied with the Christmas Eve supper in the kitchen. No one would catch Corrine eavesdropping.

"Come, Corrine," Christina called, "the popcorn is finally ready and Mara has brought the cranberries. It's time to decorate the tree!"

Ilona grabbed Corrine's arm and tried to tug her into the drawing room. But Corrine resisted. "No, we need to find out what they're talking about."

Ilona released Corrine's arm and grinned. "She's right, Christina. Besides, it should be more fun to listen in. Maybe we'll figure out more of what they're up to. I don't know what to do with all those fruits and nuts, anyway."

Christina rolled her eyes and cast a last glance toward the drawing room before allowing Corrine and Ilona to draw her along. They crept up the stairs carefully, Corrine trailing her fingertips over the wainscoting. As they crested the landing, the voices arrowed out through the transom above Uncle William's study door.

Uncle William said, "You don't understand, Thea. If you take those girls to Scotland, you are not just endangering your reputation. You endanger their very lives! I know the destruction of Falston wasn't your fault, but you must think of the consequences!"

"What are you saying, William? That I am thoughtless? That I am not fully cognizant of the danger? Believe me, I know it all too well!"

Christina's dark eyes gleamed. She smothered a giggle behind her hand. Corrine ignored her and listened more closely.

"Then why do you persist in this course?" William asked. "Is it because *Father* Joseph says you must?"

"Do not bring him into this, William."

"Why? Because you would not have me speak scathingly of your beloved priest?"

"William!"

The three girls exchanged glances. Ilona gave Corrine a knowing wink. Before their school had been destroyed, they had wondered if the headmistress and chaplain were secretly in love.

"I'm tempted to call him in here to account for himself," Uncle William said.

"He has no accounting to do." A rustle of skirts suggested that Miss Brown had shifted her position in the room.

"He most certainly does! He has gone against the rulings of the Council time and time again. He has endangered you. . He has even deliberately endangered young, helpless girls! And look at the result!" Miss Brown made a noise of protest, but Corrine's uncle, ever the relentless lawyer, continued. "I have half a mind not to allow my niece on this expedition. I am not convinced that an offensive approach is the best solution."

"But, William, you can't deny her," Miss Brown said, finally managing to interject. "You know . . . " And here Miss Brown's voice lowered. Corrine strained to hear. This was always how it was—they talked about her but never talked *to* her. Despite all she'd been through, Corrine still had to discover their plans for her through scraps of overheard conversation. For a while she heard only murmurs, then: "She bears the bloodmark. You know she is the one he seeks. And you also know that you cannot protect her; my studies have shown that the women of your line are far more powerful than the men."

"But she doesn't know how to use the power!"

"All the more reason to let her be schooled!" Miss Brown said.

"And you feel you must take her to the old haunts of the Unhallowed to do it?"

"What choice is there? The entrance to the rath here is closed. Rory took Falston's rathstone with him to Scotland. We must get it back! Besides, I've already cabled Sir James," Miss Brown said. "He's sending one of his people to escort us to his estate . . . "

Behind Corrine, there was a step and a breath at the top of the stairs. She and her friends turned.

"Miz Corrine, I *know* you girls aren't listening at your

uncle's study door!" Betsy, her uncle's maid, said. Her voice was loud enough to alert Miss Brown and Uncle William that they were being spied upon.

Betsy stood with her hands on her sharp hips, daring Corrine to lie. "Now go on! Get that tree decorated!" She flapped her apron at them.

Without answering her, Corrine, Ilona, and Christina ran downstairs to Corrine's room, nearly toppling Father Joe as he came up the stairs. Christina giggled as she passed him, but Corrine glared at her feet, annoyed that they'd been caught before she quite understood what Miss Brown was trying to say.

They raced into Corrine's room before Uncle William could come out on the landing to shout at them for their impertinence. Ilona shut the door behind them and they all jumped into the middle of the creaky bed.

They burrowed together under the down coverlet to smother their giggling as well as to keep out the December chill. "It is true," Christina said, her voice nearly slurring into her native French in excitement. "Miss Brown and Father Joe—"

"And your Uncle William—" Ilona interrupted.

"In a love triangle," Christina continued. "How romantic!"

Having just been the recent victim of a disastrous love triangle herself, Corrine was not so sure it sounded all that romantic. "I don't think—" she began.

But Ilona said, "Oh, it's—how do you say?—plain as day. Your uncle's in love with Miss Brown!"

"Oh, yes," Corrine said, drawing the covers tighter around the back. "I knew that, even before I came to Falston." The photograph of Miss Brown, so lovingly taken, so carefully placed on her uncle's desk, had proven that. But that wasn't the thing most at stake now.

"You did?" Christina said. She gripped Corrine's knee, redirecting her attention. "And you never told us?"

"Well . . . There were things that seemed more important."

"How did you know?" Ilona asked.

"He had her tintype on his desk. It looked like it was taken a long time ago. She was wearing a ball gown, and . . . she smiled. I think perhaps my uncle took the photograph himself."

Christina sighed. "So he has loved her for a long time secretly?"

"I suppose so," Corrine said. What had Miss Brown meant about her studies into her family line? What did she mean about the women being more powerful than the men? And why did Uncle William dismiss this? Corrine tried not to relive the events that had brought her to this strange conversation. Two nights ago, she had explained to her friends what had really happened at Falston inasmuch as she understood it. Somehow, she had attracted the attention of the Unhallowed Prince, who led the vampiric Unhallowed Fey. Somehow, the Prince's bloody-handed Captain had followed her to Falston, where she had been tricked to believe that the Falston witches were the evil threat. Somehow, the Prince and his minions had managed to convince her to steal not one, but *two* of the precious rathstones that allowed entrance into the Fey worlds.

And every one of her actions had led to the destruction of Miss Brown's Falston Reformatory School for Young Ladies, the ice-rimed ruins of which they had left behind in Culpeper.

With the three of them, it had become stuffy under the coverlet. *"Mon Dieu,"* Christina cried, "it is hot!" She fell back on the bed, throwing the blanket onto the other two, who were subsequently forced to wriggle out from under it.

Corrine emerged from the blanket to find Christina on her side, her head propped on her hand. Her sober expression was more becoming of a French diplomat's daughter than her earlier giggling. After Christina had accused her of deliberately getting their secret society into trouble at school, Corrine had worried that they'd never be friends again, but with the destruction of Falston, Christina had seen the truth—that Corrine had been a pawn in a plot that involved supernatural forces beyond any of their imaginations. Corrine was relieved that Christina trusted her now.

"But, Corrine," Christina asked, "what did she mean about a bloodmark?"

"And 'she is the one he seeks,' 'she has power'? What does that mean?" Ilona asked. At Corrine's glance, Ilona combed her fingers through her hair nervously. It was slowly growing out, but was still too short in back to put up.

Corrine sighed. "I don't know much," Corrine said. "But if I tell you, you have to promise not to talk about it in front of them. I think they're still afraid you might say something to your parents." Neither Christina nor Ilona had ever expressed the least interest in betraying her or the Council's secrets to their families after the destruction of Falston, but Corrine worried that perhaps she wasn't being careful enough. Goodness knew, she hardly believed all of this herself sometimes.

"We won't," Christina whispered.

"They saw something in my eye right after I woke up—a bloodmark, they called it," Corrine continued.

Ilona peered at her left eye, the one with the misshapen pupil. "Do you mean that silver mark there?"

"Yes. It was red at first, but I noticed in the mirror yesterday that it had turned silver. Like a scar."

Ilona stared. "Mmm . . . yes, I see." Her scrutiny discomfited Corrine, soshe shifted her gaze to the floral still life that hung over the bed.

"Does it give you some kind of power?" Christina asked, releasing the coverlet's pale roses.

"No," Corrine said. "At least not that I know of. Not that they'll tell me." Miss Brown had said she had some kind of power. But what?

"But we should expect further visits from the . . . Unhallowed?" Ilona tripped over the last word, still unfamiliar with the term.

"In all likelihood. I think, for some reason, after I gave the second rathstone to . . . to Rory,"—she could still barely bring herself to say his name—"the Council thought the Unhallowed were finished with Falston, that somehow they would leave us in peace."

"But they were wrong," Ilona said.

Corrine closed her eyes, hearing the hooves of the ghost horses as they burst through Falston's gates. Again, the three veiled women bent over her.

"Yes," she said, opening her eyes and looking at her friend. "Very wrong."

"And now it seems your uncle does not want you to go into further danger," Christina said.

Corrine prickled with surprise. Her uncle had seemed distant and angry with her much of the time she had spent recuperating from the swamp fever in his former home. She understood a little now of why that might have happened. He guarded tremendous secrets, secrets that she was only just beginning to discover.

"Does seem that way," Corrine said. Yet, he had sent her into danger last time, knowing full well the one who followed her and what could happen if the bloody-handed Captain caught her. Had he really believed Falston's iron gates and the protection of its rathstone were that powerful?

"What will you do?" Christina asked.

"About what?"

"If he won't let you go to Scotland . . . "

Corrine thought. The Captain could follow her anywhere; the Prince knew how to visit her in her dreams. Though she had seen neither of them in waking or dreams since leaving Falston, she was sure the respite wouldn't last.

"What will we do without you?"

Corrine had been concerned that her friends might be separated from her after the incident at Falston, but their parents had shown no interest in having their daughters returned to them.

"Will he send us to our parents?" Ilona growled, echoing her thoughts.

Corrine shook her head. "I think he'll let me go." she said. "I think he'll let all of us go. Miss Brown will convince him, I'm certain of it."

"But will he be able to convince her to marry him?" Ilona said.

Before Corrine could answer, a feather pillow hit her squarely across the mouth.

Later that afternoon, the girls sat together in the drawing room by the fire. The naked Christmas tree waited in the corner, while Christina sat on the piano bench, threading a string of cranberries and popcorn onto a garland.

"This will never be finished in time," Ilona said, holding up its pitiful end.

Corrine cut snowflakes from paper with her sewing scissors. Ilona looked helplessly at the bowl of fruit and nuts on the table.

"We must try," Christina said. "At home . . . "

Christina trailed off, biting her lip.

"What?" Corrine said. "What would you do?"

Christina looked as if she wanted to cry, but she ducked her head and pushed cranberries onto the string as if her life depended on it instead. An envelope had arrived this morning from her father that had contained money but little else. Such coldness had hurt her more deeply than she would ever say.

"Come now," Corrine said. She dropped her snowflake and scissors and went to Christina's side. She put her hand on Christina's arm. "Tell us what your Christmas was like. I'm sure it was grand." Corrine thought of Christmases past—her old woolen stocking hanging alone by the fire, the few boughs of greenery scattered throughout the house, her mother and Nora singing, the surprise snows in Maryland . . . All probably nothing compared to the glamor Christina must have enjoyed with her family in France.

"Yes," Christina said, glancing upward. "At our Paris house, we would go to the midnight mass and come back to *Le Réveillon.* And we would have oysters and *buche de Noel* and . . . "

Christina fell silent as Siobhan, Falston's former laundry maid, entered the drawing room with a basket of pine cones.

She set them near the bowl of fruit Ilona still contemplated. "Miss Brown said as you might want these she collected, too," Siobhan said. She glanced at Corrine, nervous questions in her eyes that Corrine knew would remain unspoken. Siobhan was still fragile, likelier to startle than to smile.

The sound of carriage wheels in the drive drove them to the window. Siobhan trailed a little behind them.

A young man climbed out of the carriage, looking quite the worse for wear. His dark hair stuck out from under his hat at stiff angles, and his wool suit, though serviceable, was ragged. His face was tight, careworn as though he hadn't slept well in a good while. Corrine noticed that unlike most men, he was clean-shaven. In fact, his face almost looked as smooth as a woman's. Perhaps it meant he was young, but his ill health made him appear older, so that that Corrine wasn't sure quite what his age was.

Siobhan hissed and hurried out of the room without another word.

Corrine turned back to watch the man just as the driver handed him his valise, the only piece of luggage he seemed to possess. The man bent in a fit of coughing and spat into the bushes as the driver climbed back into his seat and clucked to the horses.

Betsy came then, opening the door before the man could even knock. Corrine shrank from the window and huddled with Ilona and Christina, watching as Betsy showed the man up the stairs toward Uncle William's study. Corrine caught a hazel glance and a wolfish half-smile before he was gone.

The girls looked at each other.

"Who was that?" Ilona mouthed.

Corrine shrugged. Uncle William had clients and colleagues who visited him all the time, though it did seem odd that one of them would come on Christmas Eve. She went to her snowflakes, scattered in a pile across the Queen Anne table.

Not long after the girls had put the final touches on the Christmas tree, Betsy called them to supper. Gilt frames, crystal, and silverware glimmered in the lamp and candle flames. A white horse reared in the shadows of an oil painting over the teak and mahogany-inlaid buffet. Corrine's spine tingled as she moved toward the table. The china and silver sparkled on the table.

Uncle William sat at the head, with the strange man sitting close to him. Corrine took the seat farthest from him, next to Father Joe.

The strange young man rose and bowed as the girls entered. Corrine could see that he'd changed his travel-worn suit for kilt, jacket, and tartan, though she had no idea how they had fit in his small valise.

"This is Euan MacDougal," Uncle William said, as the girls settled themselves into their chairs. "He is the gillie, or gamekeeper, for Sir James Campbell on his estates in Scotland. And a fine fencing master, so I hear."

Mr. MacDougal's lips quirked at the last. "Ladies." His voice was breathy and dark, with none of Rory's affected brogue. His gaze swept across them. He barely glanced at Christina as he resumed his seat. Corrine was impressed. She was accustomed to everyone—particularly men—staring at Christina.

"Did you have a fair journey, Mr. MacDougal?" Father Joe asked.

Mr. MacDougal blanched, almost as though the thought of travel nauseated him. He coughed and said, "I'm afraid I'm a bit worse for the wear, Father. I've a yenning for the old Highland soil. The high seas don't take too kindly to me."

Father Joe nodded as he settled his napkin in his lap. "I understand," he said.

Mr. MacDougal peered at him. The wolfish half-smile she'd seen earlier curved his lips. "I believe you do at that."

"We're sorry to have taken you away from your home," Miss Brown said.

A draft of cold brushed Corrine's shoulders, like someone watching her from beyond the window.

"It's no trouble, no trouble at all. Sir James thought a bit of the sea air would do me good, cure this lung fever. Guess he didn't reckon on all the bad weather."

Miss Brown nodded, looking at him with concern.

"I am sorry to hear your school was burned down," Mr. MacDougal said to Miss Brown. "Sir James spoke of it. A great fire in the midst of winter . . ." He clucked sympathetically.

Miss Brown looked at him and smiled hesitantly. "Thank you, Mr. MacDougal." Corrine guessed what her fellow Council members thought. How much did he know? What had Sir James told him? Corrine wondered if her uncle had known Mr. MacDougal when he had known Sir James. The gamekeeper's age was impossible to tell.

"You'll be starting a new school in Scotland then?" Mr. MacDougal asked.

Corrine couldn't exchange glances with Christina and Ilona, but out of the corner of her eye she saw their heads turn toward Uncle William.

Uncle William cleared his throat. Miss Brown lifted her

chin as she looked at him. "We hope to," she said.

"We are still discussing it," Uncle William said. He locked eyes with Miss Brown.

" 'Twould be a pity were you to change your mind, Mr. McPhee," Mr. MacDougal said. "We've been making the estate fit for the presence of the young ladies. And I've come a long way to escort nothing but my tartan and kilt home again."

Uncle William's expression hardened. "We shall see." His tone was disapproving. Unwilling to meet his gaze, Corrine stared at her glass of cordial, which glowed in the light like a ruby heart.

Before Uncle William could say more, Mara, Falston's other servant, arrived with a steaming tureen of oyster stew that looked large enough for a small child to swim in. Tall as she was, Mara's knobby arms scarcely seemed capable of bearing such weight, but she set the tureen on the table as gracefully as if it were a feather pillow. Raphael, the little boy who had helped tend Uncle William's gardens at the old house, brought a basket of freshly-baked rolls. Uncle William's maid Betsy carried in pickled vegetables and a salver of butter.

Christina clapped her hands at the sight of the steaming tureen. "Oysters!" She exclaimed something else in French, and Uncle William smiled, inclining his head. "At least we can attempt to make the evening pleasurable for you, my dear," he said.

Mara ladled the stew into each bowl with an expert flick of the wrist that kept the stew from spattering across the fine linens. Corrine sniffed the milky sea-breath of stewed oysters appreciatively.

Father Joe said grace, giving special thanks for the coming miracle of Christmas. While he did so, Corrine looked around the table at Miss Brown's careful composure, Uncle William sulking, and Father Joe's solemn expression. Mr. MacDougal stared at his bowl, green with nausea. Oysters clearly weren't his favorite dish. Ilona leaned out to wink at her, and Corrine grinned, but bowed her head again when Father Joe put his hand in a light warning on Corrine's arm. When grace was over, they fell to, and the silence between the clinking spoons and butter knives was nearly fatal. Corrine's discomfiting feeling of being watched intensified.

Finally, Corrine could stand it no more. She turned as discreetly as possible, and nearly choked on an oyster as it slid down her throat. The darkness outside the window wavered, pulsing in aortic rhythm. The lamplight tricked out eight gleaming eyes staring from atop the throbbing body. What had seemed like a mess of dead vines over the windowpane resolved into blunt, oscillating jaws. As she watched, the jaws parted and a tube emerged—a long, venom-filled saber.